Chapter 1: Summer has Arrived

Thursday, June 20,2024

10:45 am

Finally, the first day of summer has arrived. This school year was so exhausting for me, and Mrs. Richardson has been a thorn in my side. She reminds me so much of my mother, they are both just so annoying. Anyway, I wonder what Jayden is doing for the summer. He is so fine. I can't imagine not being able to spend time with him this summer. I know Rebecca likes him too but not more than I do. I would kill to have him all to myself so she better not get too close. Besides, she already has a boyfriend. I think he's weird but that's another story.

11:05 am

Just got off the phone with my bestie. She is coming over to do my hair once my mom leaves for work. My mom is just always in our business and she thinks I'm having sex but I am still a virgin. Just because she lost her virginity at 14 she thinks history will repeat itself lol. She really needs a man. It's been so long since dad left, so she says. I think he died before I was born because I have never seen him. Either that or she just doesn't know who my father is. I wouldn't put it past her, my mom is weird like that. Anyway I am about to jump in the shower and get myself ready for the day.

12:15 pm

Mom just left, I can't believe she actually gave me $100. My mom hasn't given me money since my 12th birthday. That was 2 years ago and it was only $20. Honestly I can't complain, she is all I have in this world, and as a single mom she does all that she can to make sure I have a roof over my head and food to eat. She believes the 3 most important things to maintain in life are: Food, Clothing and Shelter. My mom has taught me a lot over the years. I just can't stand her most of the time but I can't imagine life without her. Ok, I'm getting a little too emotional. I don't want to start soaking up my phone screen. What I'm really thinking about is how long I should be holding on to this money because only the Lord knows when I'll get $100 again. I wish I could work for the summer but in this town you have to be 15 years old to get a Summer job. Sucks for me because I won't be 15 until September. Wait, was that the doorbell? I think my bestie has arrived. Time to get my hair done.

1:03 pm

OMG, I swear I look like a whole new person, I wish Jayden could see me. I know he would acknowledge me now. I have the best bestie ever, she always looks out for me. She also did my lashes and my make up. I totally think I'm in love with myself all over again. I was literally in the mirror for almost an hour lol. She wants to go to the mall to find boys but I told her Jayden is the only boy I want and need. She is a low key hater because her famous words are "girl, Jayden does not want you" but Little does she know. I'm gonna get him before the summer is out and if he acts right I might let him take my V card when I turn 15. I hope he doesn't find a girl, I would be so upset I might die, or that bitch will lol. Ok, my bestie is downstairs screaming for me to hurry up. She is thirsty to find a man. First We're going to grab lunch then hit the mall.

Chapter 2: So Annoying

Thursday, June 20, 2024

1:46 pm

Omg, I just had the best shrimp tacos ever. My mom would definitely love it here. The waiter was so fine. I think I've seen him somewhere before, but anyway my bestie has been in the bathroom for quite some time now. Once she comes out we'll be walking over to the mall. I'm just so nervous right now because I know if I was to see Jayden at the mall I would literally pass out. I don't know why I'm so obsessed with him, maybe because he hasn't said a word to me all school year. It seems like all the boys that do give me attention I don't want them at all, but the one boy that gives me no attention I seem to be head over heels for. What can I do to make him at least look my way? Should I show more body and dress a little sexier? Even though I know my mom would kill me if she saw me wearing short shorts and a crop top. Yes, she is that kind of mom. Very over protective. Maybe because I am her only child, but I am also a teenager. I mean, Can I Live? Ok, Here comes my bestie now, I wonder who she's on the phone with.

2:11 pm

Just got to the mall. My bestie is in Bath & Body Works buying her mom a birthday gift. She is so thoughtful. That's why I love her so much. She's like the big sister I never had. Honestly she deserves as much love as she gives. I hope she does find a boyfriend. She did say she was on the phone with some boy while she was in the bathroom at the restaurant. He is supposed to be meeting her here. He also has a friend with him she says, but I don't care, I'm all about Jayden. She wants me to look out for him while she's inside and I think I see him. Not gonna lie he's kind of cute, if that's him with that other cute boy. She did say he was tall with blonde hair. I'm gonna introduce myself.

2:23 pm

Omg, I had to use the bathroom so badly. Those shrimp tacos went right through me. I'm glad I had a chance to get away because his friend is so annoying. He can't stop talking about himself. He comes off like a real narcissist. He thinks I care about how much money he has and the Mercedes Benz that he drives that probably belongs to his dad. I just can't stand a spoiled rich kid. Bragging like he works hard for anything, so annoying. I guess that's why I am so attracted to Jayden. I swear he's like the Aladdin to my

Jasmine. Every time I see him I just think of flying carpets and golden lamps, like seriously. He makes me feel like I'm in a whole new world. OMG, someone just busted in the bathroom crying and screaming on the phone. Sounds like relationship problems. Let me get out of here.

2:32 pm

I am so annoyed right now. This boy is still talking about himself. He hasn't asked me anything about myself not once. So while he's talking I'm just typing. Can this moment be over any sooner. Aww, Look at my bestie over there laughing and smiling with her new boo looking so happy. Meanwhile I'm stuck here with sir talk a lot. Wait, I wonder where she thinks she is going with that boy. Trust me she is definitely not leaving me here with this bimbo.

Chapter 3: Missing In Action

3:00 pm

I swear, I've been looking all over this mall for my bestie and haven't been able to find her anywhere. Every time I call her phone it goes straight to voicemail. I don't know how long she's been knowing that boy, but I do know that I just met him today. He comes off as nice but it's the nice ones that I don't trust. Plus with a friend like he has I definitely wouldn't trust him no further than I could see him. Come to think of it, his friend just randomly got a phone call in the middle of all that rambling then suddenly got up and left like it was some kind of emergency. Now I'm starting to get worried.

3:59 pm

A whole hour has gone by and I still haven't seen or heard from my bestie. At this point I am beyond worried, I am scared. I want to call the police but I don't want to make a claim and then she shows up. So what I'm going to do is wait until 4:30. It just turned 4 o'clock. I'm gonna go grab a coffee from Starbucks to keep myself calm. If I don't see or hear from her by 4:30 I am calling the police. Is that Rebecca? I did not know she worked at Starbucks. Let's see if she'll give me a free coffee.

4:48 pm

It is now 4:48 and I just got off the phone with 911. They said that the Police should be here shortly. I sure do hope so. I am getting very anxious and impatient. I mean, where could she have possibly gone with that boy? I hope she didn't go into the family restroom with him, that would be very disgusting of her, but I know my bestie is nothing like that. Unlike some girls we know she has Love and Respect for herself. That's why we are besties, we are one and the same. Though it's not like her to just disappear on me like this. I swear when I see her I am going to strangle her and that boy she's with, but all jokes aside I hope she is okay. Wait, what if he kidnapped her. No, seriously what if he and his friend planned this all along? He gets her to meet with him here, bring his friend along to distract me while he gets her somewhere alone. Then he calls his friend and makes it seem like there's some kind of emergency so that he just ups and leaves me alone. Now I'm here looking like a dummy, searching all over for my bestie while she's probably with those two boys screaming for help while being taken against her own will. I swear I have the mind of a detective but I have to stop watching First 48, I'm probably just overreacting or, am I? I mean, what if I'm right. What if this was all a set up and my bestie has really been kidnapped. O' Thank God, I just saw two officers walk into the mall. I'm going to go speak with them. I think that's officer Whitley, our friend Stanely's dad. I'm pretty sure he can help.

4:52 pm

Ugh, Could this day get any worse, They were simply no help at all. Officer Whitley said that she hasn't been missing for more than 48 hours so they can't put out a missing persons report or do much about the situation. Talk about serving and protecting huh. I am so over with this day. Please lord don't let my bestie be kidnapped. I would hate to think that into existence. My mom always says "what you think about is what you bring about". You know what? I'm gonna go to her house to see if her mom has seen or heard from her. I'm pretty sure her phone must've died and she had to get home in time to drop off her mom's birthday gift before she leaves town. Yeah, that sounds much better.

CHAPTER 4: Have You Seen Her?

Thursday, June 20, 2024

5:23 pm

So, you are not gonna believe what just happened. While on my way to my bestie's house I get a phone call from a random number. Looks like one of those call & text free numbers if you asked me. At first I wasn't going to answer the call, but I suddenly decided to answer. I said "hello" and all I heard was a soft whispering voice saying "HAVE YOU SEEN HER?". Immediately I went into panic mode and started screaming and yelling at whoever was on the other end of the phone. Just so happens that officer Whitley and his partner were driving by on their way to my bestie's house to speak with her mom when they saw me in the middle of the street making a scene. Officer Whitley quickly stopped and jumped out to see what was going on with me. I told him that I just received a random phone call from someone whispering the words "HAVE YOU SEEN HER?". Officer Whitley says "seen who?" I said "who else?" I believe some boy and his friend have kidnapped my bestie and are now playing games as if this is some kind of joke. Officer Whitley told me to get into the back of his car as he was already on his way to my bestie's house to speak with her mom and see if she has seen or heard from her daughter.

5:46 pm

When we arrived at my besties house her moms car was already gone. I told officer Whitley that my bestie's mom was supposedly going out of town for her birthday weekend. Which is why me and my bestie went to the mall so she could get her mom a gift before she left town. Officer Whitley jumped out of the car and proceeded to knock on the door as if what I just told him didn't matter. A part of me was relieved because I felt that officer Whitley was now committed to helping me find my Bestie. Another part of me was still shaken up after receiving that phone call. Suddenly my phone rings again and it's the same number, I yell out to officer Whitley he grabs the phone and answers it. He hears the same exact whispering voice saying "HAVE YOU SEEN HER?". Officer Whitley quickly lashed out just as I did earlier. He said "when I find out who you are you are going away for a long time pal" and hung up. Now I suddenly started to feel served and protected. There's nothing like an officer doing his job. Especially an officer who is the father of a friend you've known since the first grade.

7:15 pm

I'm just now getting home. Officer Whitley and his partner dropped me off to make sure I got home safely. He told me not to worry, he'll be out all night and all day tomorrow until he finds my bestie. Honestly I don't care what he says, I'm so worried and scared right now. I just hope my bestie is okay, I can only imagine what she is going through or even how she is feeling right now. The crazy part is that her mom has left town not even knowing that her daughter is missing.

9:26 pm

Just got out of the shower. It felt so good. I definitely needed that. This has been like the worst day of my life. I'm not sure if I will be able to sleep comfortably tonight knowing that my bestie is somewhere out here alone with no help. Please protect and watch over her. Bring her home safely. She doesn't deserve what has happened to her, she is such a good person with a pure heart. She would never hurt anyone Lord, please don't let anyone hurt her. And if those boys are behind her reason for missing I ask that you give them the ultimate punishment that they deserve. Wait, what was that? I wonder who is knocking at my door this late.

CHAPTER 5: Knock Knock

Thursday, June 20, 2024

9:38 pm

I swear I heard someone knocking at my front door, but when I asked who it was no one answered. Then I heard another knock and asked once again "who is it?" No one replied. I hesitated to open the door at first but my gut said "open it now". When I suddenly opened the door no one was there. I looked all around and all I found was a piece of paper on the ground. I slowly picked up the piece of paper that was folded in four. I unfolded the paper and what was on it was an address with a message below it saying "Come alone". Now this is starting to feel like a movie. So much suspense is flowing through me right now. I mean, who knocks on someone's door twice then runs off leaving a creepy note like this. They are lucky my mom isn't home because she would go straight to this address and shoot up everyone who lives there with no questions asked, just for playing such a silly game. That's if this is even a real address to an actual location. Honestly I'm not sure what to do or think. I do know that I am willing to do whatever it takes to save my bestie. It is now 9:42pm. My mom will be home by midnight. I can take an uber to this address and pay the uber driver extra to stay and wait for me.

First I'm gonna need some money transferred into my cash app account, because my mom only gave me $100 in cash. Let me call her real quick.

9:56 pm

Oh my goodness my mom is really turning into someone I never met before. I can't believe she actually sent me another $100 through cash app. I think I'm beginning to like her again. My uber will be here in 10 minutes, let me go downstairs to the kitchen. I think I should at least take a knife with me. The way I'm feeling I might have to kill someone tonight. As a matter of fact my mom keeps a small can of mace in her party purse for when she goes out to party. She started packing mace ever since that one night she was attacked by a crazy man a few years ago while leaving a birthday party she had put together for one of her friends. Though my mom gets on my nerves I love the fact that she is such a fighter and far from a push over. I guess that's why I am the way I am. Like mother, like daughter. I believe my uber just pulled up. Let me put on my sneakers and head out.

10:08 pm

Omg, this uber stinks so bad. This has got to be the filthiest uber car I've ever been in. This is so embarrassing, wherever I'm going I just know that by the time I get there I will be smelling like this filth. I just showered and now I feel so dirty. The best thing about this ride is the music. I can't wait to get out. The uber driver has already agreed to wait for me. I already gave him officer Whitley's phone number and told him if I'm not out within 20 minutes he needs to call officer Whitley and let him know that I am in danger.

10:23 pm

We are 2 minutes away from the address, I am so scared and nervous, but just the thought of me saving my bestie's life is keeping me sane. Ok, we are pulling up to the address, it's so dark outside you would think these people would have their outside lights on. Wait, is that someone sitting on the stoop? I can't really see his face but I have my mace ready.

CHAPTER 6: Sudden Surprise

Thursday, June 20, 2024

10:37 pm

So, the creepy note with the address on it didn't turn out to be what I thought it would be. I thought it would lead to me rescuing my bestie. My heart was definitely trembling in fear, oh what a feeling. Can you believe it was my ex boyfriend brian throwing an AirBNB first day of summer surprise party. Almost everyone from the school is here, at least everyone that matters. I feel some sort of relief but not totally relieved because I'm still wondering where my bestie could be. Wait, what if she's here, at the party. I'm going to walk around and see if I can find her. Omg i just saw Jayden walk by. My heart is pounding so fast I don't know what to do. Wait, he just looked at me and now he's heading my way.

10:49 pm

Have you ever heard of Heaven on Earth? Well i just experienced it for 5 minutes. I can't believe I actually had a conversation with the man of my dreams. His voice, his smile, his eyes, his lips. I mean, everything about him is so perfect. He told me how beautiful he thinks I am and that he wishes we can hang out sometime before summer ends. I am floating on cloud

9. Cupid has struck again. One thing I couldn't help but notice was that he kept smelling around me as if he smelt a bad odor. Damn, I forgot I was in that filthy and smelly uber car. OMG the uber driver might still be outside and it's been 40 minutes since I left him. As if things couldn't get any worse now there's some idiot outside banging on the front door.

10:54 pm

What have I done? This is so embarrassing. Now Officer Whitley is at the front door asking for a young girl that got dropped off by an uber to this address. Luckily no one knew it was me. I'm going to sneak to the bathroom and stay there until he leaves.

11:23 pm

Ok, I'm upstairs hiding in the bathroom shower. Two people just busted in here kissing and moaning. They have to be drunk I can tell. What if it's my bestie? It kind of sounds like her. I swear if that's her I will strangle her so bad it's not even funny. I'm about to take a peek. As I peek from behind the shower curtain you won't believe who I see. The slut of all sluts. It's Rebecca's trifling self kissing on my ex boyfriend Brian. How could she just cheat on her boyfriend as if he doesn't even matter. I swore I saw him downstairs earlier smh. I probably would be furious if Brian was still mine but he's not. Besides, he's a cheater as well so I guess that would make them both perfect for each other. Being that they are both sluts. I just hope Jayden hasn't left the party yet. I want to see him again and possibly get his phone number this time. Just to spend a day with him will make my entire summer. Finally Rebecca and Brian are out of the bathroom. Yuk, I just can't stand her. Let me go back downstairs and see if anyone has seen my bestie today.

Friday, June 21,2024

12:14 am

So I have spoken to almost everyone here and no one has seen or heard from my bestie all day. I seem to be the only one that was with her today besides those two boys. Where could this girl be? Omg it's 12:15 am and my mom is blowing up my phone. she is probably worried sick about me.

CHAPTER 7: Grounded

My mom is totally pissed off with me. I stayed out past my curfew and also attended a party that lord knows she would have never allowed me to go to. Like I said, she's very overprotective. She's afraid that I might get attacked by some crazy man just as she did. She usually doesn't allow me out after sun down unless I'm at my bestie's house. I could've lied and said I was there but she knows my bestie's mom is out of town for the weekend. When I got home I tried to sit my mom down and explain to her what happened today, but she was not trying to listen to me. I am now grounded for the entire weekend. How am I supposed to find my bestie now? I know I said that I am willing to do whatever it takes to find her, but going against my mom will really be the ultimate test of my loyalty to my bestie. I'm beginning to feel hopeless and helpless. I swear I just want to cry myself to sleep. I hope I'll wake up in the morning and everything will be back to normal. There has to be a major lesson to learn behind all of this. Like stranger danger especially with a cute teenage boy that looks trustworthy. Would Jayden do something like that to me? I'm starting to wonder, but I just can't see it happening. Besides the boy that my bestie was with, I've never seen him before so I know she hasn't. I wonder if she met him online. What if she was catfished? Okay, I'm thinking too much. Time for me to go to bed. Maybe I can explain to my mom in the morning when she is not so upset. Goodnight Bestie, wherever you are just know that I love you so much.

3:56 am

I just woke up from a nightmare. It is now 3:56 in the morning. This nightmare felt so real. It wasn't about my bestie at all. It was about that bitch Rebecca. I caught her having sex with Jayden and I snapped immediately. I grabbed her by her neck and squeezed until her whole head fell off her body. Jayden was so afraid and upset. He proceeded to curse me out and tell me how crazy I am and how he doesn't even like me. I got so angry I pulled a knife from my purse and stabbed him 37 times. Then suddenly Officer Whitley shows up and tries to arrest me. I managed to grab his gun from his holster and shot him dead in the face. Then my mother came in yelling at me saying I'm grounded for the rest of my life so I also shot her. Then I fled the scene. No matter where I went there were TV's everywhere with news channels casting my photo saying I was wanted for multiple murders. I don't know how many bullets were in that gun but I shot over 100 TV's until I collapsed and everything went dark. When I opened my eyes I saw a big red dragon goat like monster. Everything in my gut was telling me that I've just seen the Devil himself. He started to congratulate me on a Job well done and offered me a position to work alongside him. He pulled out a contract that was at least 100 feet long. On the contract were the names of everyone who attended the AirBnB party. He wanted me to kill them all for not inviting him to the party which I thought was weird. Then he told me if I was to honor and complete the task on the contract he would give me my bestie back safe and sound. The last thing he said was "now let's see if you are really willing to do whatever it takes to get your bestie back" that's when I woke up. I am not going back to bed at all. In fact I'm going to take a nice cold shower.

CHAPTER 8: She's Alive

Friday, June 20, 2024

6:13 am

It is 6:13 in the morning and I just got a text from that same call & text free number from yesterday. The text message says "SHE'S ALIVE". When I read that my heart completely dropped. I texted back "Prove it" and a picture of my bestie was sent. She seemed to look unbothered. Now my mind is really scattering for clues. Looking deep into the photo since they say a picture is worth a thousand words. Suddenly my phone rings and I answer it immediately. It's my Bestie but she is talking as if nothing happened. As if she wasn't missing yesterday and had me losing my mind looking all over town for her. I yelled at her asking her where she had been. She started talking like her memory was erased. She told me she didn't even remember being with me yesterday. Now I am totally confused and upset. I asked her where she was and she said that she was home in her bed and had just woken up. I want to go over to her house so badly and get to the bottom of this situation but I am grounded and not allowed to leave the house. As we are talking she starts to slur her words as if she is either drunk or drugged, then the call drops. I got another text message saying "come to my house I need you".

Now I have to figure out a plan. When my mom wakes up I will ask her if she has plans to go out today and if she does I can sneak over to my bestie's house to make sure she is really ok. I know something just isn't right.

11:32 am

Great news, my mom is leaving at noon to go to a wine tasting event with a few of her friends a few towns over. That gives me enough time to check on my bestie and make it home before my mom gets back. I am so anxious. My mom still doesn't believe anything I told her last night but it's ok. Today I get to the bottom of it all and get my bestie back.

11:43 am

I just received another text. This one says "don't come here". Another text comes in and it's an address that looks like the same address from the party last night. What in the heck is going on? I decided to call the number and got no answer. I then called my bestie's phone and it's still going to voicemail. Now I'm getting nervous all over again. This has to be a real sick twisted game. I mean, what did I do to deserve this? As soon as my mom leaves I'm getting dressed and going to my bestie's house first. I swear she better be home. If she is not home I will have the Uber driver take me to the other address. It is day time so I don't think I would need him to wait for me. Plus I get to save money that I definitely do not have.

12:23 pm

My mom is finally gone. I'm heading downstairs to my Uber. I hope it is not the same Uber from last night because I'm seeing the same name. Wait, let me not forget my mace, and I will pack a knife just in case. Suddenly my phone rings, and it's my mom telling me not to do anything stupid while she is gone. Little does she know, it's definitely too late for that. Let me go get in this Uber and save my bestie. She is definitely going to owe me a big explanation after this.

CHAPTER 9: You Have Some Explaining To Do

Friday, June 21, 2024

1:36 pm

Omg, I can't believe it's the same stinking, filthy Uber from last night. I'm not even gonna trip out about it. Just the fact that I'm getting closer to seeing my bestie is putting my mind somewhat at ease. The car is still filthy and smelly but the music is still good. I just zoned out until we arrived at my bestie's house. After 10 minutes of singing in the back seat we finally pulled up to my bestie's house. I gladly hopped out of the Uber and told the driver to wait for me. I get to the front door and start banging on the door in both anger and excitement. Screaming for my bestie to come and open up the door. Calling her from the window and everything. After about a few minutes of banging, knocking and screaming I was getting no answer at the door. The Uber driver then starts to yell out to me "no one is home, let's go I have more calls waiting". Obviously he was rushing me so I hopped back in the Uber and we proceeded to go to the address from last night. This car is making me so sick I think I'm going to throw up. I'm about to make him pull over.

1:52pm

Damn, I must've thrown up everything I ate yesterday. Though this car is awful, the Uber driver is so polite. He came out to help me. He even held my hair back so I wouldn't get vomit in my hair. He also gave me a bottle of water. I feel so bad because I was prejudging just because his car is filthy. He's a nice guy. Maybe I owe him an apology but not today. Right now I am on a mission. Here we go again, 2 minutes away from the address and I'm starting to get more anxious and nervous.

2:01pm

Here we are. But wait is that who I think it is? Tell me that is not my ex boyfriend Brian standing outside talking to that Bimbo sir talk a lot from the mall yesterday. Oh yea, he definitely has some explaining to do.

2:23pm

I'm inside the house now, but I jumped out of that Uber as if it was on fire. Maybe it wasn't actually on fire but I sure do know that I certainly was. I approached both losers and asked "what is going on here and where the hell is my Bestie?" Sir talk a lot was trying to smooth talk me and calm me down as if I didn't have a reason to be highly upset. He said "Calm down, your bestie is right up stairs with my boy, she's in good hands". He then said "I see you couldn't handle those gummies yesterday". Right then and there is when I lost it. I lashed out something horrible. I punched him square in his face so hard that he fell to the ground and started snoring. That's when my ex boyfriend Brian grabbed me and shoved me into the house. Brian was yelling at me but I was so mad I wasn't hearing a word he was saying. I took a few breathers and then I calmly sat down on the living room couch and asked Brian "please tell me where my bestie is" he said "she's upstairs about to come down and talk to you". Brian then proceeded to tell me that my bestie was worried sick about me saying that she lost me at the mall after we all ate a few gummies, but that is impossible because I don't remember eating any gummies at the mall yesterday. I remember seeing her getting up and disappearing with that boy. Wait, now I can't seem to remember what happened after that. I yelled at Brian to get my Bestie out here now. Some one definitely Has some explaining to do.

CHAPTER 10: The Blackout

I hear someone finally coming down the stairs. I just know it's my bestie. So I turn around and look up and guess who I see. Bozo number 2 that happened to be with my bestie all day and all night. I am so furious because now I feel like they are playing a game on me. Bozo number 1 finally wakes up and comes back into the house cursing me out. Everyone is holding him back. I calmly ask the boy that was with my bestie where she is and he tells me she is upstairs resting. I ask kindly "can you please take me to her?" He says "yes, but first I need you to sit down and let me explain all of what is going on here". I say "oh please do".

He proceeds to tell me the most bogus story I ever heard. He said that when we were all at the mall together we all decided to eat gummies that his friend brought along. He then said while me and his friend were sitting down talking he took my friend over to scoops to get her some ice cream. All he remembers is his friend coming to him panicking saying that I was over by the cell phone case stand tweaking out of my mind. So they all rushed over to come and get me. He said when they arrived I was already gone. Supposedly they were looking all up and down the mall trying to find me. They even spoke to two officers trying to get them involved in a search for me. I rudely interrupted him saying you are so full of shit. You took my bestie from me and had me looking all over town for her. You text me from a random call & text free number playing games with my head. Also I'm the one who had got the police involved, not you. You two are criminals for all I know. Now I'm going to ask you one more time to take me to my bestie. If you don't I'm going upstairs on my own and getting her the hell out of here.

Everyone was standing around silent so I started to run up the steps. As I am running up the stairs my ex boyfriend Brian runs after and tries to stop me. I kicked him so hard that he flew all the way to the bottom step breaking his neck. I was too upset to feel sorry or even care if he was alive. When I finally got upstairs it was a long hallway with about 8 bedrooms. I started banging on each room door and if no one opened I would kick the door in. I made it to the first 3 rooms kicking in each door. They were all completely empty. But when I got to the 4th room and kicked it open I started to see a few students from the party last night. Now I'm raging kicking in room door after room door until I finally get to the last room. I kicked the door open and you won't believe who I saw. Once again the slut of all sluts, Rebecca, this time she was having sex with the love of my life, Jayden. That's when I totally blacked out.

Suddenly I woke up and everyone who was at the party was now standing over me. They all were in some sort of shock. As I looked around I started to feel heaving wetness all over me. When I looked down at my clothes I was completely covered in blood. I asked everyone what happened? That's when my bestie slowly walked through the crowd crying so hard like I never saw her cry before. She said " you killed them" I said "killed who" she said "Rebecca and Jayden" I started crying saying "how did I kill them? That's impossible". She said "you strangled Rebecca to death with your bare hands, then you pulled a knife from your purse and stabbed Jayden 37 times' '.

And That's all I remember.

Detective Hathaway: Ok. We got the whole confession on tape. I'm sorry to say Ms. Adams but you are being charge for the murders of Brian Richards, Rebecca Hensley and Jayden Maldonado

Mikayla Adams has been sentenced to 55 years in prison. For the murders of 3 fellow high school students. She was only 14 years of age.

Contents

Study Package Booklet 7 - Waves

Wave - I

(571 - 632)

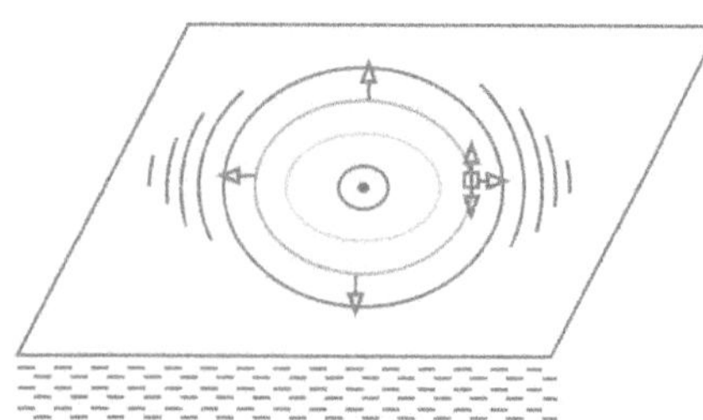

Fig. 9.1

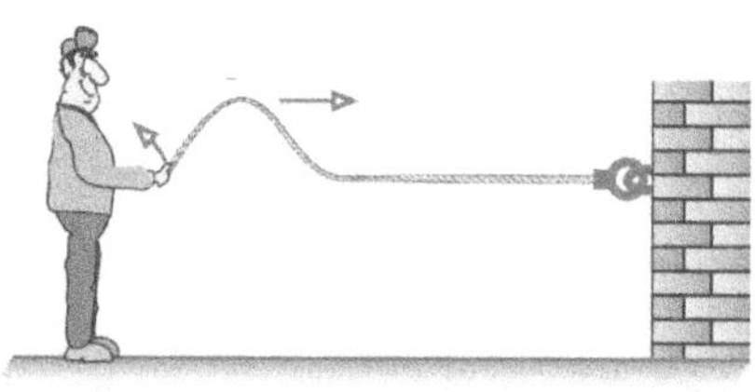

A wave pulse

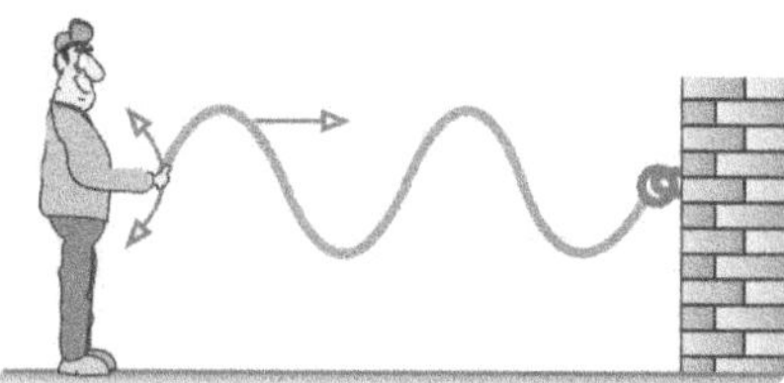

Progressive or travelling wave

Fig. 9.2

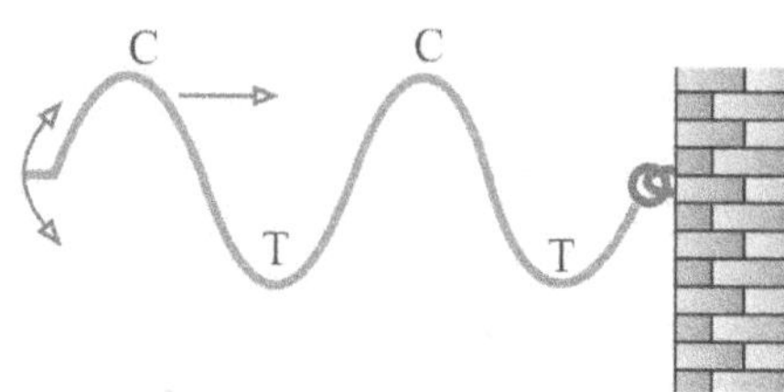

Fig. 9.3 Transverse wave in stretched string.

9.1 INTRODUCTION

When a stone is dropped into water, its surface gets disturbed. A disturbance is produced at the point where

the stone enters into water. This disturbance does not confine to that place along where stone is dropped but it spreads out. The disturbance spreads in the form of the concentric circles of ever-increasing radii eventually reach all the parts and strike the boundary of the pond.

Now let us put a wooden block on the disturbed water surface. The wooden block moves up and down as the ripples pass but does not move outward along with the ripples. This clearly indicates that the particles of water do not move outward with the disturbance. Up and down motion of wooden block as the wave disturbance passes on the water surface.

Thus a disturbance which communicated from one to another place without transfer of medium is called wave motion. Such a wave which require material medium for its propagation is called mechanical wave. The wave which requires no material medium for its propagation is called electromagnetic wave. Remember that mechanical wave can travel only in a medium which has elasticity.

Properties of medium require for wave motion

If a wave is to travel through a medium such as water, air, string, it must cause the particles of medium to oscillate as it passes through the medium. For this to happen, the medium must have inertia so that kinetic energy can be stored. Then, the particles can overshoot their mean position. After being displaced, the particles tend to regain the original position. For this the medium must store potential energy, which require elasticity to do this. Thus for the propagation of wave, medium must have **inertia and elasticity** . These two properties of medium decides the speed of the wave.

9.2 PULSE AND WAVE

Take a long string and attach it to a wall at its one end. Give a quick jerk to the other end of the string. A hump is produced in the string, such a disturbance that is sudden and lasts for the short duration is called a **pulse**. If jerks are continuously produced, a wave move along the string is called **progressive wave**.

There are two type of waves.

1. **Mechanical waves :** These waves require material medium for their propagation. Sound waves, waves in stretched string are the examples of mechanical waves.

2. **Non-mechanical or electromagnetic waves:** These waves require no medium for their propagation. Light waves are electromagnetic waves.

There are two types of mechanical waves

(i) Transverse waves :

A transverse wave is the one in which the particles of medium execute oscillations in a direction perpendicular to the direction of propagation of wave. Transverse waves can travel only in solids and surface of liquids.

In case of waves in stretched string, the points like C where upward displacement is maximum are called crests. Similarly the points like T, having maximum downward displacement are called troughs.

(ii) Longitudinal waves :

Take a slinky and hold its free end on his hand (see *Fig. 9.4*). Give a sudden jerk to the free end to the right, the slinky is suddenly compressed. A compression pulse travel along the slinky. Apply push and pull periodically on the free end of the slinky, compressions (*C*) and rarefactions (*R*) start travelling towards the fixed end of the slinky. Such a wave is called longitudinal waves.

Thus in a longitudinal wave particles of medium execute oscillations in the direction of propagation of wave. Longitudinal waves can travel in solids, liquids and gases. Sound waves in air are longitudinal.

9.3 Graphical Representation of Simple Harmonic Wave

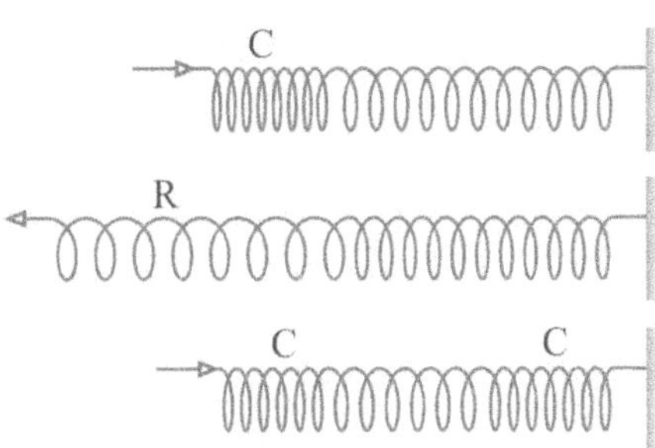

Fig. 9.4. Longitudinal wave in slinky.

The particles of the medium in transverse and longitudinal waves also oscillate about their mean positions. They execute simple harmonic motion. When the oscillation of the particles of the medium is simple harmonic, the waves that they produced are called **simple harmonic waves**.

Displacement - time graph of harmonic wave

The simple harmonic motion of oscillating particles is represented by the equation,

$$y = A\sin\frac{2\pi}{T}t$$

where *A* is the amplitude of oscillating particle which here is called amplitude of wave, *T* is the time period of oscillation.

The value of *y* at different time is given in the following table.

Time, t	Displacement, y
0	0
$\dfrac{T}{4}$	A
$\dfrac{T}{2}$	0
$\dfrac{3T}{4}$	$-A$
T	0

Displacement - distance graph of harmonic wave

You have studied that in transverse waves, the displacement of the oscillating particles are perpendicular to the direction of propagation of wave. On the other hand, in longitudinal waves, the particles of medium oscillate along the direction of propagation of wave. Thus, both transverse and longitudinal waves are simple harmonic waves and can be represented graphically as follows.

Characteristics of harmonic waves

(a) **Amplitude :** The amplitude of a wave is the magnitude of maximum displacement of the oscillating particles of the medium on either side of their mean position. It is usually represented by letter A. Its SI unit is metre (m).

(b) **Wavelength :** The distance between two consecutive crests or two consecutive troughs is called wavelength. Or the distance between two consecutive compressions or two consecutive rarefactions is called wavelength. It is usually represented by Greek letter lambda, λ. Its SI unit is metre (*m*).

(c) **Time period :** The time taken by crest or trough to move a distance equal to one wavelength is called time period. In case of longitudinal wave, the time taken by compression or rarefaction to travel a distance equal to one wavelength is called the time period. This time period of the wave is the same as the period of the particle which is take to complete an oscillation. Time period is usually represented by *T*. Its SI unit is second (*s*).

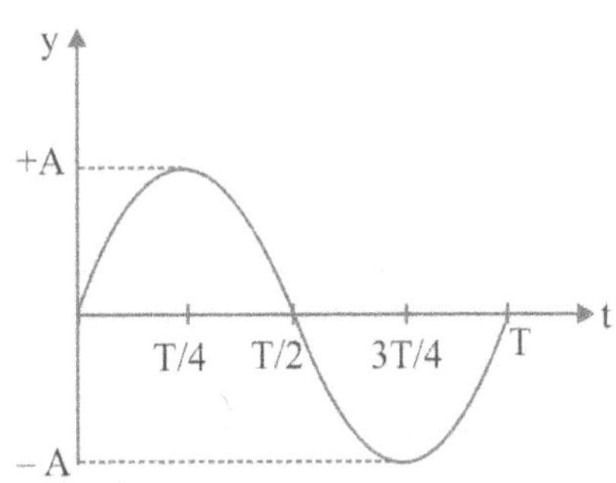

Fig. 9.5 (a)

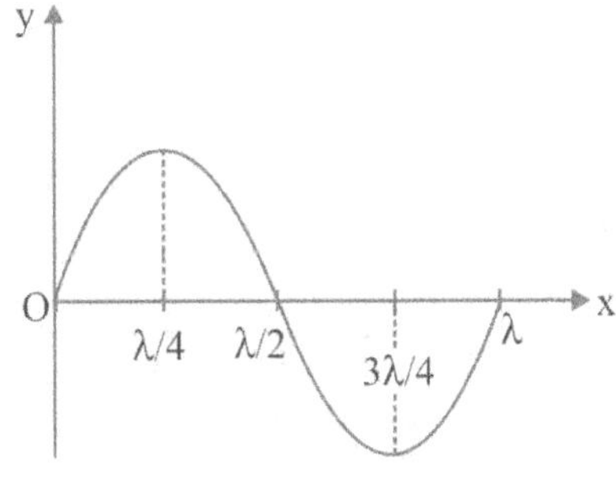

Fig. 9.5 (b)

(d)   **Frequency :** Frequency of the wave is equal to the frequency of oscillation of the particles of the medium. The frequency of an oscillating particle is the number of oscillations completed by the particle of the medium in one complete wavelength. Thus the frequency of a wave may be regarded as the number of complete wavelength traversed in one second. The SI unit of frequency is hertz (Hz).

(e)   **Wave velocity:**

It is the distance travelled by the wave in one second. The wave velocity is usually represented by v. Its SI unit is metre/ second (m/s).

Relationship between wave velocity, frequency and wavelength

We have defined that wave velocity is the distance moved by wave in one second. Also we know that the distance travelled by wave in time T is equal to the wavelength of the wave, so

$$\text{Wave velocity} = \frac{\text{Distance travelled}}{\text{Time taken}}$$

or
$$v = \frac{\lambda}{T}$$

As
$$\frac{1}{T} = f$$

$$\therefore \quad v = f\lambda$$

Thus wave velocity is the product of frequency and wavelength of wave.

Ex. 1

(a)   A wave transfer momentum. Can it transfer angular momentum?

(b)   Frequency is the most fundamental property of a wave. Why?

(c)   Which of the following is not a wave characteristic: Reflection, refraction, interference, diffraction, polarisation, rectilinear propagation?

(d)   What is a non-dispersive medium? Give an example.

(e)   We always see lightening before we hear thundering. Why?

(f)   What is the difference between wave velocity and particle velocity?

Sol.

(a)   As the particles of the medium have translational motion, no rotatory motion when wave travels, so there is no transfer of angular momentum.

(b)   When wave travels from one medium to other , its speed and wavelength change. But frequency does not change. This is the reason that frequency is the fundamental property of a wave.

(c)   Rectilinear propagation is not a wave characteristic.

(d)   If speed of a wave in any medium is independent of frequency, then mediums called non-dispersive. For example, air is a non-dispersive medium for sound waves.

(e)   The speed of light (3×10^8m/s) is much greater than the speed of sound (340m/s). So, the flash of light reaches us much earlier than the sound of thunder .

(f)   The wave velocity is constant $v = f\lambda$ in a given medium while the particle velocity changes harmonically with time. The particle velocity is zero at the extreme position.

Ex. 2   A narrow pulse (for example, a short pip by a whistle) is sent across a medium.

(a)   Does the pulse have a definite
(i) frequency, (ii)   wavelength, (iii) speed of propagation?

(b)   If the pulse rate is 1 after every 20 s, (that is the whistle is blown for a split of second after every 20s), is the frequency of the note produced by the whistle equal to 1/20 or 0.05 Hz

Sol.

(a)   A narrow pulse does not have a definite wavelength or frequency. But being a sound, it has a definite speed.

(b)   The frequency of the note produced by the whistle is not equal to 1/20 or 0.05 Hz, it is only the frequency of pulse repetition.

Ex. 3

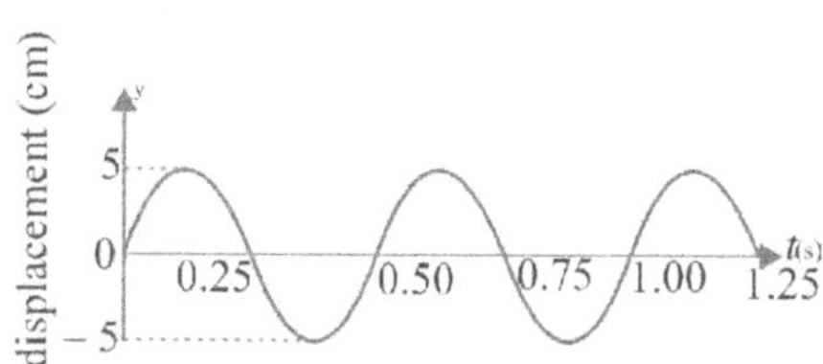

Fig. 9.6

A wave is travelling along the x -axis, whose displacement-time graph is shown in *Fig. 9.6*. Find period and frequency of wave.

Sol.

The time period of wave
$$T = 0.50 \text{ s}$$

The frequency of oscillation

$$f = \frac{1}{T} = \frac{1}{0.50} = 2 \, Hz \quad \textbf{Ans.}$$

Ex. 4   A source of wave produces 40 crests and 40 troughs in 0.4 second. Find the frequency of the wave.

Sol.

The total number of waves produced in 0.4 s is 40.

$$\therefore \quad \text{The frequency of wave, } f = \frac{n}{t} = \frac{40}{0.4}$$

$$= 100 \text{ Hz} \quad \textbf{Ans.}$$

Ex. 5   A boat at anchor is rocked by waves whose consecutive crests are 100 m apart. The wave velocity of the moving crests is 20 m/s. What is the frequency of rocking of the boat?

Sol.

Given, wavelength of wave, $\lambda = 100$ m

and wave velocity, $v = 20$ m/s

$\therefore$ Frequency of rocking of boat = frequency of wave

or $f = \dfrac{v}{\lambda} = \dfrac{20}{100} = 0.20$ Hz   *Ans.*

Ex. 6 A longitudinal wave is produced on a toy slinky. The wave travels at a speed of 30 cm/s and the frequency of the wave is 20 Hz. What is the minimum separation between the consecutive compressions of the slinky?

Sol.

Given, speed of wave, $v = 30$ cm/s

and frequency of wave, $f = 20$ Hz

$\therefore$ Wavelength of wave, $\lambda = \dfrac{v}{f} = \dfrac{30}{20} = 1.5$ cm

Thus the separation between the consecutive compressions

$$= 1.5 \text{ cm}. \qquad \textit{Ans.}$$

Ex. 7 Earthquakes generates sound waves inside the earth. Unlike a gas, the earth can experience both transverse (*S*) and longitudinal (*P*) sound waves. Typically the speed of S wave is about 4.0 km/s, and that of *P* wave is 8.0 km/s. A seismograph records P and S waves from an earthquake. The first *P* wave arrives 4 min before the first S wave. Assuming the waves travel in straight line, how far away does the earthquake occur?

Sol.

Suppose the earthquake occurs at a distance x km from the seismograph. Time taken by the S wave to reach the seismograph

$$t_1 = \dfrac{x}{4} \text{ s}$$

Time taken by the *P* wave to reach the seismograph

$$t_2 = \dfrac{x}{8} \text{ s}$$

As $t_1 - t_1 = 4 \times 60$s

$\therefore$ $\dfrac{x}{4} - \dfrac{x}{8} = 4 \times 60$

or $x = 1920$ km   *Ans.*

9.4 SOUND

Sound is a form of energy which creates the sensation of hearing in human ears. Sound can be produced by vibrating turning fork, by colliding bodies, by mouth etc. In production of sound one form of energy changes into sound energy e.g. when we clap, a sound is produced. In this process muscular energy changes into sound energy.

Sound waves are longitudinal waves

When sound waves propagate the density as well as the pressure of the medium at a given time varies with the distance, above and below their average values. The figure represents variation of density and pressure of a medium when sound wave propagates. At some regions of medium the density as well as pressure is high. These regions are called compressions. At some regions of medium the density as well as pressure is law. These regions are called rarefactions. In the figure peak represents the regions of maximum compression (pressure amplitude) and trough represents the rarefaction. The distance between two consecutive compressions (*C*) or two consecutive rarefactions (*R*) is called the wavelength, λ .

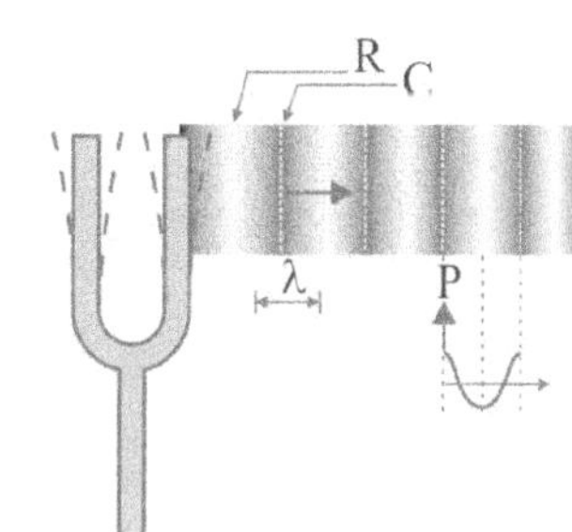

Fig. 9.7

 Waves may be one-dimensional, two dimensional or three dimensional according to the propagation of energy in one, two or three dimensions. Thus, transverse waves in stretched string or longitudinal waves along a rod are one dimensional, surface waves or ripples on water are two dimensional and sound waves produced by horn are three dimensional.

9.5 WAVE FRONT

A plane or surface on which particles of the medium are in an identical state of motion at a given instant, i.e., in the same phase, is called a wave front.

In an isotropic medium, the wave front is always perpendicular to the direction of the wave motion and the position of a given wave front shifts outwards with the wave speed. A line normal to the wave front thus gives the direction of propagation of the wave is called a ray. The wave front may have different shapes. One dimensional waves like waves in stretched string produces plane wave front and such waves are called plane waves . A point source produces spherical wave front. All wave front at a large distance from the source become plane wave front.

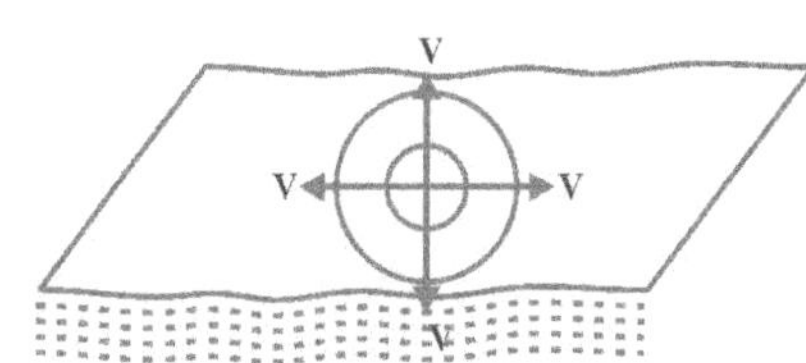

(i) Plane wave front

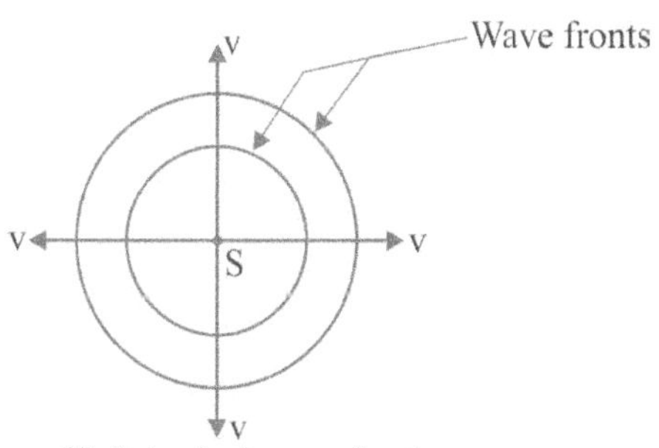

(ii) Spherical wave front

Fig. 9.8

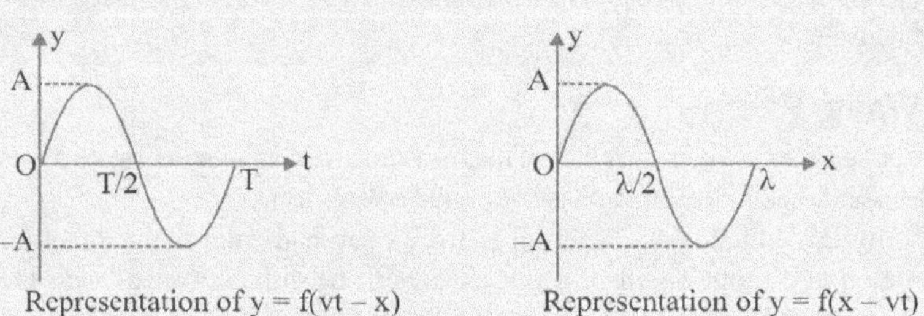

Fig. 9.9

9.6 EQUATION OF A TRAVELLING WAVE

Consider a disturbance travels along positive direction of x with a constant speed v. It travels a distance x in time $\dfrac{x}{v}$. Let the displacement of the particle at a distance x from the origin at any time t is y. The same amount of displacement of the particle situated at the origin was at $\left(t - \dfrac{x}{v}\right)$. Therefore we can write

$$y(x,t) \;=\; y\left(x = 0,\, t - \frac{x}{v}\right).$$

The displacement of the particle at x at time t i.e., $y(x, t)$ can simply be written as y, and so wave equation can be written as

$$y \;=\; f\left(t - \frac{x}{v}\right) \qquad\qquad \ldots(1)$$

Equation (1) represents a wave travelling in the positive x - direction. Such a wave is called a travelling or progressive wave. In such a wave time t and x must appear in the wave equation in the combination $\left(t - \dfrac{x}{v}\right)$. For example $y = \left(t - \dfrac{x}{v}\right)$, $y = Ae^{-\left(\frac{t - x/v}{T}\right)}$, $y = A\sin\dfrac{(t - x/v)}{T}$. The equations $y = A\sin(ax^2 - bt)$, $y = A\sin\left(\dfrac{x^2 - v^2 t^2}{L}\right)$ do not represent travelling wave. The equation of wave travelling in negative x -direction can be written as

$$y \;=\; f\left(t + \frac{x}{v}\right). \qquad\qquad \ldots(2)$$

The wave equation can also be written as

$$y \;=\; f\left(\frac{vt - x}{v}\right)$$

As v is constant, so we can write

$$y \;=\; f(vt - x)$$

or $\qquad\qquad y \;=\; g(x - vt) \qquad\qquad \ldots(3)$

Note :

1. The equation $y = f(vt - x)$ represents the displacement of the particle at $x = 0$ as time passes:

Fig. 9.10

2. The equation $y = g(x - vt)$ represents the displacements of different particles of the medium at any time.

9.7 PLANE PROGRESSIVE HARMONIC WAVE OR SINUSOIDAL WAVE : $y = A\sin(\omega t - kx)$

In the process of travelling of wave if particles of the medium vibrate simple harmonically about their mean positions, then the wave is called plane progressive harmonic wave or sinusoidal wave. In harmonic wave of given frequency, all particles have same amplitude but phase of oscillation changes from one particle to the next. The displacement of a oscillating particle at x = 0 and at any instant of time can be written as :

$$y = A\sin\omega t \qquad \dots(1)$$

$$\text{or} \qquad y = A\cos\omega t \qquad \dots(2)$$

where A is the amplitude of the particle. The displacement of any particle at x at time t will be

$$y = f\left(t - \frac{x}{v}\right)$$

The required equation can be obtained by replacing t by $\left(t - \dfrac{x}{v}\right)$ in the equation $y = A\sin\omega t$. Thus we have

$$y = A\sin\omega\left(t - \frac{x}{v}\right) \qquad \dots(3)$$

$$= A\sin\left(\omega t - \frac{\omega}{v}x\right)$$

But

$$\frac{\omega}{v} = \frac{2\pi f}{f\lambda} = \frac{2\pi}{\lambda} = k$$

k is called **propagation constant** or **angular wave number**.

Hence

$$y = A\sin(\omega t - kx) \qquad \dots(4)$$

Equation (3) can be written in the following forms:

$$y = A\sin\frac{\omega}{v}(vt - x)$$

or

$$y = A\sin\frac{2\pi}{\lambda}(vt - x) \qquad \dots(5)$$

Also

$$y = A\sin 2\pi\left(\frac{v}{\lambda}t - \frac{x}{\lambda}\right)$$

As

$$\frac{v}{\lambda} = f = \frac{1}{T}$$

$$\therefore \qquad y = A\sin 2\pi\left(\frac{t}{T} - \frac{x}{\lambda}\right) \qquad \dots(6)$$

9.8 INITIAL PHASE

If the particle of the medium does not start from mean position at $t = 0$, then there needs an information regarding with its initial displacement. This can be possible by introducing a quantity ϕ_0, is called initial phase. Thus if ϕ_0 is the initial phase, then the wave equation can be written as

$$y = A\sin(\omega t - kx + \phi_0)$$

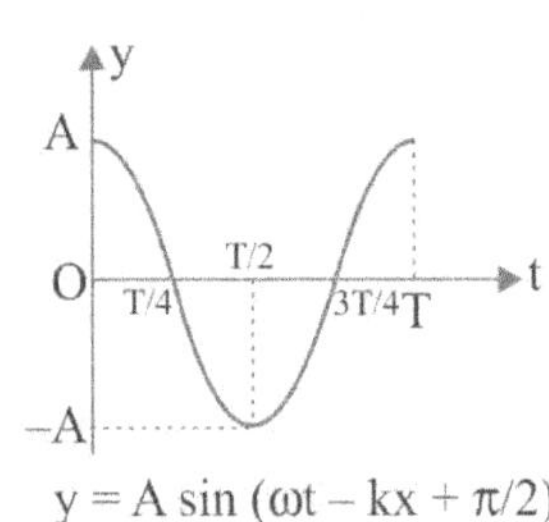

$$y = A \sin(\omega t - kx + \pi/2)$$

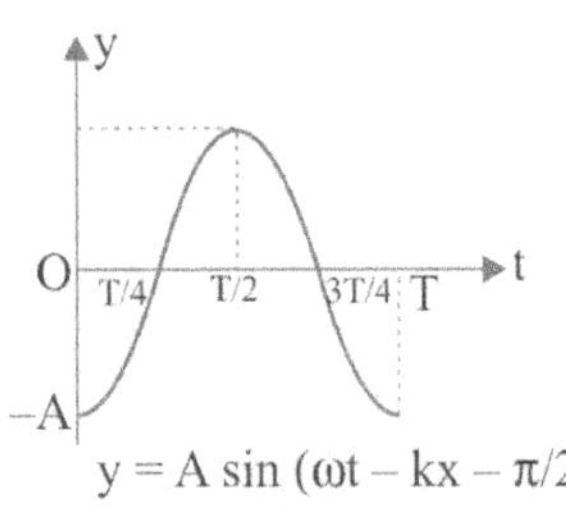

$$y = A \sin(\omega t - kx - \pi/2)$$

Fig. 9.11

Positive and negative phase:

If　　at $x = 0, t = 0$; $y = A$, then

$$A = A \sin(\omega \times 0 - 0 + \phi_0)$$

or $$\phi_0 = \frac{\pi}{2} \qquad \text{(Positive phase)}$$

If　　at $x = 0, t = 0$; $y = -A$, then

$$-A = A \sin(\omega \times 0 - k \times 0 + \phi_0)$$

or $$\phi_0 = -\frac{\pi}{2} \qquad \text{(Negative phase)}$$

The equation of wave corresponding to $\phi_0 = \dfrac{\pi}{2}$ becomes

$$y = A \sin\left(\omega t - kx + \frac{\pi}{2}\right)$$

$$= A \cos(\omega t - kx)$$

and for $$\phi_0 = -\frac{\pi}{2}$$

$$y = A \sin\left(\omega t - kx - \frac{\pi}{2}\right)$$

or $$y = -A \cos(\omega t - kx)$$

9.9 Phase and Phase Difference

Phase of a wave: The phase of a harmonic wave is a quantity that gives complete information regarding with wave at any time and at any position. It is equal to the argument of the sine or cosine function representing the wave. In wave equation $y = A \sin(\omega t - kx + \phi_0)$, the phase of the wave $\phi = (\omega t - kx + \phi_0)$

Clearly, the phase of a wave is periodic both in time and space. At any position x, it changes with time and at any time t, it changes with position.

Phase change with position:

We have $$\phi = \omega t - kx + \phi_0$$

At any time t, the phase change $\Delta\phi$ can be obtained by differentiating above equation

$$\therefore \qquad \Delta\phi = -k\Delta x$$

Thus the phase difference between two particles separated by distance Δx is given by

$$\Delta\phi = -k\Delta x = -\frac{2\pi}{\lambda}\Delta x$$

The negative sign indicates that farther the particle is located from the origin in the positive x-direction, the more it lags behind in phase.

Phase change with time:

We have $$\phi = \omega t - kx + \phi_0$$

At any position x, the phase change $\Delta\phi$ with time can be obtained by differentiating above equation.

$$\therefore \qquad \Delta\phi = \omega \Delta t = \frac{2\pi}{T}\Delta t$$

Fig. 9.12

Δx	$\Delta\phi$	Δt	$\Delta\phi$
0	0	0	0
$\dfrac{\lambda}{4}$	$\dfrac{\pi}{2}$	$\dfrac{T}{4}$	$\dfrac{\pi}{2}$
$\dfrac{\lambda}{2}$	π	$\dfrac{T}{2}$	π
λ	2π	T	2π

Ex. 8 What is the phase difference between the particles 1 and 2 located as shown in *Fig. 9.13*.

Sol.

The distance between the particles

$$\Delta x = \left(\frac{\lambda}{2} - \frac{\lambda}{8}\right) + \frac{\lambda}{4}$$

$$= \frac{5\lambda}{8}$$

$$\therefore \ \Delta\phi = \frac{2\pi}{\lambda}.\Delta x$$

$$= \frac{2\pi}{\lambda} \times \frac{5\lambda}{8}$$

$$= \frac{5\pi}{4} \qquad \textit{Ans.}$$

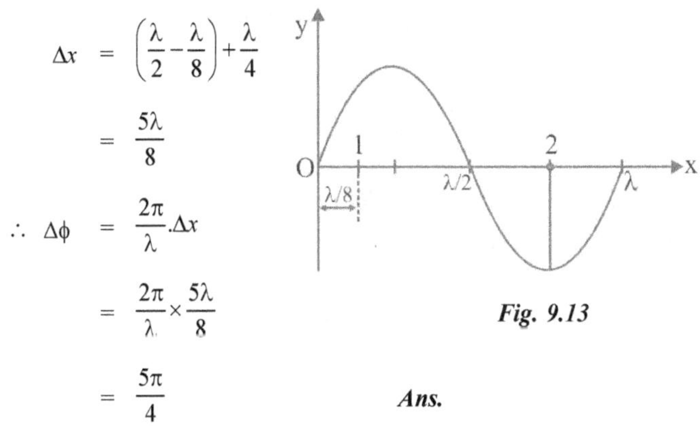

Fig. 9.13

Ex. 9 A wave of frequency 500 cycles/s has a phase velocity of 360 m/s . (a) How far apart are two points 60° out of phase? (b) What is the phase difference between two displacements at a certain point at times 10^{-3} s apart?

Sol.

(a) Given $\Delta\phi = 60° = \dfrac{\pi}{3}$ rad and $\lambda = \dfrac{v}{f} = \dfrac{360}{500} = 0.72$ m

We know that,

$$\Delta\phi = \frac{2\pi}{\lambda}\Delta x$$

$$\therefore \quad \Delta x = \Delta\phi \frac{\lambda}{2\pi} = \frac{\pi}{3} \times \frac{0.72}{2\pi}$$

$$= 0.12\text{m} \qquad \textit{Ans.}$$

(b) Phase difference with time is given by

$$\Delta\phi = \frac{2\pi}{T}.\Delta t$$

Here $\quad T = \dfrac{1}{f} = \dfrac{1}{500} = 0.002\text{s}$

$$\therefore \quad \Delta\phi = \frac{2\pi}{0.002} \times 10^{-3}$$

$$= 3.14 \text{ rad} = 180° \qquad \textit{Ans.}$$

9.10 PARTICLE VELOCITY AND ACCELERATION

Particle velocity : In the process of wave motion, the particle velocity changes with time. It can be obtained by differentiating displacement of the particle w.r.t. time.

$$\therefore \quad v_p = \frac{dy}{dt} = \frac{d}{dt}[A\sin(\omega t - kx)]$$

or $\quad v_p = \omega A\cos(\omega t - kx) \qquad ...(1)$

or $\quad v_p = \omega A\sin\left(\omega t - kx + \frac{\pi}{2}\right) \qquad ...(2)$

(i) Clearly particle velocity v_p changes simple harmonically with time while wave velocity $v = f\lambda$ remain constant.

(ii) The particle velocity leads displacement in phase by $\dfrac{\pi}{2}$ radian.

(iii) The maximum particle velocity, $v_0 = \omega A$.

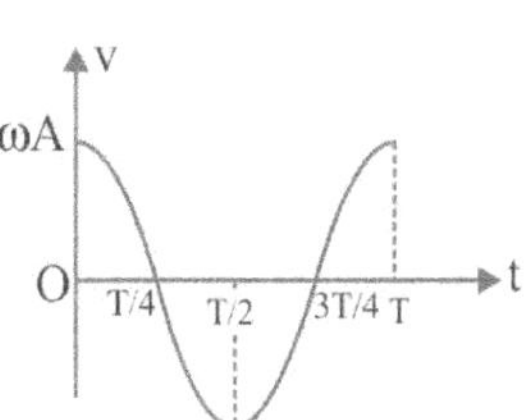

velocity vs. time graph of a particle.

Fig. 9.14

Slope of displacement curve: It is defined by $\dfrac{dy}{dx}$.

Thus slope, $\quad \dfrac{dy}{dx} = \dfrac{d}{dx}[A\sin(\omega t - kx)]$

or $\quad \dfrac{dy}{dx} = -kA\cos(\omega t - kx) \qquad ...(3)$

Dividing equation (1) by (3), we get

$$\frac{v_p}{dy/dx} = \frac{-\omega A}{kA} = -v$$

or

$$v_p = -v\left(\frac{dy}{dx}\right) \qquad \ldots(4)$$

or particle velocity at a point = – (wave velocity) × (slope of displacement curve at that point)

Particle acceleration : The acceleration of the particle can be obtained by differentiating particle velocity. Thus

$$a = \frac{dv_p}{dt} = \frac{d}{dt}[-\omega A\cos(\omega t - kx)]$$

or

$$a = -\omega^2 A\sin(\omega t - kx)$$

As

$$y = A\sin(\omega t - kx)$$

$\therefore$

$$a = -\omega^2 y$$

Also

$$a = \omega^2 A\sin(\omega t - kx + \pi)$$

(i) The maximum value of particle acceleration $a_0 = \omega^2 A$.

(ii) The particle acceleration leads particle velocity by $\dfrac{\pi}{2}$ and displacement by π radian.

Note:

1. For a wave travelling along positive x - axis, we can write
$$y = A_{0y}\sin(\omega t - kx) \text{ for transverse wave}$$
and
$$y = A_{0x}\sin(\omega t - kx) \text{ for longitudinal wave.}$$

2. In wave equation displacement y can be replaced by pressure, electric field, magnetic field. For electric field we can write
$$E = E_0\sin(\omega t - kx)$$

3. As $v_p = -v\left(\dfrac{dy}{dx}\right)$, so for positive slope, the velocity is negative and vice-versa.

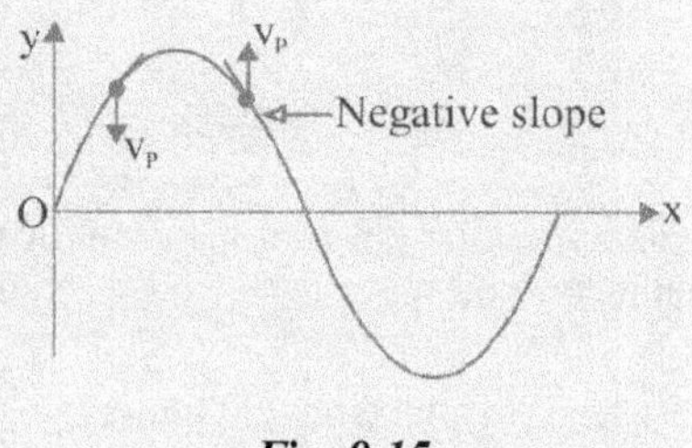

Fig. 9.15

9.11 WAVE EQUATION, $y = A \sin (kx - \omega t)$

The equation

$$y = A\sin(kx - \omega t) \qquad \ldots(1)$$

can be used to find the displacements of all the particles of the wave as a function of time. If this equation is used to represent a wave in stretched string, then it can tell us the shape of the wave at any given time and how that shape changes as the wave moves along the string.

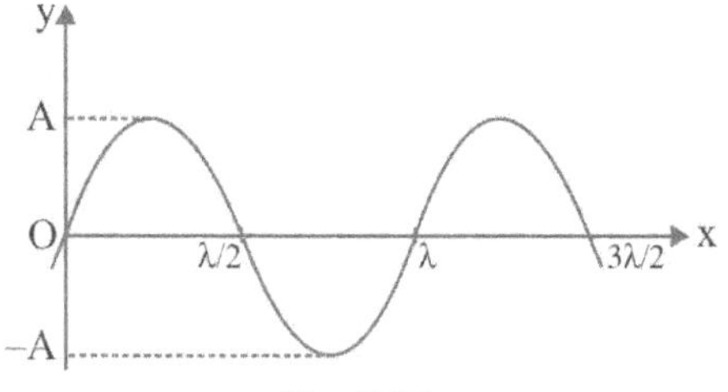

Fig. 9.16

9.12 THE SPEED OF A TRAVELLING WAVE

Consider a wave travelling along positive x - direction. *Fig. 9.17* shows two snap shots of the wave at a small interval of time Δt. Let Δx is the movement of entire wave pattern in time Δt, then wave speed is defined as

$$v = \frac{\Delta x}{\Delta t} \qquad \ldots(2)$$

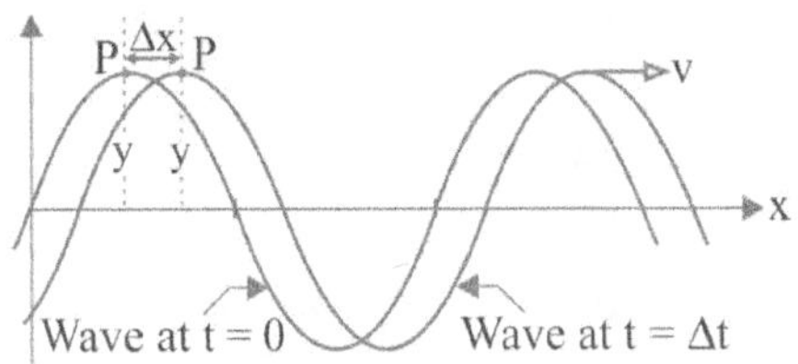

Fig. 9.17

As the wave move, each point of the moving wave form, retain its displacement. In figure point P moves to P′ in time Δt, but its displacement y remain constant.

Therefore, $\qquad \sin(kx - \omega t) = $ constant

or $\qquad (kx - \omega t) = $ a constant $\qquad \ldots(3)$

Differentiating equation (3) w.r.t. time, we get

$$k\frac{dx}{dt} - \omega = 0$$

or $$\frac{dx}{dt} = v = \frac{\omega}{k} \qquad \ldots(4)$$

Note:

It should be remembered that although argument $(kx - \omega t)$ is constant, but both x and t are changing.

Equation (1) represents a wave moving along positive x -direction. A wave travelling in the negative x -direction is described by the equation

$$y = A\sin[-(kx + \omega t)] \qquad \ldots(5)$$

For wave speed, $\dfrac{d}{dt}[-(kx + \omega t)] = 0$

or $$\frac{dx}{dt} = v = -\frac{\omega}{k}, \qquad \ldots(6)$$

here negative indicates that wave is moving along negative x-direction.

Thus general equation of a travelling harmonic wave (transverse or longitudinal) can be written as:

$$y(x, t) = y = g(kx \pm \omega t) \qquad \ldots(7)$$

Note:

The wave equations $y = A\sin(\omega t - kx)$ and $y = A\sin(kx - \omega t)$ have phase difference of π radian, but when we speak of a moving wave, we mean displacement of all the particles at any time, and therefore $y = A\sin(kx - \omega t)$ should be used according to the rule.

9.13 NON-SINUSOIDAL WAVES

1. **Square wave:** In square wave, there is a sharp over shot at $t = 0$ and at $t = \dfrac{T}{2}$.

   For a square wave (at $x = 0$)

   $$y = +A \quad \text{for} \quad 0 < t < \frac{T}{2}$$

   and $$= 0 \quad \text{for} \quad t = \frac{T}{2},$$

   and $$= -A \quad \text{for} \quad \frac{T}{2} < t < T$$

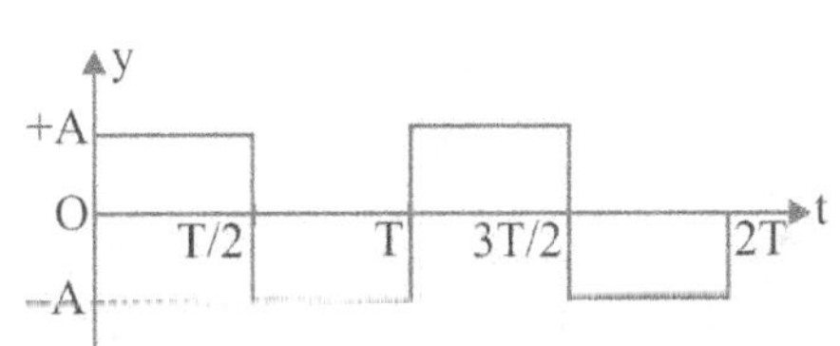

Fig. 9.18. Square wave.

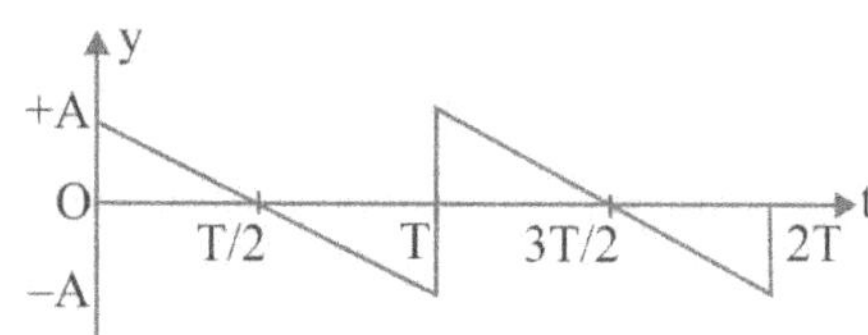

Fig. 9.19. Saw-tooth wave.

2. **Saw-tooth wave:** It can be represented by the equation

$$\text{At } x = 0 \quad y = A\left(1 - \frac{t}{T}\right) \qquad \text{for} \qquad 0 < t < T$$

$$y = A, \qquad \text{at} \qquad t = 0,$$
$$\text{and} \qquad y = 0, \qquad \text{at} \qquad t = T/2$$

Differential equation of wave:

An equation will represent a wave if it satisfy the following differential equation.

$$\frac{\partial^2 y}{\partial t^2} = v^2 \frac{\partial^2 y}{\partial x^2}$$

where v is the wave velocity or **phase velocity**.

Note:

If any function of x and t satisfy the differential equation but if not finite, then it will not represent a wave. For example $y = \ln(x + vt)$ etc. satisfy the differential equation, but not represent wave.

Ex. 10 Show that the function $y(x,t) = Ae^{-B(x-vt)^2}$ represents a travelling wave.

Sol.

Given
$$y = Ae^{-B(x-vt)^2} \qquad ...(i)$$

$$\therefore \quad \frac{\partial y}{\partial t} = Ae^{-B(x-vt)^2} \times (-2B)(x-vt) \times (-v)$$

$$= 2ABv(x-vt)e^{-B(x-vt)^2}$$

and
$$\frac{\partial^2 y}{\partial t^2} =$$

$$2ABv\left[(x-vt)e^{-B(x-vt)^2} \times (-2B)(x-vt)(-v) + e^{-B(x-vt)^2} \times (-v)\right]$$

$$= 2ABv^2 e^{-B(x-vt)^2}[2B(x-vt)^2 - 1] \cdots \text{(ii)}$$

Now
$$\frac{\partial y}{\partial x} = -2ABe^{-B(x-vt)^2} \times (x-vt)$$

and
$$\frac{\partial^2 y}{\partial x^2} = 2ABv^2 e^{-B(x-vt)^2} \times [2B(x-vt)^2 - 1] \quad ...(iii)$$

On comparing equations (ii) and (iii), we get

$$\frac{\partial^2 y}{\partial t^2} = v^2 \frac{\partial^2 y}{\partial x^2}$$

Also the given function is finite for each value of t, so it will represent a wave.

Ex. 11 Show that (i) $y = x^2 + v^2t^2$, (ii) $y = (x + vt)^2$, (iii) $y = (x - vt)^2$ and (iv) $y = 2 \sin x \cos vt$ are each a solution of one dimensional wave equation but not (v) $y = x^2 - v^2 t^2$ and (vi) $y = \sin 2x \cos vt$.

Sol.

(i) Differentiating expression (i) twice w.r.t.t, we have

$$\frac{\partial^2 y}{\partial t^2} = 2v^2$$

and differentiating expression (i) twice w.r.t. x, we have

$$\frac{\partial^2 y}{\partial x^2} = 2$$

Clearly,
$$\frac{\partial^2 y}{\partial t^2} = v^2\left(\frac{\partial^2 y}{\partial x^2}\right)$$

Thus expression (i) is a solution of the one-dimensional wave equation.

Similar treatment can be done for (ii), (iii) and (iv).

Note: The expression (iv) satisfies differential equation of wave, but it does not represent progressive wave. It represents stationary wave.

(v) Differentiating expression (v) twice w.r.t. we have

$$\frac{\partial^2 y}{\partial t^2} = -2v^2$$

and differentiating expression (v) twice w.r.t. x, we have

$$\frac{\partial^2 y}{\partial x^2} = 2$$

Clearly $\dfrac{\partial^2 y}{\partial t^2} \neq v^2 \dfrac{\partial^2 y}{\partial x^2}$, so the expression (v) is not a solution of the one dimensional wave equation.

(vi) Differentiating expression (vi) twice w.r.t. t, we have

$$\frac{\partial^2 y}{\partial t^2} = -v^2 \sin 2x \cos vt = -v^2 y$$

and
$$\frac{\partial^2 y}{\partial x^2} = -4 \sin 2x \cos vt = -4y$$

Clearly $\dfrac{\partial^2 y}{\partial t^2} \neq v^2 \dfrac{\partial^2 y}{\partial x^2}$, and therefore the expression is not a solution of the one dimensional wave equation.

Ex. 12 The shape of a wave pulse at time t is given by the function $f(x) = \dfrac{2x}{1 + ax^2}$, where $a = 1$ cm^{-2}. The wave is travelling along positive x-axis with velocity of 4 cm/s. Graph the wave function at times, $t = 0$s, 2s and 3s.

Sol.

Wave pulse at any time t can be obtained by putting $x - vt$ in place of x. Thus we wave

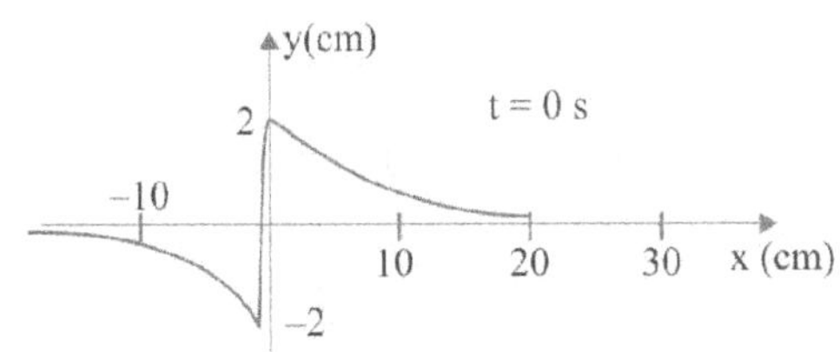

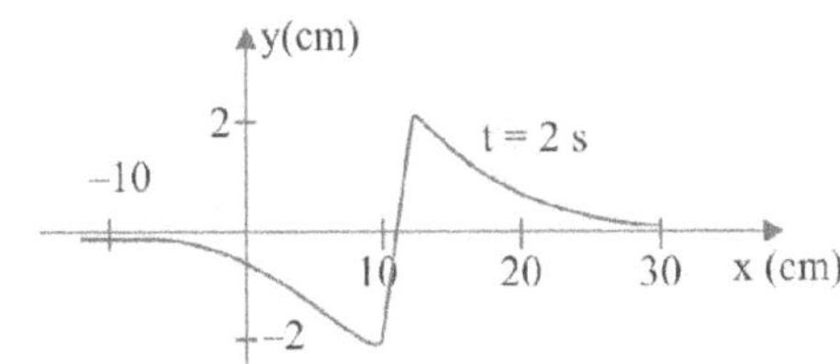

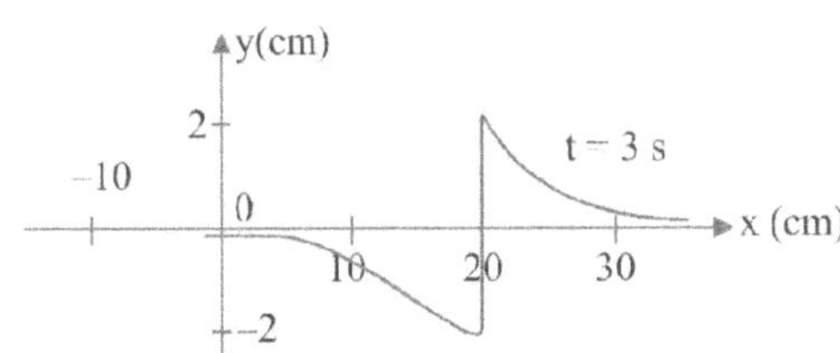

Fig. 9.20

$$y = \frac{2(x - vt)}{1 + a(x - vt)^2}$$

At $t = 0$ s, $\quad y = \dfrac{2x}{[1 + (1)x^2]}$

$$= \frac{2x}{1 + x^2}$$

At $t = 2$ s, $\quad y = \dfrac{2[x - 4 \times 2]}{\left[1 + (1)\{x - 4 \times 2\}^2\right]}$

$$= \frac{2(x - 8)}{\left[1 + (x - 8)^2\right]}$$

At $t = 3$s, $\quad y = \dfrac{2(x - 4 \times 3)}{\left[1 + (1)\{x - 4 \times 3\}^2\right]}$

$$= \frac{2(x - 12)}{\left[1 + (x - 12)^2\right]}$$

The wave function at given times are shown in *Fig. 9.20*.

Ex. 13 The equation of a wave travelling on a string stretched along the x-axis is given by

$$y = Ae^{-\left(\frac{x}{a} + \frac{t}{T}\right)^2}$$

where is the maximum of pulse located at $t = T$?

Sol.

The maximum of the pulse is $y = A$, when

$$e^{-\left(\frac{x}{\alpha} + \frac{t}{T}\right)^2} = 1$$

or $\qquad \left(\dfrac{x}{a} + \dfrac{t}{T}\right) = 0$

At $\quad t = T, \qquad \dfrac{x}{a} + 1 = 0$

$\therefore \qquad\qquad x = -a \qquad\qquad$ *Ans.*

Ex. 14 *Fig. 9.21* shows a snapshot of a vibrating string at $t = 0$. The particle P is observed moving up with velocity $20\sqrt{3}$ cm/s. The tangent at P makes an angle 60° with the x-axis. Find

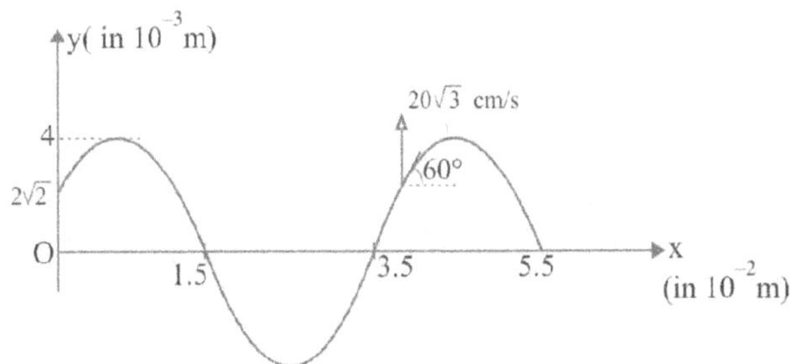

Fig. 9.21

(a) the direction in which wave is moving,

(b) equation of wave.

Sol.

(a) Suppose $\qquad y = A \sin(kx - \omega t + \phi) \qquad$ ...(i)

Given (from figure), at $t = 0$, $x = 0$; $y = 2\sqrt{2}$ and $A = 4$

$\therefore \qquad 2\sqrt{2} = 4 \sin(0 - 0 + \phi_0)$

which gives $\qquad \phi_0 = \dfrac{\pi}{4}$ or $\dfrac{3\pi}{4}$

We know that particle velocity

$$v_p = -v\left(\frac{dy}{dx}\right)$$

or $\qquad 20\sqrt{3} = -v \times \tan 60°$

$\therefore \qquad v = -20$ cm/s

It indicates that wave is travelling along negative x-axis.

(b) From the figure, $\quad \lambda = (5.5 - 1.5) = 4$ cm

$\therefore \qquad f = \dfrac{v}{\lambda} = \dfrac{20}{4} = 5\text{s}^{-1}$

Propagation constant

$$k = \frac{2\pi}{\lambda} = \frac{2\pi}{4} = \frac{\pi}{2}$$

and

$$\omega = 2\pi f = 2\pi \times 5$$
$$= 10\pi \text{ rad/s}$$

On substituting these values in equation (i), we get

$$y = 4\sin\left(\frac{\pi x}{2} - 10\pi t + \frac{\pi}{4}\right)$$

and

$$= 4\sin\left(\frac{\pi x}{2} - 10\pi t + \frac{3\pi}{4}\right) \quad Ans.$$

Ex. 15 For a travelling harmonic wave $y = 2.0 \cos(10t - 0.0080x + 0.35)$, where x and y are in cm and t in s. What is the phase difference between oscillatory motion at two points separated by a distance of (i) 4m, (ii) 0.5 m (iii) $\frac{\lambda}{2}$, (iv) $\frac{3\lambda}{4}$?

Sol.

Given $y = 2.0 \cos(10t - 0.0080x + 0.35)$
The standard equation of travelling harmonic wave can be written as
$$y = A \cos(\omega t - kx + \phi)$$
On comparing two equations, we have
$$\omega = 10 \text{ rad/s}$$
and
$$k = 0.0080 \text{ m}^{-1}$$

or

$$\frac{2\pi}{\lambda} = 0.0080$$

$$\therefore \quad \lambda = \frac{2\pi}{0.0080} = \frac{2\pi}{0.0080 \times 100} \text{ m}$$

$$= \frac{2\pi}{0.80}$$

Phase difference

$$\Delta\phi = \frac{2\pi}{\lambda} \times \Delta x$$

(i) When $\Delta x = 4$ m, $\quad \Delta\phi = \dfrac{2\pi}{(2\pi/0.80)} \times 4 = 3.2$ rad

(ii) When $\Delta x = 0.5$ m, $\Delta\phi = \dfrac{2\pi}{(2\pi/0.80)} \times 0.5 = 0.40$ rad

(iii) When $\Delta x = \dfrac{\pi}{2}$, $\Delta\phi = \dfrac{2\pi}{\lambda} \times \dfrac{\lambda}{2} = \pi$ rad

(iv) When $\Delta x = \dfrac{3\lambda}{4}$, $\Delta\phi = \dfrac{2\pi}{\lambda} \times \dfrac{3\lambda}{4} = \dfrac{3\pi}{2}$ rad.

Ex. 16

A transverse harmonic wave on a string is described by $y(x, t) = 3.0 \sin(36t + 0.018x + \frac{\pi}{4})$, where x, y are in cm and t in s. The positive direction of x is from left to right.
(i) Is this a travelling or a stationary wave? If it is travelling, what are the speed and direction of its propagation.
(ii) What are its amplitude and frequency?
(iii) What is the initial phase at the origin?
(iv) What is the least distance between two successive crest in the wave?

Sol.

Given $\quad y = 3.0\sin\left(36t + 0.018x + \dfrac{\pi}{4}\right)$ ...(i)

The standard equation of a harmonic wave travelling along negative x-direction is

$$y = A\sin(\omega t + kx + \phi_\circ) \quad ...(ii)$$

On comparing equations (i) and (ii), we have
$$\omega = 36 \text{ rad/s, } k = 0.018/\text{m}$$

and

$$\phi_0 = \frac{\pi}{4} \text{ rad}$$

(i)

$$v = \frac{\omega}{k} = \frac{36}{0.018}$$
$$= 2000 \text{ cm/s} = 20 \text{ m/s}$$

(ii)

$$A = 3.0 \text{ cm}$$

$$f = \frac{\omega}{2\pi} = \frac{36}{2\pi} = 5.73 \text{ s}^{-1}$$

(iii) Initial phase $\quad \phi_0 = \dfrac{\pi}{4} \text{ rad}$

(iv) Least distance between two successive crests

$$= \lambda = \frac{2\pi}{k} = \frac{2\pi}{0.018} = 349.0 \text{ cm}$$
$$= 3.49 \text{ m} \quad Ans.$$

Ex. 17 A travelling harmonic wave on a string is described by

$$y = 7.5 \sin\left(0.0050\, x + 12\, t + \frac{\pi}{4}\right).$$

(i) What are the displacement and velocity of oscillation of a point at $x = 1$cm, and $t = 1$s? Is this velocity equal to the velocity of wave propagation?
(ii) Locate the points of the string, which have the same transverse displacement and velocity as the $x = 1$cm point $t = 2$s, 5s, 11s.

Sol.

Given $\quad y = 7.5\sin\left(0.0050x + 12t + \dfrac{\pi}{4}\right)$ ...(i)

The standard equation of a travelling wave is
$$y = A\sin(\omega t + kx + \phi_0) \quad ...(ii)$$
On comparing equations (i) & (ii), we get

$A = 7.5$ cm, $\omega = 12$ rad/s, $k = 0.0050$ cm^{-1} and $\phi_0 = \dfrac{\pi}{4}$ rad.

(i) At $x = 1$cm and $t = 1$s, displacement of the particle

$$y = 7.5\sin\left(0.0050 \times 1 + 12 \times 1 + \frac{\pi}{4}\right)$$
$$= 7.5 \sin 12.79 = 1.67 \text{ cm} \quad Ans.$$

The velocity of the particle

$$v_p = \frac{dy}{dt}$$

$$= \frac{d}{dt}\left[7.5\sin\left(0.0050x + 12t + \frac{\pi}{4}\right)\right]$$

$$= 7.5 \times 12\cos\left(0.0050x + 12t + \frac{\pi}{4}\right)$$

$$= 90\cos\left(0.0050x + 12t + \frac{\pi}{4}\right)$$

At $x = 1$ cm and $t = 1$s

$$v_p = 90\cos\left(0.0050 \times 1 + 12 \times 1 + \frac{\pi}{4}\right)$$

$$= 90\cos 12.79 = 87.76 \text{ cm/s}$$

Velocity of propagation

$$v = \frac{\omega}{k} = \frac{12}{0.0050} = 2400 \text{ m/s}$$

Clearly velocity of the particle is not equal to the velocity of wave.

(ii)   As $k = \dfrac{2\pi}{\lambda} = 0.0050$

$\therefore$ $\lambda = \dfrac{2\pi}{0.0050} = 1256.64$ cm

All points located at distance $\eta\lambda$ (where η is an integer) from the point $x = 1$ cm have the same transverse displacement and velocity.

Ex. 18 The *Fig. 9.22* shows two snap shots, each of a wave travelling along a particular string . The phase for the waves are given by

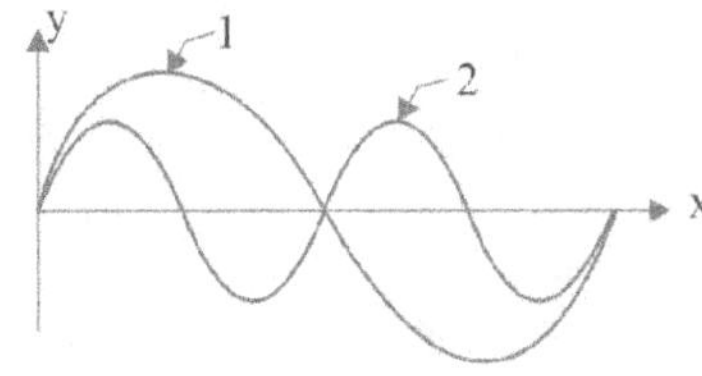

Fig. 9.22

(a) $4x - 8t$
(b) $8x - 16t$. Which phase corresponds to which wave in the figure?

Sol.

The standard equation of a plane progressive wave is $y = A\sin(kx - \omega t)$, the phase of the wave is $(kx - \omega t)$.

(a)   Comparing $4x - 8t$ with $(kx - \omega t)$, we get

$$\omega = 8 \text{ and } k = 4$$

$\therefore$ $$\lambda_1 = \frac{2\pi}{k} = \frac{2\pi}{4} = \frac{\pi}{2}$$

(b)   Comparing $8x - 16t$ with $(kx - \omega t)$, we get

$$\omega = 16 \text{ and } k = 8$$

$\therefore$ $$\lambda_2 = \frac{2\pi}{k} = \frac{2\pi}{8} = \frac{\pi}{4}$$

Clearly $\lambda_1 = 2\lambda_2$, $\therefore$ snap-shots 1 and 2 correspond to a and b respectively.

9.14 SPEED OF TRANSVERSE WAVE

If a wave is to propagate through a medium, it must cause the particles of the medium to oscillate as it passes. The oscillations of the medium possess kinetic energy and potential energy both. For that to happen, the medium must possess mass for kinetic energy and elasticity for potential energy. Thus mass and elasticity of the medium determine the wave speed.

Consider a transverse wave moving from left to right along a string with speed v. For the purpose, we can choose the reference frame attached to moving pulse. In this frame the string appears to move from right to left (see *Fig. 9.23*).

Consider a small element of the string of length $\Delta\ell$, forming an arc of a circle of radius R and subtending an angle θ at the centre of that circle. A force F pulls the string on this

element at each end. The net force $2F\sin\dfrac{\theta}{2}$ acts vertically downwards on the pulse. The

particles on the arc (pulse) are made to rotate in a circle due to this force exerted by neighbouring parts of the element. By Newton's second law

$$2F\sin\frac{\theta}{2} = \frac{mv^2}{R}$$

If μ is the mass per unit length of the string, then mass of the element, $m = \mu\Delta\ell$. For

small θ, $\sin\dfrac{\theta}{2} = \dfrac{\theta}{2}$. In view of these relations, we get

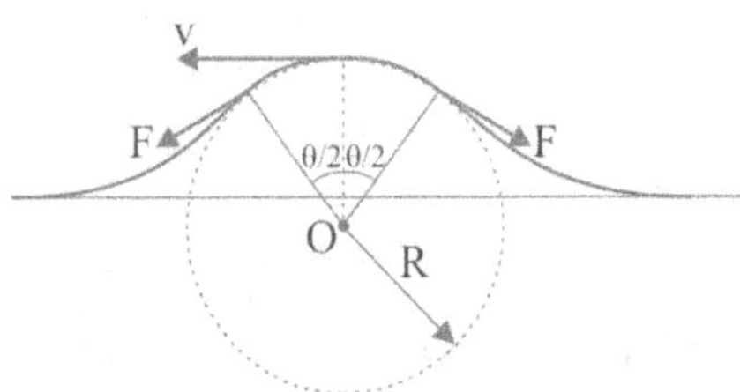

Fig. 9.23. A pulse viewed in a frame attached to the pulse.

$$2F \times \frac{\theta}{2} = \frac{(\mu \Delta \ell) v^2}{R}$$

As

$$\frac{\Delta \ell}{R} = \theta,$$

$\therefore$

$$F = \mu v^2$$

or

$$v = \sqrt{\frac{F}{\mu}}$$

> **Note:**
>
> 1. The wave shape in stretched string is sinusoidal, but on being small element, we have assumed it as circular.
> 2. If A is the area of cross-section of string and ρ is the density, then
>
> $$\mu = (A \times 1 \times \rho) = A\rho, \therefore v = \sqrt{\frac{F}{A\rho}}. \text{ As } \frac{F}{A} = \text{stress}, v = \sqrt{\text{Stress} / \text{Density}}.$$

Speed of transverse waves in solid

The speed of transverse wave in solid medium is determined by modulus of rigidity η of the material of the solid and density ρ of the solid (determine the inertia property). Thus the speed of transverse wave in solid is given by

$$v = \sqrt{\frac{\eta}{\rho}}$$

Ex. 19 A copper wire is held at the two ends by rigid supports. At 30°C, the wire is just taut with negligible tension. Find the speed of transverse waves in the wire at 10°C.

$(\alpha = 1.7 \times 10^{-5}/°C, Y = 1.4 \times 10^{11} N/m^2 \text{ and } \rho = 9 \times 10^3 kg/m^3)$

Sol.

The thermal stress in the wire corresponds to change in temperature Δt is

$$F = Y\alpha\Delta t$$

If A is the cross-sectional area of the wire, then tension produced in the wire

$$F = fA = Y\alpha\Delta tA$$

Speed of transverse wave in the wire

$$v = \sqrt{\frac{F}{\mu}} = \sqrt{\frac{Y\alpha\Delta tA}{(A \times 1)\rho}}$$

$$= \sqrt{\frac{Y\alpha\Delta t}{\rho}}$$

$$= \sqrt{\frac{1.4 \times 10^{11} \times 1.7 \times 10^{-5} \times 10}{9 \times 10^3}}$$

$$= 51.42 \text{ m/s } \textit{Ans.}$$

Ex. 20 A uniform rope of length 12m and mass 6 kg hangs vertically from a rigid support. A block of mass 2 kg is attached to the free end of the rope. A transverse pulse of wavelength 0.06 m is produced at the lower end of the rope, what is the wavelength of the pulse when it reaches the top of the rope?

Sol.

The force at any section of the rope is the weight suspended from the section. If F_A and F_B are the tensions at ends A and B respectively, then

$$F_A = 2g \text{ and } F_B = 8g$$

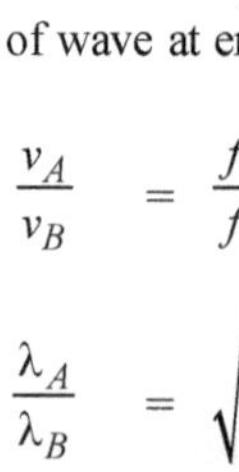

B
6 kg
A
2kg

Fig. 9.24

If v_A and v_B are the speeds of wave at ends A and B respectively, then

$$\frac{v_A}{v_B} = \frac{f\lambda_A}{f\lambda_B} = \frac{\sqrt{F_A/\mu}}{\sqrt{F_B/\mu}}$$

or

$$\frac{\lambda_A}{\lambda_B} = \sqrt{\frac{F_A}{F_B}} = \sqrt{\frac{2g}{8g}} = \frac{1}{2}$$

$\therefore$

$$\lambda_B = 2\lambda_A$$

$$= 2 \times 0.06$$

$$= 0.12 \text{ m} \qquad\qquad \textit{Ans.}$$

Ex. 21 A uniform rope of mass 0.1 and length 2.45 m hangs from a ceiling.
(i) Find the speed of transverse wave in the rope at a point 0.5 m distance from lower end.
(ii) Calculate the time taken by a transverse wave to travel the full length of the rope.

Sol.

Given length of the rope $\ell = 2.45$m . If μ is the mass per unit length of the rope, then mass of the y length of the rope, $m = \mu y$

$\therefore$ Tension at the point y from the free end $F = mg = \mu y g$

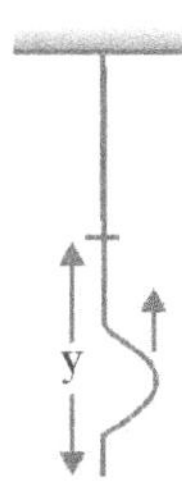

Fig. 9.25

The speed of transverse wave, $v = \sqrt{\dfrac{F}{\mu}}$

$$= \sqrt{\dfrac{\mu y g}{\mu}} = \sqrt{gy}$$

(i)   At $y = 0.5$m ,

$$v = \sqrt{9.8 \times 0.5} = 2.21 \text{ m/s}\quad \textit{Ans.}$$

(ii)   We can write $\dfrac{dy}{dt} = \sqrt{gy}$

or $dt = \dfrac{dy}{\sqrt{gy}}$

or $\displaystyle\int_0^t dt = \int_0^{2.45} \dfrac{dy}{\sqrt{gy}}$

$\therefore$ $t = \dfrac{2}{\sqrt{g}} |\sqrt{y}|_0^{2.45}$

$$= \dfrac{2}{\sqrt{g}}\left(\sqrt{2.45} - 0\right)$$

$$= 1 \text{ s}\qquad\qquad \textit{Ans.}$$

Ex. 22 A wave pulse starts propagating in the positive x direction along a non-uniform wire of length 10 m with a mass per unit length given by $m = m_0 + \alpha\, x$ and under a tension of 100 N. Find the time taken by the pulse to travel from the lighter end ($x = 0$) to the heavier end. ($m_0 = 10^{-2}$ kg/ m and $\alpha = 9 \times 10^{-3}$kg/m^2).

Sol.

The speed of transverse wave is given by

$$v = \sqrt{\dfrac{F}{\mu}}$$

Fig. 9.26

Here $F = 100$ N and $\mu = m = m_0 + \alpha x$

$\therefore$ $v = \sqrt{\dfrac{100}{(m_0 + \alpha x)}}$

or $\dfrac{dx}{dt} = 10\dfrac{1}{(m_0 + \alpha x)^{1/2}}$

or $dt = \dfrac{1}{10}(m_0 + \alpha x)^{1/2} dx$

$$\int_0^t dt = \dfrac{1}{10}\int_0^{10}(m_0 + \alpha x)^{1/2} dx$$

$$t = \dfrac{1}{10}\left|\dfrac{(m_0 + \alpha x)^{3/2}}{(3/2)\alpha}\right|_0^{10}$$

$$= \dfrac{1}{15\alpha}\left[(m_0 + \alpha \times 10)^{3/2} - m_0 3/2\right]$$

$$= \dfrac{1}{15 \times 9 \times 10^{-3}}\left[(10^{-2} + 9\times 10^{-3}\times 10)^{3/2} - (10^{-2})^{3/2}\right]$$

$$= 0.23 \text{ s}\qquad\qquad \textit{Ans.}$$

Ex. 23 The amplitude of a wave disturbance propagating along positive x -axis is given by $y = \dfrac{1}{(1+x^2)}$ at $t = 0$ and $y = \dfrac{1}{1+(x-2)^2}$ at $t = 4$ s, where x and y are in metre. The shape of wave disturbance does not change with time. Find velocity of the wave.

Sol.

The equation of the wave at any time t can be obtained by putting $(x - vt)$ in place of x in the given expression, so we have

$$y = \dfrac{1}{1+(x-vt)^2}\qquad\qquad \text{...(i)}$$

Given $y = \dfrac{1}{1+(x-2)^2}$ at $t = 4$s ...(ii)

On comparing equations (i) and (ii) , we get

$$vt = 2$$

As $t = 4$s, $\therefore$ $v = \dfrac{2}{t} = \dfrac{2}{4} = 0.5 \text{ m/s}\quad \textit{Ans.}$

Ex. 24 A pulse is propagating on a long stretched string along its length taken as positive x -axis. Shape of the string at $t = 0$ is given by,

$$y = \sqrt{a^2 - x^2}\quad \text{when } |x| \geq a$$

$$= 0 \qquad\quad \text{when } |x| \leq 0$$

Study the propagation of this pulse if it travelling in positive x- direction with v.

Sol.

The given equation can be written as
$$y^2 = a^2 - x^2$$
or
$$x^2 + y^2 = a^2$$
It represents a circular shape of the pulse.

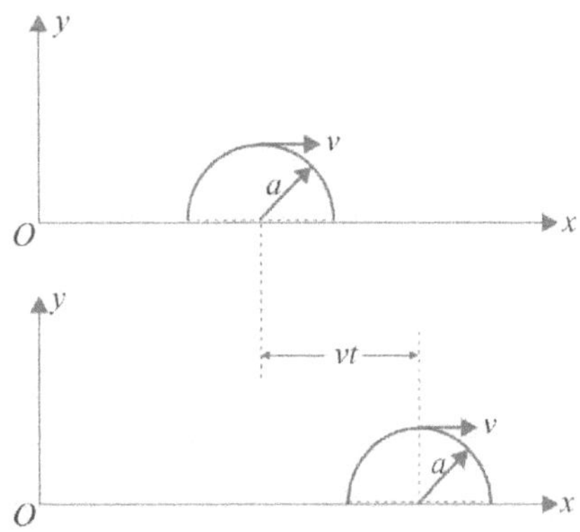

Fig. 9.27

The wave shape at any time can be obtained by putting $(x - vt)$ in place of x in the given equation, so we can write

$$y = \sqrt{a^2 - (x - vt)^2}$$

$$\text{when } |(x - vt)| \geq a$$

$$= 0 \qquad \text{when } |x - vt| \leq 0$$

The wave shape at any time t is shown in *Fig. 9.27*.

Ex. 25 A circular loop of string rotates about its axis on a frictionless horizontal plane at a uniform rate so that the tangential speed of any particle of the string is v. If a small transverse disturbance is produced at a point of the loop, with what speed (relative to the string) will this disturbance travel on the string?

Sol.

Suppose F is the tension in the string due to its rotation. Choose a small element of the string of length ℓ. If μ is the mass per unit length of the string, then mass of the element,
$$m = \mu\ell = \mu(R\theta).$$
Using Newton's second law for the element, we have

$$2F \sin\frac{\theta}{2} = \frac{mv^2}{R}$$

For small θ, $\qquad \sin\frac{\theta}{2} = \frac{\theta}{2}$

$$\therefore \qquad 2F\left(\frac{\theta}{2}\right) = \frac{mv^2}{R}$$

or $\qquad\qquad F\theta = (\mu R\theta)\dfrac{v^2}{R}$

$$\therefore \qquad F = \mu v^2$$

The speed of the disturbance

Fig. 9.28

$$\sqrt{\frac{F}{\mu}} = \sqrt{\frac{\mu v^2}{\mu}} = v \qquad\qquad \textit{Ans.}$$

9.15 SOUND WAVES

Sound waves, we mean the longitudinal waves in air which, when strike the ear, produce the sensation of hearing. The human ear is sensitive to waves in the frequency range from about 20 to 20000 Hz.

The sound waves in an elastic medium can be described by a wave function of displacement

$$y = A\cos(kx - \omega t), \qquad\qquad ...(1)$$

here cosine function is taken to make the final wave equation positive. In practice, it is easier to measure pressure variation in a sound wave than the displacement, so it becomes necessary to develop a relation between these two quantities.

Figure shows an oscillating element of air of thickness Δx and cross-sectional area S. Let the element is displaced towards right by an amount Δy.

The volume of the element

$$V = S\Delta x$$

The change in volume of the element due to its displacement Δy
$$\Delta V = S\Delta y.$$

This change in volume occurs because the displacement of the two faces of the element are not equal. The bulk modulus B of the medium is given by

$$B = \frac{\Delta P}{\left(-\dfrac{\Delta V}{V}\right)}$$

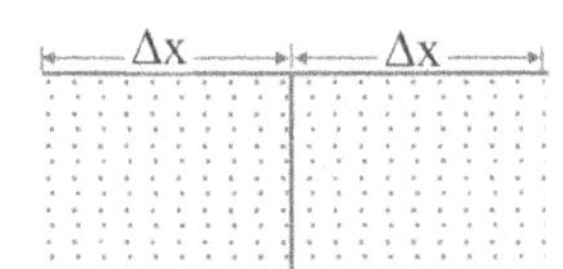

Fig. (a) A tube filled with air at normal pressure

Fig. (b) The element happens to be displaced a distance Δy

Fig. 9.29

or $\qquad\qquad \Delta P = -B\left(\dfrac{\Delta V}{V}\right)$

After substituting the values of ΔV and V in above equation, we get

$$\Delta P = -B\frac{S\Delta y}{S\Delta x}$$

$$= -B\frac{\Delta y}{\Delta x}$$

For small Δx, $\dfrac{\Delta y}{\Delta x} \to \dfrac{\partial y}{\partial x}$. The symbol ∂ is used for partial differentiation.

$$\therefore \qquad \Delta P = -B\frac{\partial y}{\partial x} \qquad \qquad ...(2)$$

Substituting y from equation (1) , we get

$$\Delta P = -B\frac{\partial\left[A\cos(kx-\omega t)\right]}{\partial x}$$

$$= ABk\sin(kx-\omega t) \qquad ...(3)$$

The maximum amount by which pressure differs (usually from atmospheric pressure), that is maximum value of ΔP, is called the pressure amplitude, denoted ΔP_m, so equation (3) can be written as;

$$\Delta P = \Delta P_m \sin(kx-\omega t) \qquad ...(4)$$

where $\Delta P_m = ABk$. The equation (4) is also called pressure wave. The equation can also be written as;

$$\Delta P = \Delta P_m \cos(kx-\omega t-\pi/2) \quad ...(5)$$

If P_0 be the normal pressure of the air, then pressure varies between $(P_0-\Delta P_m)$ to $(P_0+\Delta P_m)$ or (P_0-ABK) to (P_0+ABk).

Relationship between P and v_p

The particle velocity is given by the equation

$$v_P = \omega A\cos(\omega t-kx) \qquad ...(6)$$

The maximum velocity, called the velocity amplitude v_0, is given by $v_{0P}=\omega A$ and pressure amplitude $P_0=ABk$,

$$\therefore \qquad \frac{P_0}{v_0} = \frac{Bk}{\omega}$$

As $\qquad \dfrac{\omega}{k}=v$, so $\qquad P_0 = \dfrac{Bv_{0P}}{v}$

$$\text{Pressure amplitude} = \left[\frac{\text{Bulk modulus}\times\text{velocity amplitude}}{\text{Wave speed}}\right]$$

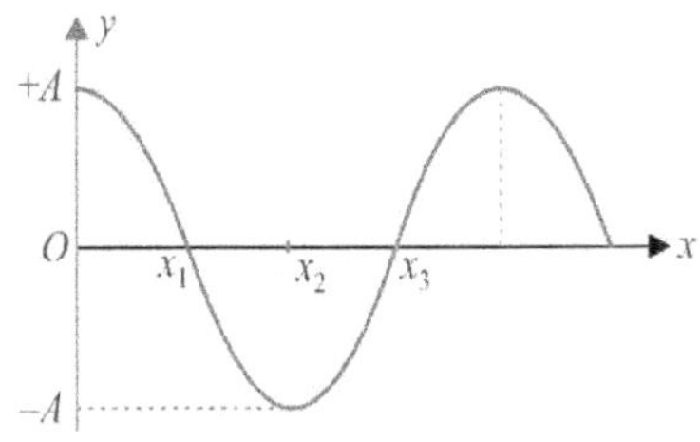

(a) A plot of displacement function for $t=0$.

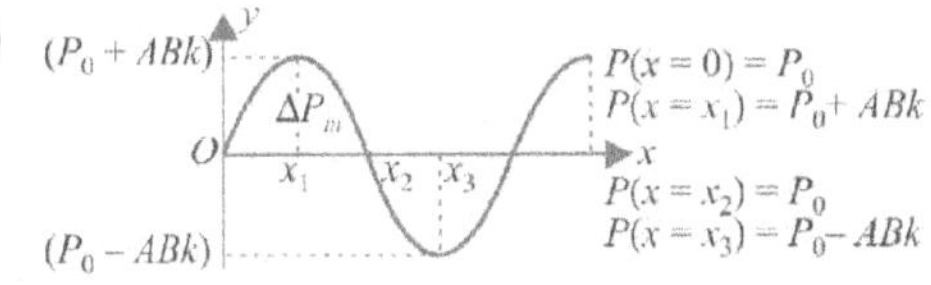

(b) A plot of the pressure variation.

Fig. 9.30

9.16 THE SPEED OF LONGITUDINAL WAVE

Consider a long tube filled with air. Let a single pulse travels towards left with a speed v. To understand easily, let us take a frame attached to the moving pulse. In this frame pulse appears stationary and the air is moving towards right with a speed v.

Let the normal air pressure be P and the pressure inside the pulse be $P+\Delta P$, taking ΔP positive for the compression. Take an element of air of thickness Δx and face area S, moving toward the pulse at a speed v. As the element of air enters the pulse, its speed changes from v to $v+\Delta v$, in which Δv is negative. The speed decreases due to a region of higher pressure.

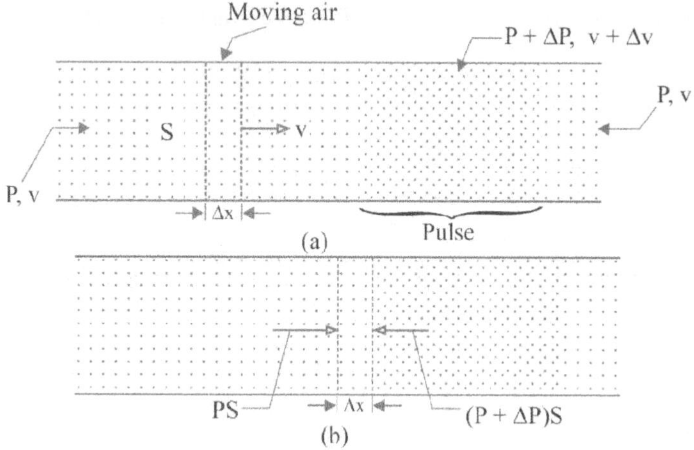

Fig. 9.31

If Δt is the time in which rear face of air element reaches the pulse, then $\Delta x = v\Delta d$ ...(1)
The net force on the element

$$F_{net} = PS - (P + \Delta P)S$$

or
$$F_{net} = \Delta PS \qquad ...(2)$$

The mass of the air element

$$\Delta m = \text{density} \times \text{volume}$$
$$= \rho(S\Delta x) = \rho Sv\Delta t \qquad ...(3)$$

Using Newton's second law for the element of mass Δm, we have

$$F_{net} = \Delta m \times a$$

or
$$-\Delta PS = (\rho Sv\Delta t)\frac{\Delta v}{\Delta t}$$

or
$$\Delta P = -\rho v\Delta v$$

or
$$\rho v = -\frac{\Delta P}{\Delta v}$$

or
$$\rho v^2 = -\frac{\Delta P}{(\Delta v / v)} \qquad ...(4)$$

The volume of the air element $V = S\Delta x = Sv\Delta t$, and the compression as it enters the pulse,

$$\Delta V = S\Delta v\Delta t .$$

Thus

$$\text{volumetric strain } \frac{\Delta V}{V} = \frac{S\Delta v\Delta t}{Sv\Delta t} = \frac{\Delta v}{v} \qquad ...(5)$$

Substituting this value in equation (4), we have

$$\rho v^2 = -\frac{\Delta P}{(\Delta V / V)} = B$$

After rearranging , we get

$$v = \sqrt{\frac{B}{\rho}} \qquad ...(6)$$

9.17 Speed of Sound : Newton's Formula

By his observations, Newton obtained a formula for speed of sound in air as :

$$v = \sqrt{\frac{P}{\rho}}, \qquad ...(1)$$

where P is the isothermal elasticity of the air. He argued that when sound propagates through air, the temperature of air remain constant. By Newton's formula the speed of sound at one atmosphere is

$$v = \sqrt{\frac{1.013 \times 10^5}{1.29}} \simeq 280 \, m/s$$

This value is less than the experimental value 332 m/s. Hence Newton's formula requires some correction, which was made by Laplace in 1816.

9.18 LAPLACE'S CORRECTION

French scientist Laplace pointed out that when sound propagates in air the heat of the medium remain constant instead of temperature. So he replaced isothermal elasticity by adiabatic elasticity, B_{ad}. The corrected formula is :

$$v = \sqrt{\frac{B_{ad}}{\rho}} \qquad \qquad ...(2)$$

For the adiabatic change, $PV^\gamma = $ constant
Differentiating both sides, we get

$$P(\gamma V^{\gamma-1}) \, dV + V^\gamma \, dP = 0$$

or
$$\gamma \, PdV + VdP = 0$$

or
$$\frac{dP}{\left(\dfrac{-dV}{V}\right)} = \gamma P$$

As
$$\frac{dP}{\left(\dfrac{-dV}{V}\right)} = B_{ad}$$

$\therefore$
$$B_{ad} = \gamma P \qquad \qquad ...(3)$$

where $\gamma = C_p / C_v$, is the ratio of specific heats.
Hence Laplace formula for the speed of sound in air (gas) is

$$v = \sqrt{\frac{\gamma P}{\rho}} \qquad \qquad ...(4)$$

For air $\gamma = \dfrac{7}{4}$, so the speed of sound in air at STP will be

$$v = \sqrt{\gamma}\sqrt{\frac{P}{\rho}} = \sqrt{\frac{7}{5}} \times 280$$

$$= 332 \, m/s$$

This value is in very close agreement with the experimental value.

Note :

1. Speed of longitudinal wave in a solid is given by, $v = \sqrt{\dfrac{B + \dfrac{4}{3}\eta}{\rho}}$, where η is the modulus of rigidity and B is the bulk modulus.

2. Speed of longitudinal wave in solid rod is given by, $v = \sqrt{\dfrac{Y}{\rho}}$, where Y is the Young's modulus of the material of the rod.

Speed of sound in different mediums

Solid	Steel	5960(m/s)
	Aluminium	6420
Liquid	Water	1498
Gas	Air	340
	Oxygen	316

Ex. 26 At a pressure of 10^5 N/m^2, the volume strain of water is 5×10^{-5}. Calculate the speed of sound in water. Density of water is 10^3 kg/m^3.

Sol. Bulk modulus of water

$$B = \frac{\text{Normal stress}}{\text{Volume strain}}$$

$$= \frac{10^5}{5 \times 10^{-5}} = 2 \times 10^9 \, \text{N/m}^2$$

Speed of sound in water

$$v = \sqrt{\frac{B}{\rho}} = \sqrt{\frac{2 \times 10^9}{10^3}}$$

$$= 1414 \text{ m/s} \qquad \textit{Ans.}$$

9.19 FACTORS AFFECTING SPEED OF SOUND IN GAS

(i) **Pressure**: The speed of sound in a gas is given by

$$v = \sqrt{\frac{\gamma P}{\rho}}$$

We know, $\qquad PV = nRT = \frac{m}{M} RT$

At constant temperature, $\quad P\Delta V = \frac{\Delta m}{M} RT$

$\therefore \qquad\qquad P = \frac{\Delta m}{\Delta V} \frac{RT}{M}$

or $\qquad\qquad P = \rho \frac{RT}{M}$

or $\qquad\qquad \frac{P}{\rho} = \text{constant}$

i.e, with the change in pressure, the density also changes in such proportion, so that $\dfrac{P}{\rho}$ remains constant. Hence pressure has no effect on the speed of sound in a gas.

(ii) **Effect of density :** For two gases of densities ρ_1 and ρ_2 at same pressure with γ_1 and γ_2,

$$\frac{v_1}{v_2} = \sqrt{\frac{\gamma_1}{\gamma_2} \times \frac{\rho_2}{\rho_1}} \, .$$

(iii) **Temperature :** We have got $\quad \dfrac{P}{\rho} = \dfrac{RT}{M}$

$\therefore \qquad\qquad v = \sqrt{\frac{\gamma RT}{M}}$

Clearly $\qquad\qquad v \propto \sqrt{T}$

Hence the speed of sound in a gas is proportional to the square root of its absolute temperature. If v_0 and v_t are the velocities of sound in gas at $0°$C and $t°$C respectively, then

$$v_0 = \sqrt{\frac{\gamma R(273 + 0)}{M}}$$

and $\qquad\qquad v_t = \sqrt{\frac{\gamma R(273 + t)}{M}}$

$$\therefore \qquad \frac{v_t}{v_0} = \left(\frac{273+t}{273}\right)^{\frac{1}{2}}$$

$$= \left(1+\frac{t}{273}\right)^{\frac{1}{2}}$$

For small value of t

$$v_t \approx v_0\left(1+\frac{1}{2}\frac{t}{273}\right)$$

or $\qquad v_t = v_0 + \frac{v_0 t}{546}$

But $v_0 = 332$ m/s,

$$\therefore \qquad v_t - v_0 = \frac{332t}{546} = 0.61t$$

When $t = 1°C$, $\qquad v_t - v_0 = 0.61$ m/s

Hence the velocity of sound in air increases by 0.61 m for every 1°C rise in temperature.

(iv) **Humidity :** With the increase in humidity, the density of air decreases. As the speed of sound in air is

$$v \propto \frac{1}{\sqrt{\rho}},$$

$\therefore$ the speed of sound will increase.

(v) **Frequency :** With the change in frequency of the sound wave, wavelength inversely changes, so that $f\lambda = v$ (constant). Thus the speed of sound is independent of its frequency.

(vi) **Wind :** As the sound is carried by air, so its speed is affected by the wind velocity. Suppose the wind is blowing with a velocity v_ω at an angle θ with the direction of propagation of the sound. Clearly, the component of wind velocity in the direction of sound is $v_\omega \cos\theta$.

$\therefore$ Resultant velocity of sound $= v + v_\omega \cos\theta$

When the wind blows in the direction of sound $(\theta° = 0)$, resultant velocity $= v + v_\omega$

When wind blows in the opposite direction of sound $(\theta = 180°)$, resultant velocity $= v - v_\omega$.

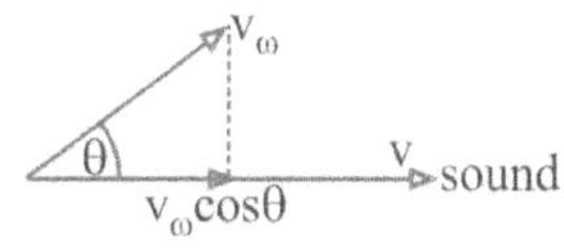

Fig. 9.32

Ex. 27 At what temperature will the speed of sound be double its value at 273°K?

Sol.

We have, $\qquad \dfrac{v_2}{v_1} = \sqrt{\dfrac{T_2}{T_1}}$

Given $\qquad v_2 = 2v_1$

$$\therefore \qquad \frac{2v_1}{v_1} = \sqrt{\frac{T_2}{T_1}}$$

or $\qquad T_2 = 4T_1 = 4(273) = 1092$ K *Ans.*

Ex. 28 A tuning fork of frequency 220 Hz produces sound waves of wavelength 1.5 m in air at STP. Calculate the increase in wavelength, when temperature of air is 27°C.

Sol.

Given $f = 220$ Hz, $\lambda_0 = 1.5$ m at $T_0 = 273$ K

Speed of sound at STP, $\qquad v_0 = f\lambda_0 = 220 \times 1.5 = 330$ m/s.

Final temperature, $\qquad T = 273 + 27 = 300$ K

Let v the speed of sound at this temperature, then

$$\frac{v}{v_0} = \sqrt{\frac{T}{T_0}}$$

$$\therefore \qquad v = v_0 \sqrt{\frac{T}{T_0}}$$

$$= 330\sqrt{\frac{300}{273}} = 346.1 \text{ m/s}$$

Final wavelength, $\qquad \lambda = \dfrac{v}{f} = \dfrac{346.1}{220} = 1.57 \text{ m}$

The increase in wavelength $= \lambda - \lambda_0 = 1.57 - 1.50 = 0.07 \text{ m}$ *Ans.*

Ex. 29 A sample of oxygen at NTP has volume V and a sample of hydrogen at NTP has volume $4V$. Both the gases are mixed and the mixture is maintained at NTP. If the speed of sound in hydrogen at NTP is 1270 m/s, calculate the speed of sound in the mixture.

Sol.

If V_H and V_m are the velocities in hydrogen and mixture respectively, then

$$\frac{v_m}{v_H} = \sqrt{\frac{\rho_H}{\rho_m}} \qquad \ldots(i)$$

Density of mixture, $\qquad \rho_m = \dfrac{\rho_o V_o + \rho_H V_H}{V_o + V_H}$

where ρ_o and V_o are the density and volume of the oxygen.

$$\rho_m = \frac{\rho_H V_H \left(1 + \dfrac{\rho_o}{\rho_H} \times \dfrac{V_o}{V_H}\right)}{V_H \left(1 + \dfrac{V_o}{V_H}\right)}$$

or $\qquad \dfrac{\rho_m}{\rho_H} = \dfrac{\left(1 + \dfrac{\rho_o}{\rho_H} \times \dfrac{V_o}{V_H}\right)}{\left(1 + \dfrac{V_o}{V_H}\right)}$

$$= \frac{1 + 16 \times \dfrac{1}{4}}{1 + \dfrac{1}{4}} = 4$$

or $\qquad \dfrac{\rho_H}{\rho_m} = \dfrac{1}{4}$

From equation (i),

$$v_m = v_H \sqrt{\frac{1}{4}} = \frac{v_H}{2}$$

$$= \frac{1270}{2} = 635 \text{ m/s} \quad \textit{Ans.}$$

Ex. 30 The absolute temperature of air in a region linearly increases from T_1 and T_2 in a space of width d. Find the time taken by sound wave to goes through the region in terms of T_1, T_2, d and the speed v of sound at 273 K.

Sol.

The variation of temperature with the distance is shown in *Fig. 9.33*. Consider a section of air at a distance x from the end at temperature T_1.

The temperature at this section $\quad T = T_1 + \left(\dfrac{T_2 - T_1}{d}\right)x$

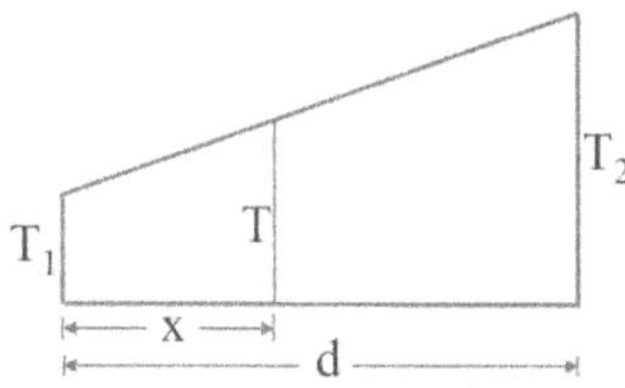

Fig. 9.33

The speed of sound at any temperature is given by

$$v_t = \sqrt{\frac{\gamma R T}{M}}$$

At $\qquad$ 273 K, $v = \sqrt{\dfrac{\gamma R \times 273}{M}}$

$$\therefore \qquad v_t = v\sqrt{\frac{T}{273}}$$

or $\qquad \dfrac{dx}{dt} = \dfrac{v}{\sqrt{273}}\left[T_1 + \dfrac{T_2 - T_1}{d}x\right]^{\frac{1}{2}}$

or $\qquad \displaystyle\int_0^t dt = \dfrac{\sqrt{273}}{v}\int_0^d \dfrac{dx}{\left[T_1 + \left(\dfrac{T_2 - T_1}{d}\right)x\right]^{\frac{1}{2}}}$

or $\qquad t = \dfrac{2\sqrt{273}}{v}\dfrac{\left|\left\{T_1 + \left(\dfrac{T_2 - T_1}{d}\right)x\right\}^{\frac{1}{2}}\right|_0^d}{\left(\dfrac{T_2 - T_1}{d}\right)}$

$$= \frac{2d\sqrt{273}\left(\sqrt{T_2} - \sqrt{T_1}\right)}{v} \cdot \frac{1}{T_2 - T_1}$$

$$= \frac{2d}{v}\frac{\sqrt{273}}{\sqrt{T_2} + \sqrt{T_1}} \qquad \textit{Ans.}$$

9.20 ENERGY OF A PROGRESSIVE WAVE

We know that, in wave motion, the energy derived from the source is transferred from one part of the medium to other part of the medium. The work done by the source in any way gets associated with two kinds of the energy of the medium; kinetic energy and potential energy.

1. In taut string, the forces due to tension in the string continuously do work to transfer energy from regions with energy to regions with no energy. The oscillating string element possesses both its maximum kinetic energy and its maximum elastic potential energy at $y = 0$. The oscillating element has maximum speed and hence kinetic energy at $y = 0$ and also maximum stretching and hence maximum potential energy at $y = 0$. The regions of the string at maximum displacement have no energy.

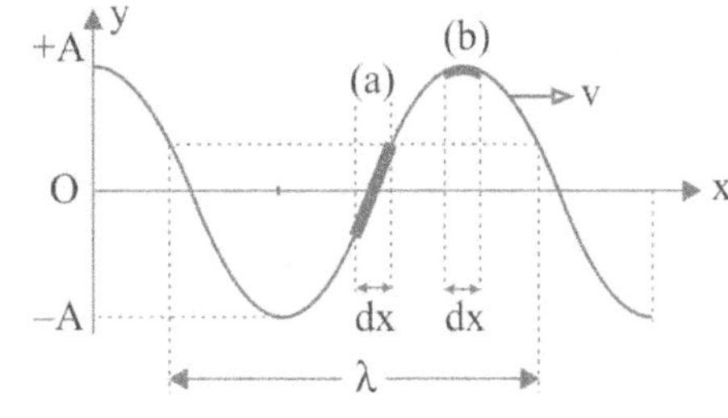

Fig. 9.34

Explanation:

It is clear from the figure that the string element (b), its length has its normal undisturbed value dx, so its potential energy is minimum. However when the element passes through its $y = 0$ position, it is stretched to its maximum, and possess maximum potential energy.

2. In case of sound wave energy is transferred due to work done by the source by creating pressure difference in the medium.

9.21 POWER TRANSMISSION

Consider a thin element of the medium of mass dm parallel to the wave front (it may be string element or air element). If μ is the mass per unit length of the medium, then $dm = \mu dx$.

Kinetic energy: The kinetic energy dK associated with the element

$$dK = \frac{1}{2}dmv_P^2 = \frac{1}{2}(\mu dx)v_P^2 \qquad ...(1)$$

where v_p is the speed of the oscillating element. v_P can be obtained as;

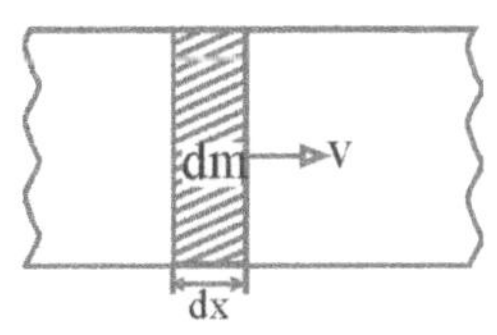

Fig. 9.35

$$v_p = \frac{\partial y}{\partial t} = \frac{\partial}{\partial t}[A\sin(kx - \omega t)]$$

$$= -\omega A\cos(kx - \omega t)$$

$$\therefore \quad dK = \frac{1}{2}(\mu dx)\omega^2 A^2 \cos^2(kx - \omega t)$$

The rate at which kinetic energy is carried by the wave

$$\frac{dK}{dt} = \frac{1}{2}\mu\left(\frac{dx}{dt}\right)\omega^2 A^2 \cos^2(kx - \omega t)$$

or

$$\frac{dK}{dt} = \frac{1}{2}\mu v\omega^2 A^2 \cos^2(kx - \omega t) \qquad ...(2)$$

The average rate at which kinetic energy is carried can be obtained as:

The average value of $\cos^2(kx - \omega t)$ over the wavelength.

$$\frac{\displaystyle\int_0^\lambda \cos^2(kx - \omega t)dx}{\displaystyle\int_0^\lambda dx} = \frac{1}{2}$$

$$\therefore \quad \text{Power,} \qquad P_{\text{kinetic}} = \left(\frac{dK}{dt}\right)_{av} = \frac{1}{4}\mu v\omega^2 A^2 \qquad ...(3)$$

Potential energy : The force acting on the element

$$F = (dm) \times \text{acceleration}$$

$$= (\mu dx) \times \frac{\partial^2 y}{\partial t^2}$$

$$= \mu dx \times \frac{\partial^2}{\partial t^2}[A\sin(kx - \omega t)]$$

$$= \mu dx\left[-\omega^2 A\sin(kx - \omega t)\right]$$

$$= \mu dx \omega^2 y$$

The work done in a small displacement dy of the element

$$dW = Fdy = \mu dx \omega^2 y dy$$

Work done during the displacement 0 to y

$$W = \mu dx \omega^2 \int_0^y y dy$$

$$= \frac{1}{2}\mu dx \omega^2 y^2$$

$$= \frac{1}{2}\mu dx \omega^2 [A\sin(kx - \omega t)]^2$$

$$= \frac{1}{2}\mu dx \omega^2 A^2 \sin^2(kx - \omega t)]$$

This work done must be stored up in the medium in the form of potential energy. Thus potential energy

$$U = \frac{1}{2}\mu dx \omega^2 A^2 \sin^2(kx - \omega t)$$

The rate at which potential energy carried

$$\frac{dU}{dt} = \frac{1}{2}\mu\left(\frac{dx}{dt}\right)\omega^2 A^2 \sin^2(kx - \omega t)$$

$$= \frac{1}{2}\mu v \omega^2 A^2 \sin^2(kx - \omega t)$$

The average rate at which potential energy carried can be obtained as:
The average value of $\sin^2(kx - \omega t)$ over the wavelength

$$\frac{\int_0^\lambda \sin^2(kx - \omega t)dx}{\int_0^\lambda dx} = \frac{1}{2}$$

$\therefore$ Power, $\qquad P_{\text{potential}} = \left(\frac{dU}{dt}\right)_{av} = \frac{1}{4}\mu v \omega^2 A^2$ ...(4)

Total power transmitted: The average power, which is the average rate at which energy of both kinds is transmitted by the wave, is then

$$P_{av} = P_{\text{kinetic}} + P_{\text{potential}}$$

or $\qquad P_{av} = \frac{1}{2}\mu v \omega^2 A^2$ ...(5)

If ρ is the volume density and S is the area across which power transmitted, then

$$\mu = \rho S$$

$\therefore \qquad P_{av} = \frac{1}{2}(\rho S)v\omega^2 A^2 = \frac{1}{2}\rho v S \omega^2 A^2$ ...(6)

9.22 INTENSITY OF SOUND

The intensity I of a sound wave (or any other wave) at any point of a surface is the sound energy transferred through unit surface area perpendicular to the direction of propagation of wave in unit time.

Or it can be defined as the power transferred through unit surface area perpendicular to the direction of propagation of wave. If P is the power transferred through surface area S, then intensity of wave can be written as

$$I = \frac{P}{S}$$

SI unit of intensity is W/m^2. We have already derived that

$$P = \frac{1}{2}\rho v S \omega^2 A^2$$

$$\therefore \quad I = \frac{P}{S} = \frac{1}{2}\rho v \omega^2 A^2 \qquad \qquad ...(1)$$

For sound wave

$$\Delta P_m = ABk$$

$$\therefore \quad A = \frac{\Delta P_m}{Bk}$$

Substituting this value in equation (1), we get

$$I = \frac{1}{2}\rho v \omega^2 \left(\frac{\Delta P_m}{Bk}\right)^2$$

$$= \frac{1}{2}\rho v \omega^2 \frac{\Delta P_m^2}{B^2 k^2}$$

As $\qquad K = \dfrac{\omega}{v}$ and $B = v^2 \rho$

$$\therefore \quad I = \frac{1}{2}\rho v \omega^2 \frac{\Delta P_m^2}{B^2 \dfrac{\omega^2}{v^2}}$$

$$\therefore \quad I = \frac{v \Delta P_m^2}{2B} = \frac{\Delta P_m^2}{2\rho v} \qquad \qquad ...(2)$$

Variation of intensity with distance

Let us assume that mechanical energy of the sound waves is conserved as they spread from the source.

1. The plane or one dimensional wave travels without change in intensity, i.e., with its amplitude undiminished, the intensity of the wave remains the same throughout. For power of source P and surface S, the intensity

$$I = \frac{P}{S}$$

As S remain constant, so I remain constant.

2. The power P of the line source will spread over a cylindrical surface. The surface area of the cylinder of radius r is $2\pi rL$, where L is the length of the line source. The intensity is given by

$$I = \frac{P}{S} = \frac{P}{2\pi rL} \qquad \qquad ...(1)$$

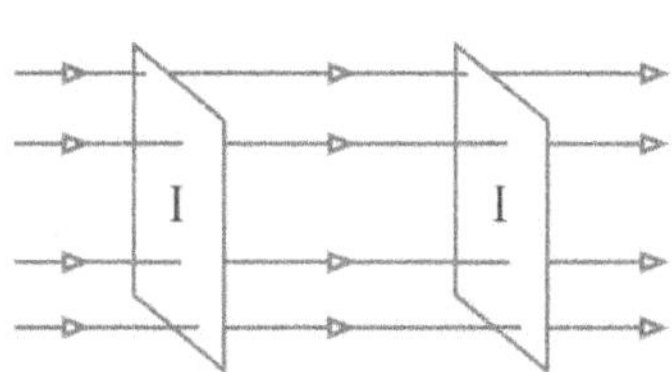

Fig. 9.36. A plane wave

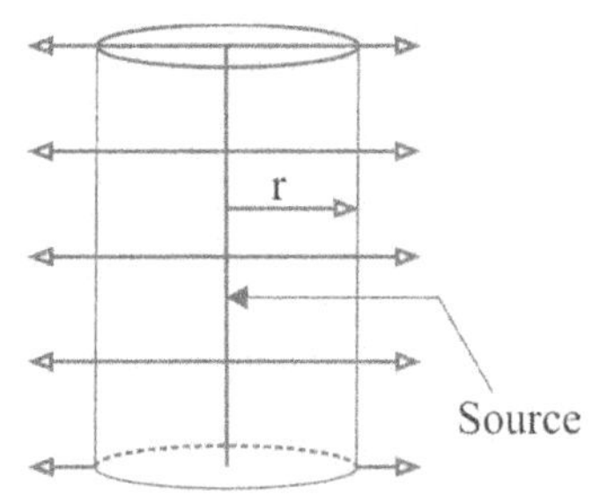

Fig. Line source of power P

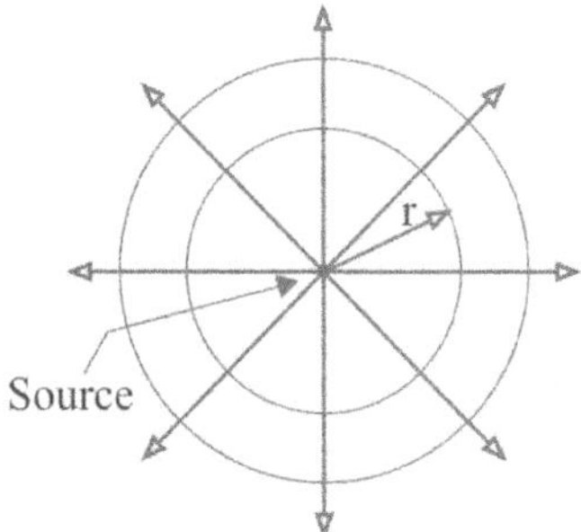

Fig. A point source of power P.

Fig. 9.37

Clearly, $\qquad\qquad I \propto \dfrac{1}{r}.$

As $\quad I \propto A^2, \qquad\qquad \therefore\ A \propto \dfrac{1}{\sqrt{r}}$

3. The power P of the point source will spread over the spherical surface. The intensity of the source at a distance r from the source is given by

$$I \;=\; \frac{P}{4\pi r^2} \qquad\qquad\qquad ...(2)$$

Clearly $I \propto \dfrac{1}{r^2}$. As $I \propto A^2, \quad \therefore\ A \propto \dfrac{1}{r}.$

Note :

In view of these facts, we can write the following wave equations

(i) $\quad y = \dfrac{A}{r^\circ}\sin(kx - \omega t)$ for plane progressive wave.

(ii) $\quad y = \dfrac{A}{\sqrt{r}}\sin(kx - \omega t)$ for waves from a line source.

(iii) $\quad y = \dfrac{A}{r}\sin(kx - \omega t)$ for waves from point or spherical source.

Ex. 31 The maximum pressure amplitude ΔP_m that the human ear can tolerate in loud sounds is about 28 Pa. What is the displacement amplitude A for such a sound in air of density $\rho = 1.21$ kg/m^3, at a frequency of 1000 Hz and a speed of 343 m/s?

Sol.

The pressure amplitude is related to displacement amplitude as

$$\Delta P_m \;=\; ABk$$

$$=\; Av^2\rho \times \frac{\omega}{v}$$

$$=\; Av\rho \times 2\pi f$$

$\therefore\quad$ Displacement amplitude

$$A \;=\; \frac{\Delta P_m}{v\rho(2\pi f)}$$

$$=\; \frac{28}{343 \times 1.21 \times 2\pi \times 1000}$$

$$=\; 1.1 \times 10^{-5}\ \text{m} \qquad\qquad \textit{Ans.}$$

Ex. 32 A line source of sound of length 10 m, emitting a pulse of sound that travels radially outward from the source. The power of the source is $P = 1.0 \times 10^4$ W. What is the intensity I of the sound when it reaches a distance of 10m from the source.

Sol.

The intensity at a distance r from a line source is given by

$$I \;=\; \frac{P}{2\pi r L}$$

$$=\; \frac{1.0 \times 10^4}{2\pi \times 10 \times 10} \;=\; 15.92\ \text{W/m}^2\ \textit{Ans.}$$

Sound level: The decibel scale

The lowest intensity of sound that can be perceived by the human ear is called threshold of hearing . For a sound of frequency 10 kHz, the threshold of hearing is, $I_0 = 10^{-12}$ W/m^2. The ratio of intensities of the loudest to faintest sound is 10^{12}. Humans can hear over a large range of intensities.

Instead of expressing the intensity I of a sound wave, it is more convenient to express of its sound level β , which is defined as

$$\beta \;=\; (10\,dB)\log\frac{I}{I_0}$$

Here dB is the abbreviation for decibel, the unit of sound level. The unit bel was introduced in honour of Alexander Graham Bell.

$(\beta_2 - \beta_1)$: Let β_1 and β_2 are the sound levels corresponding to sound intensities I_1 and I_2 respectively, then

$$\beta_1 = 10 \log \frac{I_1}{I_0}$$

and

$$\beta_2 = 10 \log \frac{I_2}{I_0}$$

$\therefore$

$$\beta_2 - \beta_1 = 10 \left(\log \frac{I_2}{I_0} - \log \frac{I_1}{I_0} \right)$$

or

$$\beta_2 - \beta_1 = 10 \log \left(\frac{I_2}{I_1} \right)$$

Ex. 33 If the intensity is increased by a factor 100, by how many decibels is the sound level increased?

Sol.

We know that

$$\beta_2 - \beta_1 = 10 \log \left(\frac{I_2}{I_1} \right)$$
$$= 10 \log 100$$
$$= 10 \times 2 = 20 \, dB \qquad \textit{Ans.}$$

SOUND LEVELS OF DIFFERENT SOUNDS

Source of sound	Sound levels in decibels
1. Threshold of hearing	0
2. Rustle of leaves	10
3. Whisper	15-20
4. Normal conversation	60-65
5. Heavy traffic	70-80
6. Roaring of loin	90
7. Thunder	100-110
8. Painful sound	130 and above
9. Rocket launch	160

Ex. 34 A sound level at a point 5.0 away from a point source is 40 *dB*. What will be the level at a point 50 m away from the source?

Sol.

The ratio of intensities of sound

$$\frac{I_1}{I_2} = \frac{r_2^2}{r_1^2} = \left(\frac{50}{5} \right)^2 = 100$$

$$\beta_2 - \beta_1 = 10 \log \left(\frac{I_2}{I_1} \right)$$
$$= 10 \log 100 = 10 \times 2$$
$$= 20 \, dB \qquad \textit{Ans.}$$

9.23 DOPPLER EFFECT

You might have observed that when a train blowing its whistle approaches you, standing on a railway platform, the pitch of the whistle appears to rise and it appears to drop as the train moves away from you. Doppler was the first to analyse this apparent change in frequency and he stated that whenever there is a relative motion between source of sound, the observer and the medium; the frequency of sound as received by the observer is different from the frequency of sound emitted by the source. This apparent change in the frequency of sound due to relative motion between source and observer is called **Doppler effect**.

Doppler effect is a wave phenomenon, it holds for sound waves as well as for light waves. Doppler effect in sound depends on three factors:

(i) Velocity of the source v_s (ii) Velocity of the observer v_o (iii) Velocity of the medium or wind v_ω.

Apparent frequency when the source moves towards the stationary observer :

Consider a source produces sound of frequency f. If v is the speed of sound in air then the wavelength of the sound wave

$$\lambda = \frac{v}{f} = vT$$

Now suppose the source S moves towards stationary observer O with a speed v_s. In one time period T, S moves a distance v_sT, before it emits next pulse. As a result the wavelength becomes

$$\lambda' = vT - v_sT$$
$$= \frac{(v - v_s)}{f}$$

Because of this changed wavelength, frequency of the sound appears to change. If f' is the apparent frequency, then

$$f' = \frac{v}{\lambda'} = f\left(\frac{v}{v - v_s}\right) \qquad \dots(1)$$

If the source moves away from the observer, then

$$f' = f\left(\frac{v}{v + v_s}\right) \qquad \dots(2)$$

Alternate method:

At $t = 0$, suppose the source is at a distance L from the observer and emits a compressional pulse. It reaches the observer at time

$$t_1 = \frac{L}{v}$$

The source emits next compressional pulse after a time T. In the mean time, the source has moved a distance v_sT towards the observer and is now a distance $L - v_sT$ from the observer. The next compressional pulse reaches the observer at time

$$t_2 = T + \frac{L - v_sT}{v}$$

The time interval between two successive compression pulses

$$T' = t_2 - t_1 = T + \frac{L - v_sT}{v} - \frac{L}{v}$$
$$= T\left(1 - \frac{v_s}{v}\right) = T\left(\frac{v - v_s}{v}\right)$$

The apparent frequency

$$f' = \frac{1}{T'} = \frac{fv}{v - v_s} \qquad \left[\frac{1}{T} = f\right]$$

Apparent frequency when observer moves towards the stationary observer:

Consider a source produces sound of frequency f. If v is the speed of sound in air, then the wavelength of the sound wave

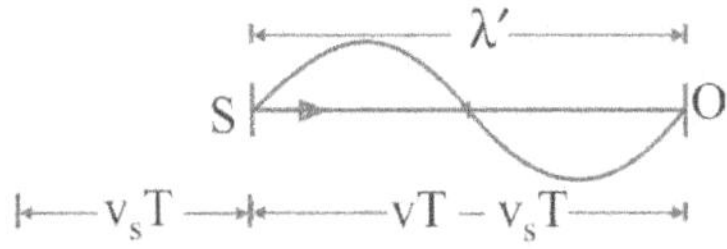

(a) When source and observer both stationary.

(b) When source moves towards stationary observer.

Fig. 9.38

$$\lambda = \frac{v}{f}$$

Now suppose the observer O moves towards stationary source with a speed of v_O. The speed of sound relative to observer

$$v' = v + v_O$$

As the source is stationary, so wavelength of the sound wave remain same. Because of the increased relative speed of the sound, the frequency appears to increase . Thus apparent frequency

$$f' = \frac{v'}{\lambda} = \frac{v + v_O}{v / f}$$

or

$$f' = f\left(\frac{v + v_O}{v}\right) \qquad \qquad ...(3)$$

If the observer moves away from the stationary source, then

$$f' = f\left(\frac{v - v_O}{v}\right) \qquad \qquad ...(4)$$

General Doppler effect equation:
The apparent frequency can be written as ;

$$f' = f\left(\frac{v \pm v_O}{v \pm v_s}\right) \qquad \qquad ...(5)$$

9.24 DOPPLER EFFECT IN LIGHT

The speed of light c is invariant irrespective of the motion of source or observer. Therefore the apparent change in frequency or wavelength of light does not depend on the fact whether source is moving or observer is moving . It depends on relative velocity between them.

The change in wavelength can be obtained by

$$\frac{\Delta\lambda}{\lambda} = \frac{v}{c} \qquad \qquad ...(1)$$

where $c \rightarrow$ speed of light

         $v \rightarrow$ velocity of source w.r.t. observer

         $\lambda \rightarrow$ actual wavelength of light

As $f\lambda = c$ (constant), so $\dfrac{\Delta f}{f} = -\dfrac{\Delta\lambda}{\lambda} \qquad \qquad ...(2)$

Red shift and blue shift:

When source of light moves away from the observer the wavelength of light coming from the source appears to increase . It is known as red shift, and $\lambda' = \lambda + \Delta\lambda$.

When source is approaching towards the observer, then the wavelength of light coming from the source is appears to decrease. It is known as blue shift, and $\lambda' = \lambda - \Delta\lambda$.

Doppler effect in sound is asymmetric:

Suppose a source of sound moves towards a stationary observer with a speed v', then the observed frequency

$$f' = f\frac{v}{v - v'}$$

Now if the observer moves towards the stationary source with the same speed v', then the observed frequency

$$f'' = f\frac{v + v'}{v}$$

Clearly, $f' \neq f''$. That is the observed frequency in two cases is different, although the relative speed between them is same. For this reason, the Doppler effect in sound is said to asymmetric. However, the Doppler effect in light is symmetric. This is because the observed frequency or wavelength depends only on relative speed between source and observer.

> **Note:**
>
> No Doppler effect is observed in the following situations:
> (i)   When both the source and the observer move in the same direction with the same speed.
> (ii)   When both the source and the observer are at rest and wind is alone is blowing.
> (iii)   When the distance between source and observer remain constant. When either the source or the observer is at the centre of a circle and other is moving along it with an uniform speed.
> (iv)   The Doppler effect is noticeable when v_0 or $v_s < v$. It does not hold when the speed of the source or the observer becomes equal or greater than the speed of the wave.

9.25 SOME IMPORTANT CASES OF DOPPLER EFFECT

1.
$$f' = f\left(\frac{v - v_o}{v - v_s}\right) \qquad \xrightarrow{v_s}_{s} \qquad \xrightarrow{v_o}_{o}$$

 and
$$\lambda' = \lambda\left(\frac{v - v_s}{v}\right)$$

2.
$$f' = f\left(\frac{v + v_o}{v - v_s}\right) \qquad \xrightarrow{v_s} \qquad \xleftarrow{v_o}$$

 and
$$\lambda' = \lambda\left(\frac{v - v_s}{v}\right)$$

3.
$$f' = f\left(\frac{v - v_o}{v + v_s}\right) \qquad \xleftarrow{v_s} \qquad \xrightarrow{v_o}$$

 and
$$\lambda' = \lambda\left(\frac{v + v_s}{v}\right)$$

4.
$$f' = f\left(\frac{v + v_o}{v + v_s}\right) \qquad \xleftarrow{v_s} \qquad \xleftarrow{v_0}$$

 and
$$\lambda' = \lambda\left(\frac{v + v_s}{v}\right)$$

5.   Moving source crosses a stationary observer

 Apparent frequency before crossing, $\quad f_1 = f\dfrac{v}{v - v_s}$

 Apparent frequency after crossing, $\quad f_2 = f\dfrac{v}{v + v_s}$

 Change in apparent frequency, $\quad \Delta f = f_1 - f_2$

Fig. 9.39

$$= fv\left(\frac{1}{v-v_s} - \frac{1}{v+v_s}\right) = \frac{2fvv_s}{v^2 - v_s^2}$$

$$= \frac{2fvv_s}{v^2 - v_s^2}$$

for $\quad v_s << v \qquad\qquad \Delta f = \frac{2fv_s}{v}$

6. Observer crosses a stationary source

Apparent frequency before crossing $\quad f_1 = f\left(\dfrac{v+v_O}{v}\right)$

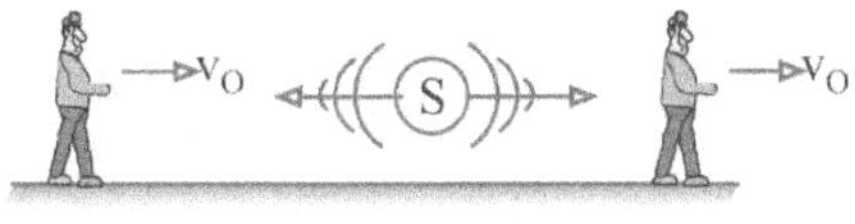

Fig. 9.40

Apparent frequency after crossing $\quad f_2 = f\left(\dfrac{v-v_O}{v}\right)$

Change in apparent frequency $\qquad \Delta f = f_1 - f_2 = \left(\dfrac{2fv_O}{v}\right)$

7. When source is moving in a direction making an angle θ w.r.t. the observer Velocity of source towards observer $-v_s\cos\theta$. The apparent frequency heard by the observer at rest

$$f' = f\left(\frac{v}{v-v_s\cos\theta}\right)$$

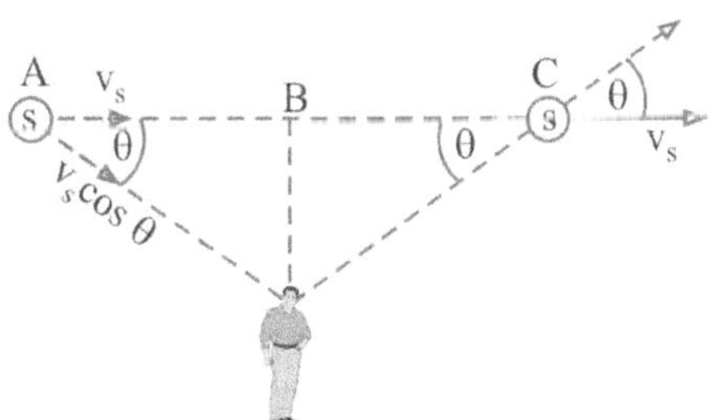

Fig. 9.41

As source moves along line ABC,

at B; $\theta = 90°$, $\qquad\qquad \therefore \quad f' = f.$

At C, $\qquad\qquad f' = f\left(\dfrac{v}{v+v_s\cos\theta}\right).$

8. Apparent frequency before crossing the function J

$$f' = f\left(\frac{v+v_o\cos\theta_2}{v-v_s\cos\theta_1}\right)$$

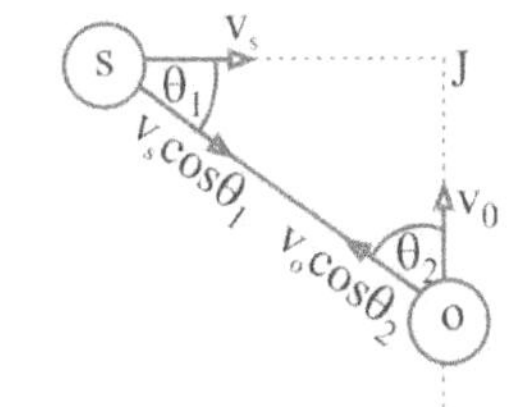

Fig. 9.42

9. (a) When source moves on a circular path and observer is standing at the centre of the circular path. Since there is no relative motion between source and observer, so the frequency perceived by the observer at the centre will be same as the frequency of the source.

(b) Observer is standing very far away from the circular path.
When the source approaching towards the observer

$$f' = f\left(\frac{v}{v-v_s}\right)$$

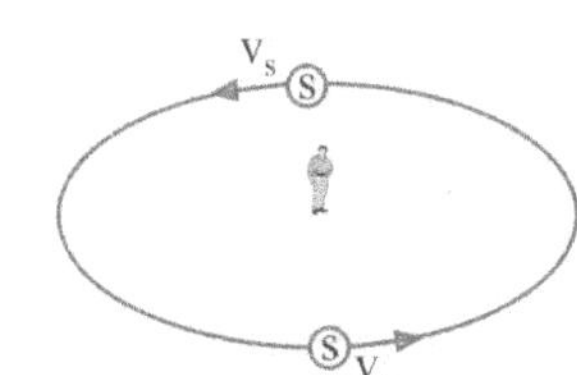

Fig. 9.45

and $\qquad\qquad f' = f\left(\dfrac{v}{v+v_s}\right)$

when source is receding from the observer.

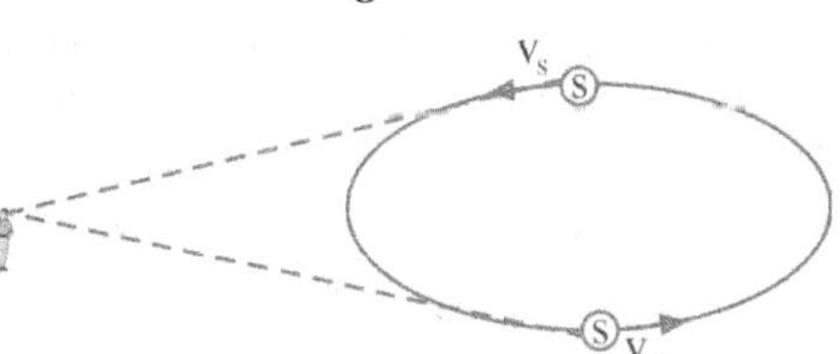

Fig. 9.46

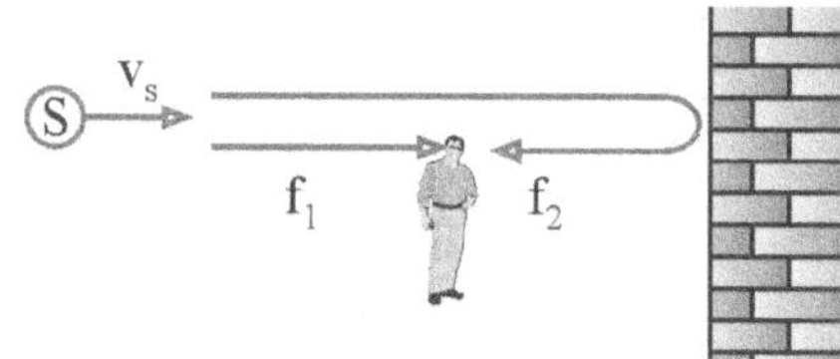

Fig. 9.47

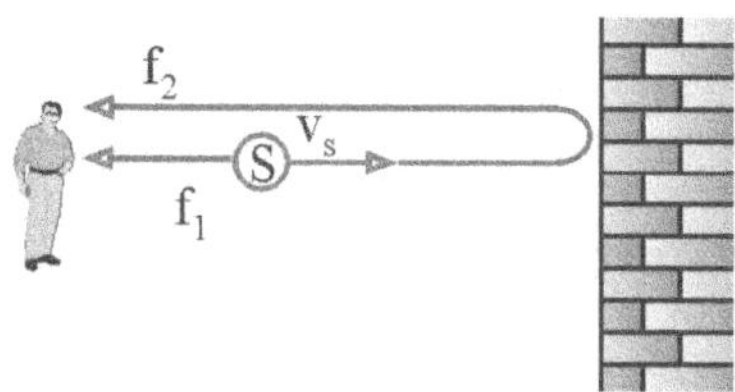

Fig. 9.48

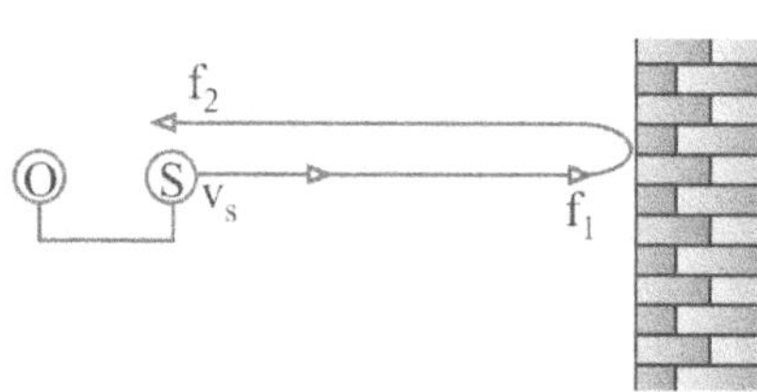

Fig. 9.49

10.   Source is moving towards a wall :

(a)   Observer in between source and wall.
The frequency of direct sound perceived

$$f_1 = f\left(\frac{v}{v - v_s}\right)$$

The frequency of reflected sound perceived

$$f_2 = f\left(\frac{v}{v - v_s}\right)$$

$$\therefore \qquad \Delta f = 0$$

(b)   Source in between observer and wall: The frequency perceived of direct

sound $\qquad f_1 = f\left(\frac{v}{v + v_s}\right)$

The frequency perceived of reflected sound

$$f_2 = f\frac{v}{(v - v_s)}$$

$$\Delta f = f_1 - f_2 = fv\left(\frac{1}{v - v_s} - \frac{1}{v + v_s}\right) = \frac{2 f v v_s}{v^2 - v_s^2}$$

(c)   When observer is moving together with source:
The frequency of sound perceived at wall

$$f_1 = f\left(\frac{v}{v - v_s}\right)$$

Frequency of the reflected sound perceived

$$f_2 = f_1\left(\frac{v + v_o}{v}\right)$$

$$= f\left(\frac{v + v_o}{v - v_s}\right)$$

Also $\qquad v_S = v_o$

11.   If wind is blowing with velocity v_ω, then

$$f' = f\left[\frac{(v \pm v_\omega) - v_0}{(v \pm v_\omega) - v_s}\right]$$

Take (+) sign with v_ω when wind is blowing from source towards observer, and
when wind is blowing from observer toward source.

Ex. 35 **A source emitting a sound of frequency f is placed at a
large distance from an observer. The source starts moving towards
the observer with a uniform acceleration a . Find the frequency
heard by the observer corresponding to the wave emitted just after
the source starts. The speed of sound in the medium is v.**

Sol.

Let initially source is at a distance L from the observer. Let first wave
front starts from the source at $t = 0$. The first wave front will reach the

observer $t_1 = \dfrac{L}{v}$. The second similar wave front is emitted after a time T.

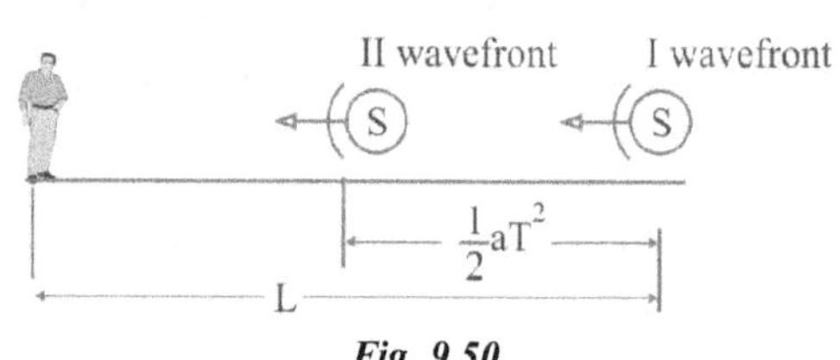

Fig. 9.50

The distance moved by the source in this time $\dfrac{1}{2}aT^2$.

The separation between source and observer becomes $\left(L - \dfrac{1}{2}aT^2\right)$.

That it is the distance of second wavefront from the observer.

Time taken by second wavefront to reach the observer $t = \left(\dfrac{L - \dfrac{1}{2}aT^2}{v}\right)$

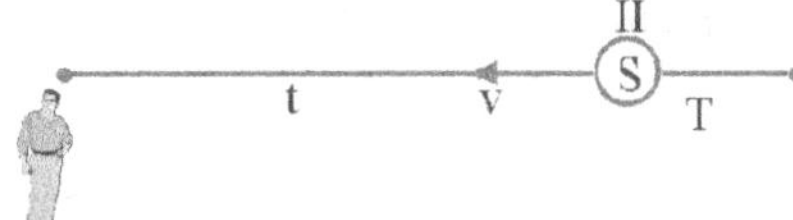

Fig. 9.51

Time taken by second wavefront from initial position of source

$$t_2 = \left(\dfrac{L - \dfrac{1}{2}aT^2}{v}\right) + T$$

Time interval between two successive wavefronts is

$$\Delta t = t_2 - t_1 = T - \dfrac{1}{2}\left(\dfrac{a}{v}\right)T^2$$

Hence , frequency received by observer

$$f' = \dfrac{1}{\Delta t} = \dfrac{1}{T - \dfrac{1}{2}\left(\dfrac{a}{v}\right)T^2}$$

or $\qquad f' = \dfrac{2vf^2}{2vf - a} \qquad \left(as\ T = \dfrac{1}{f}\right)$

Ex. 36 A train approaching a hill at a speed 40 km/ h sounds a whistle of frequency 580 Hz, when it is at distance of 1 km from the hill. Wind with speed of 40 km/h is blowing in the direction of motion of the train. Find (a) frequency of whistle as heard by an observer on the hill (b) the distance from the hill at which echo from the hill is heard by the driver and its frequency. Velocity of sound in air = 1200 km/h.

Sol.

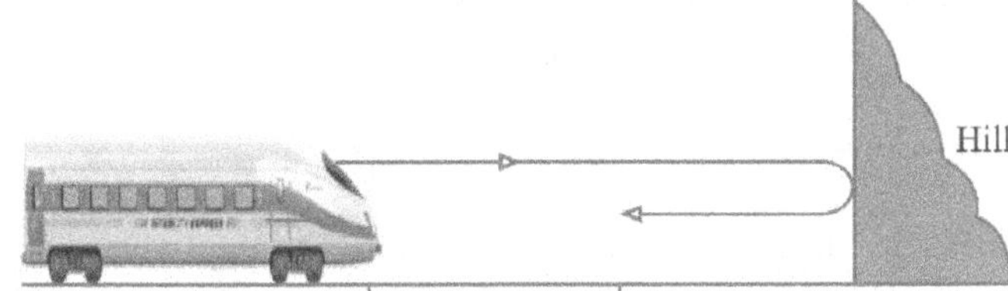

Fig. 9.52

(a)   The frequency of sound as heard by the observer at hill

$$f_1 = f\left[\dfrac{(v + v_\omega)}{(v + v_\omega) - v_s}\right]$$

$$= 580\left[\dfrac{1200 + 40}{1200 + 40 - 40}\right]$$

$$= 599.3\ \text{Hz} \qquad Ans.$$

(b)   Let x is the distance moved by the train in the duration sound come back after reflection from hill.

$\therefore$ Time of motion of sound $=$ time of motion of train

or $\left(\dfrac{1}{1200 + 40}\right) + \dfrac{(1 - x)}{(1200 - 40)} = \dfrac{x}{40}$

After solving, we get $\quad x = 0.0646\ \text{km}$

Distance from the hill $\quad = 1 - x$

$\qquad = 1 - 0.0646\ \text{km}$

$\qquad = 0.9354\ \text{km}$

The frequency as heard by the driver:

Let f_1 is the frequency as observed at the hill

$$f_1 = f\left[\dfrac{(v + v_\omega)}{(v + v_\omega) - v_s}\right]$$

$$= 580\left(\dfrac{1200 + 40}{1200 + 40 - 40}\right)$$

$$\simeq 599.3\ \text{Hz}.$$

This frequency is reflected back and wind opposes the sound

$\therefore \qquad f_2 = f_1\left[\dfrac{(v - v_\omega) + v_0}{(v - v_\omega)}\right]$

$$= 599.3\left[\dfrac{1200 - 40 + 40}{1200 - 40}\right]$$

$$= 620\ \text{Hz} \qquad Ans.$$

Ex. 37 *Fig. 9.53 shows a source of sound moving along the x - axis at a speed of 22 m/s continuously emitting a sound of frequency 2.0 kHz which travels in air at a speed of 330 m/s. A listener Q stands on the y -axis at a distance of 330 m from the origin. At t = 0, the source crosses the origin at P. (a) When does the sound emitted from the source at P reach the listener at Q? (b) What will be the frequency heard by the listener at this instant ? (c) Where will the source be at this instant?*

Sol.

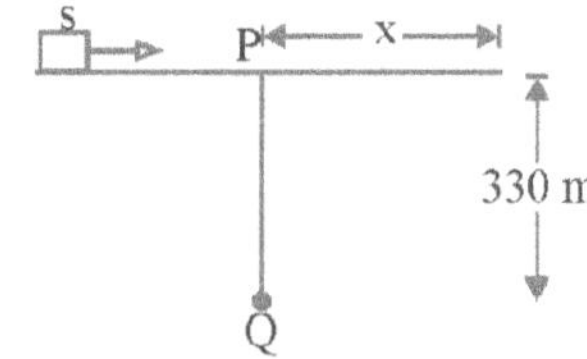

Fig. 9.53

(a)   Sound produced at P takes time to reach

$$Q = \dfrac{330}{330} = 1\text{s}$$

(b)   The frequency of sound as heard by listener = 2 kHz.

(c)   When sound arrive at Q, the source will move a distance

$$x = v_s \times t$$

$$= 22 \times 1$$

$$= 22\ \text{m} \qquad Ans.$$

Ex. 38 A source emitting sound at frequency 4000 Hz, is moving along the y - axis with a speed of 22 m/s . A listener is situated on the ground at the position (660 *m*, 0). Find the frequency of the sound received by the listener at the instant the source crosses the origin. Speed of sound in air = 330 m/s .

Sol.

Let sound produced at P will reach the listener at the instant when source crosses the origin.

Time of motion of sound from P to listener

$$= \text{time of motion of source from } P \text{ to origin}$$

or $\qquad \dfrac{y}{22} = \dfrac{\sqrt{y^2 + 660^2}}{330} \qquad \left[\cos\theta = \dfrac{44}{\sqrt{44^2 + 660^2}} = \dfrac{44}{661.5} \right]$

After solving

$$y = 44 \text{ m}$$

The frequency heard by the listener

$$f' = f \dfrac{v}{v - v_s \cos\theta}$$

$$= 4000 \dfrac{330}{330 - 22\cos\theta}$$

$$= 4018 \text{ Hz} \qquad\qquad \textit{Ans.}$$

Fig. 9.54

Ex. 39 An astronaut is approaching the moon. He sends a radio signal of frequency 5×10^9 Hz and finds that the frequency shift in echo received is 10^3 Hz. Find his speed of approach.

Sol. The frequency shift as observed on moon

$$\dfrac{\Delta f}{f} = \dfrac{v}{c} \Rightarrow \Delta f = \dfrac{v}{c} f$$

Now moon becomes source of frequency $f_1 = (f + \Delta f)$ the shift in frequency in reflected light is observed,

$$\Delta f = \dfrac{vf}{c}$$

Therefore total shift observed $= 2\Delta f = 2f\dfrac{v}{c}$

$$\therefore \qquad 10^3 = 2 \times 5 \times 10^9 \times \dfrac{v}{3 \times 10^8}$$

$$\Rightarrow \qquad v = 30 \text{ m/s} \qquad\qquad \textit{Ans.}$$

Ex. 40 A bat is fitting about in a cave, navigating via ultrasonic bleeps. Assume that the sound emission frequency of the bat is 40 kHz. During one fast sweep directly towards a flat wall surface, the bat is moving at 0.03 times the speed of sound in air. What frequency does the bat hear reflected off the wall?

Sol.

The frequency of the sound reflected from the wall as perceived by the bat

$$f' = f\dfrac{v + v_o}{v - v_s} = 40\left(\dfrac{v + 0.03v}{v - 0.03v} \right)$$

$$= 42.47 \text{ kHz} \qquad\qquad \textit{Ans.}$$

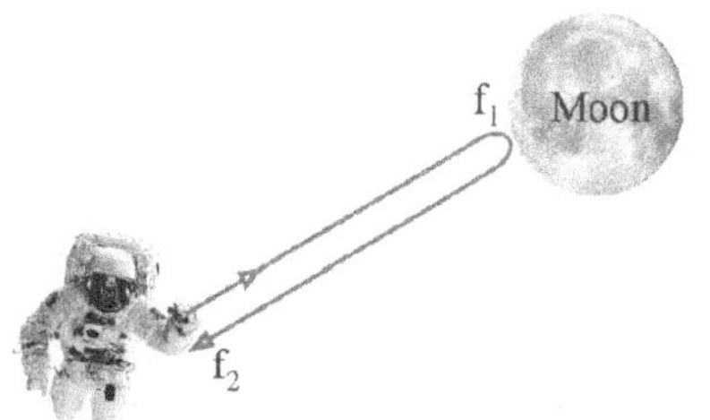

Fig. 9.55

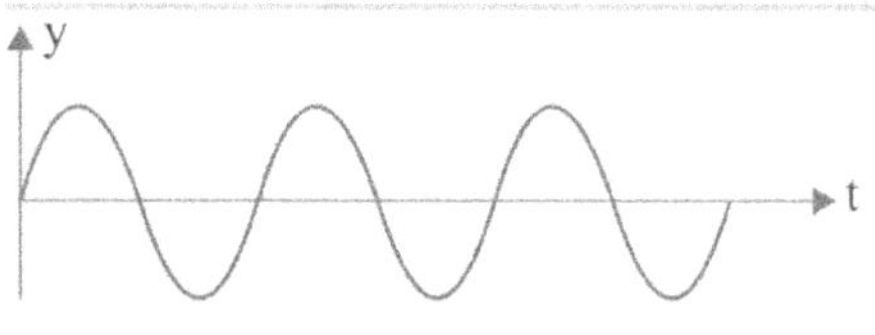

(a) Wave shape of low pitch sound

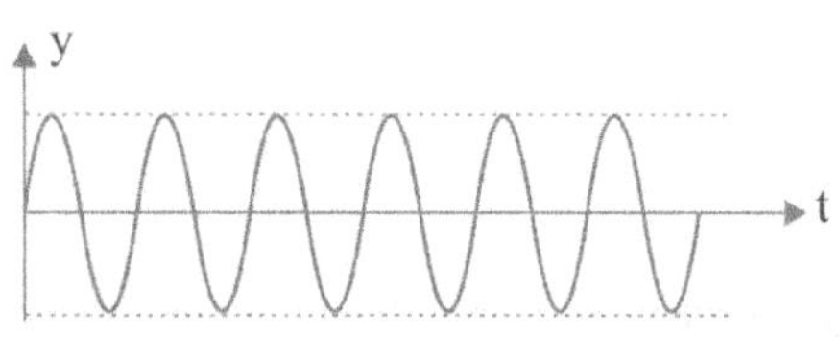

(b) Wave shape of high pitch sound

Fig. 9.56

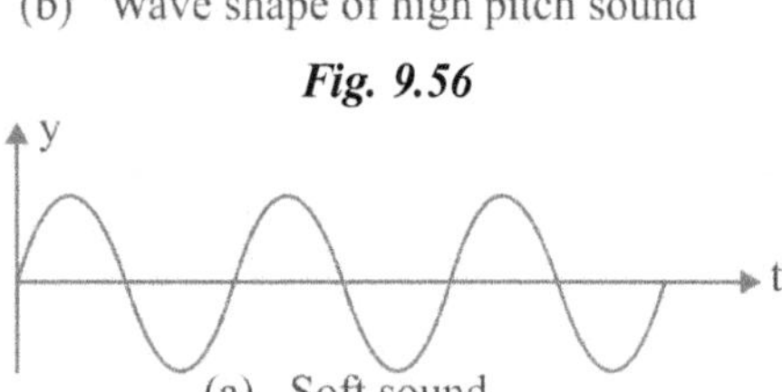

(a) Soft sound

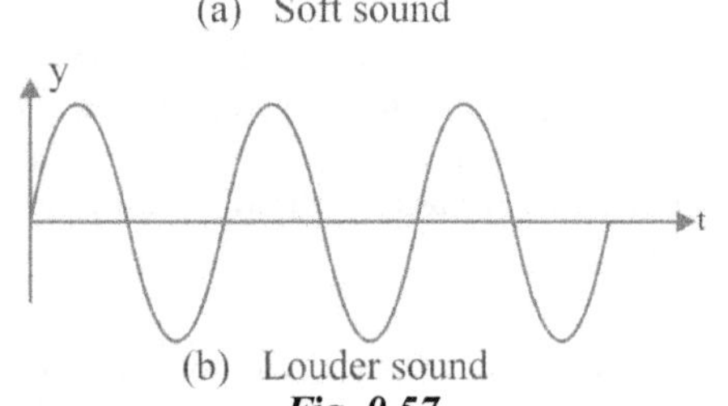

(b) Louder sound

Fig. 9.57

9.26 CHARACTERISTICS OF SOUND

Sounds produce by adults and children are different , still both the sounds travel at the same speed. This is due to the different characteristics associated with the sound. Pitch is one of the characteristics.

Pitch : Pitch is the characteristic which distinguishes between shrill and grave sound. The faster the vibration of source, the higher is the frequency and the higher is the pitch. Pitch of sound produced by children is greater than the pitch of sound produced by adults.

Loudness : It is the sensation produced on the ears. It depends on the amplitude of the sound wave. The sound produced by greater energy has larger amplitude and therefore more loudness. The following figure represents wave shapes of a loud and a soft sound of the same frequency.

Musical sound: A sound which produces pleasing effect on the ears is called musical sound.

Musical interval: The ratio of the frequencies of two notes is called musical interval. Two notes with musical interval 1:1 are called unision. Some other common musical intervals are;

(a) Octave $(1:2)$ (b) majortone $(8:9)$

(c) minortone $(9:10)$ (d) semitone $(15:16)$

Musical scale: A series of notes arranged such that their fundamental frequencies have definite ratios is called a musical scale. The most widely used musical scale is diatonic scale. It consists of eight notes, called sargam. The first note of frequency 256 Hz is called keynote or fundamental and last note of frequency 512 Hz is an octave of the first note.

Indian name:	Sa	Re	Ga	Ma	Pa	Dha	Ni	Sa
Frequency $_{(Hz)}$:	256	288	320	$341\frac{1}{3}$	384	$426\frac{2}{3}$	480	512
Intervals:		9/8	10/9	6/15	9/8	10/9	9/8	16/15

Quality or timbre:

Quality of sound distinguishes one sound from another having the same pitch and loudness. The sound which is more pleasant is said to be a rich quality. The sounds of sitar and violin can be distinguished by their quality.

9.27 REFLECTION OF SOUND

When wave strikes to any boundary, it reflected back into the same medium. The wave is reflected in such a way that angle of reflection is equal to the angle of incidence of the wave. If i and r are the angle of incidence and angle of reflection, then by law of reflection, we have

$$\angle i = \angle r.$$

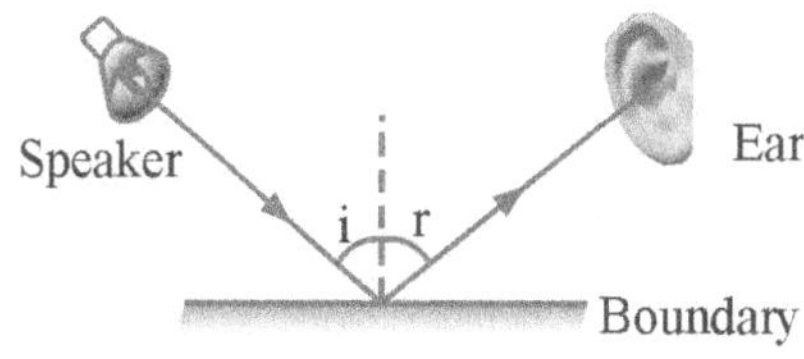

Fig. 9.58

Echo :

If we clap in front of a large wall or hill, we will hear the same sound again a little later. This repetition of sound after reflection from large obstruction is called **echo**. The sensation of sound persists in our brain nearly for 0.1s. To hear an echo the time interval between original sound and the reflected sound must be at least 0.1s.

Let x be minimum distance between source of sound and obstruction. If v is the speed of sound in air, then time taken by sound to reach the obstruction and back to the listner is

$$t = \frac{2x}{v}$$

At room temperature, $v = 340$ m/s

$$\therefore \quad t = \frac{2x}{340}$$

To hear echo,

$$\frac{2x}{340} = 0.1$$

or
$$x = \frac{0.1 \times 340}{2}$$

or
$$x = 17m$$

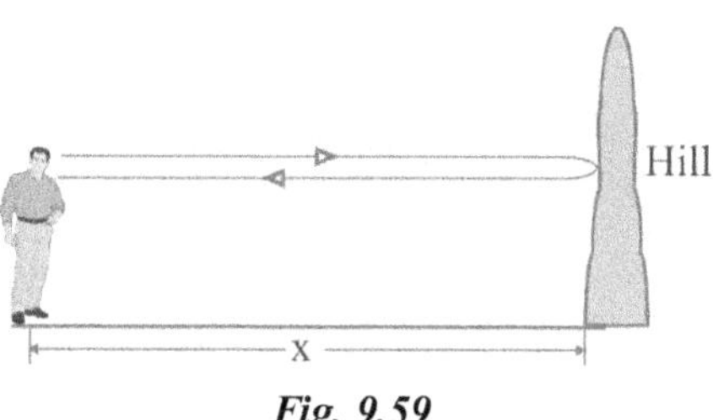

Fig. 9.59

9.28 REVERBERATION

The sound created in a big hall will persist by repeated reflections from the walls and roof until it is reduced to a value where it is no longer audible. The persistence of audible sound after the source has ceased to emit sound is called reverberation.

In a picture hall or in auditorium, excessive reverberation causes overlapping of sounds and therefore is highly undesirable. To control reverberation, the walls and roof of the structure are generally covered with sound absorbing materials like, fiberboard, rough plaster etc.

Reverberation time :

The time for which sound persists after the source has stopped producing sound is called reverberation time (T).

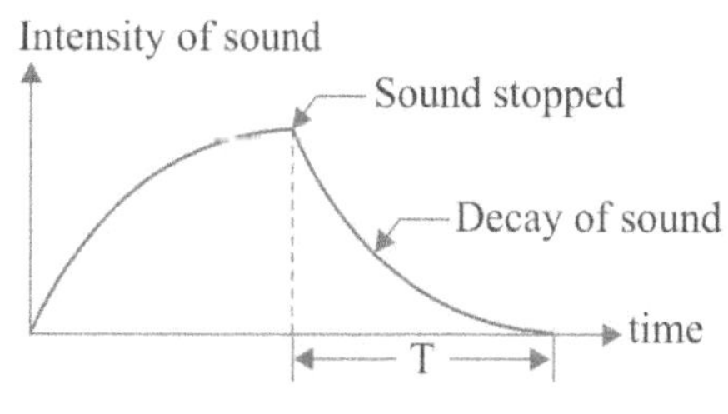

Fig. 9.63

According to Sabine law, the reverberation of a hall is given by

$$T = \frac{0.16V}{\sum a_i s_i}$$

Where V is the volume of the hall and $\sum a_i s_i$ is the total absorption of the hall. Here s and a are the surface area and absorption coefficient respectively.

Method for controlling reverberation time

(i)   Covering walls and doors with sound absorbent materials like asbestos, card board etc.

(ii)   Providing rough texture paint on the walls.

(iii)   Providing curtains on the doors and windows

(iv)   By increasing number of audience.

(v)   Floor with rough tiles.

Acoustical requirements of a building

 These are as follows:

(i)   There should be no echo.

(ii)   The reverberation time neither be too low nor too high. For lecture room, it is 2 second.

(iii)   There should no extraneous sound in the building.

(iv)   The total quality of sound should not be altered.

9.29 RANGE OF HEARING

Normal human ears can hear the sound of frequency 20 Hz to 20000 Hz. Sound of frequency less than 20 Hz is called infrasonic . Sound of frequency greater than 20000 Hz is called **ultrasound**. Children under the age of five and dogs, owls can hear upto 25 kHz. Whales and elephants produce sound in the infrasonic range. Rhinoceroes make communication between themselves by using a frequency as low as 5 Hz.

9.30 ULTRASOUND

Frequencies higher than 20000 Hz are called ultrasound. Ultrasound can be produced by Galton's whistle. Some animals, such as dolphins, porpoises can produced ultrasound. Bats can produce and hear ultrasound.

Applications of Ultrasound

On being high frequency waves, ultrasound possesses high intensity, and therefore can penetrate any solid or liquid medium.

1.   Ultrasound can kill bacteria and therefore can be used for water purification.

2.   To detect cracks in metal and in thick walls: Ultrasound can be used to detect cracks in walls of huge structure like atomic power plant. The cracks or holes inside the metal blocks or RCC walls which are invisible from outside reduces the strength of the structure.

Ultrasonic waves are allowed to pass through the walls and detectors are used to detect the transmitted waves .If there is a crack in the wall, the ultrasound gets reflected back indicating the presence of defect (see *Fig. 9.64*).

3.   Echocardiography:

By making ultrasound of some specific intensity, these are made to reflect from

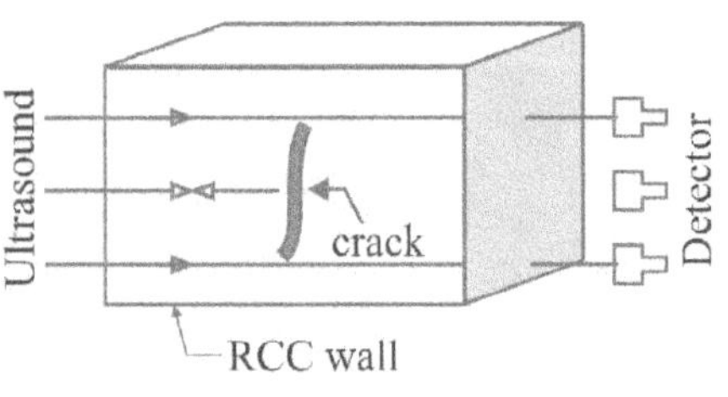

Fig. 9.64

various parts of the heart and form its image. This technique is known as echocardioigraphy.

4. Ultrasound may be used to break stones formed in the kidney. The crushed stone later get flushed out with urine.

5. Sonography:

   Ultrasonography is used for examination of the factor during frequency to detect congenial defects and growth abnormalities.

9.31 SONAR

SONAR stands for **SO**und **N**avigation **A**nd **R**anging. SONAR is a device which is used to find depth of sea or to detect the position of submarine hidden inside water. Sonar consists of a transmitter and a detector. They are installed in a ship (see *Fig. 9.65*).

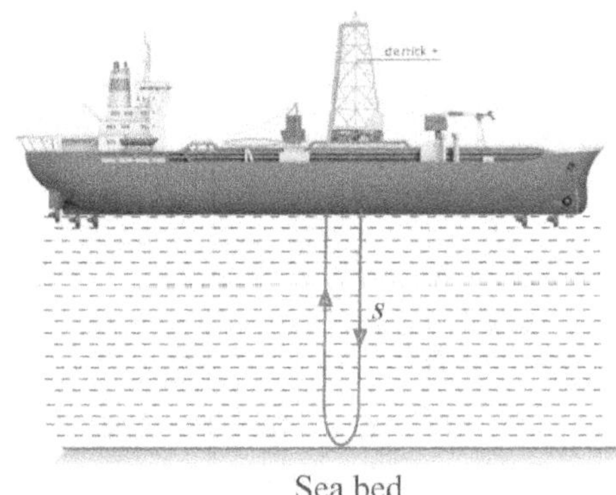

Fig. 9.65. Ultrasound sent by the transmitter and received by the detector.

The transmitter produces ultrasonic waves and transmit them. These waves propagate through water and after striking from the object inside water, get reflected back and are recorded by the detector. The distance of the object (submarine etc) can be calculated by knowing the speed of sound in water and the time interval between transmission and reception of the ultrasound in water . The total distance travelled by ultrasound is $2d$.

$$\therefore \qquad 2d = v \times t$$

or

$$d = \frac{vt}{2}$$

9.32 SHOCK WAVES

If an object moves with a speed greater than the speed of sound, then it is called supersonic. Mach studied such objects and introduced a dimensionless parameter, called **Mach number,** which is defined as:

$$\text{Mach number} = \frac{\text{speed of object}}{\text{speed of sound}}$$

or

$$M = \frac{v_0}{v}$$

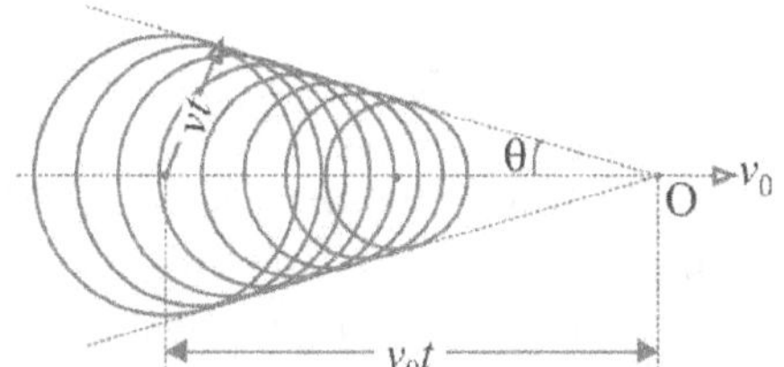

$M = 2$ means, the speed of object is twice the speed of sound. As speed of sound in air is nearly 1200 km/h, so $v_0 = 2400$ km/h. When such an object moves , it produces energetic disturbance (wave front) in the backward direction of motion of the object . The wave front extend in three dimensions and forms a cone called the Mach cone. A shock wave is said to exist along the surface of this cone. Shock waves are too energetic,

Fig. 9.66. Shock waves

they can break the glass panels or can damage the buildings. Figure shows a shock wave and the half cone angle θ, called the Mach cone angle, is given by

$$\sin\theta \;=\; \frac{vt}{v_0 t} \;=\; \frac{1}{M} \quad \text{(Mach cone angle)}$$

or

$$\theta \;=\; \sin^{-1}\left(\frac{1}{M}\right)$$

Ex. 41 Two men are equi distance from the face of a plane vertical cliff and are 300 m apart. One of them fires a pistol, the other hears the echo one second after hearing the direct sound. The velocity of sound is 330 m/s . Calculate the distance of the man from the cliff.

Sol. Let two men are standing at A and B, and the distance of each man from the cliff is x.

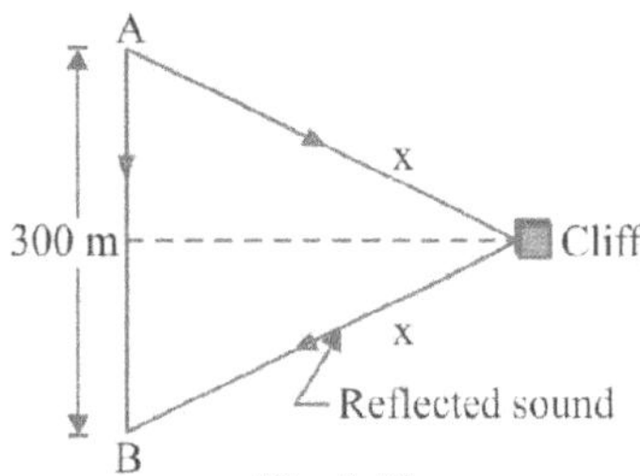

Fig. 9.60

The time taken by direct sound from A to B,

$$t_1 \;=\; \frac{300}{330}\ \text{s}$$

The time taken by the reflected sound

$$t_2 \;=\; \frac{2x}{330}$$

According to the given condition

$$t_2 - t_1 \;=\; 1$$

or $\qquad \dfrac{2x}{330} - \dfrac{300}{330} \;=\; 1$ or $x = 315$ m $\qquad$ *Ans.*

Ex. 42 A road runs between two parallel rows of buildings. A motorist moving just in the middle with a velocity of 30 km/h, sounds the horn. He hears an echo one second after sounding the horn. Find the distance between the two rows of the buildings. The velocity of sound = 330 m/s .

Sol.

Suppose 2 y is the distance between two rows of the buildings. The distance travelled by car in 1 second

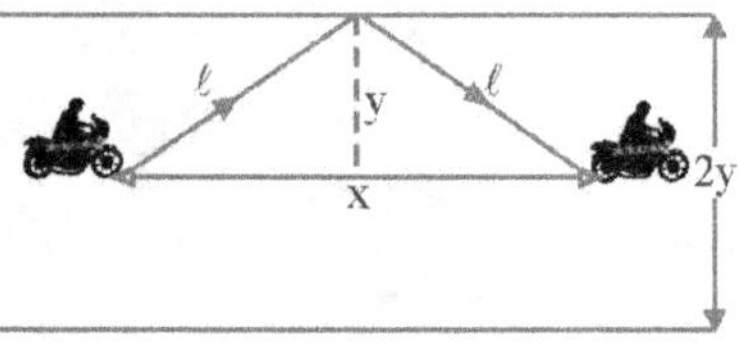

Fig. 9.61

$$x \;=\; \left(30 \times \frac{5}{18}\right) \times 1 = 8.33 \text{ m}$$

The distance travelled by sound in 1 second

$$2\ell \;=\; 330 \times 1 = 330 \text{ m}$$
$$\therefore \qquad \ell \;=\; 165 \text{ m}$$

From the figure $\qquad y \;=\; \sqrt{\ell^2 - \left(\frac{x}{2}\right)^2}$

$$=\; \sqrt{165^2 - \left(\frac{8.33}{2}\right)^2}$$

$$=\; 164.95 \text{ m}$$

Thus the distance between two rows of the buildings $2y = 329.9$ m

Ans.

Ex. 43 Why is the sound produced in air not heard by a person deep inside the water?

Sol.

The speed of sound in water is nearly four times the speed of sound in air. From Snell's law

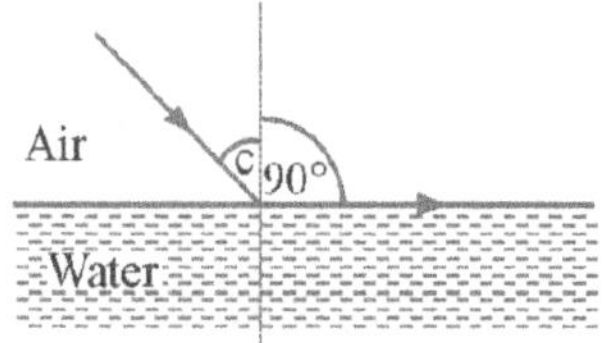

Fig. 9.62

$$_a\mu_w \;=\; \frac{\sin i}{\sin r} \;=\; \frac{v_a}{v_w} \;=\; \frac{1}{4} = 0.25$$

Critical angle $c = \sin^{-1}(\mu) \;=\; \sin^{-1}(0.25) = 14°$.

Thus most of the sound produced in air and incident at an angle $i \geq 14°$ gets reflected back in air and very small amount is refracted into water. Hence a person inside water cannot hear the sound produced in air.

Review of formulae & Important Points

1. **The velocity of wave** in a medium is given by $v = f\lambda$

2. **Equation of plane progressive wave,** $y = A\sin(\omega t - kx)$

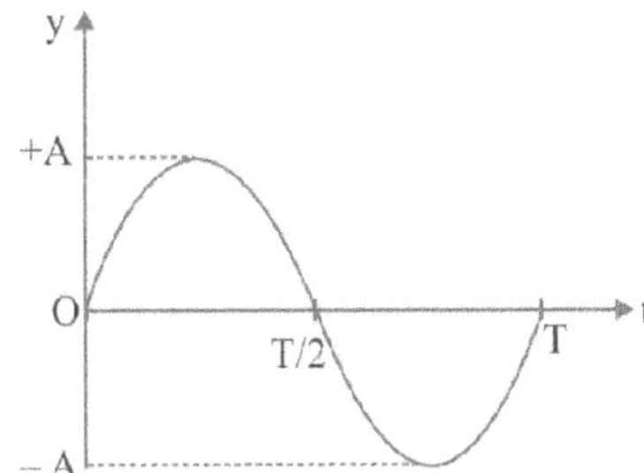

Above equation represents displacement of the particles at a distance x from the origin as time passes, and $y = A\sin(kx - \omega t)$, represents the displacements of all the particles of the wave at any time. In general we can write,

$$y = A\sin(\omega t - kx + \phi_0)$$

If at $t = 0$, $x = 0$, $y = y_0$, then

$$\phi_0 = \sin^{-1}(y_0/A).$$

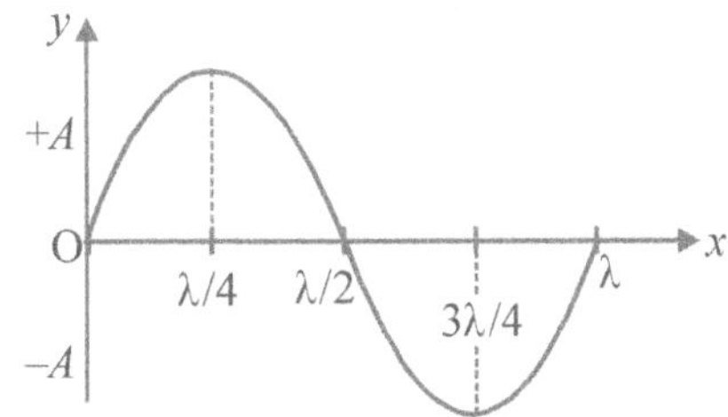

3. **Other equations of wave**

   (i) $\quad y = A\sin\dfrac{2\pi}{\lambda}(vt - x)$

   (ii) $\quad y = A\sin 2\pi\left(\dfrac{t}{T} - \dfrac{x}{\lambda}\right)$

   Differential equation of a wave : $\dfrac{\partial^2 y}{\partial t^2} = v^2 \dfrac{\partial^2 y}{\partial x^2}$

4. **Phase difference, $\Delta\phi$**
   (i) Between two particles at any time

   $$\Delta\phi = \dfrac{2\pi}{\lambda}\Delta x$$

   (ii) Between two times of a particle

   $$\Delta\phi = \dfrac{2\pi}{T}\Delta t$$

5. **Sound waves or pressure waves**

   $$\Delta P = \Delta P_m \sin(kx - \omega t), \quad \Delta P_m = ABk$$

6. **Speed of sound waves in air**

   $$v = \sqrt{\dfrac{\gamma P}{\rho}}, \text{ for air } \gamma = 1.4.$$

   Also $\quad v = \sqrt{\dfrac{\gamma RT}{M}}$

7. **Speed of transverse wave in stretched string**

   $$v = \sqrt{\dfrac{F}{\mu}} = \sqrt{\dfrac{stress}{Y}}$$

8. **Power transmitted**

   $$P_{av} = \dfrac{1}{2}\rho v S\omega^2 A^2$$

9. **Intensity of wave**

   $$I = \dfrac{P}{S} = \dfrac{1}{2}\rho v\omega^2 A^2 = 2\pi^2 f^2 A^2 \rho v$$

10. **Variation of intensity with distance**

    (i) For point source, $\quad I \propto \dfrac{1}{r^2}$

    (ii) For line source, $\quad I \propto \dfrac{1}{r}$

11. **Sound level** : The decibel scale

    $$\beta = 10\log\left(\dfrac{I}{I_0}\right) \text{ decibel}$$

    and $\quad \beta_2 - \beta_1 = 10\log\left(\dfrac{I_2}{I_1}\right)$

12. **Doppler effect in sound**
    (i) When source moves towards stationay observer

    $$f' = f\left(\dfrac{v}{v - v_s}\right)$$

    (ii) When observer moves towards stationary source

    $$f' = f\left(\dfrac{v + v_0}{v}\right), \quad \lambda' = \lambda$$

    In general,

    $$f' = f\left(\dfrac{v - v_0}{v - v_s}\right)$$

13. **Doppler effect in light**

    $$\dfrac{\Delta\lambda}{\lambda} = \dfrac{-\Delta f}{f} = \dfrac{v}{c}$$

    where $v \rightarrow$ relative speed between source and observer.
    $c \rightarrow$ speed of light.

14. Sound of frequency greater than 20000 Hz is called ultrasound. Ultrasound can be used for navigation and sonography.

15. **Mach number**

    $$M = \dfrac{\text{Speed of the object}(v_0)}{\text{Speed of the sound}(v)}$$

    Mach angle is defined as :

    $$\sin\alpha = \left(\dfrac{1}{M}\right)$$

Wave - I

MCQ Type 1

Exercise 9.1

LEVEL - 1

Only one option correct

1. Ultrasonic, infrasonic and audible waves travel through a medium with speeds v_u, v_i and v_a respectively, then
   (a) v_u, v_i and v_a are equal
   (b) $v_u \geq v_a \geq v_i$
   (c) $v_u \leq v_a \leq v_i$
   (d) $v_a \leq v_u$ and $v_u = v_i$

2. A tuning fork of frequency 480 Hz is used to vibrate a sonometer wire having natural frequency 410 Hz. The wire will vibrate with a frequency
   (a) 410 Hz
   (b) 480 Hz
   (c) 820 Hz
   (d) 960 Hz

3. Figure shows the displacement of a string element located at, say, $x = 0$ as a function of time. The time moment(s) at which element is moving downward

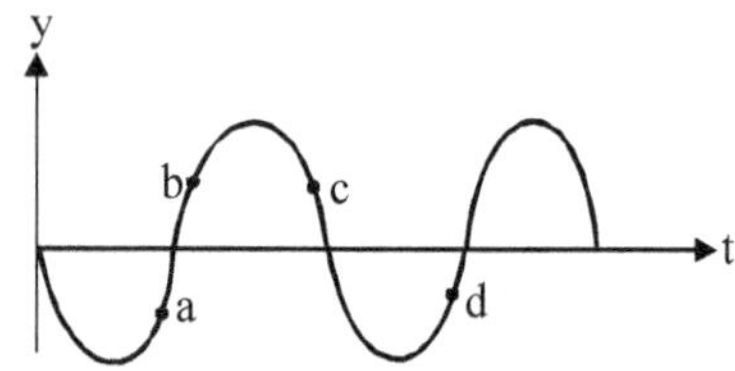

   (a) a
   (b) b
   (c) c
   (d) d

4. The following four waves are sent along strings (x in metre and t in second). Which of them is moving fastest ?
   (1) $y_1 = (1 \text{ mm}) \sin (x - 3t)$
   (2) $y_2 = (2 \text{ mm}) \sin (4x - t)$
   (3) $y_3 = (3 \text{ mm}) \sin (2x - t)$
   (4) $y_4 = (4 \text{ mm}) \sin (x - 2t)$
   (a) (1)
   (b) (2)
   (c) (3)
   (d) (4)

5. Which of the following statements is wrong ?
   (a) Sound travels in straight line
   (b) Sound is a form of energy
   (c) Sound travels in the form of waves
   (d) Sound travels faster in vacuum than in air

6. What is the wavelength of the wave shown in figure, where each segment of the wave has length b

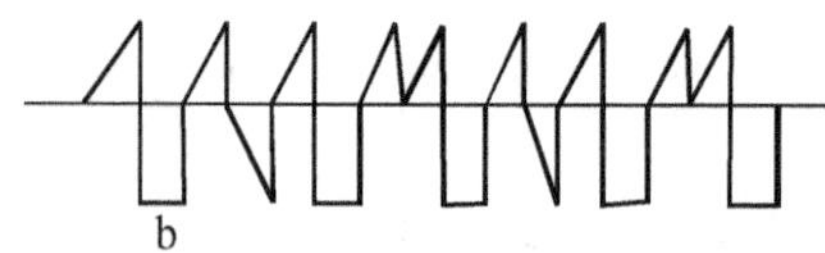

   (a) $4\,b$
   (b) $5\,b$
   (c) $6\,b$
   (d) $7\,b$

7. A man sets his watch by a whistle that is 2 km away. How much will his watch be in error (speed of sound in air 330 m/s)
   (a) 3 s fast
   (b) 3 s slow
   (c) 6 s fast
   (d) 6 s slow

8. The distance between two consecutive crests in a wave train produced in a string is 5 cm. If 2 complete waves pass through any point per second, the velocity of the wave is
   (a) 10 cm/s
   (b) 2.5 cm/s
   (c) 5 cm/s
   (d) 15 cm/s

9. When sound waves travel from air to water, which of the following remains constant ?
   (a) Velocity
   (b) Frequency
   (c) Wavelength
   (d) All the above

10. The frequency of a sound wave is f and its velocity is v. If the frequency is increased to $4\,f$, the velocity of the wave will be
    (a) v
    (b) $2\,v$
    (c) $4\,v$
    (d) $\dfrac{v}{4}$

11. What will be the wave velocity, if the radar gives 54 waves per min and wavelength of the given wave is 10 m
    (a) 4 m/s
    (b) 6 m/s
    (c) 9 m/s
    (d) 5 m/s

12. Velocity of sound in air
    I. Increases with temperature.
    II. Decreases with temperature.
    III. Increases with pressure.
    IV. Is independent of pressure.
    V. Is independent of temperature.
    Choose the correct answer
    (a) Only I and II are true
    (b) Only I and III are true
    (c) Only II and III are true
    (d) Only I and IV are true

13. v_1 and v_2 are the velocities of sound at the same temperature in two monoatomic gases of densities ρ_1 and ρ_2 respectively. If $\dfrac{\rho_1}{\rho_2} = \dfrac{1}{4}$, then the ratio of velocities v_1 and v_2 will be
    (a) $1 : 2$
    (b) $4 : 1$
    (c) $2 : 1$
    (d) $1 : 4$

14. The temperature at which the speed of sound in air becomes double of its value at 0°C is
    (a) 273 K
    (b) 546 K
    (c) 1092 K
    (d) 0 K

15. Water waves are
    (a) Longitudinal
    (b) Transverse
    (c) Both longitudinal and transverse
    (d) Neither longitudinal nor transverse

Answer Key	1	(a)	3	(c)	5	(d)	7	(d)	9	(b)	11	(c)	13	(c)	15	(c)
Sol. from page 624	2	(b)	4	(a)	6	(d)	8	(a)	10	(a)	12	(d)	14	(c)		

16. Sound travels in rocks in the form of
    (a) Longitudinal elastic waves only
    (b) Transverse elastic waves only
    (c) Both longitudinal and transverse elastic waves
    (d) Non-elastic waves

17. The waves in which the particles of the medium vibrate in a direction perpendicular to the direction of wave motion is known as
    (a) Transverse waves (b) Longitudinal waves
    (c) Propagated waves (d) None of these

18. The rate of transfer of energy in a wave depends
    (a) Directly on the square of the wave amplitude and square of the wave frequency
    (b) Directly on the square of the wave amplitude and root of the wave frequency
    (c) Directly on the wave amplitude and square of the wave frequency
    (d) None of these

19. Which of the following is not the transverse wave ?
    (a) X - rays (b) γ - rays
    (c) Visible light wave (d) Sound wave in a gas

20. Sound waves of wavelength greater than that of audible sound are called
    (a) Seismic waves (b) Sonic waves
    (c) Ultrasonic waves (d) Infrasonic waves

21. Oxygen is 16 times heavier than hydrogen. Equal volumes of hydrogen and oxygen are mixed. The ratio of the velocity of sound in the mixture to that in oxygen is
    (a) $\sqrt{\dfrac{32}{17}}$ (b) $\sqrt{\dfrac{17}{32}}$
    (c) $\sqrt{8}$ (d) $\sqrt{\dfrac{1}{8}}$

22. 'SONAR' emits which of the follwoing waves
    (a) Radio waves (b) Ultrasonic waves
    (c) Light waves (d) Magnetic waves

23. A travelling wave in a stretched string is described by the equation $y = A \sin (kx - \omega t)$. The maximum particle velocity is
    (a) $A\omega$ (b) $\dfrac{\omega}{k}$
    (c) $\dfrac{d\omega}{dk}$ (d) $\dfrac{x}{t}$

24. The displacement y of a wave travelling in the x-direction is given by $y = 10^{-4} \sin \left(600\, t - 2\, x + \dfrac{\pi}{3}\right)$ metre, where x is expressed in metre and t in second. The speed of the wave-motion in m/s is
    (a) 200 (b) 300
    (c) 600 (d) 1200

25. A wave of frequency 400 Hz has a phase velocity of 300 m/s. Two points on this wave are out of phase by 60°. The separation between these two points is
    (a) 1.25 cm (b) 12.5 cm
    (c) 0.25 cm (d) 2.25 cm

26. A whistle giving out 450 Hz approaches a stationary observer at a speed of 33 m/s. The frequency heard by the observer in Hz is
    (a) 409 (b) 429
    (c) 517 (d) 500

27. A whistle of frequency 500 Hz tied to the end of a string of length 1.2 m revolves at 400 rev/min. A listener standing some distance away in the plane of rotation of whistle hears frequencies in the range (speed of sound = 340 m/s) :
    (a) 436 to 586 (b) 426 to 574
    (c) 426 to 584 (d) 436 to 674

28. A train moves towards a stationary observer with speed 34 m/s. The train sounds a whistle and its frequency registered by the observer is f_1. If the train's speed is reduced to 17 m/s, the frequency registered is f_2. If the speed of sound is 340 m/s, then the ratio f_1 / f_2 is
    (a) $\dfrac{18}{19}$ (b) $\dfrac{1}{2}$
    (c) 2 (d) $\dfrac{19}{18}$

29. A small source of sound moves on a circle as shown in the figure and an observer is standing on O. Let f_1, f_2 and f_3 be the frequencies heard when the source is at A, B and C respectively. Then

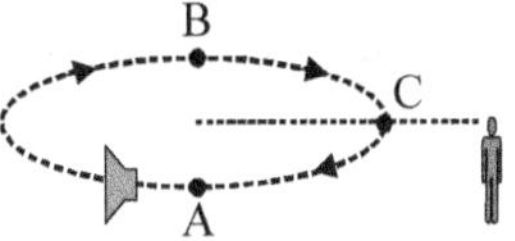

    (a) $f_1 > f_2 > f_3$ (b) $f_2 > f_3 > f_1$
    (c) $f_1 = f_2 > f_3$ (d) $f_2 > f_1 > f_3$

30. Intensity level of a sound of intensity I is 30 dB. The ratio I / I_0 is (where I_0 is the threshold of hearing)
    (a) 3000 (b) 1000
    (c) 300 (d) 30

31. Each of the properties of sound listed in column A primarily depends on one of the quantities in column B. Choose the matching pairs from two columns

Column A	Column B
Pitch	Waveform
Quality	Frequency
Loudness	Intensity

    (a) Pitch-waveform, Quality-frequency, Loudness- intensity
    (b) Pitch-frequency, Quality-waveform, Loudness- intensity
    (c) Pitch-intensity, Quality-waveform, Loudness- frequency
    (d) Pitch-waveform, Quality-intensity, Loudness- frequency

Answer Key	16	(c)	18	(a)	20	(d)	22	(b)	24	(b)	26	(d)	28	(d)	30	(b)
Sol. from page 624	17	(a)	19	(d)	21	(a)	23	(a)	25	(b)	27	(a)	29	(b)	31	(b)

32. A star is moving away from the earth with a velocity of 100 km/s. If the velocity of light is 3×10^8 m/s, then the shift of its spectral line of wavelength 5700 Å due to Doppler's effect will be
(a) 0.63 Å
(b) 1.90 Å
(c) 3.80 Å
(d) 5.79 Å

33. Two sound waves having a phase difference of $60°$ have path difference of
(a) 2λ
(b) $\lambda/2$
(c) $\lambda/6$
(d) $\lambda/3$

34. A wave of frequency 500 Hz has velocity 360 m/sec. The distance between two nearest points $60°$ out of phase, is
(a) 0.6 cm
(b) 12 cm
(c) 60 cm
(d) 120 cm

35. On increasing the tension of a stretched string by 2.5 N, the frequency is altered in the ratio 3 : 2. The original stretching force is
(a) 6 N
(b) 2 N
(c) 4 N
(d) 5 N

36. The particles of a medium vibrate about their mean positions whenever a wave travels through that medium. The phase difference between the vibrations of two such particles
(a) Varies with time
(b) Varies with distance separating them
(c) Varies with time as well as distance
(d) Is always zero

37. A transverse wave propagating in a string is decribed by the equation $y = 0.021 \sin(x + 30t)$, where x and y are in metre and t in second. If the linear density of the vibrating string is 1.3×10^{-4} kg/m, the tension in the string is
(a) 0.21 N
(b) 0.12 N
(c) 0.64 N
(d) 2.1 N

38. The phase difference between two waves represented by
$y_1 = 10^{-6} \sin [100t + (x/50) + 0.5]$m
$y_2 = 10^{-6} \cos [100t + (x/50)]$m
where x is expressed in metre and t is expressed in second, is approximately.
(a) 1.5 rad
(b) 1.07 rad
(c) 2.07 rad
(d) 0.5 rad

39. A motor cycle starts from rest and accelerates along a straight path at 2m/s^2. At the starting point of the motor cycle there is a stationary electric siren. How far has the motor cycle gone when the driver hears the frequency of the siren at 94% of its value when the motor cycle was at rest (Speed of sound $= 330 \text{ ms}^{-1}$)
(a) 49 m
(b) 98 m
(c) 147 m
(d) 196 m

Answer Key	32	(b)	34	(b)	36	(b)	38	(b)
Sol. from page 624	33	(c)	35	(b)	37	(b)	39	(b)

LEVEL -2

1. A transverse wave is described by the equation
$$y = y_0 \sin 2\pi\left(ft - \frac{x}{\lambda}\right)$$
.The maximum particle velocity is four times the wave velocity if
(a) $\lambda = \dfrac{\pi y_0}{4}$
(b) $\lambda = \dfrac{\pi y_0}{2}$
(c) $\lambda = \pi y_0$
(d) $\lambda = 2\pi y_0$

2. Which one of the following does not represent a travelling wave ?
(a) $y = \sin(x - vt)$
(b) $y = y_m \sin k(x + vt)$
(c) $y = y_m \log(x - vt)$
(d) $y = f(x^2 - vt^2)$

3. A wave represented by the given equation
$$y = A \sin\left(10\pi x + 15\pi t + \frac{\pi}{3}\right),$$
where x is in metre and t is in second.

The expression represents
(a) A wave travelling in the positive x direction with a velocity of 1.5 m/s.
(b) A wave travelling in the negative x direction with a velocity of 1.5 m/s.
(c) A wave travelling in the negative x direction with a wavelength of 0.2 m.
(d) A wave travelling in the positive x direction with a wavelength of 0.2 m.

4. A siren placed at a railway platform is emitting sound of frequency 5 kHz. A passenger sitting in a moving train A records a frequency of 5.5 kHz while the train approaches the siren. During his return journey in a different train B the records a frequency of 6.0 kHz while approaching the same siren. The ratio of the velocity of train B to that of train A is
(a) $\dfrac{242}{252}$
(b) 2
(c) $\dfrac{5}{6}$
(d) $\dfrac{11}{6}$

Answer Key	1	(b)	2	(d)	3	(b)	4	(c)
Sol. from page 625								

5. A train has just completed a U-curve in a track which is a semicircle. The engine at the forward end of the semicircular part of the track while the last carriage is at the rear end of the semicircular track. The driver blows a whistle of frequency 200 Hz. Velocity of sound is 340 m/s. Then the apparent frequency as observed by a passenger in the middle of a train when the speed of the train is 30 m/s is

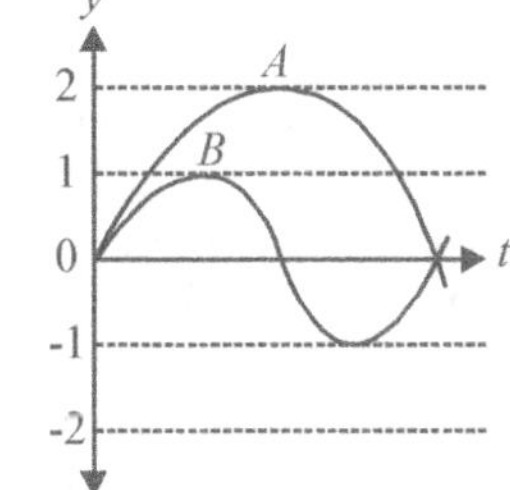

(a)   209 Hz

(b)   288 Hz

(c)   200 Hz

(d)   181 Hz

6. The displacement-time graphs for two sound waves A and B are shown in the figure. Then the ratio of their intensities I_A / I_B is equal to

(a)   1 : 4

(b)   1 : 16

(c)   1 : 2

(d)   1 : 1

7. In a plane progressive harmonic wave particle speed is always less than the wave speed if

(a)   Amplitude of wave is less than $\dfrac{\lambda}{2\pi}$.

(b)   Amplitude of wave is greater than $\dfrac{\lambda}{2\pi}$.

(c)   Amplitude of wave is less than λ

(d)   Amplitude of wave is greater than $\dfrac{\lambda}{\pi}$.

8. The ratio of intensities between two coherent sound sources is $4 : 1$. The difference of loudness in decibels (dB) between maximum and minimum intensities, when they interfere in space is

(a)   10 log (2)   (b)   20 log (3)

(c)   10 log (3)   (d)   20 log (2)

9. Two men are equidistance from the phase of a plane vertical cliff and are 300 m apart. One of them fires a pistol, the other hears the echo one second after hearing the direct sound. The velocity of sound is 330 m/s. The distance of the men from the cliff is

(a)   300 m   (b)   415 m

(c)   350 m   (d)   315 m

10. A source of sound of frequency 600 Hz is placed inside water. The speed of sound in water is 1500 m/s and in air is 300 m/s. The frequency of sound recorded by an observer who is standing in air is

(a)   200 Hz   (b)   3000 Hz

(c)   120 Hz   (d)   600 Hz

11. When a longitudinal wave propagates through a medium, the particles of the medium execute simple harmonic oscillations about their mean positions. These oscillations of a particle are characterised by an invariant

(a)   Kinetic energy

(b)   Potential energy

(c)   Sum of kinetic energy and potential energy

(d)   Difference between kinetic energy and potential energy

12. The amplitude of a wave disturbance propagating in the positive x-direction is given by $y = \dfrac{1}{\left(1 + x^2\right)}$ at $t = 0$ and $y = \dfrac{1}{1 + (x - 1)^2}$ at $t = 2s$, where x and y are in metre. The shape of the wave disturbance does not change during the propagation. The velocity of the wave is

(a)   0.25 m/s   (b)   2.5 m/s

(c)   0.5 m/s   (d)   5 m/s

13. A person speaking normally produces a sound intensity of 40 dB at a distance of 1 m. If the threshold intensity for reasonable audibility is 20 dB, the maximum distance at which he can be heard clearly is

(a)   4 m   (b)   5 m

(c)   10 m   (d)   20 m

14. The rope shown at an instant is carrying a wave travelling towards right, created by a source vibrating at a frequency f. Consider the following statements

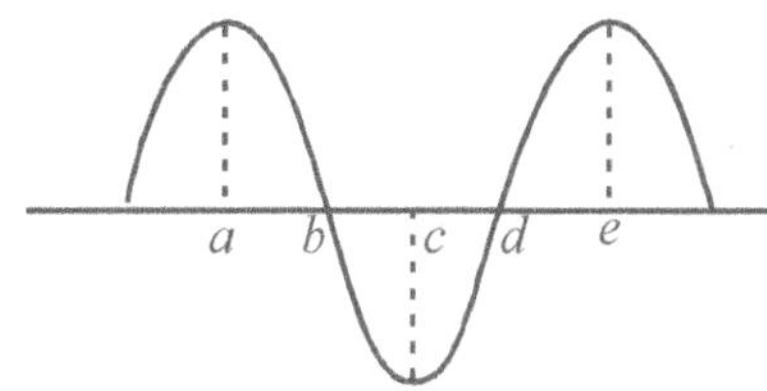

I.   the speed of the wave is $4\,f \times ab$

II.   the medium at a will be in the same phase as d after $\dfrac{4}{3f}\,s$

III.   the phase difference between b and e is $\dfrac{3\pi}{2}$

Which of these statements are correct ?

(a)   I, II and III   (b)   II only

(c)   I and III   (d)   III only

15. A uniform rope of length 12m and mass 6 kg hangs vertically from a rigid support. A block of mass 2kg is attached to the free end of the rope. A transverse pulse of wavelength 0.06m is produced at the lower end of the rope. The wavelength of the pulse when it reaches the top of the rope is

(a)   0.012 m   (b)   0.06 m

(c)   0.24 m   (d)   0.12 m

Wave - I   MCQ Type 2   *Exercise 9.2*

1. The intensity of a progressing plane wave in loss-free medium is
   (a) directly proportional to the square of amplitude of the wave
   (b) directly proportional to the velocity of the wave
   (c) directly proportional to the square of frequency of the wave
   (d) inversely proportional to the density of the medium

2. A transverse sinusoidal wave of amplitude a, wavelength λ and frequency f is travelling on a stretched string. The maximum speed of any point on the string is $v/10$, where v is the speed of propagation of the wave. If $a = 10^{-3}$ m and $v = 10$ ms^{-1}, then λ and f are given by
   (a) $\lambda = 2\pi \times 10^{-2}$ m   (b) $\lambda = 10^{-3}$ m
   (c) $f = \dfrac{10^3}{2\pi}$ Hz   (d) $f = 10^4$ Hz

3. A sound wave of frequency f travels horizontally to the right. It is reflected from a large vertical plane surface moving to the left with a speed v. The speed of sound in the medium is c, then
   (a) the frequency of the reflected wave is $\dfrac{f(c+v)}{c-v}$
   (b) The wavelength of the reflected wave is $\dfrac{c(c-v)}{f(c+v)}$
   (c) the number of waves striking the surface per second is
   $$\dfrac{f(c+v)}{c}$$
   (d) the number of beats heard by a stationary listener to the left of the reflecting surface is $\dfrac{f\,v}{c-v}$

4. In a wave motion $y = a\sin(kx - \omega t)$, y can represent
   (a) electric field   (b) magnetic field
   (c) displacement   (d) pressure

5. The equation $y = 4 + 2\sin(6t - 3x)$ represents a wave motion with
   (a) amplitude 6 units   (b) amplitude 2 units
   (c) wave speed 2 units   (d) wave speed 1/2 units

6. In a plane progressive harmonic wave
   (a) phase difference between displacement and acceleration of particle is zero
   (b) phase difference between displacement and acceleration of particle is π
   (c) phase difference between displacement and velocity of particle is $\pi/2$
   (d) phase difference between velocity and acceleration of particle is $\pi/2$

7. The speed of sound in a gas
   (a) doesn't depend on the pressure of the gas
   (b) varies directly with the square root of the absolute temperature of the gas
   (c) varies inversely with the square root of the density of the gas
   (d) changes with the change in frequency of the sound wave

8. A mixture of two diatomic gases exists in a closed cylinder. The volumes and velocities in the two gases are V_1, V_2 and c_1, c_2 respectively. ρ_1 and ρ_2 are the densities of the two gases. Then
   (a) the density of the mixture of gases is $\left(\dfrac{\rho_1 V_2 + \rho_2 V_1}{\rho_1 + \rho_2}\right)$
   (b) the density of the mixture of gases is $\left(\dfrac{\rho_1 V_1 + \rho_2 V_2}{V_1 + V_2}\right)$
   (c) the velocity of sound in the mixture is $c_1 c_2 \sqrt{\dfrac{V_1 + V_2}{V_1 c_2^2 + V_2 c_1^2}}$
   (d) the velocity of sound in the mixture is $c_1 c_2 \sqrt{\dfrac{V_1 c_1^2 + V_2 c_2^2}{V_1 + V_2}}$

9. In the figure shown an observer O_1 floats (static) on water surface with ears in air while another observer O_2 is moving upwards with constant velocity $v_1 = v/5$ in water.
   The source moves down with constant velocity $v_s = v/5$ and emits sound of frequency f.
   The velocity of sound in air is v and that in water is $4v$. For the situation shown in figure

   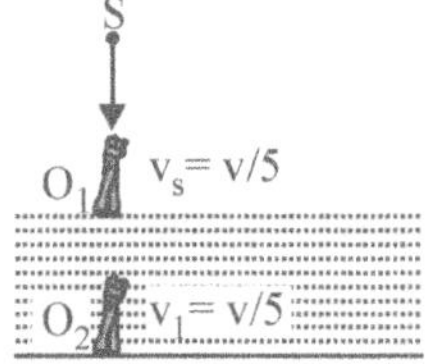

   (a) The wavelength of the sound received by O_1 is $4v/5f$
   (b) The wavelength of the sound received by O_1 is v/f
   (c) The frequency of the sound received by O_2 is $21f/16$
   (d) The wavelength of the sound received by O_2 is $16v/5f$

10. A stationary observer receives a sound of frequency $f_0 = 2000$ Hz. The apparent frequency f varies with time as shown in figure. Speed of sound $= 300$ m/s. Choose the correct alternative (s)?

    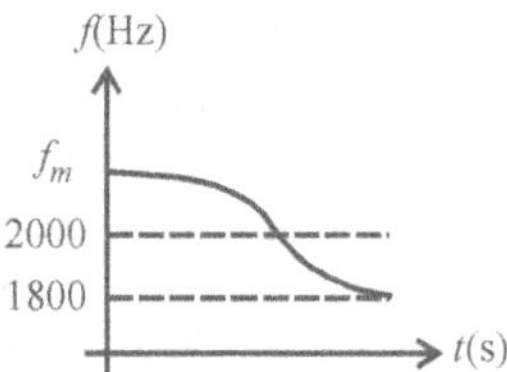

    (a) speed of source is 66.7 m/s
    (b) f_m shown in figure cannot be greater than 2500 Hz
    (c) speed of source is 33.33 m/s
    (d) f_m shown in figure cannot be greater than 2250 Hz

Answer Key	1	(a, b, c)	3	(a, b, c)	5	(b, c)	7	(a, b, c)	9	(a, c, d)
Sol. from page 626	2	(a, c)	4	(a, b, c, d)	6	(b, c, d)	8	(b, c)	10	(c, d)

11. Choose the correct option (s) ?
   (a) When a source of sound moves towards a stationary observer, the wavelength of the sound as heard by the observer is less than the original wavelength of the source.
   (b) When both observer and the source of sound moves towards each other, the wavelength of the sound as heard by the observer is less than the wavelength of the original sound.
   (c) When both observer and the source of sound moves away from each other, the wavelength of the sound as heard by the observer is less than the wavelength of the original sound.
   (d) When an observer moves away from a stationary source, the wavelength of the sound heard by the observer is less than the wavelength of the original sound.

12. As a wave propagates
   (a) the wave intensity remains constant for a plane wave.
   (b) the wave intensity decreases as the inverse of the distance from the source for a spherical wave.
   (c) the wave intensity decreases as the inverse square of the distance from the source for a spherical wave.
   (d) total intensity of the spherical wave over the spherical surface centered at the source remains constant at all times.

Answer Key
Sol. from page 626

11	(a, b, c)	12	(c, d)

Wave - I   Statement Questions   *Exercise 9.3*

Read the two statements carefully to mark the correct option out of the options given below:
(a) If both the statements are true and the *statement - 2* is the correct explanation of *statement - 1*.
(b) If both the statements are true but *statement - 2* is not the correct explanation of the *statement - 1*.
(c) If *statement - 1* true but *statement - 2* is false.
(d) If *statement - 1* is false but *statement - 2* is true.

1. **Statement 1**
   Transverse wave are not produced in fluids.
   Statement 2
   Fluid possess no rigidity.
2. **Statement 1**
   Sound wave can not propagate through vacuum but light waves can.
   Statement 2
   Sound waves cannot be polarised but light waves can be polarised.
3. **Statement 1**
   Particle velocity and wave velocity both are independent of time.
   Statement 2
   For the propagation of wave motion, the medium must have the properties of elasticity and inertia.
4. **Statement 1**
   The change in air pressure affect the speed of sound.
   Statement 2
   The speed of sound in a gas is proportional to the square root of pressure.
5. **Statement 1**
   The speed of sound in solids is maximum though their density is large.
   Statement 2
   The modulus of elasticity of solid is large.

6. **Statement 1**
   Sound travels faster on a hot summer day than on a cold winter day.
   Statement 2
   Velocity of sound is directly proportional to the square root of its absolute temperature.
7. **Statement 1**
   The base of Laplace correction was that exchange of heat between the region of compression and rarefaction in air is not possible.
   Statement 2
   Air is a bad conductor of heat and velocity of sound in air is large.
8. **Statement 1**
   Compression and rarefaction involve changes in density and pressure.
   Statement 2
   When particles are compressed, density of medium increases and when they are rarefied, density of medium decreases.
9. **Statement 1**
   In the case of a stationary wave, a person hear a loud sound at the nodes as compared to the antinodes.
   Statement 2
   In a stationary wave all the particles of the medium vibrate in phase.

Answer Key
Sol. from page 627

1	(a)	3	(d)	5	(a)	7	(c)	9	(c)
2	(b)	4	(d)	6	(a)	8	(a)		

Wave - I 

Passage & Matrix

Exercise 9.4

PASSAGES

Passage for (Q. 1 - 3) :
Answer the following questions using the informations given below.
Molecular weight of air = 28.8
Molecular weight of water vapour = 18
γ of dry air = 1.4
γ of water vapour = 1.33
Standard pressure = 760 mm of Hg
Standard temperature = 0°C
Vapour pressure at 0°C = 4.8 mm of Hg
Velocity of sound in air at STP = 332 m/s

1. If ρ_m and ρ_d be the densities of the moist and dry air respectively, then
   (a) $\rho_m = 0.251 \rho_d$ (b) $\rho_m = 0.997 \rho_d$
   (c) $\rho_m = 0.755 \rho_d$ (d) $\rho_m = 0.355 \rho_d$.

2. If γ_m and γ_d be the adiabatic exponent for moist and dry air respectively then

   (a) $\dfrac{\gamma_m}{\gamma_d} = 0.99$ (b) $\dfrac{\gamma_m}{\gamma_d} = 0.95$

   (c) $\dfrac{\gamma_m}{\gamma_d} = 0.92$ (d) $\dfrac{\gamma_m}{\gamma_d} = 0.75$

3. The speed of sound in moist air at STP is
   (a) 329.5 m/s (b) 330.25 m/s
   (c) 331.7 m/s (d) 333.7 m/s

Passage for (Q. 4 - 6) :
Two trains A and B are moving with speeds 20 m/s and 30 m/s respectively in the same direction on the same straight track, with B ahead of A. The engines are at the front ends. The engine of train A blows a long whistle. Assume that the sound of the whistle is composed of components varying in frequency from $f_1 = 800$ Hz to $f_2 = 1120$ Hz, as shown in the figure. The spread in the frequency (highest frequency – lowest frequency) is thus 320 Hz. The speed of sound in still air is 340 m/s.

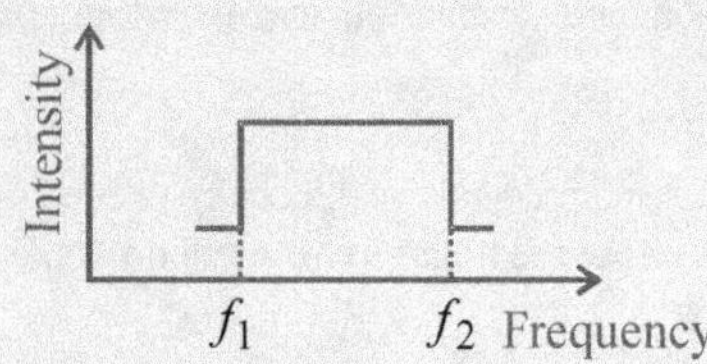

4. The speed of sound of the whistle is
   (a) 340 m/s for passengers in A and 310 m/s for passengers in B
   (b) 360 m/s for passengers in A and 310 m/s for passengers in B
   (c) 310 m/s for passengers in A and 360 m/s for passengers in B
   (d) 340 m/s for passengers in both the trains

5. The distribution of the sound intensity of the whistle as observed by the passengers in train A is best represented by

   (a) 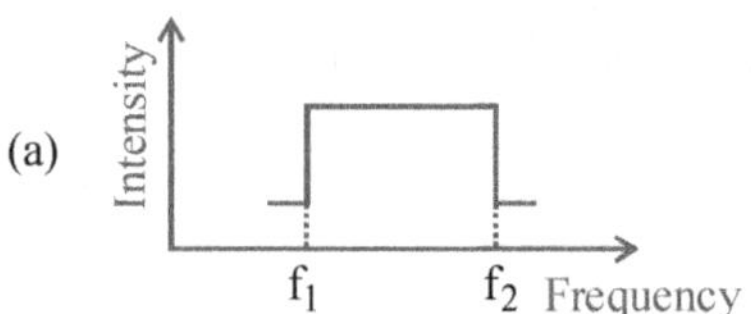

   (b) 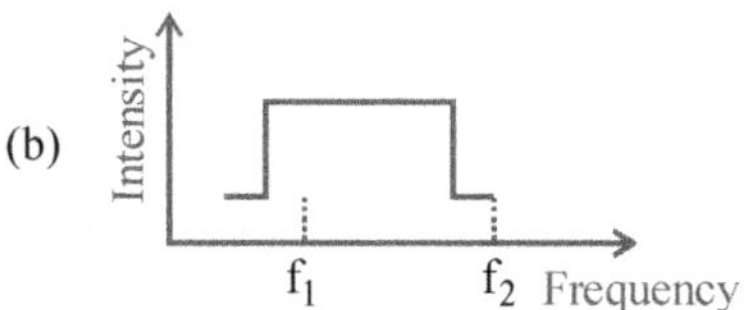

   (c) 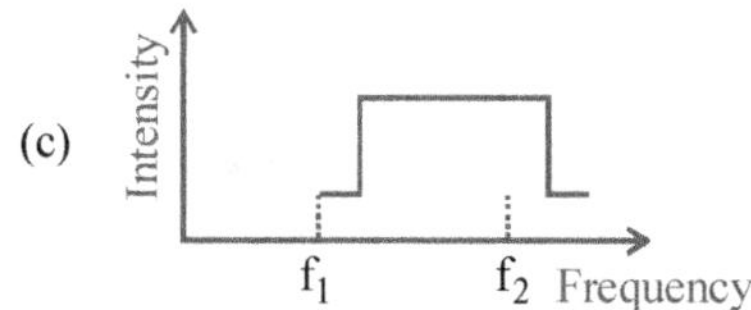

   (d) 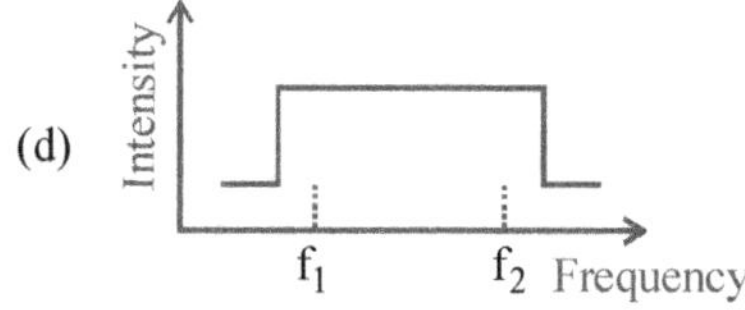

6. The spread of frequency as observed by the passengers in train B is
   (a) 310 Hz (b) 330 Hz
   (c) 350 Hz (d) 290 Hz

Passage for (Q. 7 - 9) :
A train standing at the outer signal of a railway station blows a whistle of frequency 400 Hz in still air.

7. What is the frequency of the whistle for a platform observer when the train approaches the platform with a speed of 10 m/s
   (a) 300 Hz (b) 412.12 Hz
   (c) 350 Hz (d) 360.50 Hz

8. What is the frequency of the whistle for a platform observer when the train recedes from the platform with a speed of 10 m/s ?
   (a) 400.60 Hz (b) 528.75 Hz
   (c) 574.65 Hz (d) none of these

9. What is the frequency of sound in each case ?
   (a) 340 Hz (b) 350 Hz
   (c) 360 Hz (d) 370 H

Answer Key	1	(b)	3	(c)	5	(a)	7	(b)	9	(a)
Sol. from page 627	2	(a)	4	(b)	6	(a)	8	(c)		

Passage for (Q. 10 - 12) :
A heavy but uniform rope of length L is suspended from a ceiling.

10. Write the velocity of a transverse wave travelling on the string as a function of the distance from the lower end.

(a) $\sqrt{gx}$

(b) $\sqrt{g/x}$

(c) $\sqrt{2gx}$

(d) none of these

11. If the rope is given a sudden sideways jerk at the bottom, how long will it take for the pulse to reach the ceiling ?

(a) $\sqrt{4L/g}$

(b) $\sqrt{2L/g}$

(c) $\sqrt{L/2g}$

(d) $\sqrt{L/3g}$

12. A particle is dropped from the ceiling at the instant the bottom end is given the jerk. Where will the particle meet the pulse ?

(a) $L/3$

(b) $L/2$

(c) $L/4$

(d) $L/5$

Passage for (Q. 13 - 15) :
A long wire PQR is made by joining two wires PQ and QR of equal radii. PQ has length 4.8 m and mass 0.06 kg. QR has length 2.56 m and mass 0.2 kg. The wire PQR is under a tension of 80 N. A sinusoidal wave–pulse of amplitude 3.5 cm is sent along the wire PQ from the end P. No power is dissipated during the propagation of the wave pulse. Calculate

13. The time taken by the wave–pulse to reach the other end R of the wire.

(a) 0.145

(b) 0.245

(c) 0.450

(d) 0.600

14. The amplitude of the reflected wave–pulses after the incident wave–pulse crosses the joint Q is

(a) 1.5 cm

(b) 2.5 cm

(c) 3.0 cm

(d) 4.5 cm

15. The amplitude of the transmitted wave–pulses after the incident wave–pulse crosses the joint Q.

(a) 1.0 cm

(b) 1.5 cm

(c) 2.0 cm

(d) 2.5 cm

16. Match the columns I and II

Column I	Column II
A. $y = 4\sin(5x - 4t) + 3\cos(4t - 5x + \pi/6)$	(p) Particles at every position are performing SHM
B. $y = 10\cos\left(t - \dfrac{x}{330}\right)\sin(100)\left(t - \dfrac{x}{330}\right)$	(q) Equation of travelling wave
C. $y = 10\sin(2\pi x - 120t) + 10\cos(120t + 2\pi x)$	(r) Equation of standing wave
D. $y = 10\sin(2\pi x - 120t) + 8\cos(118t - 59/30\pi x)$	(s) Equation of Beats

17.. In the equation, $y = A\sin 2\pi(ax + bt + \pi/4)$ match the following:

Column I	Column II
A. Frequency of wave	(p) a
B. Wavelength of wave	(q) b
C. Phase difference between two points $\dfrac{1}{4a}$ distance apart	(r) π
D. Phase difference of a point after a time interval of $\dfrac{1}{8b}$	(s) $\pi/2$
	(t) none

18. Regarding speed of sound in gas match the following

Coloumn I	Coloumn II
A. Temperature of gas is made 4 times and pressure 2 times	(p) speed becomes $2\sqrt{2}$ times
B. Only pressure is made 4 times without change in temperature	(q) speed becomes 2 times
C. Only temperature is changed to 4 times	(r) speed remains unchanged
D. Molecular mass of the gas is made 4 times	(s) speed remains half

19. Source has frequency f. Source and observer both have same speed. For the apparent frequency observed by observer match the following

Column -1	Column -2
A. Observer is approaching the source but source is receding from the observer	(p) more than f
B. Observer and source both approaching towards each other	(q) less than f
C. Observer and source both receding from each other	(r) equal to f
D. Source is approaching but observer is receding	

Answer Key	10	(a)	12	(a)	15	(c)	16	A→(p, q); B→(s); C→(p, r); D→(s)	18	A→(q); B→(r); C→(q); D→(s)
Sol. from page 627	11	(a)	13	(a)			17	A→(q); B→(t); C→(s); D→(t)	19	A→(r); B→(p);C→(q);D→(r)

Wave - I   # Subjective Integer Type   *Exercise 9.5*

Solutions from page 629

1. Speed of sound in air is 332 m/s at STP. What will be its value in hydrogen at STP, if density of hydrogen at STP is $1/16^{th}$ that of air ?

   Ans. 1328 m/s.

2. A gas is a mixture of two parts by volume of hydrogen and one part by volume of nitrogen. If the velocity of sound in hydrogen at 0°C is 1300 m/s, find the velocity of sound in the gaseous mixture at 27°C.

   Ans. 591 m/s.

3. The sirens of two fire engines have a frequency of 600 Hz each. A man hears the sirens from the two engines, one approaching him with a speed of 36 km/h and the other going away from him at a speed of 54 km/h. The difference in frequency of two sirens heard

   by the man is $\dfrac{83.2}{x} Hg$. Find the value of x . ? Take the speed of sound to be 340 m/s.

   Ans. 2. Hz.

4. A particle on a stretched string supporting a travelling wave, takes 5.0 ms to move from its mean position to the extreme position. The distance between two consecutive particles, which are at their mean positions Q, is 2.0 cm. Find the wave speed.

   Ans. 2.0 m/s.

5. An aeroplane is going towards east at a speed of 510 km/h at a height of 2000 m. At a certain instant, the sound of the plane heared by a ground observer appears to come from a point vertically above it. Where is the plane at this instant? Speed of the sound in air = 340 m/s.

   Ans. 833 m.

6. A train approaching a railway crossing at a speed of 120 km/h sounds a short whistle at frequency 640 Hz when it is 300 m away from the crossing. The speed of sound in air is 340 m/s. What will be the frequency heard by a person standing on a road perpendicular to the track through the crossing at a distance of 400 m from the crossing ?

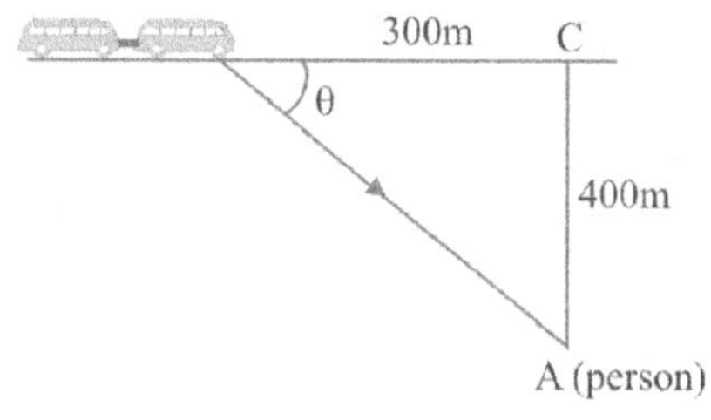

   Ans. 680 Hz.

7. A string of length 40 cm and weighing 10 g is attached to a spring at one end and to a fixed wall at the other end. The spring has a spring constant of 160 N/m and is stretched by 1.0 cm. If a wave pulse is produced on the string near the wall, the time it will take

   to reach the spring is $\dfrac{1}{x}$. The value of x is ?

   Ans. 20 s.

8. A wire of 9.8×10^{-3} kg mass per metre passes over a frictionless pulley fixed on the top of an inclined frictionless plane which makes an angle of 30° with the horizontal . Masses M_1 and M_2 are tied at the two ends of the wire. The mass M_1 rests on the plane and the mass M_2 hangs freely vertically downwards. The whole system is in equilibrium. Now a transverse wave propagate along the wire with a velocity of 100 m/s. Find the value of masses M_1.

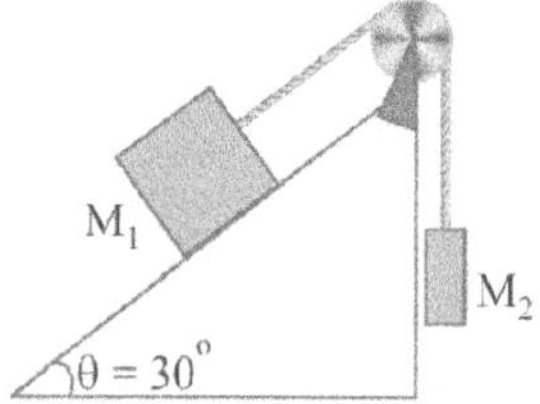

   Ans. $M_1 = 20$ kg.

9. Two sound waves have intensities 5×10^{-10} W/m² and 1×10^{-6} W/m². By how many decibels is the louder sound above the other ?   *Ans.* 33 dB.

1. You have learnt that a travelling wave in one dimension is represented by a function $y = f(x, t)$ where x and t must appear in the combination $x - vt$ or $x + vt$, i.e. $y = f(x \pm vt)$. Is the converse true ? Examine if the following functions for y can possibly represent a travelling wave :

(i) $(x - vt)^2$

(ii) $\log\,[(x + vt)/x_0]$

(iii) $\exp\,[-(x + vt)\,/\,x_0]$

(iv) $1\,/\,(x + vt)$

Ans. Functions (i), (ii) and (iv) are not finite for all values of x and t, hence they cannot represent a travelling wave. Only function (iii) satisfies the condition to represent a travelling wave.

2. Given below are some functions of x and t to represent the displacement (transverse or longitudinal) of an elastic wave. State which of these represent (i) a travelling wave, (ii) a stationary wave or (iii) none at all :

(a) $y = 2 \cos (3x) \sin (10\,t)$

(b) $y = 2\sqrt{x - vt}$

(c) $y = 3 \sin (5x - 0.5t) + 4 \cos (5x - 0.5t)$

(d) $y = \cos x \sin t + \cos 2x \sin 2t$

Ans. (a) stationary wave (b) it cannot represent any type of wave (c) it represents a travelling wave of amplitude 5 unit. (d) it represents the superposition of two stationary waves.

3. Explain why or how :

(a)   in a sound wave, a displacement node is a pressure antinode and vice versa

(b)   bats can ascertain distance, directions, nature, and sizes of the obstacles without any "eyes"

(c)   a violin note and sitar note may have the same frequency, yet we can distinguish between the two notes

(d)   Solids can support both longitudinal and transverse waves, but only longitudinal waves can propagate in gases, and

(e)   the shape of a pulse gets distorted during propagation in a dispersive medium.

Ans. (d) gases do not possess shear elasticity.

   (e) the shape of a pulse gets distorted during propagation in a dispersive medium.

4. What is the ratio of the velocity of sound in hydrogen ($\gamma = 7/5$) to that in helium gas ($\gamma = 5/3$) at the same temperature ?

Ans. $\sqrt{42\,/\,5}$.

5. The equation of a plane progressive wave is

$$y = 10 \sin 2\pi\,(t - 0.005\,x)$$

where y and x are in cm and t in second. Calculate the amplitude, frequency, wavelength and velocity of the wave.

Ans. $A = 10$ cm , $f = 1$ Hz, $\lambda = 200$ cm, $v = 200$ cm/s.

6. A displacement wave is represented by $y = 0.25 \times 10^{-3} \sin$ $(500\,t - 0.025\,x)$, where y, t and x are in cm, sec and metre respectively. Deduce (i) amplitude (ii) period (iii) angular frequency, and (iv) wavelength. Also deduce the amplitude of paticle velocity and particle acceleration.

Ans. (i) $A = 0.25 \times 10^{-3}$ cm (ii) 0.01257 s (iii) 500 rad/s (iv) 251.2 cm (v) 0.125 cm/s (vi) 62.5 cm/s^2.

7. One end of a long string of linear mass density 8.0×10^{-3} kg/m is connected to an electrically driven tuning fork of frequency 256 Hz. The other end passes over a pulley and is tied to a pan containing a mass of 90 kg. The pulley end   absorbs all the incoming energy so that reflected waves at this end have negligible amplitude. At $t = 0$, the left end (fork end) of the string $x = 0$ has zero transverse displacement ($y = 0$) and is moving along positive $y-$ direction. The amplitude of the wave is 5.0 cm. Write down the transverse displacement y as function of x and t that describes the wave on the string.

Ans. $y = 0.05 \sin (16.1 \times 10^2\,t - 4.84\,x)$, x and y are in m.

8. A SONAR system fixed in a submarine operates at a frequency 40.0 kHz. An enemy submarine moves towards the SONAR with a speed of 360 km/h. What is the frequency of sound reflected by a submarine? Take the speed of sound in water to be 1450 m/s.

Ans. 45.93 kHz.

9. A whistle of frequency 540 Hz rotates in a circle of radius 2 m at an angular speed of 15 rad/s. What is the lowest and highest frequency heard by a listener a long distance away at rest w.r.t. centre of the circle ? Can the apparent frequency be ever equal to the actual frequency ? Take v = 330 m/s.

Ans. 495 Hz, 594 Hz, yes.

10. The displacement of the particle at $x = 0$ of a stretched string carrying a wave in the positive $x-$ direction is given by $f(t) = A \sin$ $(t\,/\,T)$. The wave speed is v. Write the wave equation.

$$Ans.\quad f(x,T) = A\sin\left(\frac{t}{T} - \frac{x}{vT}\right).$$

11. A wave pulse is travelling on a string with a speed v towards the positive x – axis. The shape of the string at $t = 0$ is given by $g(x) = A \sin (x/a)$, where A and a are constants.

(a)   What are the dimension of A and a?

(b)   Write the equation of the wave for a general time t, if the wave speed is v.

$$Ans.\; (a)\;(L, L)\quad (b)\; f(x, t) = A \sin \frac{x - vt}{a}.$$

12. A wave propagates on a string in the positive x – direction at a velocity v. The shape of the string at $t = t_0$ is given by $g(x, t_0) = A \sin (x/a)$. Write the wave equation for a general time t.

$$Ans.\; f(x,t) = A\sin\frac{x - v(t - t_0)}{a}.$$

13. Figure shows a plot of the transverse displacements of the particles of a string at $t = 0$ through which a travelling wave is passing in the positive x– direction. The wave speed is 20 cm/s. Find

(a) the amplitude,   (b) the wavelength

(c) the wave number and   (d) the frequency of the wave.

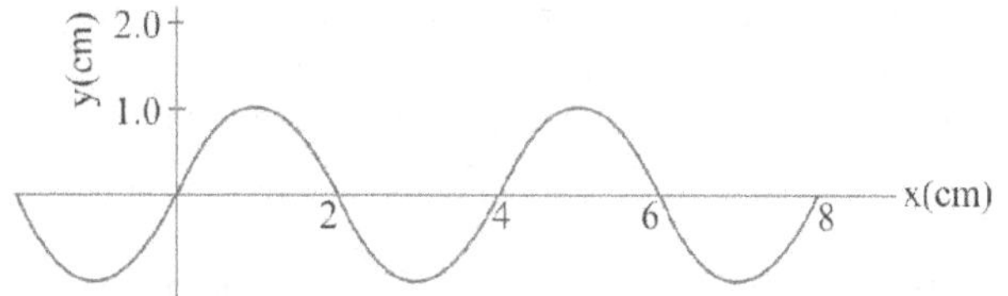

Ans. (a) 1.0 cm (b) 4 cm (c) 1.6 cm^{-1} (d) 5 Hz .

14. Calculate the bulk modulus of air from the following data about a sound wave of wavelength 35 cm travelling in air. The pressure at a point varies between $(1.0 \times 10^5 \pm 14)$ Pa and the particles of the air vibrate in simple harmonic motion of amplitude 5.5×10^{-6} m.

Ans. 1.4×10^5 N/m^2.

15. A bat emitting an ultrasonic wave of frequency 4.5×10^4 Hz flies at a speed of 6 m/s between two parallel walls. Find the two frequencies heard by the bat and the beat frequency between the two. The speed of sound is 330 m/s.

Ans. 4.67×10^4 Hz, 4.34×10^4 Hz, 3270 Hz.

16. A small source of sound S of frequency 500 Hz is attached to the end of a light string and is whirled in a vertical circle of radius 1.6 m. The string just remains tight when the source is at the highest point.

(a) An observer is located in the same vertical plane at a large distance at the same height as the centre of the circle. The speed of sound in air = 330 m/s and g = 10 m/s^2. Find the maximum frequency heard by the observer.

(b) An observer is situated at a large distance vertically above the centre of the circle. Find the frequencies heard by the observer corresponding to the sound emitted by the source when it is at the same height as the centre.

Ans. (a) 506 Hz (b) 490 Hz and 511 Hz.

17. A transverse mechanical harmonic wave is travelling on a string. Maximum velocity and maximum acceleration of a particle on the string are 3 m/s and 90 m/s^2 respectively. If the wave is travelling with a speed of 20 m/s on the string. Write wave function describing the wave.   ***Ans.*** $y = 0.1 \sin (30\, t \pm 1.5\, x)$.

18. Two gases with different densities but same atomicity are mixed in proportions V_1 and V_2 by volume. Prove that the velocity of sound in a mixture will be given by

$$c = c_1 c_2 \sqrt{\left\{ \frac{V_1 + V_2}{V_1 c_2^2 + V_2 c_1^2} \right\}}$$

where c_1 and c_2 are velocities of sound in pure gases respectively.

19. (a) Find the speed of sound in a mixture of 1 mole of helium and 2 mole of oxygen at 27°C.

(b) If the temperature is raised by 1 K from 300 K, find the percentage change in the speed of sound in the gaseous mixture ($R = 8.31$ J/mol K).

Ans. (a) 400.9 m/s (b) 0.167 % .

20. A source of sound is moving along a circular orbit of radius 3 m with an angular velocity of 10 rad/s. A sound detector located far away from the source is executing linear simple harmonic motion along the line BD with an amplitude $BC = CD = 6$ m. The frequency of oscillation of the detector is $5/\pi$ per second. The source is at the point A when the detector is at the point B. If the source emits a continuous sound wave of frequency 340 Hz, find the maximum and the minimum frequencies recorded by the detector.

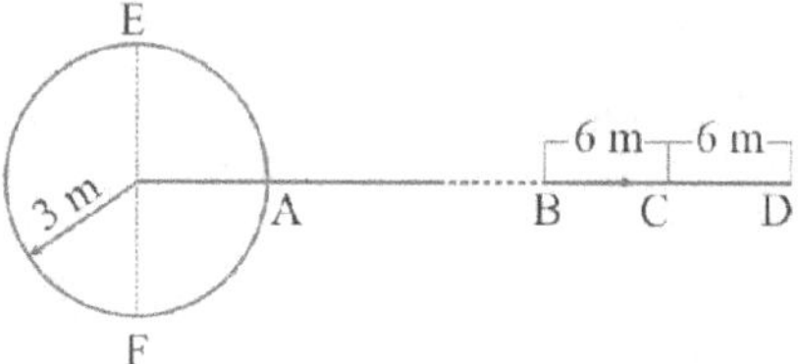

Ans. 442 Hz, 255 Hz .

21. A band playing music at a frequency f is moving towards a wall at a speed v_b. A motorist is following the band with a speed v_m. If v is the speed of sound, obtain an expression for the beat frequency heard by the motorist.

$$\textit{Ans. } x = \frac{2v_b(v + v_m) f}{v^2 - v_b^2}$$

22. A boat is travelling in a river with a speed 10 m/s along the stream flowing with a speed 2 m/s. From this boat, a sound transmitter is lowered into the river through a rigid support.The wavelength of the sound emitted from the transmitter inside the water is 14.45 mm. Assume that attenuation of sound in water and air is negligible.

(a) What will be the frequency detected by a receiver kept inside downstream ?

(b) The transmitter and the receiver are now pulled up into air. The air is blowing with a speed 5 m/s in the direction opposite the river stream. Determine the frequency of the sound detected by the receiver.(Temperature of the air and water = 20°C; density of river water = 10^3 kg/m^3; Bulk modulus of the water = 2.088×10^9 Pa; Gas constant $R = 8.31$ J /mol–K; Mean molecular mass of air = 28.8×10^{-3} kg/mol; C_p/C_v for air = 1.4)

Ans. (a) 10^5 Hz, 100696 Hz, (b) 103040 Hz.

23. A train is running exacting on a semicircular rails at a speed of $v/20$ where v is speed of sound in air. At an instant the driver of the engine at one end of semicircle and guard at the other end. At this instant the driver blows a whistle whose real frequency is 400 Hz. Calculate the frequency of the whistle as heard by the guard, a passanger in the middle of the train and a workman on the track in front of the train.

Ans. 400 Hz, 400 Hz, 421 Hz.

Hints & Solutions

1. (a) Speed of sound does not change with frequency $f\lambda$ = constant.

2. (b) The sonometer wire is forced to vibrate by tunning fork, so its frequency becomes 480 Hz.

3. (c) At point c, the slope $\dfrac{dy}{dt}$ is negative, so the element at this point moves downward.

4. (a) On comparing the given equation with,
$y = A\sin(kx - \omega t)$, we get

$$v_1 = \frac{\omega}{k} = \frac{3}{1} = 3 \text{ m/s}$$

$$v_2 = \frac{1}{4} \text{ m/s}; \quad v_3 = \frac{1}{2} \text{ m/s}; \quad v_4 = \frac{2}{1} = 2\text{m/s};$$

5. (d) Sound cannot be travelled in vacuum.

6. (d) By the observation you can find $\lambda = 7b$.

7. (d) The time taken by sound to travel 2km,

$$t = \frac{2000}{300} \approx 6 \text{ s (slow)}$$

8. (a) $v = f\lambda = 2 \times 5 = 10$ cm/s.

9. (b) Frequency is the fundamental characteristic which does not change from one to other medium.

10. (a) Speed of sound will not change with frequency. If frequency of sound changes, its wavelength is also changes, and so $f\lambda = v$, constant in a medium.

11. (c) $v = f\lambda = \dfrac{54}{60} \times 10 = 9$ m/s.

12. (d) $v = \sqrt{\dfrac{\gamma RT}{M}}$, so $v \propto \sqrt{T}$. Also $\dfrac{P}{\rho}$ is constant and so,

$$v = \sqrt{\frac{\gamma P}{\rho}} \text{ , is a constant.}$$

13. (c) As $v = \sqrt{\dfrac{\gamma P}{\rho}}$, $\therefore \dfrac{v_1}{v_2} = \sqrt{\dfrac{\rho_2}{\rho_1}} = \sqrt{4} = 2.$

14. (c) As $v_0 = \sqrt{\dfrac{\gamma RT}{M}}$ and $2v_0 = \sqrt{\dfrac{\gamma RT'}{M}}$

$$\therefore \frac{T'}{T} = 4 \Rightarrow T' = 4T = 4 \times 273 = 1092 \text{ K.}$$

15. (c) Sound waves in water are transverse at the surface and longitudinal along depth.

16. (c) Sound can travel longitudinally as well as transversly in solids.

17. (a) Transverse waves.

18. (a) The intensity of wave, $I = 2\pi^2 f^2 A^2 \rho v$, so $I \propto f^2$ and $I \propto A^2$.

19. (d) Sound waves in air are longitudinal.

20. (d) The wavelength of infrasonic wave is shorter than audible sound.

21. (a)
$$\rho_{mixture} = \frac{M_o + M_H}{V_o + V_H} = \frac{\rho_o V_o + \rho_H V_H}{V_o + V_H}$$

$$= \frac{\rho_o V_o\left(1 + \dfrac{\rho_H}{\rho_o} \times \dfrac{V_H}{V_o}\right)}{V_o\left(1 + \dfrac{V_H}{V_o}\right)}$$

or $\quad \dfrac{\rho_{mixture}}{\rho_o} = \left[\dfrac{1 + \dfrac{1}{16} \times 1}{1 + 1}\right] = \dfrac{17}{32}$

$\therefore \quad \dfrac{v_{mixture}}{v_o} = \sqrt{\dfrac{\rho_o}{\rho_{mixture}}} = \sqrt{\dfrac{32}{17}}$

22. (b) SONAR emits ultrasonic waves.

23. (a) The maximum particle velocity is given by $v_{max} = \omega A$.

24. (b) On comparing with standard equation of wave
$y = A \sin(\omega t - kx + \phi_0)$, we get
$\omega = 600$ rad/s and $k = 2/m$

$$\therefore \quad v = \frac{\omega}{k} = \frac{600}{2} = 300 \text{ m/s.}$$

25. (b)
$$\lambda = \frac{v}{f} = \frac{300}{400} = 0.75\text{m}$$

$$\therefore \quad \Delta x = \Delta\phi \times \frac{\lambda}{2\pi} = \frac{(60/180) \times 0.75}{2\pi} = 0.125\text{m}$$

26. (d) $f' = f\left(\dfrac{v}{v - v_s}\right) = 450\left(\dfrac{332}{332 - 33}\right) \approx 500$ Hz.

27. (a) $v = \omega r = (2\pi f)\, r = 2\pi \times \dfrac{400}{60} \times 1.2 = 50.24$ m/s.

$$f_1 = f\frac{v}{v - v_s} = 500\left(\frac{340}{340 + 50.24}\right) = 436 \text{ Hz.}$$

and $\quad f_2 = f\dfrac{v}{v - v_s} = 500\left(\dfrac{340}{340 - 50.24}\right) = 586$ Hz.

28. (d) $f_1 = f\dfrac{v}{v - v_s} = f\dfrac{340}{340 - 34} = f \times \dfrac{340}{306}$

and $\quad f_2 = f\dfrac{v}{v - v_s} = f\dfrac{340}{340 - 17} = f \times \dfrac{340}{323}$

$$\therefore \quad \frac{f_1}{f_2} = \frac{19}{18}$$

29. (b) At A, source is moving away, and at B it is approaching the observer, and so
$$f_1 < f_3 < f_2$$

30. (b)   We know that $\beta = 10 \log \dfrac{I}{I_0}$

or $30 = 10 \log \dfrac{I}{I_0}$

$\therefore$ $\dfrac{I}{I_0} = 10^3 = 1000$

31. (b)   Explanation is in the theory of the chapter.

32. (b) $\dfrac{\Delta\lambda}{\lambda} = \dfrac{v}{c}$

$\therefore$ $\Delta\lambda = \dfrac{v}{c}\lambda = \dfrac{100 \times 10^3 \times 5700}{3 \times 10^8} = 1.90\,\text{Å}$

33. (c) $\Delta x = \dfrac{\Delta\phi \times \lambda}{2\pi} = \dfrac{\left(\dfrac{60 \times \pi}{180}\right) \times \lambda}{2\pi} = \dfrac{\lambda}{6}$

34. (b) $\lambda = \dfrac{360}{500} = \dfrac{18}{25}\,\text{m}$

$\Delta x = \dfrac{\Delta\phi \times \lambda}{2\pi} = \dfrac{\dfrac{\pi}{3} \times \dfrac{18}{25}}{2\pi}$

$= 0.12\,\text{m}$

35. (b) $\dfrac{3}{2} = \sqrt{\dfrac{F + 2.5}{F}}$

on solving, $F = 2\,\text{N}.$

36. (b) $\Delta\phi = \dfrac{2\pi}{\lambda} \cdot \Delta x$; so phase difference between the vibrations of two such particles varies with distance between them.

37. (b) $v = \sqrt{\dfrac{F}{\mu}} = \dfrac{\omega}{k} = \dfrac{30}{1}$

$\therefore$ $F = 30^2 \times \mu = 30^2 \times 1.3 \times 10^{-4}$

$= 0.12\,\text{N}$

38. (b) $\Delta\phi = \phi_2 - \phi_1 = \dfrac{\pi}{2} - 0.5$

$= 1.07\,\text{rad.}$

39. (b) $f' = f\,\dfrac{v - v_0}{v}$ (M) $\xrightarrow{2\text{m/s}^2}$ - - - - - - (M) $\rightarrow$

or $0.94 = \left(\dfrac{330 - v_0}{330}\right)$

$\therefore$ $v_0 \approx 19.8\,\text{m/s}$

Now $19.8^2 = 0 + 2 \times 2 \times x \Rightarrow x = 98\,\text{m}.$

Solutions **EXERCISE 9.1 LEVEL -2**

1. (b) $[v_P]_{max} = 4v$

or $\omega A = 4v$

or $2\pi f y_0 = 4 \times (f\lambda)$

$\therefore$ $\lambda = \dfrac{\pi y_0}{2}$

2. (d)   To represent a travelling wave, the equation must satisfy the differential equation

$$\dfrac{\partial^2 y}{\partial t^2} = v^2 \dfrac{\partial^2 y}{\partial x^2}$$

So $\dfrac{\partial^2 y}{\partial t^2} = \dfrac{\partial^2 (x^2 - vt^2)}{\partial t^2} = -2v,$

and $\dfrac{\partial^2 y}{\partial x^2} = 2$

The given equation does not satisfy the condition of travelling wave.

3. (b) $y = A\sin(10\pi x + 15\pi t + \pi/3),$

On comparing with standard equation, we get

$k = 10\pi$ and $\omega = 15\pi.$

$v = \dfrac{\omega}{k} = \dfrac{15\pi}{10\pi} = 1.5\,\text{m/s}.$

4. (c) $5.5 \times 10^3 = 5 \times 10^3\,\dfrac{v + v_A}{v}$ ...(i)

and $6 \times 10^3 = 5 \times 10^3\,\dfrac{v + v_B}{v}$ ...(ii)

On substituting, $v = 332$ and simplifying, we get

$\dfrac{v_B}{v_A} = 5/6.$

5. (c)   The line of motion of engine is perpendicular to line of motion of the observer at that instant, so $f' = f = 200$ Hz.

6. (d) $A_A = 2,\ f_A = f$

and $A_B = 1,\ f_B = 2f$

$\therefore$ $\dfrac{I_A}{I_B} = \dfrac{f_A^2\,A_A^2}{f_B^2\,A_B^2} = 1$

7. (a) $v_P < v$

or $\omega A < f\lambda$

or $A < \dfrac{f\lambda}{\omega}$ or $\dfrac{\lambda}{2\pi}$

8. (b) $\dfrac{A_1}{A_2} = \sqrt{\dfrac{4}{1}} = \dfrac{2}{1}$

$\dfrac{I_{max}}{I_{min}} = \dfrac{(A_1 + A_2)^2}{(A_1 - A_2)^2} = \dfrac{(2+1)^2}{(2-1)^2} = 9$

$\beta = 10 \log 9 = 20 \log 3$

9. (d) $\dfrac{\sqrt{150^2 + x^2}}{300} - \dfrac{330}{330} = 1$

$\therefore$ $x = 315\,\text{m}.$

10. (d)   Frequency of the sound will not change in water.

11. (c)   The sum of their KE and PE is a constant.

12. (c)   The general equation of wave disturbance can be written as

$y = \dfrac{1}{1 + (x - vt)^2}$. So

$vt = 1$ at $t = 2,$

$\therefore$ $v = \dfrac{1}{t} = \dfrac{1}{2} = 0.5\,\text{m/s}.$

13. (c)

$$40 = 10\log\frac{I_1}{I_0} \;,\therefore\; \frac{I_1}{I_0} = 10^4$$

and

$$20 = 10\log\frac{I_2}{I_0} \;,\therefore\; \frac{I_2}{I_0} = 10^2$$

$$\therefore \quad \frac{I_1}{I_2} = 100.$$

Also

$$\frac{I_1}{I_2} = 100 = \frac{r_2^2}{r_1^2} = \frac{r_2^2}{1^2}$$

or $\quad r_2 = 10$ m.

14. (c)

(I) $\quad \lambda = 4(ab); \;\therefore\; v = f\lambda = f \times 4\,(ab)$

(II) $\quad \Delta t = \dfrac{3T}{4} = \dfrac{3}{4n}$

(III) $\quad \Delta\phi = \dfrac{2\pi}{\lambda}\times\Delta x = \dfrac{2\pi}{\lambda}\times\dfrac{3\lambda}{4} = \dfrac{3\pi}{2}$

15. (d)

$$f = \frac{v_A}{\lambda_A} = \sqrt{2g/\mu}\,/0.06 \;\;...(i)$$

Also

$$f = \frac{v_B}{\lambda_B} = \sqrt{8g/\mu}\,/\lambda_B \;\;...(ii)$$

From above equations, we get

$$\lambda_B = 0.12 \text{ m}$$

Solutions EXERCISE 9.2

1. (a,b,c)

$$I = 2\pi^2 f^2 A^2 \rho v$$

2. (a, c)

$$\omega a = \frac{v}{10} = \frac{10}{10} = 1$$

$$\omega = \frac{1}{a} = \frac{1}{10^{-3}} = 10^3$$

or

$$f = \frac{w}{2\pi} = \frac{10^3}{2\pi} \text{ hz.}$$

Also

$$\lambda = \frac{v}{f} = \frac{10}{10^3/2\pi} = 2\pi \times 10^{-2} \text{ m.}$$

3. (a, b, c)

$$f_1 = f\frac{c+v}{c}$$

and

$$f_2 = f_1\frac{c}{c-v} = f\left(\frac{c+v}{c-v}\right)$$

The wavelength of reflected wave

$$\lambda = \frac{c}{f_2} = \frac{c(c-v)}{f(c+v)}$$

The number of waves striking the surface per second

$$f_1 = \frac{f(c+v)}{c}$$

4. (a,b,c,d) y may be electric field, magnetic field, displacement or pressure.

5. (b, c) The equation, $y = 4 + 2\sin(6t - 3x)$

Here $\quad A = 2, \omega = 6, k = 3$

$$\therefore \quad v = \frac{\omega}{k} = \frac{6}{3} = 2 \text{ unit.}$$

6. (b,c,d)

$$y = A\sin(kx - \omega t),$$

Velocity

$$v = -\omega A\cos(kx - \omega t)$$

$$= \omega A\sin\left(kx - \omega t + \frac{\pi}{2}\right)$$

Acceleration $\quad a = -\omega^2 A\cos(kx - \omega t)$

$$= \omega^2 A\sin(kx + \omega t + \pi)$$

Clearly, phase difference between displacement and acceleration is π and phase difference between displacement and velocity is $\pi/2$.

7. (a,b,c) Explaination in the theory of the chapter.

8. (b,c) Solution is given in exercise 9.6, question number 18

9. (a, c, d) For observer O_1,

$$\lambda_1 = \frac{v - v_s}{f} = \frac{v - v/5}{f} = \frac{4v}{5f}$$

For O_2, there is change of medium, hence at the surface of water, keeping frequency unchanged

$$\frac{v}{\lambda_u} = \frac{4v}{\lambda_w} \Rightarrow \lambda_w = 4\lambda_a = \frac{16v}{5f}$$

$$f'' = \frac{velocity\ of\ wave\ relative\ to\ observer}{\lambda_w}$$

$$= \frac{4v + \dfrac{v}{5}}{\lambda_w} = \frac{21v}{5}\cdot\frac{5f}{16v} = \frac{21f}{16}$$

10. (c, d) The graph shows the situation shown in figure. The observed frequency will initially be more than the natural frequency. When the source is at P, observed frequency is equal to its natural frequency i.e., 2000 Hz.

For region AP: $f = f_0\left(\dfrac{v}{v - v_s\cos\theta}\right)$

For PB: $f = f_0\left(\dfrac{v}{v + v_s\cos\theta}\right)$

Minimum value of f will be

$$f_{\min} = f_0\left(\frac{v}{v + v_s}\right) \quad \text{when } \cos\theta = 1$$

or $1800 = 2000\left(\dfrac{300}{300 + v_s}\right)$

Solving this, we get, $v_s = 33.33$ m/s and maximum value of f can be

$$f_{\max} = f_0\left(\frac{v}{v - v_s}\right) \quad \text{when } \cos\theta = 1$$

or $f_{\max} = 2000\left(\dfrac{300}{300 - 33.33}\right) \approx 2250$ Hz

11. (a, b, c) As per Doppler's effect, the apparent frequency heard by an observer is given by

$f' = \left(\dfrac{v + v_o}{v - v_s}\right) f,$ where symbols have their usual meanings.

In option (a), $f' = \left(\dfrac{v}{v - v_s}\right) f \Rightarrow f' > f \Rightarrow \lambda' < \lambda$

In option (b), $f' = \left(\dfrac{v + v_o}{v - v_s}\right) f \Rightarrow f' > f \Rightarrow \lambda' < \lambda$

In option (c), $f' = \left(\dfrac{v - v_o}{v + v_s}\right) f \Rightarrow f' < f \Rightarrow \lambda' > \lambda$

In option (d), $f' = \left(\dfrac{v - v_o}{v}\right) f \Rightarrow f' < f \Rightarrow \lambda' > \lambda$

12. (c,d) Explaination is given in theory.

Solutions EXERCISE-9.3

1. (a) Statement-2 is the answer of statement-1.
2. (b) Light waves on being electromagnetic need no material medium for their propagation.
3. (d) Particle velocity, $v_p = \omega A\cos(\omega t - kx)$, which depends on time, $v = \sqrt{\gamma P/\rho}$.
4. (d) With change in pressure, density of medium also changes and so P/ρ remains constant.

5. (a) Statement-2 is the answer of statement-1.
6. (a) Statement-2 is the answer of statement-1.
7. (c) When sound propagate, the medium remains adiabatic and so $\Delta Q = 0$.
8. (a) Statement-2 is the answer of statement-1.
9. (c) At nodes pressure is maximum. Particles within a loop vibrate in phase.

Solutions EXERCISE-9.4

Passage (Q. 1 - 3) :

1. (b) The velocity of sound is given by $c = \sqrt{\dfrac{\gamma RT}{\rho}} = \sqrt{\dfrac{\gamma P}{\rho}}$

In this case we have to determine ρ_{mix} as well as γ_{mix}. Denoting moist air by m and dry air by d, we have

$$c_m = \sqrt{\dfrac{\gamma_m P}{\rho_m}} \quad . c_d = \sqrt{\dfrac{\gamma_d P}{\rho_d}}$$

or $\quad c_m = c_d \sqrt{\dfrac{\gamma_m}{\gamma_d} \dfrac{\rho_d}{\rho_m}}$

Moist air can be assumed to consist of two components dry component and water vapour.

$$\rho_m = \dfrac{(P - p)M_d}{RT} + \dfrac{pM_m}{RT}$$

$$\rho_d = \dfrac{PM_d}{RT}$$

$$\dfrac{\rho_m}{\rho_d} = \dfrac{P - p}{P} + \dfrac{p}{P}\dfrac{M_m}{M_d}$$

$$= 1 - \dfrac{p}{P}\left[1 - \dfrac{18}{28.8}\right]$$

$$= 1 - 0.375\dfrac{p}{P} = 0.997$$

$\therefore \quad \rho_m = 0.997\rho_d$

2. (a) The adiabatic exponent for a mixture of gases is given by

$$\dfrac{n_1 + n_2 + \dots}{\gamma_{mix.} - 1} = \dfrac{n_1}{\gamma_1 - 1} + \dfrac{n_2}{\gamma_2 - 1} + \dots$$

where $n_1, n_2 \dots$ are number of moles of respective components. Now,

$$\dfrac{1}{\gamma_{mix.} - 1} = \dfrac{n_1}{n_1 + n_2 + \dots}\dfrac{1}{\gamma_1 - 1} + \dfrac{n_2}{n_1 + n_2 + \dots}\dfrac{1}{\gamma_2 - 1}$$

$$= \dfrac{P - p}{P}\dfrac{1}{\gamma_1 - 1} + \dfrac{p}{P}\dfrac{1}{\gamma_2 - 1}$$

where $\dfrac{p_i}{P_{total}}$ = mole fraction

Thus $\quad \dfrac{1}{\gamma_{mix.} - 1} = \dfrac{(P - p)}{P(1.4 - 1)} + \dfrac{p}{P(1.33 - 1)}$

or $\quad \gamma_{mix.} = 1 + \dfrac{2}{5}\left(1 - \dfrac{p}{5P}\right)$

Hence $\quad \dfrac{\gamma_m}{\gamma_d} = \dfrac{5}{7} + \dfrac{2}{7}\left(1 - \dfrac{p}{5P}\right)$

$$= 1 - 0.057\dfrac{p}{P} = 0.99$$

3. (c) $c_m = c_d\sqrt{\left(1 - 0.057\dfrac{p}{P}\right) \times \left(1 - 0.375\dfrac{p}{P}\right)}$

$$= 332\sqrt{1 - 0.318\dfrac{p}{P}}$$

$$= 332\sqrt{1 - 0.318 \times \frac{4.58}{760}}$$

$$= 331.7 \text{ m/s}$$

Passage (Q. 4 - 6) :

4. **(b)** The speed of sound depends on the frame of reference of the observer.

5. **(a)** Since all the passengers in train A are moving with a velocity of 20 m/s therefore the distribution of sound intensity of the whistle by the passengers in train A is uniform.

6. **(a)** $f_1 = f\left[\dfrac{v - v_0}{v - v_s}\right] = 800\left[\dfrac{340 - 30}{340 - 20}\right] = 800 \times \dfrac{31}{32}$

$$f_2 = f\left[\dfrac{v - v_0}{v - v_s}\right] = 1120 \times \dfrac{31}{32}$$

$$\therefore \quad f_2 - f_1 = (1120 - 800) \times \dfrac{31}{32} = 320 \times \dfrac{31}{32} = 310 \text{ Hz.}$$

Passage (Q. 7 – 9) :

7. **(b)**   8. **(c)**   9. **(a)**

The speed of sound will be same in both the cases i.e., 340 m/s. In the case when train is approaching the platform, the apparent frequency

$$f_1 = f\left(\frac{v}{v - v_s}\right)$$

$$= 400\left(\frac{340}{340 - 10}\right) = 412.12 \text{ Hz.}$$

When train receds, the apparent frequency

$$f_2 = f\left(\frac{v}{v + v_s}\right)$$

$$= 600\left(\frac{340}{340 + 15}\right) = 574.65 \text{ Hz.}$$

Thus $\Delta f = f_1 - f_2 \approx 41.6 Hz.$

Passage (Q. 10 – 12) :

10. **(a)**   11. **(a)**   12 **(a)**

(a) If μ is the mass per limit length of rope, then tension in the rope at a distance x from the free end
$$F = \mu x g.$$
The velocity of transverse wave

$$v = \sqrt{\frac{F}{\mu}}$$

$$= \sqrt{\frac{\mu x g}{\mu}}$$

$$= \sqrt{x g}.$$

(b) We have $\dfrac{dx}{dt} = \sqrt{xg}$

or $x^{-1/2}\,dx = \sqrt{g}\,dt$

or $\displaystyle\int_0^L x^{-1/2}dx = \sqrt{g}\int_0^t dt$

$\therefore$ $t = \sqrt{4L/g}$

Passage for (Q. 13 – 15) :

13. **(a)**   14. **(a)**   15. **(c)**

$$\mu_1 = \frac{0.06}{4.8}\text{kg/m}$$

and $$\mu_2 = \frac{0.2}{2.56}\text{kg/m}$$

The velocity of wave in wire

$$PQ, \qquad v_1 = \sqrt{\frac{F}{\mu_1}}$$

$$= \sqrt{\frac{80}{0.06/4.8}} = 80 \text{ m/s.}$$

The velocity of wave in wire

$$QR, \qquad v_2 = \sqrt{\frac{F}{\mu_2}}$$

$$= \sqrt{\frac{80}{(0.2/2.56)}} = 32 \text{ m/s.}$$

(a) The time taken by the wave-pulse to reach the other end

$$t = \frac{PQ}{v_1} + \frac{QR}{v_2}$$

$$= \frac{4.8}{80} + \frac{2.56}{32} = 0.14 \text{ s.}$$

(b) The amplitude of the reflected and transverse wave are given by

$$A_r = \left(\frac{v_2 - v_1}{v_2 + v_1}\right) A_i$$

and $$A_t = \left(\frac{2v_2}{v_1 + v_2}\right) A_i$$

After substiting the values, we get
$$A_r = 1.5 \text{ cm,}$$
$$A_t = 2.0 \text{ cm}$$

16. **(A) → p,q, (B) → s, (C)→ p, r, (D) → s**

(A) $y = 4\sin(5x - 4t) + 3\cos\left(4t - 5x + \dfrac{\pi}{6}\right)$

is super position of two coherent waves, so their equivalent will be an another travelling wave

(B) $y = 10\cos\left(t - \dfrac{x}{330}\right)\sin(100)\left(t - \dfrac{x}{330}\right)$

Lets check at any point, say at x = 0, y = (10 cos t) sin (100t) at any point amplitude is changing sinusoidally. so this is equation of beats.

(C) $y = 10\sin(2\pi x - 120t) + 10\cos(120t + 2\pi x)$

= superposition of two coherent waves travelling in opposite direction.

$\Rightarrow$ equation of standing waves

(D) $y = 10\sin(2\pi x - 120t) + 8\cos(118t - 59/30\pi x)$

= superposition of two waves whose frequency are slightly different

$(\omega_1 = 120, \omega_2 = 118) \Rightarrow$ equation of beats

17. **(A)→ q, (B)→ t, (C)→ s, (D)→t**

$$k = \frac{2\pi}{\lambda} = 2\pi a \quad \therefore \lambda = \frac{1}{a}$$

$$\omega = \frac{2\pi}{T} = 2\pi b \therefore T = \frac{1}{b} \text{ or } f = b$$

$$\Delta\phi = \frac{2\pi}{\lambda}.\Delta x = (2\pi a)\left(\frac{1}{4a}\right) = \frac{\pi}{2}$$

$$\Delta\phi = \frac{2\pi}{T}.\Delta t = (2\pi b)\left(\frac{1}{8a}\right) = \frac{\pi}{4}$$

18. **(A) → q, (B)→r, (C)→q , (D)→s**

$$v = \sqrt{\frac{\gamma RT}{M}} = \sqrt{\frac{\gamma P}{\rho}}$$

Speed does not change with change in pressure unless temperature is changed.

Solutions EXERCISE-9.5

1. We have
$$\frac{v_H}{v_{air}} = \sqrt{\frac{\rho_{air}}{\rho_H}}$$
$$\therefore \quad v_H = 4\ v_{air}$$
$$= 1328 \text{ m/s.} \quad \textit{Ans.}$$

2. We have
$$\frac{v_m}{v_H} = \sqrt{\frac{\rho_H}{\rho_m}} \qquad ...(1)$$

Here
$$\rho_m = \frac{m_H + m_N}{V_H + V_N}$$
$$= \frac{\rho_H V_H + \rho_N V_N}{V_H + V_N}$$
$$= \frac{\rho_H V_H\left(1 + \frac{\rho_N}{\rho_H} \times \frac{V_N}{V_H}\right)}{V_H\left(1 + \frac{V_N}{V_H}\right)}$$

$$\therefore \quad \frac{\rho_m}{\rho_H} = \frac{1 + \frac{28}{2} \times \frac{1}{2}}{1 + \frac{1}{2}} = \frac{16}{3}$$

Now from equation (i), we have
$$[v_m]_0 = v_H = \sqrt{\frac{3}{16}}$$
$$\frac{1300\sqrt{3}}{4} = 325\sqrt{3}$$
$$[v_m]_{27} = (v_m)_0\left(1 + \frac{t}{546}\right) \approx 591 \text{m/s.}$$

3. The speed of sound will be same in both the cases i.e., 340 m/s. In the case when train is approaching the platform, the apparent frequency
$$f_1 = f\left(\frac{v}{v - v_s}\right)$$
$$= 400\left(\frac{340}{340 - 10}\right) = 412.12 \text{ Hz.}$$

When train receds, the apparent frequency
$$f_2 = f\left(\frac{v}{v + v_s}\right)$$
$$= 600\left(\frac{340}{340 + 15}\right) = 574.65 \text{ Hz.}$$

Thus
$$\Delta f = f_1 - f_2 \approx 41.6 Hz.$$

4. Given,
$$\frac{T}{4} = 0.005$$
$$\therefore \quad T = 0.028$$
and
$$f = \frac{1}{T} = 50 \text{ Hz.}$$

Also,
$$\frac{\lambda}{2} = 2 \text{ cm.}$$
$$\therefore \quad \lambda = 4 \text{ cm.}$$
Wave speed, $\quad v = f\lambda = 50 \times 0.04 = 2$ m/s

5. The situation is shown in figure.
The time taken by the sound to reach the ground observer,

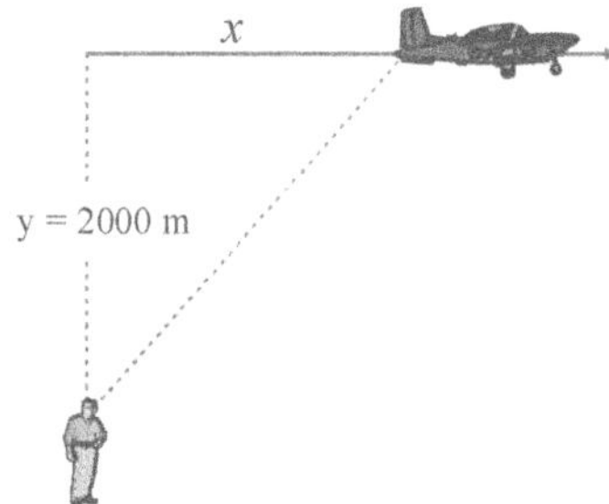

$$t = \frac{2000}{340} = 5.88 \text{ s}$$

The distance, $\quad x = vt = \left(510 \times \frac{5}{18}\right) \times 5.88 = 833$ m

6. From the geometry of the figure
$$\cos\theta = \frac{3}{5}.$$
The frequency heard by the person
$$f' = f\frac{v}{v - v_s \cos\theta}.$$

Here
$$v_s = 120 \times \frac{5}{18} = 33.3 \text{ m/s.}$$

$$\therefore \quad f' = 640 \times \frac{340}{340 - 33.3 \times \frac{3}{5}} = 680 \text{ Hz.}$$

7. The tension in the string
$$F = kx = 160 \times 0.01 = 1.6 \text{ N}$$

The mass per unit length of the string
$$\mu = \frac{10 \times 10^{-3}}{0.40} = 0.025 \text{ kg/m}$$

The speed of transverse wave

$$v = \sqrt{\frac{F}{\mu}} = \sqrt{\frac{1.6}{0.025}} = 8 \text{ m/s.}$$

The time taken by wave pulse to reach the spring

$$t = \frac{0.40}{8} = 0.05 \text{ s}$$

8. Given, the velocity of transverse wave

$$v = 100$$

$$= \sqrt{\frac{F}{\mu}} = \sqrt{\frac{F}{0.8 \times 10^{-3}}}$$

$$\therefore \qquad F = 98 \text{ N.}$$

For the equilibrium of the system

$$F = M_2 g$$
$$= M_1 g \sin 30°$$
or $$98 = M_2 g$$
$$= M_1 g \sin 30°$$
$$\therefore \qquad M_1 = 20 \text{ kg}$$
and $$M_2 = 20 \text{ kg.}$$

9. We know that $$\beta_2 - \beta_1 = 10 \log\left(\frac{I_2}{I_1}\right)$$

$$= 10 \log\left(\frac{10^{-6}}{5 \times 10^{-10}}\right) = 33 \text{ dB.}$$

Solutions EXERCISE-9.6

1. Any function will represent wave motion, if it satisfies, the differential equation

$$\frac{\partial^2 y}{\partial t^2} = v^2 \frac{\partial^2 y}{\partial x^2}$$

(i) Given; $$y = (x - vt)^2$$

$$\therefore \qquad \frac{\partial^2 y}{\partial x^2} = 2$$

and $$\frac{\partial^2 y}{\partial t^2} = 2v^2.$$

Clearly the given function will represents a travelling wave.

Do the other part similarly.

2. (a) The given function is the product of two reparate harmonic functions of x and t, so it represents a stationary wave.

(b) If does not satisfy the differential equation of wave so it will not represents any type of wave.

(c) The given functions can be expressed in the form

$$y = A \sin (\theta + \alpha)$$

where $$A = \sqrt{3^2 + 4^2} = 5,$$

$$\theta = 5x - 0.5 t$$

and $$\alpha = \tan^{-1}\left(\frac{4}{3}\right)$$

So, it will represent a travelling wave.

(d) If represents the superposition of two stationary waves; one represented by $\cos x \sin t$ and other by $\cos 2x \sin 2t$.

3. (a) At displacement node, the variation of pressure is maximum. Hence the displacement node is the pressure antinode and vice-versa.

(b) Bats can produced and detect ultrasonic waves. Bats notice the time of reflected waves and they then estimate the distance of the object from them. From the intensity of reflected waves, they can estimate the nature and size of the object.

(c) These instruments produce different overtones. Hence quality produced by them will be different.

(d) Solids possess both bulk modulus and shear modulus. So both longitudinal and transverse waves propagate through them.

(e) When a pulse passes through a dispersive medium, the wavelength of wave changes, and so the shape of the pulse changes.

4. We kmow that, velocity of sound in gas is given by

$$v = \sqrt{\frac{\gamma P}{\rho}}$$

$$\therefore \qquad \frac{v_{H_2}}{v_{H_e}} = \sqrt{\frac{\gamma_{H_2} \rho_{H_e}}{\gamma_{H_e} \rho_{H_2}}}$$

$$= \sqrt{\frac{7/5}{5/3} \times \frac{4}{2}} = \sqrt{42}/5.$$

5. Given, $$y = 10 \sin 2\pi (t - 0.005 x)$$

$$= 10 \sin (2 \pi t - 0.005 \times 2\pi x)$$

On comparing with the standard equation of the travelling wave, we get

$$y = A \sin (\omega t - kx),$$

$$A = 10 \text{ cm,}$$

$$\omega = 2\pi$$

or $$f = \frac{\omega}{2\pi}$$

$$= 1 \text{ Hz.}$$

$$k = 0.005 \times 2\pi$$

As $$k = \frac{\omega}{v},$$

$$\therefore \qquad v = \frac{\omega}{k} = \frac{2\pi}{0.005 \times 2\pi} = 200 \text{ cm/s.}$$

Also $$k = \frac{2\pi}{\lambda} = 0.005 \times 2\pi,$$

$$\therefore \qquad \lambda = 200 \text{ cm.}$$

6. Given, $\qquad y = 0.25 \times 10^{-3} \sin (500\, t - 0.025\, x)$

Compare this equation with $y = A \sin (\omega t - kx)$,

we get $\qquad A = 0.25 \times 10^{-3}$ cm,

$\qquad\qquad \omega = 500$ rad/s.

Time period $\qquad T = \dfrac{2\pi}{\omega} = \dfrac{2\pi}{500} = 0.01257$ s

Also $\qquad k = 0.025$ /m

As $\qquad k = \dfrac{2\pi}{\lambda}$

$\therefore \qquad \lambda = \dfrac{2\pi}{k} = \dfrac{2\pi}{0.025} = 251.2$ cm

Amplitude of particle velocity

$$v_{max} = \omega A$$
$$= 500 \times 0.25 \times 10^{-3} = 0.125 \text{ m/s}$$

and $\qquad a_{max} = \omega^2 A$

$$= 500^2 \times 0.25 \times 10^{-3} = 62.5 \text{ cm/s}^2.$$

7. Velocity of the transverse wave

$$v = \sqrt{\dfrac{F}{\mu}} = \sqrt{\dfrac{90g}{8 \times 10^{-3}}}$$

$$= \sqrt{\dfrac{900}{8 \times 10^{-3}}} = 335.4 \text{ m/s}$$

$$\omega = 2\pi f$$
$$= 2\pi \times 256 = 1610 \text{ rad/s}$$

$$k = \dfrac{\omega}{v} = \dfrac{1610}{335.4} = 4.8 \text{/m}$$

The equation of the wave

$$y = A \sin (\omega t - kx)$$
$$= 0.05 \sin (16.1 \times 10^2\, t - 4.8\, x)$$

8. The frequency of the reflected sound

$$f' = f\left(\dfrac{v + v_0}{v - v_s}\right)$$

$$= (40 \times 10^3)\left(\dfrac{1450 + 100}{1450 - 100}\right)$$

$$= 45.93 \times 10^3 \text{ Hz}.$$

9. The speed of the whistle

$$v_s = \omega r$$
$$= 15 \times 2 = 30 \text{ m/s}.$$

$$f_{min} = f\dfrac{v}{v + v_s}$$

$$= 540\left(\dfrac{350}{330 + 30}\right) = 495 \text{ Hz}.$$

$$f_{max} = f\dfrac{v}{v - v_s}$$

$$= 540\left(\dfrac{350}{330 - 30}\right) = 594 \text{ Hz}.$$

10. Given, $\qquad y = A \sin (t / T)$

To make the wave equation, $\dfrac{t}{T}$ should be replaced by $\left(\dfrac{t}{T} - \dfrac{x}{vT}\right)$,

which now becomes the functions of x & T. Thus wave equations becomes

$$y = A\sin\left(\dfrac{t}{T} - \dfrac{x}{vT}\right).$$

11. (a) The dimensions of A must be the dimensions of length. i.e., L. Also dimensions of

$$\dfrac{x}{a} = 1,$$

$\therefore$ dimensions of a will be the dimensions of x. i.e., L.

   (b) To make the wave equation $\dfrac{x}{a}$ should be replaced by $\dfrac{x - vt}{a}$.

Thus the wave equation becomes

$$y = f(x, t) = A\sin\dfrac{x - vt}{a}.$$

12. Given, $\qquad y = g(x, t_0) = A\sin\left(\dfrac{x}{a}\right) \qquad ...(i)$

The wave equation will be

$$y = g(x, t) = A\sin\dfrac{x - v(t - t_0)}{a} \quad ...(ii)$$

If we place $t = t_0$ in equation (ii), the equation (i) will be obtained.

13. From the figure, the amplitude of the wave

$A = 1.0$ cm, and $\qquad \lambda = 4$ cm,

wave number $\qquad k = \dfrac{2\pi}{\lambda} = \dfrac{2\pi}{4} \simeq 1.6\,\text{cm}^{-1}$

Frequency $\qquad f = \dfrac{v}{\lambda} = \dfrac{20}{4} = 5$ Hz.

14. The wave number, $k = \dfrac{2\pi}{\lambda} = \dfrac{2\pi}{0.35} = 18 \text{ m}^{-1}$

$$A = 5.5 \times 10^{-6} \text{m}.$$

Given $\qquad \Delta P_{max} = 14 \text{ N/m}^2.$

or $\qquad ABk = 14$

$\therefore \qquad B = \dfrac{14}{AK}$

$$= \dfrac{14}{5.5 \times 10^{-6} \times 18} \simeq 1.4 \times 10^5 \text{ N/m}^2.$$

15.

$$f_{min} = f\left(\frac{v - v_0}{v + v_s}\right)$$

$$= 4.5 \times 10^4 \left(\frac{330 - 6}{330 + 6}\right)$$

$$= 4.34 \times 10^4 \text{ Hz.}$$

$$f_{max} = f\left(\frac{v + v_0}{v - v_s}\right)$$

$$= 4.5 \times 10^4 \left(\frac{330 + 6}{330 - 6}\right)$$

$$= 4.67 \times 10^4 \text{ Hz.}$$

16. Velocity of the source, $v_s = \sqrt{gl} = \sqrt{10 \times 1.6} = 4$ m/s.

The maximum frequency,

$$f' = f\frac{v}{v - v_s} = 500\left(\frac{330}{330 - 4}\right) = 506 \text{ Hz.}$$

17. Given, $\quad v_{max} = \omega A = 3 \quad\quad .....(i)$

and $\quad u_{max} = \omega^2 A = 90 \quad\quad .....(ii)$

From above equations, we have

$$\omega = 30 \text{ rad/s}$$

and $\quad\quad A = 0.1$ m

The propagation constant,

$$k = \frac{\omega}{A} = \frac{30}{20} = 1.5.$$

Thus wave functions can be written as

$$y = A\sin(\omega t \pm kx) = 0.1\sin(30\,t \pm 1.5\,x).$$

18. We can write $\quad C_1 = \sqrt{\dfrac{\gamma P}{\rho_1}}$ and $\quad C_2 = \sqrt{\dfrac{\gamma P}{\rho_2}}$

$$\therefore \quad \frac{\rho_1}{\rho_2} = \frac{C_2^2}{C_1^2}$$

If ρ is the density of the mixture of gases, then

$$\rho = \frac{m_1 + m_2}{V_1 + V_2} = \frac{\rho_1 V_1 + \rho_2 V_2}{V_1 + V_2}$$

$$= \frac{\rho_1 V_1 \left(1 + \dfrac{\rho_2}{\rho_1}\dfrac{V_2}{V_1}\right)}{V_1 + V_2}$$

or $\quad \dfrac{\rho}{\rho_1} = \dfrac{V_1\left(1 + \dfrac{c_1^2}{c_2^2}\dfrac{V_2}{V_1}\right)}{V_1 + V_2} = \dfrac{V_1(V_1 C_2^2 + V_2 C_1^2)}{C_2^2(V_1 + V_2)}$

The velocity of sound in a mixture is given by

$$c = \sqrt{\frac{\gamma P}{\rho}}.$$

Also $\quad \dfrac{c}{c_1} = \sqrt{\dfrac{\rho_1}{\rho}} \quad \therefore \quad c = c_1 c_2 \sqrt{\dfrac{V_1 + V_2}{V_1 c_2^2 + V_2 c_1^2}}.$

19. (a) γ of the mixture of gases is given by

$$\frac{n_1 + n_2}{\gamma - 1} = \frac{n_1}{\gamma_1 - 1} + \frac{n_2}{\gamma_2 - 1}$$

$$\frac{1 + 2}{\gamma - 1} = \frac{1}{\dfrac{5}{3} - 1} + \frac{2}{\dfrac{7}{5} - 1}$$

$$\therefore \quad\quad \gamma = 19/13.$$

Molecular mass of the mixture of gases

$$M = \frac{n_1 M_1 + n_2 M_2}{n_1 + n_2}$$

$$= \frac{1 \times 4 + 2 \times 32}{1 + 2} = 68/3 \text{ g.}$$

The velocity of sound in the mixture of gases

$$v = \sqrt{\frac{\gamma RT}{M}}$$

$$= \sqrt{\frac{(19/13) \times 8.31 \times 300}{(68/3) \times 10^{-3}}} = 400.9 \text{ m/s}$$

(b) We have $\quad v = \sqrt{\dfrac{\gamma RT}{M}} = kT^{1/2}$

$$\therefore \quad \frac{\Delta v}{v} \times 100 = \frac{1}{2}\frac{\Delta T}{T} \times 100 = \frac{1}{2} \times \frac{1}{300} \times 100 = 0.167\%$$

20. The maximum velocity of the detector

$$v_0 = \omega A$$
$$= 2\pi f A$$
$$= 2\pi \times \frac{5}{\pi} \times 6 = 60 \text{ m/s.}$$

The velocity of the source,

$$v_s = \omega r = 10 \times 3 = 30 \text{ m/s.}$$

If source is going clockwise on the circular orbit, then maximum will be heard at E and minimum frequency at F.

Thus $\quad\quad f_{min} = f\left(\frac{v - v_0}{v + v_s}\right)$

$$= 340\left(\frac{340 - 60}{340 + 30}\right) \approx 255\,Hz.$$

and
$$f_{max} = f\left(\frac{v+v_0}{v-v_s}\right)$$

$$= 340\left(\frac{340+60}{340-30}\right) \approx 442\,Hz.$$

21. The frequency noticed at the wall
$$f_1 = f\left(\frac{v}{v-v_b}\right) \qquad \ldots(i)$$

This frequency is reflected back and picked by motorist, then
$$f_2 = f_1\left(\frac{v+v_m}{v}\right) \qquad \ldots(ii)$$

From equations (i) and (ii), we have
$$f_2 = f\left(\frac{v+v_m}{v-v_b}\right)$$

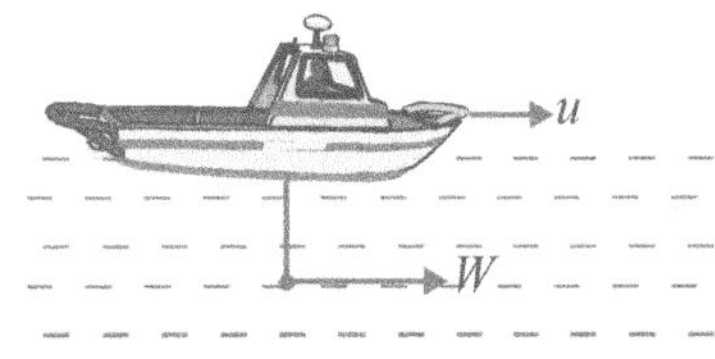

The frequency of sound noticed directly.
$$f' = f\left(\frac{v+v_m}{v+v_b}\right) \qquad \ldots(iii)$$

∴ Beat frequency
$$\Delta f = f_2 - f' = f\left(\frac{2b(v+v_m)}{v^2-v_b^2}\right)$$

22. (a) Given, speed of the boat,

$$u = 10 \text{ m/s.}$$
speed of river stream $= 2$ m/s.
Wavelength of sound wave inside water
$$\lambda\omega = 14.45 \text{ mm.}$$
Speed of sound wave inside water,

$$v = \sqrt{\frac{B}{\rho}} = \sqrt{\frac{2.088\times10^9}{10^3}} = 1445 \text{ m/s.}$$

Frequency of wave
$$f = \frac{v}{\lambda} = \frac{1445}{14.45\times10^{-3}} = 10^5 \text{ Hz.}$$

Apparent frequency
$$f' = f\left(\frac{(v+\omega)}{(v+\omega)-u}\right)$$

$$= 10^5\left(\frac{1445+2}{(1445+2)-10}\right) = 100696.$$

(b) Speed of sound in air
$$v = \sqrt{\frac{\gamma RT}{M}}$$

$$= \sqrt{\frac{1.4\times8.3\times293}{28.8\times10^{-3}}} = 344 \text{ m/s.}$$

Now apparent frequency
$$f' = f\left[\frac{v-\omega}{(v-\omega)-u}\right]$$

$$= 10^5\left[\frac{344-5}{(344-5)-10}\right] = 103040 \text{ Hz.}$$

23. In first two cases the observed frequency will be equal to the real frequency. i.e., 400 Hz.

Apparent frequency as observed by workman
$$f' = f\left[\frac{v}{v-v_s}\right]$$

$$= 400\left[\frac{v}{v-\dfrac{v}{20}}\right]$$

$$= 400\times\frac{20}{19} = 421 \text{ Hz.}$$

Wave - II

(633 - 698)

10.1 REFLECTION AND REFRACTION OF SOUND WAVES

Experiments show that the speed of light wave in air is greater than that in water. While the speed of sound wave is greater in water. These results show that water is denser medium for light wave but rarer for sound wave. Lloyd by his experiment proved that when light wave reflected from mirror, the reflected light wave suffers a phase change of π radian. This is true for sound wave also. Frequency of wave is a fundamental property, which remain constant in different mediums. If f, λ and v are the frequency, wavelength and speed in air and f', λ' and v' are the corresponding quantities in water, then

for light wave; $v' < v$, $f' = f$, $\lambda' < \lambda$ and

for sound wave; $v' > v$, $f' = f$, $\lambda' > \lambda$.

Light wave; $v' < v$, $\lambda' < \lambda$	**Sound wave; $v' > v$, $\lambda' > \lambda$.**
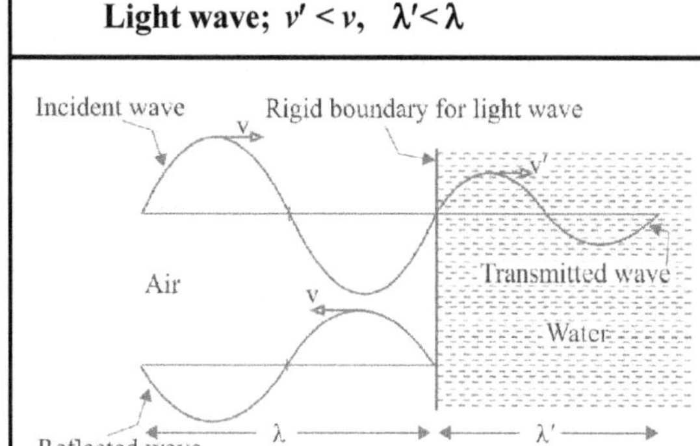 *Fig.10.1. Reflection and transmission of light wave.*	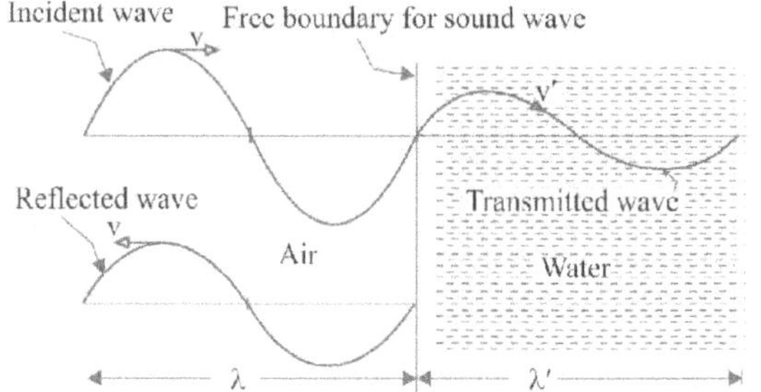 *Fig.10.2. Reflection and transmission of sound wave.*
Suppose an incident light wave $y_i = A \sin (k_a x - \omega t)$, then the equations for reflected and transmitted waves are: $$y_r = -A_r \sin (k_a x + \omega t - \pi) = A_r \sin (k_a x + \omega t)$$ and $y_t = A_t \sin (k_\omega x - \omega t)$ Also $A = A_r + A_t$. Here k_a and k_ω are propagation constants for air and water respectively.	Suppose an incident sound wave $y_i = A \sin (k_a x - \omega t)$, then the equations of reflected and transmitted waves are: $$y_r = -A_r \sin(k_a x + \omega t) \text{ and}$$ $$y_t = A_t \sin (k_\omega x - \omega t)$$ Also $A = A_r + A_t$

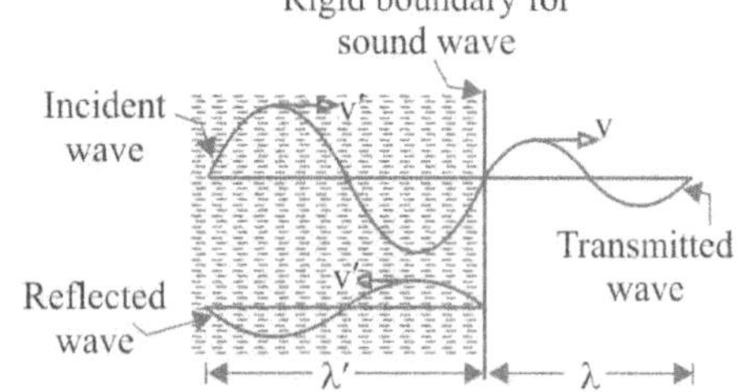

Fig.10.3. Reflection and transmission of sound wave.

When sound wave enters from water to air, it get reflected from the interface with a phase change of π radian. So we have

$$y_i = A \sin (k_\omega x - \omega t),$$

$$y_r = -A_r \sin (k_\omega x + \omega t - \pi)$$

And

$$y_t = A_t \sin (k_a x - \omega t)$$

Also

$$A = A_r + A_t$$

Refraction:

If i and r are the angles of incident and angle of refraction respectively, then for light wave;

$$\frac{\sin i}{\sin r} = \frac{v}{v'}.$$

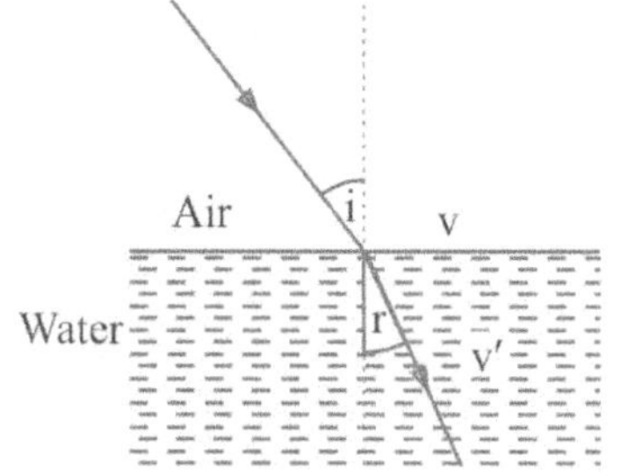

Fig. 10.4. Refraction of light wave

Here, $v' < v$, $\therefore \angle r < \angle i$

And for sound wave;

$$\frac{\sin i}{\sin r} = \frac{v}{v'}.$$

Here $v' > v$, $\therefore \angle r > \angle i$

Here straight lines are showing directions of propagation of wave.

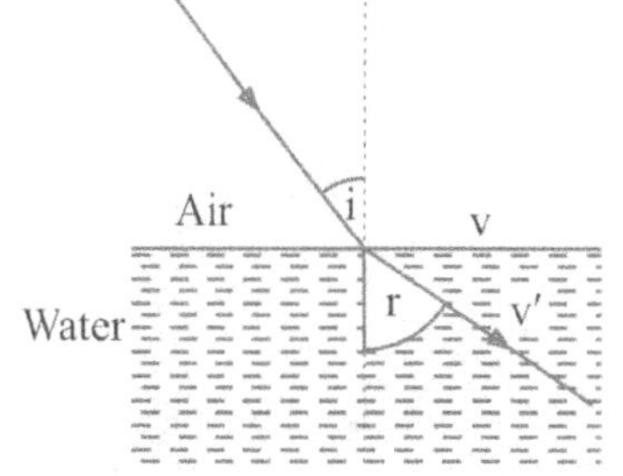

Fig.10.5 Refraction of sound wav

10.2 REFLECTION AND TRANSMISSION OF TRANSVERSE WAVE IN STRETCHED STRING

Reflection of a wave from a fixed boundary:

Consider a wave pulse travelling along a string connected to a rigid support, such as a wall. As the pulse reaches the wall, it exerts an upward force on the wall. By Newton's third law, the wall exerts an equal amount of force on the string in downward direction. Because of this downward force, an invert pulse produces which travels in reverse direction. Thus a crest is reflected as a trough.

Hence when a wave is reflected from a fixed boundary, it is reflected back with a phase difference of π radian. If an incident wave is represented by

$$y_i = A \sin (kx - \omega t),$$

then the reflected wave can be represented as

$$y_r = A \sin [(-kx - \omega t) + \pi]$$
$$= A \sin (kx + \omega t).$$

Reflection of a wave from a free boundary :

Consider a wave pulse travelling along a string connected to a light ring, which can slide without friction up and down on a vertical rod. As the crest produced in the string reaches at the ring, it rises above its mean position. In the process string stretches, and so it pulls back the ring to its mean position. Because of this a crest produces and reflected back without any phase change.

Hence when a wave is reflected from a free boundary, it suffers no phase change.

Suppose an incident wave is represented by

$$y_i = A \sin(kx - \omega t),$$

then the reflected wave can be represented as

$$y_r = -A \sin (kx + \omega t).$$

From the above discussion, it can be concluded that at the fixed boundary, the string end has no displacement, so a node is formed at the boundary. In case of free boundary, the displacement is maximum $(2A)$, so an antinode is formed at the boundary.

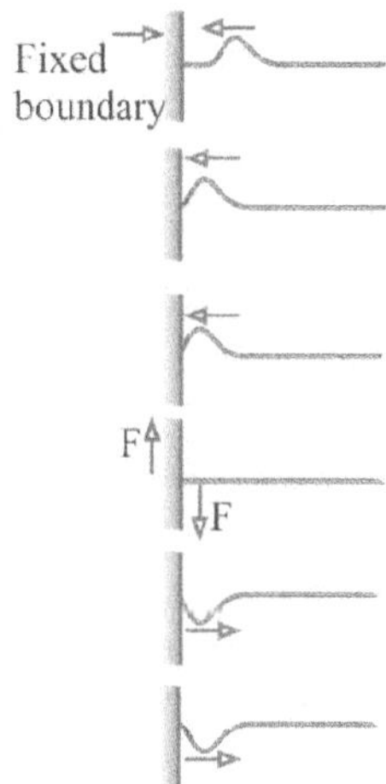

Fig.10.6. A pulse incident from the right is reflected at the left end of the string, which is tied to a wall. Note that the reflected pulse is inverted from the incident pulse.

Reflection at fixed boundary (for light wave)	Reflection at free boundary (for light wave)
1. Displacement, velocity undergo a phase change of π rad.	1. Displacement, particle velocity undergo no phase change.
2. Strain and pressure variation undergo no phase change.	2. Strain variation undergo a phase change of π rad.

Reflection and transmission :

(i)   Consider a combined string made of two parts: string A and string B, part A is thinner than B. As speed of wave $v = \sqrt{\dfrac{F}{\mu}}$, so $v_A > v_B$, i.e., a wave pulse travels faster in thinner string. For a wave pulse travelling from string A to B, the joints behaves as a rigid boundary, so the reflected wave pulse suffers a phase change of π radian, while there is no phase change in transmitted wave pulse.

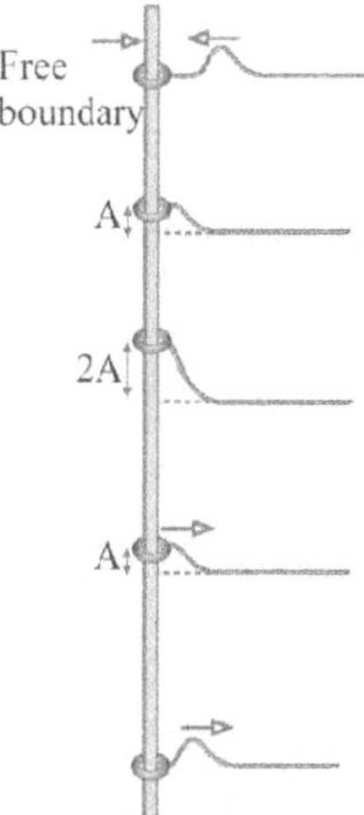

Fig. 10.7. The left end of the string is tied to a ring that can slide without friction up and down the rod.

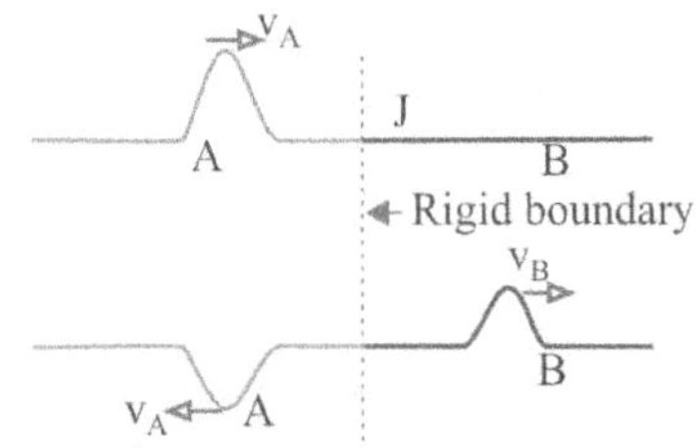

Reflected wave pulse   Transmitted wave pulse

Fig.10.8. Reflection and transmission of wave (ii) from rigid boundary.

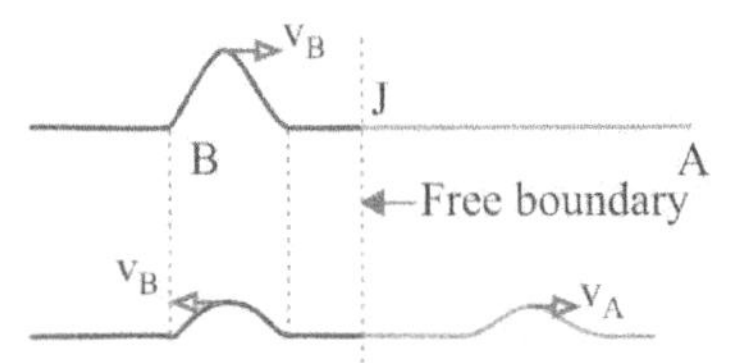

Reflected wave pulse   Transmitted wavepulse

Fig.10.9

Suppose an incident wave is represented by

$$y = A\sin(k_A x - \omega t)$$

then reflected and transmitted waves can be represented by

$$y_r = A_r \sin(k_A x + \omega t + \pi)$$

and

$$y_t = A_t \sin(k_B x - \omega t).$$

Also

$$A = A_r + A_t, \quad f_A = f_B, \ \lambda_A > \lambda_B$$

Now consider a wave pulse travelling from string B to A. Here joints behaves as a free boundary, and so the reflected wave pulse suffers no phase change. Transmitted wave pulse also has no phase change.

Suppose an incident wave pulse is represented by

$$y_i = A\sin(k_B x - \omega t)$$

then reflected and transmitted wave pulse can be represented as

$$y_r = A_r \sin(k_B x + \omega t)$$

and

$$y_t = A_t \sin(k_A x - \omega t)$$

also

$$A = A_r + A_t, f_B = f_A, \ \lambda_B < \lambda_A.$$

Ex. 1 Two wires of different linear mass densities are joined, consider junction to be at $x = 0$. An incident wave $y_i = A_i \sin(\omega t - k_1 x)$ is travelling to the right from the region $x \leq 0$. At the boundary the wave is partly reflected and partly transmitted. Find the reflected and transmitted amplitudes in terms of the incident amplitude.

Sol.

Given

$$y_i = A_i \sin(\omega t - k_1 x)$$

Medium 1   **Medium 2**

$$x = 0$$

The equation of reflected and transmitted waves are

$$y_r = A_r \sin(\omega t + k_1 x),$$
$$y_t = A_t \sin(\omega t - k_2 x)$$

We have $A_r + A_t = A_i$ ...(i)

and $y_r + y_t = y_i$ ...(ii)

Differentiating equation (ii) partially

$$\frac{\partial y_r}{\partial x} + \frac{\partial y_t}{\partial x} = \frac{\partial y_i}{\partial x}$$

or $\dfrac{\partial}{\partial x}[A_r \sin(\omega t + k_1 x)] + \dfrac{\partial}{\partial x}[A_t \sin(\omega t - k_2 x)] =$

$$\frac{\partial}{\partial x}[A_i \sin(\omega t - k_1 x)]$$

or $\quad A_r k_1 \cos\omega t - A_t k_2 \cos\omega t = -A_i k_1 \cos\omega t$ at $x = 0$

or $\qquad A_r k_1 - A_t k_2 = -A_i k_1$ ...(iii)

Solving equations (i) & (iii) , we get

$$A_r = \left(\frac{k_1 - k_2}{k_1 + k_2}\right) A_i$$

and

$$A_t = \left(\frac{2k_1}{k_1 + k_2}\right) A_i \qquad \textit{Ans.}$$

As $k = \dfrac{\omega}{v}$ and $\omega = $ constant

$$\therefore \quad A_r = \left(\frac{v_2 - v_1}{v_2 + v_1}\right) A_i$$

and

$$A_t = \left(\frac{2v_2}{v_1 + v_2}\right) A_i$$

Ex. 2   A string of length 20 cm and linear mass density 0.40 g/cm is fixed at both ends and is kept under a tension of 16N. A wave pulse is produced at $t = 0$ near an end as shown in figure, which travels towards the other end. When will the string have the shape shown in the figure again?

Sol.

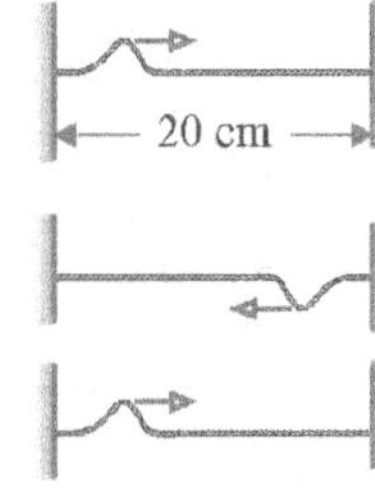

Fig. 10.10

Given $\mu = 0.40$ g/cm $= \dfrac{0.40}{1000} \times 100 = 0.040$ kg/m

Wave speed in the stretched string

$$v = \sqrt{\frac{F}{\mu}} = \sqrt{\frac{16}{0.040}} = 20 \text{ m/s}$$

The string will regain its shape after travelling the pulse a distance

$$= 20 + 20 = 40 \text{ cm}$$

Thus time spend $t = \dfrac{0.40}{20} = 0.02$ s   *Ans.*

10.3 SUPERPOSITION OF WAVES

In an orchetra, we can differentiate the sounds of different musical instruments playing simultaneously. The antenna of our television receiver is set in motion by the resultant effect of many electromagnetic waves from different broadcasting stations. Above examples show the independent behaviour of the waves and superposition of waves.

Independent behaviour of waves: When number of waves travel through a region at the same time, each wave travels independently of the other i.e., as if all other waves were absent.

Principle of superposition of waves: The principle states that when a number of waves travel through a medium simultaneously, the resultant displacement of any particle of the medium at any given time is equal to the algebraic sum of the displacements due to the individual waves.

If y_1, y_2,..., y_n are the displacements produced by waves acting separately, then the resultant displacement, when all the waves act simultaneously is given by the algebraic sum

$$y = y_1 + y_2 + ... + y_n \quad \text{(Principle of superposition)}$$

Note:

1. The principle of superposition is valid for small displacements.
2. The principle is valid for the quantities like displacement, velocity, pressure, momentum etc. but not for kinetic energy.
3. The algebraic sum is application only for one dimensional waves. For other waves $(2D$ or $3D$ waves), it will by $\vec{y} = \vec{y_1} + \vec{y_2} + ... + \vec{y_n}$.

(i) Superposition of two identical pulses travelling towards each other: To understand easily, consider two pulses moving towards each other with a constant speed of 1 m/s . Figure shows the positions of the pulses after every second. They cross each other between $t = 2$ s and 3s. At $t = 2.5$ s the two pulses superpose in such a way that the displacement of the resultant pulse is twice the displacement of either pulse, i.e., $y_{res} = y + y = 2y$.

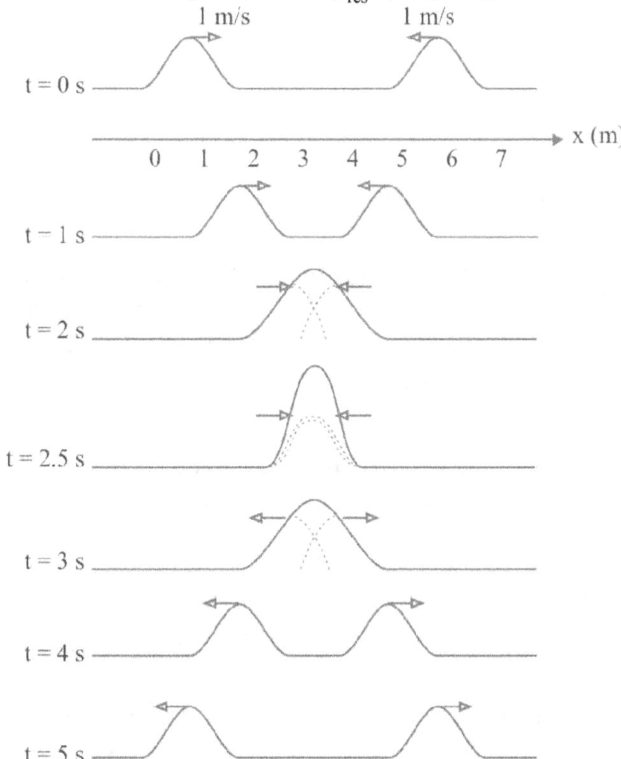

Fig.10.11. Superposition of two identical pulses traveling towards each other.

(ii) Superposition of two pulses of equal and opposite shapes travelling towards each other:

Consider two equal and opposite pulses coming towards each other with a speed of 1m/s . Figure shows the positions of the pulses $t = 0$, 1.5s, 2.5s, 3.5s & 4.5s. At 2.5 s the two pulses superpose in such a way that the displacement of the resultant pulse is zero, i.e., $y_{res} = y - y = 0$. This again shows that the resultant displacement is the algebraic sum of individual waves.

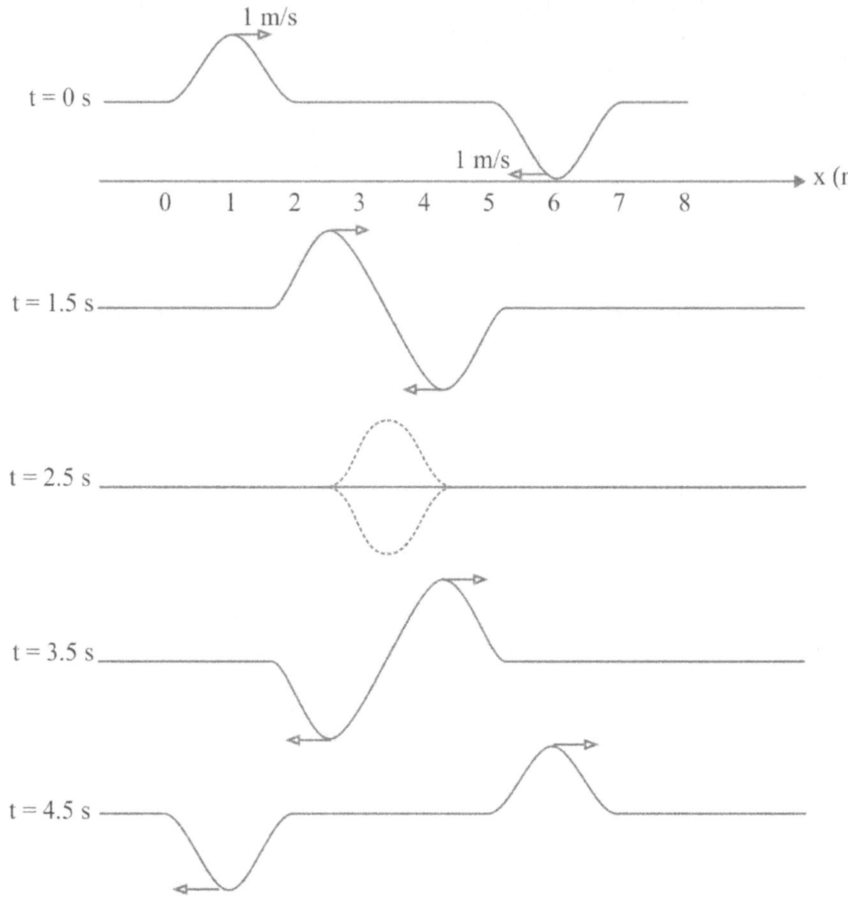

Fig.10.12. Superposition of two equal and opposite pulses travelling in opposite directions.

From the graphical treatment of superposition of wave pulses, it can be concluded that the two pulses continue to retain their individual identity after crossing each other. However, at the instant they cross each other, the appearance of the wave profile is different from the shape of individual pulse.

There are three types of superposition in our study.

(i)   When two or more waves of same frequency travel simultaneously in the same direction or nearly along the same direction in a medium, they superpose on each other, give new disturbance, called **interference of waves**.

(ii)   When two or more waves of slightly different frequencies $(f_1 \sim f_2 \ngtr 10)$ travel with the same speed in the same direction in a medium then superpose on each other, give **beats**.

(iii)   When two identical waves travel with the same speed in the opposite directions in a medium, they superpose on each other, give **stationary wave**.

Ex. 3 *Fig. 10.13* shows two rectangular wave pulses travelling in opposite directions along a string at $t = 0$. Sketch the wave functions for $t = 1, 2$ and 3s.

Sol.

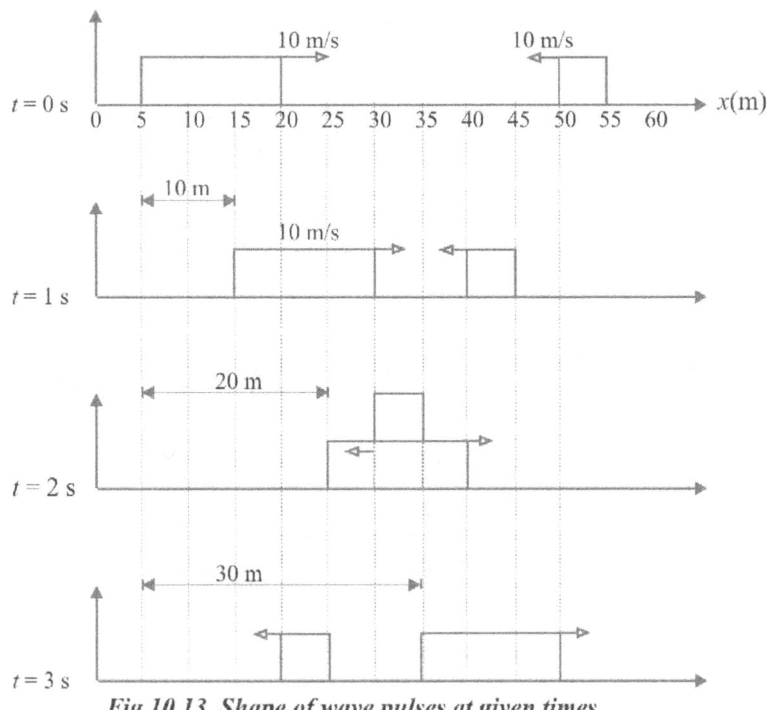

Fig.10.13. Shape of wave pulses at given times.

10.4 INTERFERENCE

Consider two harmonic waves of same frequency (coherent waves). Suppose A_1 and A_2 be the amplitudes of the waves and ϕ is the phase difference between them. It is assumed that the waves are plane and move almost along a line. Thus wave equations are

$$y_1 = A_1 \sin (kx - \omega t) \qquad ...(1)$$

and

$$y_2 = A_2 \sin (kx - \omega t + \phi) \qquad ...(2)$$

where

$$\phi = \left(\frac{2\pi}{\lambda}\right)x.$$

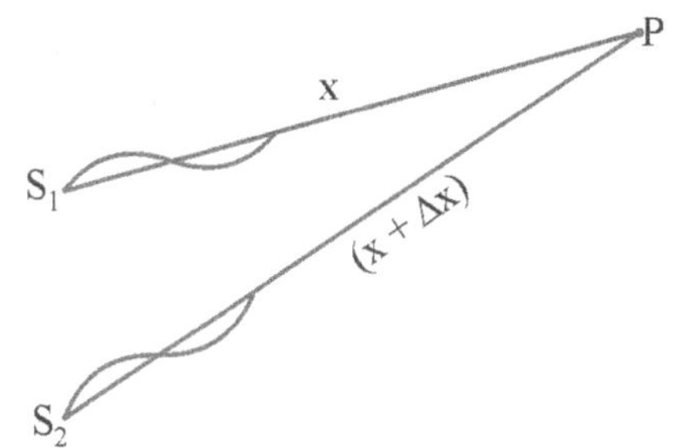

Fig. 10.14

When both the waves travel simultaneously, the resultant wave at P can be obtained by principle of superposition, i.e.,

$$y = y_1 + y_2$$

$$= A_1 \sin(kx - \omega t) + A_2 \sin(kx - \omega t + \phi)$$

$$= A_1 \sin(kx - \omega t) + [A_2 \sin(kx - \omega t)\cos\phi + A_2 \cos(kx - \omega t)\sin\phi]$$

$$= (A_1 + A_2 \cos\phi)\sin(kx - \omega t) + A_2 \sin\phi \cos(kx - \omega t)$$

Let

$$A_1 + A_2 \cos\phi = R\cos\theta \qquad ...(3)$$

and

$$A_2 \sin\phi = R\sin\theta \qquad ...(4)$$

Squaring and adding equations (3) and (4), we get

$$R = A_1^2 + A_2^2 + 2A_1 A_2 \cos\phi \qquad ...(5)$$

As $I \propto A^2$,

$$\therefore \quad I = I_1 + I_2 + 2\sqrt{I_1 I_2} \cos\phi \qquad ...(6)$$

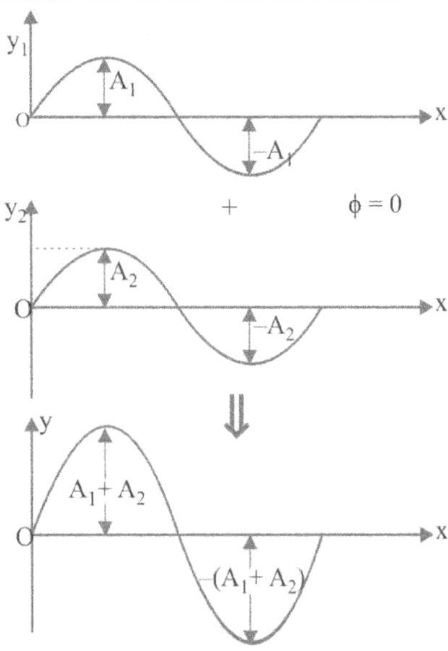

Fig10.15. Constructive interference.

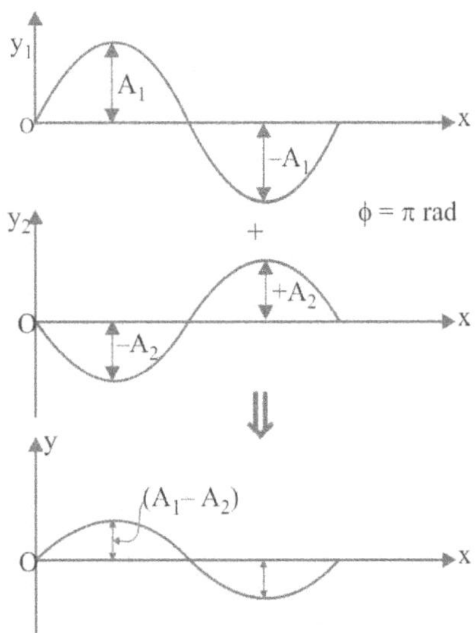

Fig.10.16. Destructive interference.

Also
$$\tan\theta = \frac{A_2\sin\phi}{A_1 + A_2\cos\phi} \qquad ...(7)$$

The resultant wave becomes

$$y = R\sin\big[(kx-\omega t)+\theta\big] \qquad ...(8)$$

Clearly the resultant wave has the same frequency and speed as the interfereing waves

Two types of interference

(i) Constructive interference:

The intensity of the resultant wave is maximum at P, if

$$\cos\phi = +1$$

or $\qquad \phi = 2\pi n$, where n $= 0, 1, 2, 3, ...$

As 2π phase difference is equal to a path difference λ, so

$$\Delta x = n\lambda$$

Thus from (5), $\qquad R_{max} = A_1 + A_2$

(ii) Destructive interference: The intensity of the resultant wave will be minimum at P, if $\qquad \cos\phi = -1$

or $\qquad \phi = (2n-1)\pi$, where $n = 1, 2, 3, ...$

and $\qquad \Delta x = (2n-1)\dfrac{\lambda}{2}$

Thus from (5), $R_{min} \qquad = A_1 - A_2$

The ratio of maximum to minimum intensities

$$\frac{I_{max}}{I_{min}} = \frac{(A_1+A_2)^2}{(A_1-A_2)^2} \qquad ...(9)$$

Note:

The distance between maxima and next minima $= \dfrac{\lambda}{2}$.

Conditions of sustained interference:

1. Mathematically interference phenomenon can takes place between two waves of same frequency and different amplitudes. But for obserable interference, the amplitudes of the waves should be equal. In this case,

$$A_1 = A_2 = A$$

$$\therefore \qquad R^2 = A^2 + A^2 + 2AA\cos\phi$$

or $\qquad R^2 = 2A^2(1+\cos\phi)$

$$= 2A^2 \times 2\cos^2\frac{\phi}{2}$$

$$R^2 = 4A^2\cos^2\frac{\phi}{2} \qquad ...(10)$$

Write $\qquad R^2 = I$ and $4A^2 = I_o$

$$\therefore \qquad I = I_o\cos^2\frac{\phi}{2} \qquad ...(11)$$

From equation (11), the maximum intensity is $4A^2$ and minimum intensity is zero. In the phenomenon of interference the energy is not destroyed but is only redistributed from the positions of minimum intensity to those of maximum intensity. At the maximum intensity positions the intensity due to the two waves should be $2A^2$ but it actually $4A^2$. As shown in figure, the intensity varies from 0 to $4A^2$ and the average is still $2A^2$. It is equal to a uniform intensity of $2A^2$ which will be present in the absence of interference phenomenon between two waves. Hence the formation of maxima and minima is due to interference of waves is in accordance with the law of conservation of energy.

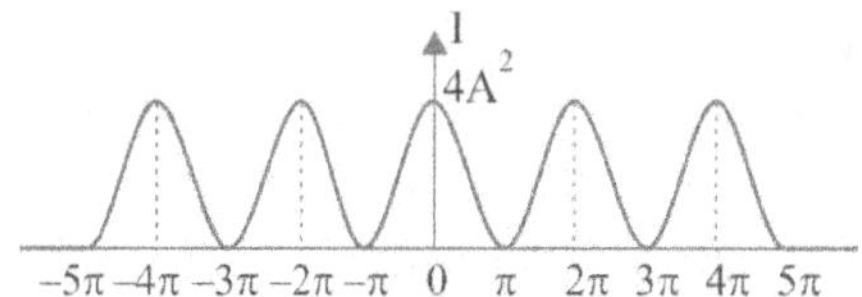

Fig.10.17. Intensity distribution in interference of two waves.

2. The phase difference between the two waves must remain constant, it will not change with time. If the phase difference between the waves continuously changes,then the positions of the maximum and minimum intensities do not remain fix.

3. The waves must travel in the same direction because with increase in obliquity between the waves, the resultant intensity decreases.

10.5 INTERFERENCE OF SOUND WAVES: QUINKE'S TUBE

Two independent sources of sound can not be coherent because they can not maintain the constant phase difference. In practice the coherent sources can be produced from a single source, as in case of Quinke's tube. Source so produced remain coherent because they produced from the same source. Quinke's tube consists of two U - tubes, one can slide over the other. In figure tube D can slide inside the tube ABC. When a source of sound (vibrating tuning fork) is held near the opening at A, the sound waves travel through the tube along two paths ABC and ADC. The resultant sound produced at C due to the interference will be maximum or minimum depending upon their path difference. The path difference between the two sounds.

$$\Delta x = ADC - ABC$$

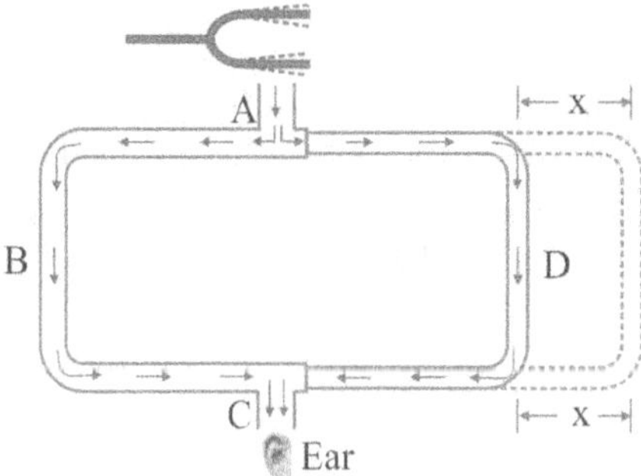

Fig.10.18 Quinke's tube set-up

If $\Delta x = n\lambda$, then maximum sound will be heard, and if $\Delta x = (2n-1)\dfrac{\lambda}{2}$, then minimum sound will be heard. But gradually sliding the tube D outwards or inwards maximum and minimum can be noticed at regular intervals.

Note:

Each x cm slide of tube will cause a path difference of $2x$. Thus for a maxima and next minima

$$\frac{\lambda}{2} = 2x \qquad \text{or } \lambda = 4x.$$

Ex. 4 The ratio of intensities of two interfering waves is 4 : 1. What will be the ratio of maximum and minimum intensities in their interference?

Sol.

If A_1 and A_2 be the amplitudes of the waves, then

$$\frac{I_1}{I_2} = \frac{A_1^2}{A_2^2} = \frac{4}{1}$$

or

$$\frac{A_1}{A_2} = \frac{2}{1}$$

$$\therefore \quad \frac{I_{max}}{I_{min}} = \frac{(A_1+A_2)^2}{(A_1-A_2)^2} = \frac{(2+1)^2}{(2-1)^2} = 9 \ \textbf{\textit{Ans.}}$$

Ex. 5 *Fig.10.20.* shows a tube structure in which a sound signal is sent from one end and is received at the other end. The frequency of the second source can be varied electronically between 2000 and 5000 Hz. Find the frequencies at which maxima of intensity are detected. The speed of sound in air 340 m/s.

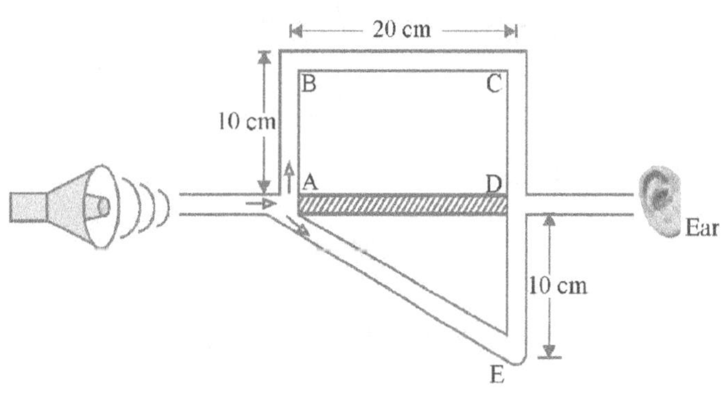

Fig. 10.19

Sol.

The path difference between the sounds going through the tubes

$$\Delta x = ABCD - AED$$
$$= (10 + 20 + 10) - (\sqrt{500} + 10)$$
$$= 7.64 \text{ cm}$$

The wavelength of the sound

$$\lambda = \frac{v}{f} = \frac{340}{f} \text{ m}$$

For maximum intensity,

$$\Delta x = n\lambda$$

or $\quad 7.64 \times 10^{-2} = n \times \dfrac{340}{f}$

$\therefore \qquad f = n\dfrac{340}{7.64 \times 10^{-2}}$

$$= n\, 4450 \text{ Hz}$$

Here $n \geq 1$. For $n = 1$, $f = 4450$ Hz and for $n = 2$, $f = 8900$ Hz. Thus the frequency within the specified range is 4450 Hz.

Ex. 6
Two simple harmonic sources separated by 20 m oscillate according to the equation

$$y_1 = 0.06 \sin \pi t \,(m)$$

and $\qquad y_2 = 0.02 \sin \pi t \,(m)$

These sources induce simple harmonic waves along a rod of speed 3 m/s. Determine the equation of motion of a particle 12 m from the first source and 8 m from the second.

Sol.   The sources are separated as shown in figure

Fig. 10.20

The equation of oscillation of a source at a distance x can be written as

$$y = A \sin \pi (t - x/v)$$

$\therefore \quad$ For source S_1, $x = 12$ m

$$y_1 = 0.06 \sin \pi \left(t - \frac{12}{3} \right)$$

$$= 0.06 \sin \pi (t - 4) = 0.06 \sin \pi t$$

and for source S_2, $x = -8$ m

$\therefore \qquad y_2 = 0.02 \sin \pi \left(t + \dfrac{-8}{3} \right) = 0.02 \sin \pi (t - 8/3)$

$$= 0.02 \sin \left(\pi t - \frac{8\pi}{3} \right) = 0.02 \sin \left(\pi t - \frac{2\pi}{3} \right)$$

The resultant displacement

$$y = y_1 + y_2 = 0.06 \sin \pi t + 0.02 \sin \left(\pi t - \frac{2\pi}{3} \right)$$

$$= 0.06 \sin \pi t + 0.02 \left(\sin \pi t \cos \frac{2\pi}{3} - \cos \pi t \sin \frac{2\pi}{3} \right)$$

$$= 0.06 \sin \pi t + 0.02 \left[\sin \pi t (-1/2) - \cos \pi t (\sqrt{3}/2) \right]$$

$$= 0.05 \sin \pi t - 0.0173 \cos \pi t \qquad \textit{Ans.}$$

Ex. 7
In a Quinke's experiment, the sound intensity has a minimum value I at a particular position. As the sliding tube is pulled out by a distance of 16.5 mm, the intensity increase to a maximum of $9I$. Take the speed of sound in air to be 330 m/s. (a) Find the frequency of the sound source. (b) Find the ratio of the amplitudes of the two waves arriving at the detector assuming that it does not change much between the position of minimum and maximum intensity.

Sol.

(a)   The separation between minimum and next maximum is $\lambda/2$. For the slide of tube by 16.5 mm will cause a path difference of 33 mm.

$\therefore \qquad \dfrac{\lambda}{2} = 33 \text{ mm} \Rightarrow \lambda = 66 \text{ mm}$

and $\qquad f = \dfrac{v}{\lambda}\; \dfrac{330}{66 \times 10^{-3}} = 5.0 \text{ kHz} \quad \textit{Ans.}$

(b) $\qquad \dfrac{I_{max}}{I_{min}} = \dfrac{9I}{I} = \dfrac{(A_1 + A_2)^2}{(A_1 - A_2)^2}$

or $\qquad \dfrac{A_1 + A_2}{A_1 - A_2} = 3$

or $\qquad \dfrac{A_1}{A_2} = 2 \qquad \textit{Ans.}$

Ex. 8
A source of sound S and a detector D are placed at some distance from one another. A big cardboard is placed near the detector and perpendicular to the line SD as shown in the *Fig. 10.21*. It is gradually moved away and it is found that the intensity changes from maximum to minimum as the board is moved through a distance of 20 cm. Find the frequency of the sound emitted. The velocity of sound in air is 336 m/s.

Sol.

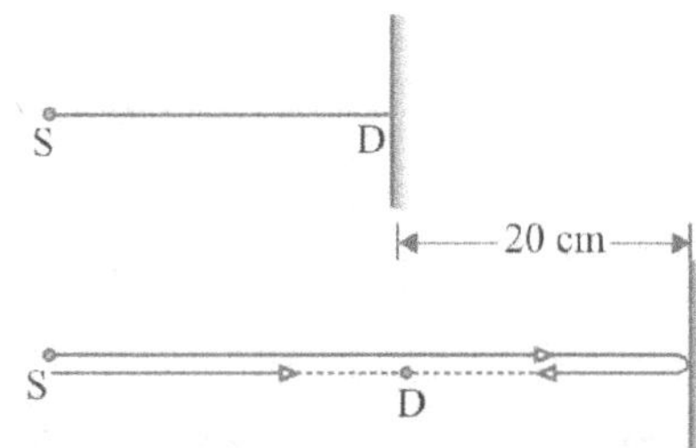

Fig. 10.21

The distance between maximum to next minimum is $\lambda/2$. When cardboard is displaced by 20 cm the path difference produces by 40 cm.

$\therefore \qquad \lambda/2 = 40 \text{ cm}$

or $\qquad \lambda = 80 \text{ cm}$

Frequency of sound $\qquad f = \dfrac{v}{\lambda} = \dfrac{336}{0.80}$

$$= 420 \text{ Hz} \qquad \textit{Ans.}$$

Ex. 9
Two sources of sound S_1 and S_2, emitting waves of equal wavelength 20.0 cm are placed with a separation of 20.0 cm between them. A detector can be moved on a line parallel to $S_1 S_2$ and at a distance of 20.0 cm from it. Initially the detector is equidistance from the two sources. Assuming that the waves emitted by the sources are in phase, find the minimum distance through which the detector should be shifted to detect a minimum of sound.

Sol.

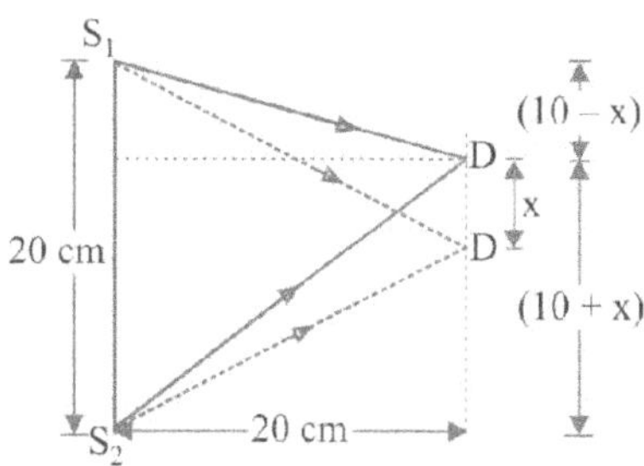

Fig. 10.22

Let the detector is shifted by x

The path difference between the sounds reach at D,

$$\Delta x = \sqrt{20^2 + (10+x)^2} - \sqrt{20^2 + (10-x)^2}$$

As detector detect the minima for the shifted position

$$\therefore \quad \Delta x = \lambda/2$$

or $\quad \sqrt{20^2 + (10+x)^2} - \sqrt{20^2 + (10-x)^2} = \dfrac{20}{2}$

After solving, we get $x = 12.6$ cm **Ans.**

Ex. 10

Two coherent narrow source emitting sound of wavelength λ in the same phase are placed parallel to each other at a small separation of 2λ. The sound is detected by moving a detector on the screen Σ at a distance D ($>> \lambda$) from the source S_1 as shown in *Fig. 10.23*. Find the distance x such that the intensity at P is equal to the intensity at O.

Sol.

The maximum path difference between the sounds can be 2λ, and minimum can be zero, when x tends to infinity. So there is only one position between them at which intensity is maximum, for which path difference between sound at P is λ.

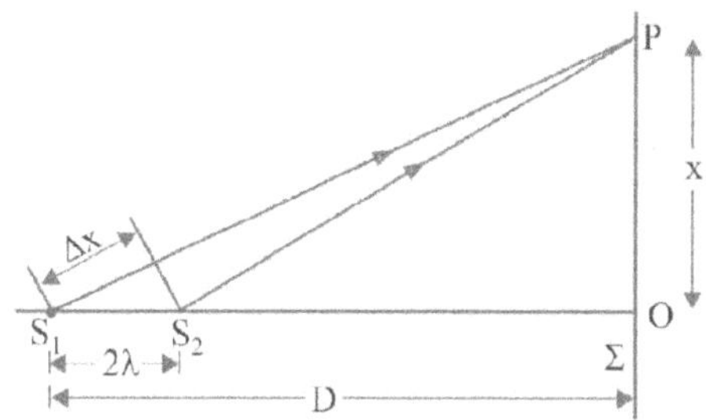

Fig. 10.23

Possible position x	Path difference Δx	Intensity
$x = 0$	2λ	Maximum
$x = ?$	λ	Maximum
$x = \infty$	0	Maximum

From the figure, path difference $\Delta x = 2\lambda\cos\theta$

where $\quad \cos\theta = \dfrac{D}{\sqrt{D^2 + x^2}}$

$\therefore \quad 2\lambda \times \dfrac{D}{\sqrt{D^2 + x^2}} = \lambda$

or $\quad x = \sqrt{3}\, D$ **Ans.**

Ex. 11

Figure shows two coherent sources S_1 and S_2 which emit sound of wavelength λ in phase. The separation between the sources is 3λ. A circular wire of large radius is placed is such a way that

S_1S_2 lies in its plane and middle point of S_1S_2 is at the centre of the wire. Find the angular position θ on the wire for which constructive interference takes place.

Sol.

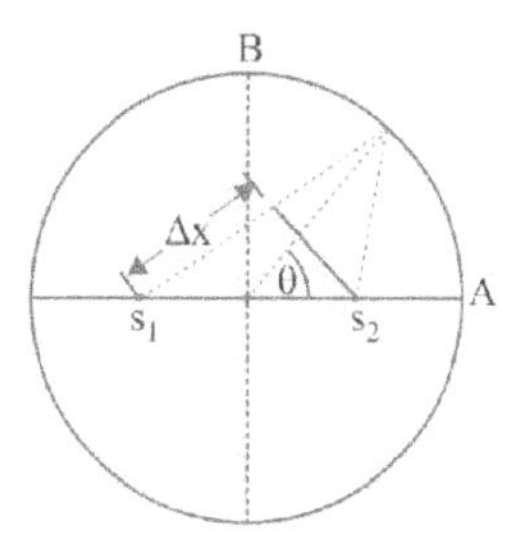

Fig. 10.24

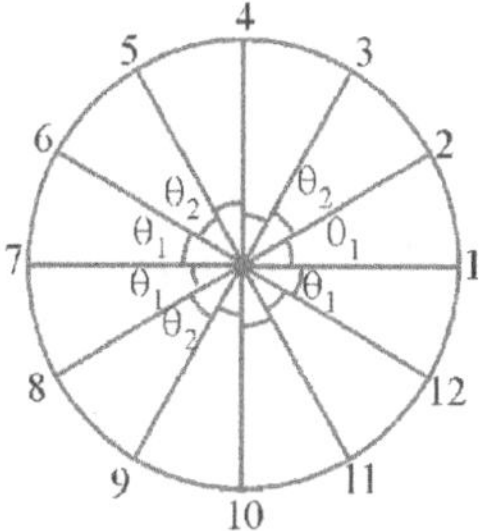

Fig. 10.25

Since θ is small, so the path difference $\Delta x = 3\lambda\cos\theta$

$$\Delta x_m = 0 \text{ for } \theta = 90° \text{ at } B$$

and $\quad \Delta x_{\max} = 3\lambda$, for $\theta = 0$ at A

For constructive interference Δx can be, $0, \lambda, 2\lambda, 3\lambda, \ldots$

There are two positions between A and B where constructive interference occurs. These are

$$\Delta x = \lambda \text{ and } 2\lambda$$

$\therefore \quad 3\lambda\cos\theta = \lambda$

or $\quad \cos\theta = \dfrac{1}{3} \Rightarrow \theta_1 = \cos^{-1}(1/3)$

and $\quad 3\lambda\cos\theta = 2\lambda \Rightarrow \theta_2 = \cos^{-1}(2/3)$

Similar positions in other quadrants can also be obtained.

Ex. 12

Three identical radio sources each of intensity I_0, vibrating in phase, are positioned, along y-axis, as shown in *Fig. 10.27*. The frequency of each source is 10^8 Hz, separation between two adjacent sources is $d = 1$ km. A detector moves parallel to y-axis at a perpendicular distance D-from the sources. The separation between two consecutive minima registered is 10 km.

(a) Determine the radiation wavelength and the distance D, the resultant intensity at maxima and minima.

(b) If the source S_2 stops radiating, what should be the new separation between the remaining two sources so that positions of maxima are unchanged?

Sol.

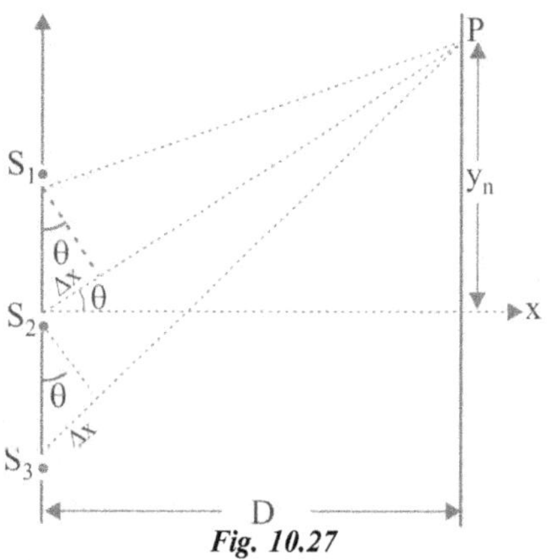

Fig. 10.27

For $D >> d$, the waves from all the sources travel approximately in the same direction. The path difference between any two consecutive sources is $d\sin\theta$. The corresponding phase difference

$\phi = \dfrac{2\pi}{\lambda}(d\sin\theta) = kd\sin\theta$. The equations of the three waves arriving at P can be written as

$$y_1 = A\sin(kx-\phi),$$
$$y_2 = A\sin(kx),$$
$$y_3 = A\sin(kx+\phi)$$

The resultant wave is given by

$$y = y_1 + y_2 + y_3$$
$$= A[\sin(kx-\phi)+\sin(kx+\phi)]+A\sin kx$$
$$= 2A\sin kx\cos(-\phi)+A\sin kx$$
$$= A(1+2\cos\phi)\sin kx$$

The amplitude of resultant wave

$$R = A(1+2\cos\phi)$$

As $I \propto R^2$ and $I_0 \propto A^2$, we have

$$I = I_0[1+2\cos(kd\sin\theta)]^2$$

For maxima

$$\cos(kd\sin\theta) = 1$$

or $\qquad kd\sin\theta = 2n\pi$

$\therefore \qquad \sin\theta = \dfrac{2n\pi}{kd} = \dfrac{n\lambda}{d}$

From figure $\sin\theta \approx \tan\theta = \dfrac{y_n}{D}$, where y_n denotes position of nth maxima. Therefore

$$\dfrac{y_n}{D} = \dfrac{n\lambda}{d}$$

or $\qquad y_n = n\dfrac{D\lambda}{d}$, where $n = 0, 1, 2, ...$

Separation between two consecutive maximas

$$\beta = y_n - y_{n-1} = \dfrac{D\lambda}{d}$$

The separation between two consecutive minima also be $\dfrac{D\lambda}{d}$.

Wavelength of radiations,

$$\lambda = \dfrac{c}{f} = \dfrac{3\times10^8}{10^8} = 3\,\text{m} \qquad \textbf{Ans.}$$

$\therefore \qquad D = \dfrac{\beta d}{\lambda} = \dfrac{(10\times10^3)\times1000}{3} = \dfrac{10000}{3}\,\text{km}$

(a) Resultant intensity at maxima
$$I_{max} = I_0[1+2\cos(2\pi n)]^2$$
$$= 9I_0$$
Resultant intensity at minima

$$I_{min} = I_0[1+2\cos(\phi)]^2 = 0, \text{ where } \phi = \dfrac{2n\pi}{3}; n = 1, 3, ...$$

(b) Let d' be the new distance between the adjacent sources, then
$$y_1 = A\sin(kx-\phi') \ ; \ y_2 = A\sin(kx+\phi')$$
where $\qquad \phi = kd'\sin\theta$
The new amplitude $R = 2A\cos(kd'\sin\theta)$

The intensity $\quad I = R'^2 = 4A^2\cos^2(kd'\sin\theta)$
$$= 4I_0^2\cos^2(kd'\sin\theta)$$

For maxima $\cos(kd'\sin\theta) = \pm1$

or $\qquad kd'\sin\theta = n\pi$

or $\qquad \dfrac{2\pi}{\lambda}d'\sin\theta = n\pi$

or $\qquad \dfrac{2\pi}{\lambda}d'\left(\dfrac{y'_n}{D}\right) = n\pi$

$\therefore \qquad y'_n = \dfrac{n\lambda D}{2d'}$

As position of maxima is unchanged
$\therefore \qquad y_n = y'_n$

$$n\dfrac{D\lambda}{d} = n\dfrac{D\lambda}{2d'}$$

$\therefore \qquad d' = \dfrac{d}{2} = \dfrac{1}{2}\,\text{km} \qquad \textbf{Ans.}$

10.6 INTERFERENCE IN TIME : BEATS

When two or more sound waves of nearly same frequency and amplitude travel along the same path in the same directions, the intensity of the resultant sound wave at any point in the medium rises and falls (technically known as waxing and waning of sound) alternately with time.

The periodic variations in the intensity of sound due to the superposition of sound waves of slightly different frequencies are called **beats**. One rise and one fall of the intensity constitute a beat. The number of beat produced per second is called beats frequency. Thus

beat frequency = difference in frequency of the two superposing waves.

or $\qquad f_{beat} = f_1 \sim f_2$

Condition of audible beats:

The persistance of hearing of our ear is (1/10)th of a second. So our ears can not differentiate the sound variation more than 10 in a second. Hence beats heard will not be distinct if the number of beats produced are more than 10 per second.

Formation of beats by graphical method

Figure shows two sound waves of frequencies f_1 and f_2. The frequency f_1 is slightly greater than f_2.

At $t = t_1$, the two waves meet in the same phase at a given point, so they produce maximum intensity with the passes of time, the phase difference between the two waves increases and so the two curves gradually become out of phase.

At $t = t_2$, the two waves are in exactly opposite phase, so they produce minimum sound intensity. Thereafter the phase difference goes on decreasing with time. At $t = t_3$, the first wave complete one more vibration than the second wave. And so they again in same phase and produce maximum intensity, and so on. The resultant wave as obtained by the superposition of the two waves is shown in *Fig. 10.28* (b). The dashed envelopes above and below it show the variation of the amplitude of the wave. The time interval from t_1 to t_3 is one beat period, because during this duration only one beat is formed. Clearly if $t_3 - t_1 = 1\text{s}$, then beat frequency $f_{\text{beat}} = f_1 - f_2 = 1$.

Analytical treatment of beats

Consider two sound waves of equal amplitudes and travelling in a medium in the same direction but of frequencies f_1 and f_2 (f_1 being slightly greater than f_2). The pressure variations due to two waves at a given points (for simplicity $x = 0$) may be represented as

$$\Delta P_1 = \Delta P_m \sin \omega_1 t = \Delta P_m \sin 2\pi f_1 t$$

and
$$\Delta P_2 = \Delta P_m \sin \omega_2 t = \Delta P_m \sin 2\pi f_2 t$$

By the principle of superposition, the net pressure variation

$$\Delta P = \Delta P_1 + \Delta P_2$$
$$= \Delta P_m \sin 2\pi f_1 t + \Delta P_m \sin 2\pi f_2 t$$
$$= 2\Delta P_m \cos 2\pi \left(\frac{f_1 - f_2}{2} \right) t . \quad \sin 2\pi \left(\frac{f_1 + f_2}{2} \right) t$$

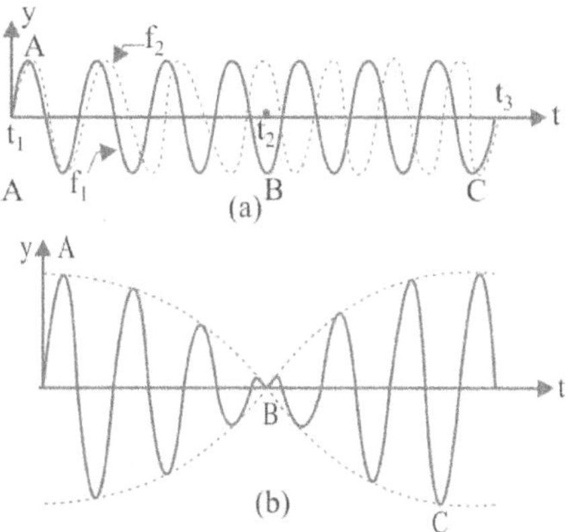

Fig.10.28. Formation of beats by graph.

Here $\dfrac{f_1 + f_2}{2} = f_{av}$ and $\dfrac{f_1 - f_2}{2} = f_{\text{mod}}$

$\therefore \qquad \Delta P = 2\Delta P_m \cos(2\pi f_{\text{mod}} t)\sin(2\pi f_{av} t)$

or $\qquad \Delta P = R\sin(2\pi f_{av} t) \qquad\qquad ...(1)$

where $R = 2\Delta P_m \cos(2\pi f_{\text{mod}} t)$ is the amplitude of the pressure variation. As f_1 is slightly greater than f_2, so $f_{\text{mod}} \ll f_{av}$, i.e., R varies very slowly with time. Hence equation (1) represents a wave of rapid oscillation of average frequency f_{av} modulated by a slowly varying oscillation of frequency f_{mod}.

The amplitude of pressure variation R of the resultant wave will be maximum, when

$$\cos 2\pi f_{\text{mod}} t = \pm 1 , \text{ and } R = \pm 2\Delta P_m$$

or $\qquad 2\pi f_{\text{mod}} t = n\pi, \ n = 0, 1, 2, ...$

or $\qquad 2\pi \left(\dfrac{f_1 - f_2}{2} \right) t = n\pi$

or
$$t = \frac{n}{f_1 - f_2} \qquad \ldots (2)$$

The instant of maxima
$$t = 0, \frac{1}{f_1 - f_2}, \frac{2}{f_1 - f_2}, \ldots\ldots$$

$\therefore$ Time interval between two successive maximas

$$\Delta t = \frac{1}{f_1 - f_2}$$

Similarly, the amplitude of pressure variation will be minimum, when
$$\cos(2\pi f_{\text{mod}}t) = 0, \text{ and } R = 0$$

or
$$2\pi \left(\frac{f_1 - f_2}{2} \right) t = (2n+1)\frac{\pi}{2}, \ n = 0, 1, 2, \ldots\ldots$$

or
$$t = \frac{(2n+1)}{2(f_1 - f_2)} \qquad \ldots (3)$$

The instant of minimas
$$t = \frac{1}{2(f_1 - f_2)}, \frac{3}{2(f_1 - f_2)}, \frac{5}{2(f_1 - f_2)}, \ldots$$

$\therefore$ The interval between two successive minimas

$$\Delta t = \frac{1}{f_1 - f_2}$$

Clearly, both maxima and minima of intensity occur alternately. Technically one maximum followed by a minimum is called a beat. Thus beat frequency

$$f_{\text{beat}} = \frac{1}{\Delta t} = f_1 - f_2.$$

Variation of intensity of resulting wave at a point

The intensity of sound wave is given by

$$I = \frac{\Delta P_m^{\;2}}{2\rho v}$$

For the resulting sound wave

$$I = \frac{[2\Delta P_m \cos(2\pi f_{\text{mod}}t)]^2}{2\rho v}$$

$$= \frac{4\Delta P_m^2 \cos^2(2\pi f_{\text{mod}}t)}{2\rho v}$$

or
$$I = I_0[\cos 2\{2\pi f_{\text{mod}}t\} + 1]$$

where
$$I_0 = \left(\frac{4\Delta P_m^{\;2}}{2\rho v} \right)$$

Clearly the intensity of the resulting wave varies between 0 to I_0 with a frequency which is double the frequency of pressure amplitude R.

Tuning fork :

A straight rod is bent to give U-shaped structure is known as tuning fork. The tuning form vibrates in three portions as shown in (*fig* 10.29)

The free ends of the fork behaves as antinodes. The junction of U-shaped rod and stem also behaves as an antinode. Tuning fork is an important source of standard frequency. It can be set into vibration when one of the prongs is struck against a hard rubber pad. Tuning forks of frequencies 256, 288, 320, 341.33, 384, 426.66, 480 and 512 Hz are commonly manufactured.

For a tuning fork of rectangular cross-section, the fundamental frequency is given by

$$f = A\sqrt{\frac{Yt}{\rho\ell^2}}$$

where $Y \to$ Young's modulus

$\rho \to$ density of material of tuning fork

$t \to$ thickness of rod

$\ell \to$ length of the tuning fork

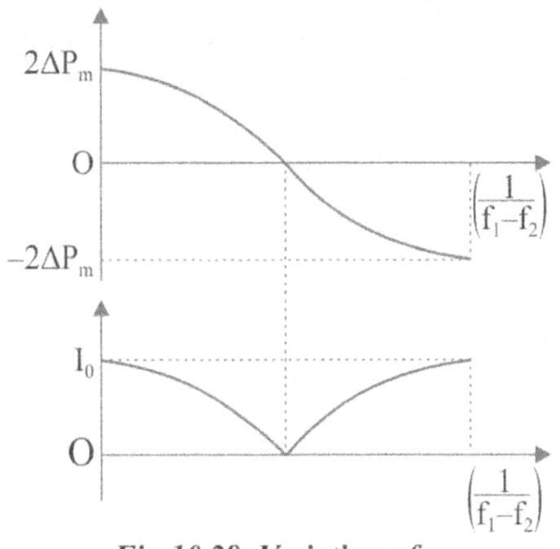

Fig.10.29. Variation of pressure amplitude and intensity of resulting sound wave.

Facts to know :

1. Why does a tuning fork have two prongs? Would the tuning fork be of any use, if one of the prongs is cut off ?

   When a tuning fork is set into vibrations, its two prongs vibrate in opposite phases. One prong of the fork is forced to vibrate by the other and vice-versa. Hence by holding its stem in the hand, a tuning fork can be set into vibrations and no external force is required to maintain its vibrations.

   If one of the prongs is cut-off, the vibrations of the tuning fork will soon die out and can be maintained only by some external periodic force.

2. What is difference between a tone and a note?

   A sound of single frequency is called a tone. A combination of tones of different frequencies is called a note.

3. What will be the speed of sound in a perfectly rigid rod?

   The Young's modulus of elasticity of a perfectly rigid rod is infinite, so speed of sound in the rod will be infinite.

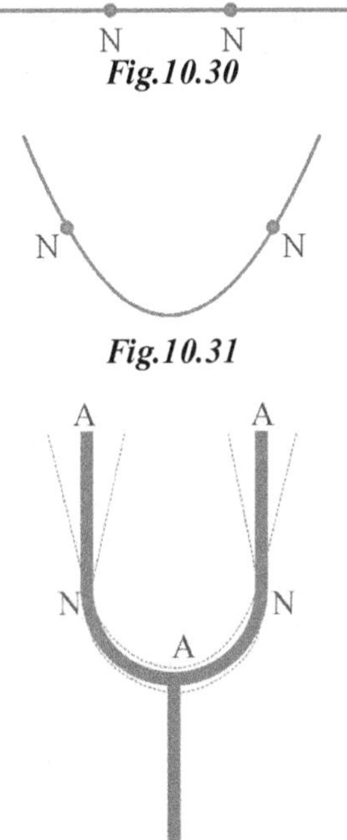

Fig.10.30

Fig.10.31

Fig.10.32

Determination of frequency of tuning fork by using beats :

Suppose a tuning fork A of known frequency f_A and fork B of unknown frequency f_B. When the two forks are sounded together, they produce f_b beats per second. Then

$$f_B = f_A + f_b \text{ or } f_A - f_b$$

The correct frequency may be determined by any of the following two methods :

(a) **Loading method :** Put the little wax to the prong of the fork B (decreases the frequency of B) and again note the number of beats per second. If the beats frequency decreases on loading the prong of the fork B of unknown in frequency, then its frequency is given by

$$f_B = f_A + f_b$$

On the other hand, if the beats frequency increases after loading, then

$$f_B = f_A - f_b$$

(b) **Filing method :** If the prong of the tuning form B is filed, its frequency increases. Again, note the number of beats per second. If on filing the prong of B, the beat frequency decreases, then

$$f_B = f_A - f_b$$

On the other hand, if beat frequency increases on filing, then $f_B = f_A + f_b$.

Ex. 13 A tuning fork of unknown frequency gives 4 beats with a tuning fork of frequency 310 Hz. It gives the same number of beats on filing. Find the unknown frequency.

Sol.

The unknown frequency of the tuning fork can be

$$= 310 \pm 4$$

or $\qquad\qquad f = 314$ or 306 Hz

Suppose $\qquad\qquad f = 314$ Hz

On filing, let it becomes $\qquad = 318$ Hz.

When it sounded together with a fork of frequency 310 Hz, beats frequency will be more than 4 per second. Therefore unknown frequency can not be 314 Hz.

Now suppose $\qquad\qquad f = 306$ Hz.

On filing, let it becomes $\qquad = 314$ Hz.

When it sounded again with a fork of frequency 310 Hz it gives 4 beats per second. So unknown frequency must be 306 Hz.

Ex. 14 When a tuning fork A of unknown frequency is sounded with another tuning fork B of frequency 256 Hz, 3 beats per second are observed. After that A is loaded with wax and sounded, the beat frequency decreases. Find the frequency of the tuning fork A.

Sol.

The frequency of the fork B can be

$$= 256 \pm 3 \text{ Hz}$$
$$= 259 \text{ Hz or } 253 \text{ Hz}$$

Suppose the frequency of the fork B

$$= 259 \text{ Hz}$$

On loading, its frequency let becomes

$$= 257 \text{ Hz}.$$

Now it will give less number of beats with the fork B. So the frequency of fork A must be 259 Hz.

Ex. 15 A set of 56 tuning forks are arranged in series of increasing frequencies. Each fork gives 4 beats/s with preceding one. If the frequency of last fork is 2 times that of the first, what is the frequency of 40th fork?

Sol.

Suppose the frequency of the first fork is f, then frequency of the last fork

$$= f + (56 - 1) \times 4 = f + 220$$

Given $\qquad (f + 220) = 2f$

$\therefore \qquad\qquad f = 220$ Hz $\qquad\qquad$ ***Ans.***

Now the frequency of the 40th fork

$$= f + (40 - 1) \times 4$$
$$= 220 + 39 \times 4$$
$$= 376 \text{ Hz} \qquad\qquad \textbf{\textit{Ans.}}$$

Ex. 16 There are three sources of sound of equal intensities with frequency $(f - 1), f, (f + 1)$ Hz. What is the beat frequency heard if all the sources are switched on simultaneously ?

Sol.

Let following are the waves (at $x = 0$) produced by the sources

$$y_1 = A \sin 2\pi(f - 1)t$$

$$y_2 = A \sin 2\pi f t$$

and $\qquad\qquad y_3 = A \sin 2\pi(f + 1)t$

According to the principle of superposition of waves, we have

$$y = y_1 + y_2 + y_3$$
$$= A[\sin 2\pi(f - 1)t + \sin 2\pi f t + \sin 2\pi(f + 1)t]$$
$$= A[\sin 2\pi(f - 1)t + \sin 2\pi(f + 1)t + \sin 2\pi f t]$$
$$= 2A \sin \frac{\{2\pi(f - 1)t + 2\pi(f + 1)t\}}{2}$$
$$\cos \frac{\{2\pi(f - 1)t - 2\pi(f + 1)t\}}{2} + A \sin 2\pi f t$$
$$= 2A \sin(2\pi f t).\cos(2\pi t) + A \sin(2\pi f t)$$
$$= [2A \cos(2\pi t) + A]\sin(2\pi f t)$$
$$= R \sin(2\pi f t)$$

where $\qquad R = [2A \cos(2\pi t) + A]$

The intensity of the wave, $\qquad I \propto R^2$

$$\propto [2A \cos(2\pi t) + A]^2$$

The intensity of the resulting wave is maximum or minimum,

if $\dfrac{dI}{dt} = 0$

or $\qquad 2[2\cos(2\pi t) + 1] \times [-2\sin(2\pi t) \times 2\pi] = 0$

which gives either,

$$2\cos(2\pi t) + 1 = 0$$

or $\qquad\qquad \sin(2\pi t) = 0$

or $\qquad\qquad \cos(2\pi t) = -1/2$

or $\qquad\qquad 2\pi t = n\pi$

or $\qquad\qquad 2\pi t = 2\pi n \pm \dfrac{2\pi}{3}$

or $\qquad\qquad t = \dfrac{n}{2}$

or $\qquad\qquad t = n \pm \dfrac{1}{3}$, where $n = 0, 1, 2, 3,$

where $\qquad\qquad n = 0, 1, 2, 3$

$\therefore \qquad\qquad t = \dfrac{1}{3}, \dfrac{2}{3}, \dfrac{4}{3}, \dfrac{5}{3}, \dfrac{7}{3}, ...$

$\therefore \qquad\qquad t = 0, \dfrac{1}{2}, 1, \dfrac{3}{2}, 2, ...$

As $\qquad\qquad R = A[2\cos(2\pi t) + 1]$

As $\qquad\qquad \sin(2\pi t) = 0$

$\therefore \qquad\qquad I = 0$

$\therefore \qquad \cos(2\pi t) = \pm\sqrt{1 - \sin^2(2\pi t)} = \pm 1$

$$I = A[2\cos 2\pi t + 1]^2$$
$$= A[2 \times (\pm 1) + 1]^2$$
$$= 9A^2, A^2, 9A^2, A^2, ...$$

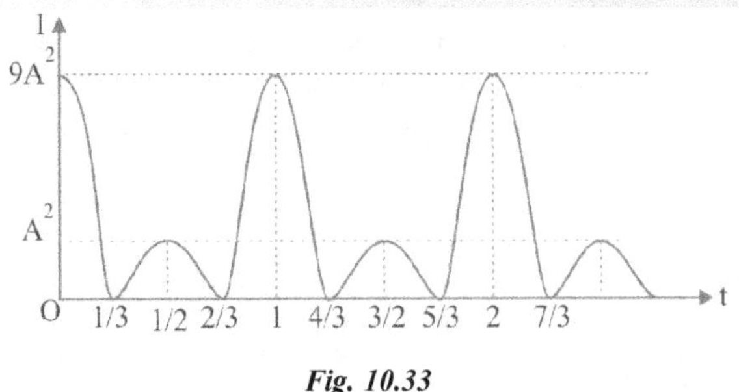

Fig. 10.33

Clearly in 1 second there are two maximas and two minimas, so beat frequency = 2 per second.

Note:

In practice the intensity A^2 in comparison to $9A^2$ is not noticeable, and therefore can be neglected. Then beat frequency in this case will be 1 beat/s.

10.7 STATIONARY WAVES

When two identical waves of same frequency travel in opposite directions with the same speed along the same path superpose each other give rise to a new wave. The resultant wave does not travel in the either direction and therefore is called **stationary or standing wave**.

The resultant wave oscillates in the same fixed position. Some particles of the medium remain permanently at rest. Their positions are called nodes. Some other particles always have maximum displacement. Their positions are called **antinode.** The positions of **nodes** and antinode do not change with time. In stationary waves, there is no transfer of energy along the medium in either direction.

Necessary condition for formation of stationary waves :

In particle a stationary wave is formed when a progressive wave and its reflected wave are superposed. So a stationary wave can be produced only in a medium which has its boundary. Two independent waves from opposite directions can not produce stationary wave.

Two types of stationary waves :

(i) **Transverse stationary wave :** When two identical transverse wave travelling in opposite directions superpose, a transverse stationary wave is formed. Example: Waves in stretched string fixed between two supports.

(ii) **Longitudinal stationary waves :** When two identical longitudinal waves travelling in opposite direction superpose, a longitudinal stationary wave is formed Example : Waves in organ pipes, waves in Kundt's tube etc.

Formation of stationary waves

Figure shows the two combing waves, one travelling to the right fig (a) the other to the left fig (b) Figure (c) shows the resultant stationary waves, obtained by using the superposition principle graphically.

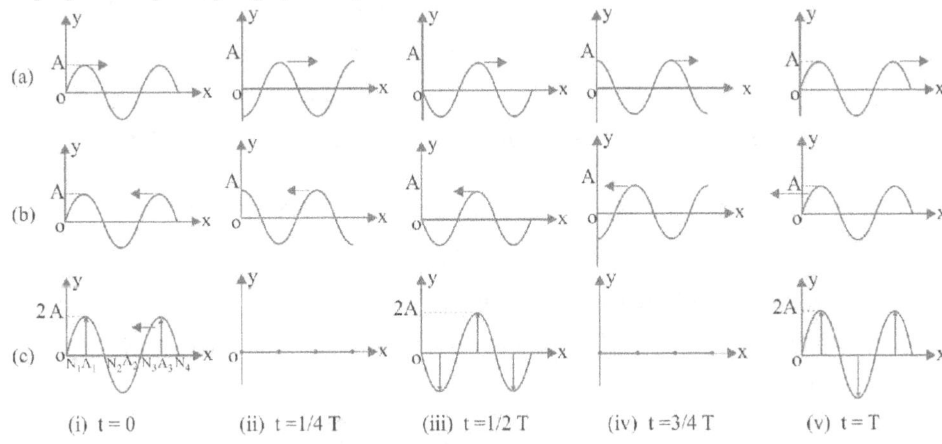

Fig. 10.34

(i)   At $t = 0$, the two waves superpose in same phase, so the amplitude of the resultant wave $(2A)$ is twice the amplitude of individual wave (A). All the particles are at their positions of maximum displacement. These position are called antinodes [fig (i)].

(ii)   At $t = \dfrac{T}{4}$, each wave has moved a distance of $\lambda/4$ in their respective direction.

The two waves now superpose in opposite phase. The amplitude of resultant wave becomes zero. All the particles of the medium are now passing through their mean position [fig (ii)].

(iii)   At $t = \dfrac{T}{2}$, each wave has moved a distance $\lambda/2$ in their respective direction. The two waves are again in same phase, so the amplitude of the resultant wave is $(-2A)$. All the particles at their positions of maximum displacement but in the direction opposite to those at $t = 0$ [fig. (iii)].

(iv)   At $t = \dfrac{3T}{4}$, each wave has moved a distance $\dfrac{3\lambda}{4}$ in their respective directions.

The two waves now again in opposite phase, so that the amplitude of resultant wave becomes zero. All the particles now again passing through their mean positions, but their directions of motion are opposite to those at $t = \dfrac{T}{4}$ (fig. iv).

(v)   At $t = T$, each wave has moved a distance λ in their respective directions. The two waves are again in same phase, so the amplitude of resultant wave is $2A$. This complete one cycle [fig (v)].

The whole cycle continues to repeat again and again. In the superposition of two identical waves from opposite directions, there are some particles are called antinodes. The positions $A_1, A_2, A_3, \ldots\ldots$ are **antinodes**. The positions N_1, N_2, N_3 $\ldots\ldots$ where the amplitude of oscillation is zero are called **nodes**. Clearly the distance between two consecutive nodes or antinodes is $\lambda/2$. The distance between node and the next antinode is $\lambda/4$.

Analytical Treatment of stationary waves

Reflection from fixed boundary:

Consider two identical waves travelling from opposite directions

$$y_1 \quad = \quad A\sin(kx - \omega t) \qquad \ldots(1)$$

and
$$y_2 \quad = \quad A\sin(kx + \omega t) \qquad \ldots(2)$$

According to the principle of superposition, the resultant wave is given by

$$y \quad = \quad y_1 + y_2$$
$$= \quad A\sin(kx - \omega t) + A\sin(kx + \omega t)$$

or
$$y \quad = \quad [2A\sin kx]\cos \omega t \qquad \ldots(3)$$

The equation does not represent a progressive wave because it does not contain the combination like $(kx \pm \omega t)$. Instead, it describes a stationary wave of frequency ω and amplitude

$$R \quad = \quad 2A\sin kx.$$

Clearly the amplitude of oscillation is not same for all the particles of the medium. It varies harmonically with the location x of the particle.

Change in R with x at any time t :

The amplitude of the stationary wave will be zero at points, where

$$\sin kx = 0$$

or

$$kx = n\pi$$

or

$$\frac{2\pi}{\lambda}x = n\pi$$

$$\therefore \qquad x = n\frac{\lambda}{2}, \text{where } n = 0, 1, 2, 3, ...$$

or

$$x = 0, \frac{\lambda}{2}, \lambda, ...$$

The positions of zero amplitude are called nodes the distance between two consecutive nodes is $\lambda/2$.

The amplitude of the stationary wave will have a maximum value of $2A$ at points, where

$$\sin kx = \pm 1$$

or

$$kx = (2n+1)\frac{\pi}{2}$$

or

$$\frac{2\pi}{\lambda}x = (2n+1)\frac{\pi}{2}$$

$$\therefore \qquad x = (2n+1)\frac{\lambda}{4}, \text{where } n = 0, 1, 2, 3, ...$$

or

$$x = \frac{\lambda}{4}, \frac{3\lambda}{4}, \frac{5\lambda}{4}, ...$$

These positions of maximum amplitude are called antinodes.

Clearly the distance between two consecutive antinodes is $\lambda/2$.

Change in R of any particle at x with time :

At the instant $t = 0, T/2, 3T/2, ...$

$$\cos\omega t = \cos\frac{2\pi}{T}t = \pm 1 .$$

Thus at these instants the displacement y becomes alternately positive and negative. That is, all the particles of the medium pass through their positions of maximum displacements twice in each cycle.

At the instant $t = T/4, 3T/4, 5T/4, ...$

$$\cos\omega t = \cos\frac{2\pi}{T}\,t = 0$$

Thus at these instants the displacement y becomes zero at all the points. That is all the particles of the medium pass through their mean positions simultaneously twice in each cycle.

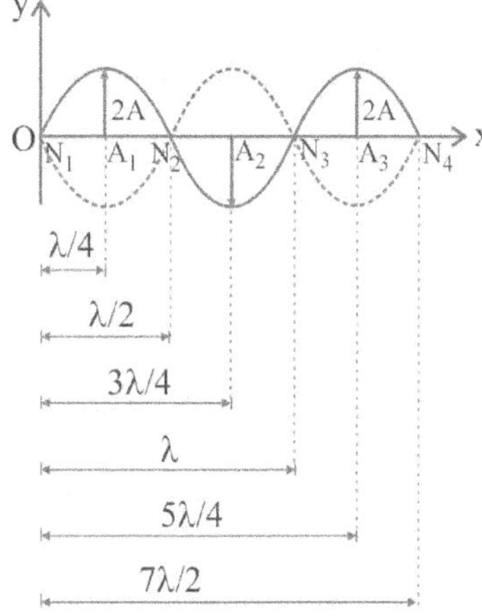

Fig. 10.35

Characteristics of stationary waves

(i)   In a stationary wave, the disturbance does not move in any direction. The conditions of crests and troughs merely appear and disappear in fixed positions to be followed by opposite conditions after every $T/2$.

(ii)   All the particles of the medium, except those at nodes, execute simple harmonic motions with the period of the wave about their mean position.

(iii)   During the formation of a stationary wave, the medium is broken into loops between equally spaced points called nodes which remain at rest and in between them are points of maximum displacement called antinodes.

(iv)   The amplitudes of the particles are different at different points. The amplitude varies gradually from zero at the nodes to the maximum at the antinodes.

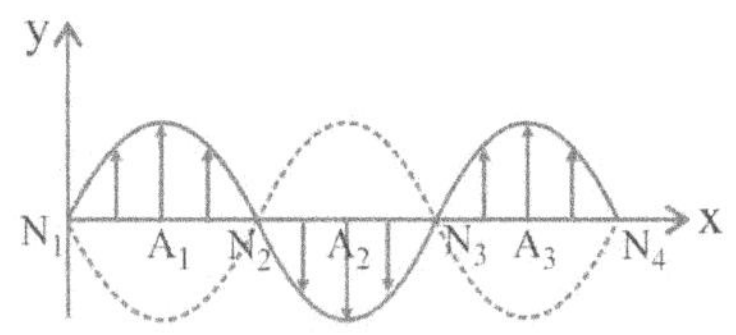

Fig.10.36. Opposite phases of the particles in consecutive segments.

(v) The maximum velocity is different at different points. Its value is zero at the nodes and gradually increases towards the antinode. All the particles attain their maximum velocities simultaneously when they pass through their mean positions.

(vi) All the particles in a particular segment between two nodes vibrate in the same phase but the particles in the neighbouring segments vibrate in opposite phases, as shown in figure.

(vii) The energy becomes alternately wholly potential and wholly kinetic in twice in each cycle. It is wholly potential when particles are at their positions of maximum displacement and wholly kinetic when the particle pass through the mean positions.

(viii) A stationary wave has the same wavelength and time period as the component waves.

(ix) The distance between two consecutive nodes and antinodes is $\lambda/2$. The distance between node and next antinode is $\lambda/4$.

Ex. 17 Consider the following wave functions :

(a) $y = A\sin(\omega t - kx)$,

(b) $y = A\sin(kx - \omega t)$,

(c) $y = A\cos(\omega t - kx)$,

(d) $y = A\cos(kx - \omega t)$,

(e) $y = A\sin(\omega t + kx)$,

(f) $y = A\cos(\omega t + kx)$.

Write the equations of reflected wave after reflection from a free and a fixed boundary. Also find the resulting stationary waves formed by the superposition of its reflected wave.

Sol.

	Incident wave $\omega = \dfrac{2\pi}{T}, k = \dfrac{2\pi}{\lambda}$	Reflected wave from free boundary, $\phi = 0$	Reflected wave from fixed boundary, $\phi = \pi$
(a)	$y = A\sin(\omega t - kx)$	$y = A\sin(\omega t + kx)$	$y = A\sin(\omega t + kx + \pi)$ $= -A\sin(\omega t + kx)$
(b)	$y = A\sin(kx - \omega t)$	$y = A\sin(-kx - \omega t)$ $= -A\sin(kx + \omega t)$	$y = A\sin(-kx - \omega t + \pi)$ $= A\sin(kx + \omega t)$
(c)	$y = A\cos(\omega t - kx)$	$y = A\cos(\omega t + kx)$	$y = A\cos(\omega t + kx + \pi)$ $= -A\cos(\omega t + kx)$
(d)	$y = A\cos(kx - \omega t)$	$y = A\cos(-kx - \omega t)$ $= A\cos(kx + \omega t)$	$y = A\cos(-kx - \omega t + \pi)$ $= -A\cos(kx + \omega t)$
(e)	$y = A\sin(\omega t + kx)$	$y = A\sin(\omega t - kx)$	$y = A\sin(\omega t - kx + \pi)$ $= -A\sin(\omega t - kx)$
(f)	$y = A\cos(\omega t + kx)$	$y = A\cos(\omega t - kx)$	$y = A\cos(\omega t - kx + \pi)$ $= -A\cos(\omega t - kx)$

(a)   Stationary wave by superposition of

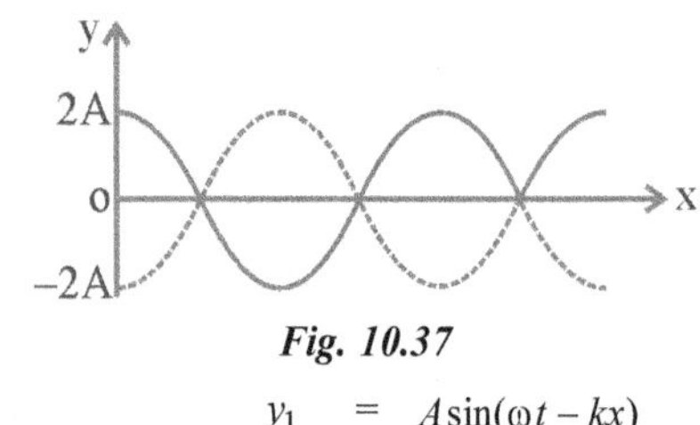

Fig. 10.37

$$y_1 = A\sin(\omega t - kx)$$

and

$$y_2 = A\sin(\omega t + kx)$$

$$y = y_1 + y_2$$

$$= A[\sin(\omega t - kx) + \sin(\omega t + kx)]$$

$$= 2A\cos kx \sin \omega t$$

The similar treatment can be done for other combination of waves to get stationary wave.

Ex. 18 The constituent waves of a stationary wave have amplitude, frequency and velocity as 10 cm, 50 Hz and 200 cm/s respectively. Write down the equation of the stationary wave for $x = 0$, there is antinode.

Sol. For the given condition, the equation of stationary wave is

$$y = 2A\cos kx \sin \omega t$$

$$= 2A\cos\frac{2\pi x}{\lambda}.\sin 2\pi ft.$$

Here $\lambda = \dfrac{v}{f} = \dfrac{200}{50} = 4$ cm and $A = 10$ cm

$$\therefore \quad y = 2 \times 10 \cos\frac{2\pi x}{4}\sin 2\pi \times 50t$$

$$= 20\cos\frac{\pi x}{2}\sin 100\pi t \; cm \;. \quad \textbf{\textit{Ans.}}$$

Ex. 19 The transverse displacement of string (clamped at its two ends) is given by

$$y(x,t) = 0.06\sin\left(\frac{2\pi x}{3}\right)\cos(120\pi t)$$

where x, y are in m and t in s. The length of the string is 1.5 m and its mass is 3.0×10^{-2} kg. Answer the following:
(a) Does the function represent a travelling or a stationary wave?
(b) Interpret the wave as a superposition of two waves travelling in opposite directions. What are the wavelength, frequency and speed of propagation of each wave?
(c) Determine the tension in the string.

Sol.

(a) The given equation

$$y(x,t) = 0.06\sin\left(\frac{2\pi x}{3}\right)\cos(120\pi t) \quad ...(i)$$

represents a stationary wave because it is the product of two separate harmonic functions of x and t.

(b) Suppose two waves

$$y_1 = A\sin\frac{2\pi}{\lambda}(x - vt)$$

and other reflected from fixed boundary

$$y_2 = A\sin\left[\frac{2\pi}{\lambda}(-x - vt) + \pi\right]$$

$$= A\sin\frac{2\pi}{\lambda}(x + vt)$$

By principle of superposition,

$$y = y_1 + y_2 = A\sin\frac{2\pi}{\lambda}(x - vt) + A\sin\frac{2\pi}{\lambda}(x + vt)$$

or

$$y = 2A\sin\frac{2\pi x}{\lambda}\cos\frac{2\pi}{\lambda}(vt) \quad ...(ii)$$

Comparing the equations (i) and (ii), we get

$$\lambda = 3m$$

and $\dfrac{2\pi v}{\lambda} = 120\pi$ or $v = 60\lambda = 60 \times 3 = 180$ m/s

Frequency $\quad f = \dfrac{v}{\lambda} = \dfrac{180}{3} = 60$ Hz.

(c) The speed of the transverse wave in the string is given by

$$v = \mathrm{v} = \sqrt{\frac{F}{\mu}}$$

$$\therefore \quad F = F = \mathrm{v}^2\mu$$

Here $\quad \mu = \dfrac{3.0 \times 10^{-2}}{1.5}$

$$= 2 \times 10^{-2}\,\text{kg/m}, \, v = 180 \text{ m/s}$$

$$F = 180^2 \times 2 \times 10^{-2} = 648 \text{ N} \quad \textbf{\textit{Ans.}}$$

Note:

1. When two waves of same frequency but different amplitudes travel from opposite directions, a stationary wave is formed. In this case there is no nodes but there are position of minimum amplitude.

$$A_{max} = A_1 + A_2$$
$$A_{min} = A_1 - A_2$$

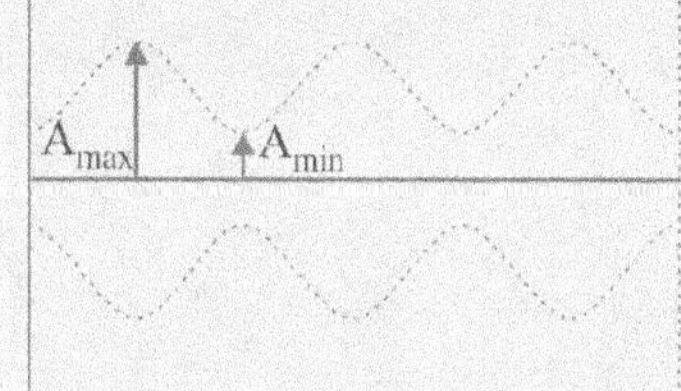

Fig. 10.38

2. All harmonics are overtones but all overtones are not harmonics. Overtones which are non-integral multiples of the fundamental are not harmonics. For fundamental frequency 200 Hz, 300 Hz is overtone but not harmonic.

3. The property of a device to reproduce the original sound in all its details is called fidelity of an instrument.

Difference between progressive and stationary waves

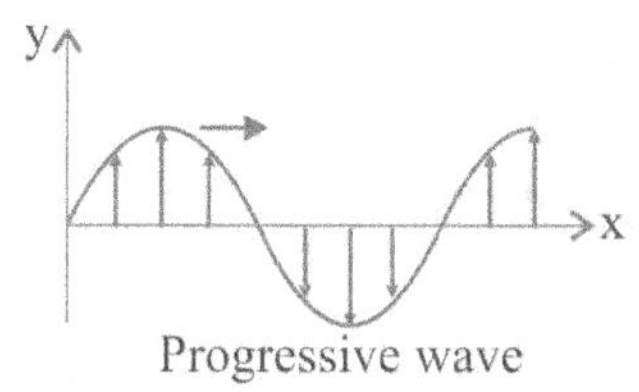
Progressive wave

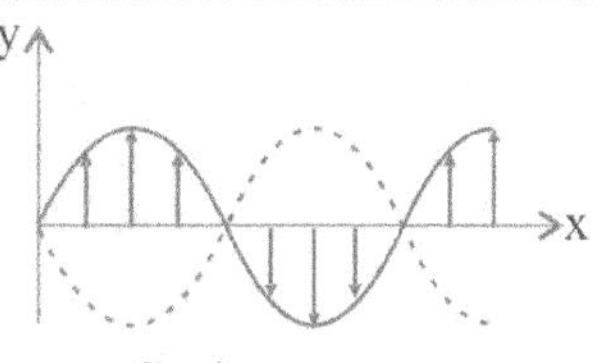
Stationary wave

Progressive wave	Stationary wave
1. The disturbance move forward with a definite speed.	1. The disturbance remain confined at its place.
2. Each particle of the medium executes SHM about its mean position with the same amplitude.	2. Except nodes, all the particles of the medium execute SHM with varying amplitude.
3. No particle of the medium is permanently at rest.	3. The particles of the medium at nodes are at rest.
4. There is continuous phase change from particle to particle.	4. All the particles between two successive nodes vibrate in same phase.
5. There is no instant when all the particles are at the mean position together.	5. All particles of the medium pass through mean position twice during each cycle.
6. There is transfer of energy from one place to another.	6. Energy of the disturbance remain confined in that region.
7. The energy averaged over one cycle is half kinetic and half potential.	7. The energy becomes alternately wholly kinetic and wholly potential twice in a cycle.

10.8 Stationary Waves in Stretched String Fixed at the Ends

Qualitative discussion : Consider a string under tension, fixed at both ends and lying along the x-axis. If the string is plucked at any point, two identical waves start from the point in opposite directions. After reflection from the fixed ends, these waves produce stationary waves. By plucking the string at different suitable points, it can be set into different modes of vibration.

Consider a string of length L under tension F. Let μ be the mass per unit length of the string. The speed of the transverse wave on the string

$$v = \sqrt{\frac{F}{\mu}}.$$

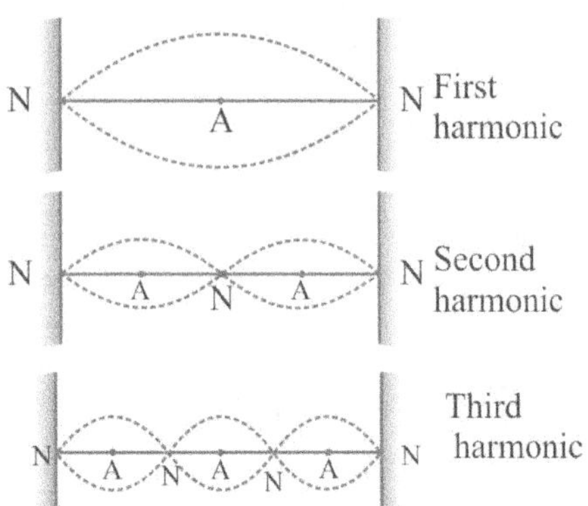

Fig. 10.39. Different modes of vibration of stretched string

As the two ends of the string are fixed, so there is a node N at each end.

First mode of vibration : If the string is plucked in the middle, it vibrates in one segment, giving its lowest or fundamental notes.

Here

$$L = \frac{\lambda_1}{2} \text{ or } \lambda_1 = 2L$$

Frequency of vibration

$$f_1 = \frac{v}{\lambda_1} = \frac{1}{2L}\sqrt{\frac{F}{\mu}} = f$$

This is the first harmonic.

Second mode of vibration : If the string is pressed in the middle and plucked at the mid-point of either half, then the string vibrates in two segments.

Here

$$L = \frac{\lambda_2}{2} + \frac{\lambda_2}{2}$$

or

$$\lambda_2 = L$$

Frequency of vibration

$$f_2 = \frac{v}{\lambda_2} = \frac{1}{L}\sqrt{\frac{F}{\mu}}$$

$$= \frac{2}{2L}\sqrt{\frac{F}{\mu}}$$

$$= 2f$$

This frequency is called first overtone or second harmonic.

Third mode of vibration : If the string is pressed at one-third of its length and plucked at the middle of the smaller length, it vibrates in three segments.

Here

$$L = \frac{\lambda_3}{2} + \frac{\lambda_3}{2} + \frac{\lambda_3}{2}$$

or

$$\lambda_3 = \frac{2L}{3}$$

Frequency of vibration

$$f_3 = \frac{v}{\lambda_3} = \frac{3}{2L}\sqrt{\frac{F}{\mu}}$$

$$= 3f$$

This frequency is called second overtone or third harmonic.

In general, if the string vibrates in P segments (loops), then

$$f_p = \frac{P}{2L}\sqrt{\frac{F}{\mu}} = Pf$$

Analytical treatment : Consider a uniform string of length L under tension F lying along the x-axis, with its ends fixed at $x = 0$ and $x = L$. Suppose a transverse wave produced in the string travels along the string along positive x-direction and get reflected at the fixed end $x = L$. The two waves can be represented as

$$y_1 = A\sin(kx - \omega t)$$

and
$$y_2 = A\sin(-kx - \omega t + \pi)$$

$$= A\sin(kx + \omega t)$$

The resultant wave is given by

$$y = y_1 + y_2$$
$$= A\sin(kx - \omega t) + A\sin(kx + \omega t)$$

or
$$y = 2A\sin(kx)\cos(\omega t) \qquad \ldots(1)$$

The ends $x = 0$ and $x = L$ are fixed, so they must be nodes. The boundary conditions are:

$$x = 0, \quad y = 0 \quad \text{for all } t$$

and
$$x = L, \quad y = 0 \quad \text{for all } t$$

The first boundary condition is satisfied automatically by the equation (1). The second boundary conditions will be satisfied if

$$y = 2A\sin(kL)\cos\omega t = 0$$

This will true for all values of t only if

$$\sin kL = 0$$

or
$$kL = n\pi, \text{ where } n = 0, 1, 2, \ldots\ldots$$

or
$$\frac{2\pi}{\lambda}L = n\pi$$

$\therefore$
$$\lambda = \frac{2L}{n} \qquad \ldots(2)$$

The frequency of vibration of the string in its nth mode

$$f_n = \frac{n}{2L}\sqrt{\frac{F}{\mu}} \qquad \ldots(3)$$

By putting $x = 1, 2, 3, \ldots\ldots\ldots$, the first, second, third, ... harmonics will be obtained, whose frequencies are in the ratio $1 : 2 : 3 : \ldots\ldots$. The first harmonic is called fundamental note. The higher harmonics are called overtones. Thus second harmonic is first overtone, third harmonic is second overtones and so on.

Nodes : In the nth mode of vibration, there are $(n + 1)$ nodes (see figure), their position from $x = 0$ end are :

$$x = 0, \frac{L}{n}, \frac{2L}{n}, \ldots\ldots, L$$

Antinodes : In the nth mode of vibration, there are n antinodes, their positions from $x = 0$ end are :

$$x = \frac{L}{2n}, \frac{3L}{2n}, \frac{5L}{2n}, \ldots\ldots\ldots\frac{(2n-1)L}{2n}.$$

Strain : It is defined by $\dfrac{dy}{dx}$.

$\therefore$
$$\text{Strain} = \frac{dy}{dx} = \frac{d}{dx}[2A\sin(kx)\cos(\omega t)]$$

$$= 2Ak\cos(kx)\cos(\omega t)$$

The strain is maximum for all values of t, for which

$$\cos kx \;=\; \pm 1 \text{ or } kx = n\pi$$

or

$$\frac{2\pi}{\lambda}x \;=\; n\pi$$

$$x \;=\; n\frac{\lambda}{2}, x = n\frac{\lambda}{2}, \text{ where } n = 0, 1, 2, 3, \ldots\ldots$$

$$\therefore \qquad x \;=\; 0, \lambda/2, \lambda, 3\lambda/2, \ldots\ldots$$

These points are nodes. Thus strain is maximum at nodes and minimum at antinodes.

Melde's experiment

The set up consists of a string which can be vibrated by an electrically maintained tuning fork. The tension in the string is produced by hanging a load on the free end of the string. There are two modes of vibration.

(i)   **Transverse mode of vibration:** In this case tuning fork vibrates perpendicular to the length of the string. The frequency of vibration of the string is equal to the frequency of the tuning fork. If f is the frequency of the tuning fork, then

$$f \;=\; \frac{P_1}{2L}\sqrt{\frac{F}{\mu}} \qquad\qquad \ldots(1)$$

where P_1 is the number of loops.

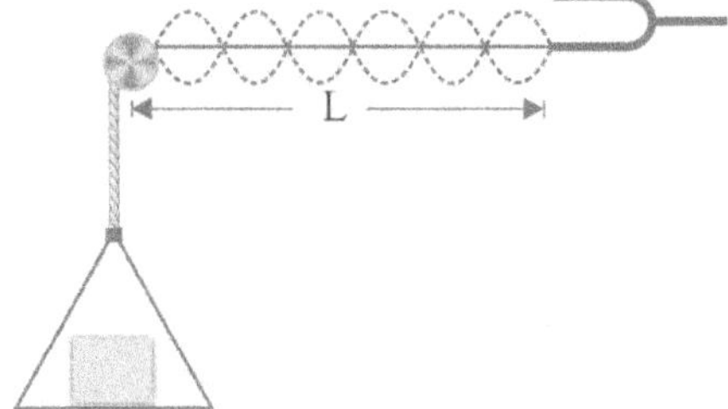

Fig. 10.40. Transverse mode of vibration of string.

(ii)   **Longitudinal mode of vibration :** In this case tuning fork vibrates along the length of the string. In one complete vibration of the tuning fork, string completes half vibration. Thus, if f is the frequency of tuning fork, then

$$\frac{f}{2} \;=\; \frac{P_2}{2L}\sqrt{\frac{F}{\mu}} \qquad\qquad \ldots(2)$$

where P_2 is the number of loops.

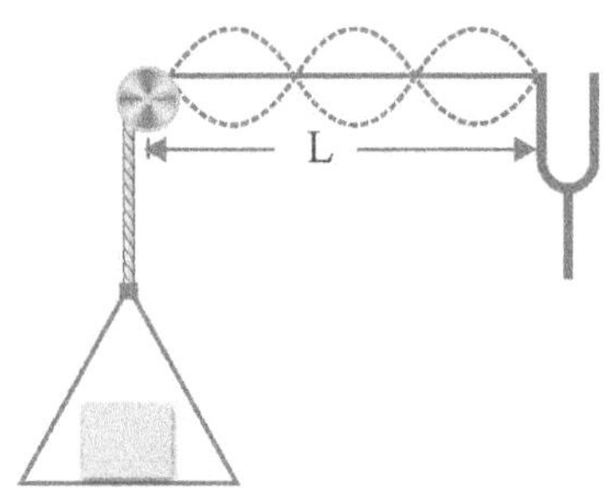

Fig. 10.41. Longitudinal mode of vibration of string.

For the same tension in the string in both the modes of vibration and for equal length of the string we have

$$P_2 \;=\; \frac{P_1}{2} \qquad\qquad \ldots(3)$$

From equation (1), $FP_1^2 \;=\; 4f^2 L^2 \mu = \text{constant}$

From equation (2), $FP_2^2 \;=\; f^2 L^2 \mu = \text{constant}$

Thus $FP^2 \;=\; \text{Constant.} \qquad\qquad \ldots(4)$

Ex. 20 Find the tension needed to produce stationary waves with four loops in a string one metre long and 0.5 g in weight, fixed to a tuning fork of frequency 200 Hz, when the prongs of the fork are vibrating perpendicular to the string.

Sol.   If string vibrates in P loops, then

$$f \;=\; \frac{P}{2L}\sqrt{\frac{F}{\mu}}$$

or $$F \;=\; \frac{4L^2 f^2 \mu}{P^2}$$

$$= \; \frac{4 \times 1^2 \times 200^2 \times \left(\dfrac{0.5 \times 10^{-3}}{1}\right)}{4^2} = 5 \text{ N } \textbf{\textit{Ans.}}$$

Ex. 21 In Melde's experiment, when a string is stretched by a piece of glass it vibrate with 7 loops. When the glass piece is completely immersed in water the string vibrates in 9 loops what is the specific gravity of glass?

Sol.

If F_1 and F_2 are the tensions in the string in the two cases, then

$$F_1 P_1^2 \;=\; F_2 P_2^2$$

or $$\frac{F_1}{F_2} \;=\; \frac{P_2^2}{P_1^2} = \frac{9^2}{7^2}$$

$$= \; \frac{81}{49}$$

If F_b is the buoyant force on the glass piece, then

$$F_b \;=\; F_1 - F_2$$

The resultant stationary wave is given by

$$\Delta P = \Delta P_1 + \Delta P_2$$
$$= \Delta P_m \sin(kx - \omega t) + \Delta P_m \sin(kx + \omega t)$$

or
$$\Delta P = 2\Delta P_m \sin(kx)\cos(\omega t)$$

For all values of t, the resultant pressure variation is zero, for which

$$\sin kx = 0$$
or
$$kx = n\pi$$

or
$$\frac{2\pi}{\lambda}x = n\pi$$

$$x = \frac{n\lambda}{2}, \text{ where } n = 0, 1, 2, 3, ...$$

$$\therefore \quad x = 0, \frac{\lambda}{2}, \lambda, \frac{3\lambda}{2}, ...$$

These points of zero pressure variation are called **pressure nodes.**

On the other hand, the pressure variation is maximum for all values of t, for which

$$\sin kx = \pm 1$$

or
$$kx = (2n+1)\frac{\pi}{2}$$

or
$$\frac{2\pi}{\lambda}x = (2n+1)\frac{\pi}{2}$$

$$x = (2n+1)\frac{\lambda}{4}, \text{ where } n = 0, 1, 2, 3, ...$$

$$\therefore \quad x = \frac{\lambda}{4}, \frac{3\lambda}{4}, \frac{5\lambda}{4}, ...$$

These points of maximum pressure variation are called **pressure antinodes.**

Note:

1. If P_0 is the normal pressure in the pipe, then at the positions of pressure nodes, the pressure will be P_0 and at the positions of pressure antinodes, it will be $P_0 \pm 2\Delta P_m$ or $P_0 \pm 2ABk$. Thus pressure at antinodes varies from $P_0 - 2ABk$ to $P_0 + 2ABk$.

2. The loud sound is heard at pressure antinode or displacement node.

Strain : We know that bulk modulus of medium (air) is

$$B = \frac{dP}{\left(-\dfrac{dV}{V}\right)} = \frac{dP}{(-dy/dx)}$$

$$\therefore \quad \text{strain} = \frac{dy}{dx} = -\frac{dP}{B}$$

$$= -\frac{\Delta P}{B}$$

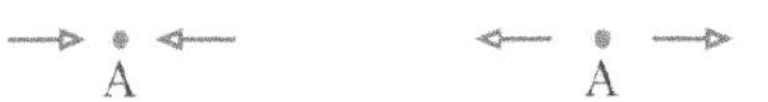

Fig.10.46. Positions of maximum strain.

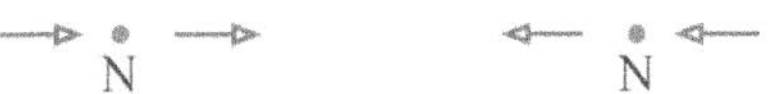

Fig.10.47. Positions of zero strain.

As ΔP is maximum $(\pm 2\Delta P_m)$ at the antinodes, so strain (positive or negative) at the pressure antinodes and zero at pressure nodes.

At antinodes due to the compressions or the rarefactions of the oppositely travelling waves, the strain becomes maximum. At nodes strain becomes zero due to the compression of one wave coming across the rarefaction of the other, as shown in figure.

End corrections : Till now we have assumed that node/ antinode is formed just at the open end. Lord Rayleigh showed that due to inertia the vibrating particles form node/ antinode little above the open end of the pipe. So an end correction is applied which is approximately $e = 0.61\,r$, where r is the radius of the pipe. Thus,

for close organ pipe, the effective length $\quad L_e = L + e$,

for open organ pipe, the effective length $\quad L_e = L + 2e$.

Close organ pipe

Fig. 10.48, shows the various modes of vibration in the form of displacement and pressure waves.

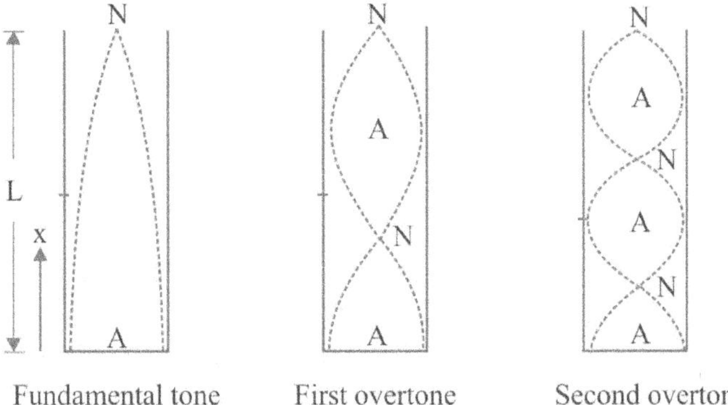

Fig.10.48. Various modes of vibration of close organ pipe showing pressure nodes and antinodes.

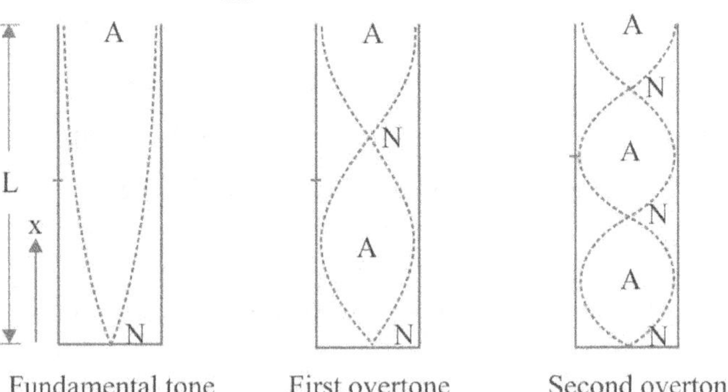

Fig.10.49 Various modes of vibration of close organ pipe showing displacement nodes and antinodes.

(i)   **First mode of vibration :** In this mode of vibration

$$L = \frac{\lambda_1}{4} \text{ or } \lambda_1 = 4L$$

Frequency, $\qquad\qquad f_1 = \frac{v}{\lambda_1} = \frac{1}{4L}\sqrt{\frac{\gamma P}{\rho}} = f\,(\text{say})$

This frequency is called first harmonic or fundamental note.

(ii) **Second mode of vibration :** In this mode of vibration

$$L = \frac{\lambda_2}{2} + \frac{\lambda_2}{4} = \frac{3\lambda_2}{4}$$

or

$$\lambda_2 = \frac{4L}{3}$$

Frequency

$$f_2 = \frac{v}{\lambda_2} = \frac{3}{4L}\sqrt{\frac{\gamma P}{\rho}} = 3f$$

(iii) **Third mode of vibration :** In this mode of vibration

$$L = \frac{\lambda_3}{2} + \frac{\lambda_3}{2} + \frac{\lambda_3}{4} = \frac{5\lambda_3}{4}$$

or

$$\lambda_3 = \frac{4L}{5}$$

Frequency ,

$$f_3 = \frac{v}{\lambda_3} = \frac{5}{4L}\sqrt{\frac{\gamma P}{\rho}} = 5f$$

This frequency is called second overtone or fifth harmonic.

Hence different frequencies produced in a closed organ pipe are in the ratio $1 : 3 : 5 : \ldots\ldots$ i.e., only odd harmonics are present in a closed organ pipes.

Analytical treatment :

Consider a cylindrical pipe of length L lying along the x-axis with its closed end at $x = 0$ and open end at $x = L$.

The sound wave sent along the pipe can be represented as

$$\Delta P_1 = \Delta P_m \sin(kx - \omega t)$$

The reflected wave from the closed end is represented by (sound wave suffers no phase change due to the reflection from closed end.).

$$\Delta P_2 = \Delta P_m \sin(-kx - \omega t)$$

$$= -\Delta P_m \sin(kx + \omega t)$$

The resultant wave is given by

$$\Delta P = \Delta P_1 + \Delta P_2$$

$$= \Delta P_m \sin(kx - \omega t) - \Delta P_m \sin(kx + \omega t)$$

or

$$\Delta P = -2\Delta P_m \cos(kx)\sin(\omega t)$$

For all values of t, the resultant pressure variation is zero, for which

$$\cos(kx) = 0$$

or

$$kx = (2n+1)\frac{\pi}{2}$$

$$\frac{2\pi}{\lambda}x = (2n+1)\frac{\pi}{2}$$

$$x = (2n+1)\frac{\lambda}{4}, \quad \text{where } n = 0, 1, 2, 3, \ldots\ldots$$

$$\therefore \qquad x = \frac{\lambda}{4}, \frac{3\lambda}{4}, \frac{5\lambda}{4}, \ldots\ldots$$

These points of zero pressure variation are called pressure nodes. On the other hand, the pressure variation is maximum for all values of t, for which

$$\cos(kx) = \pm 1$$

or

$$kx = n\pi$$

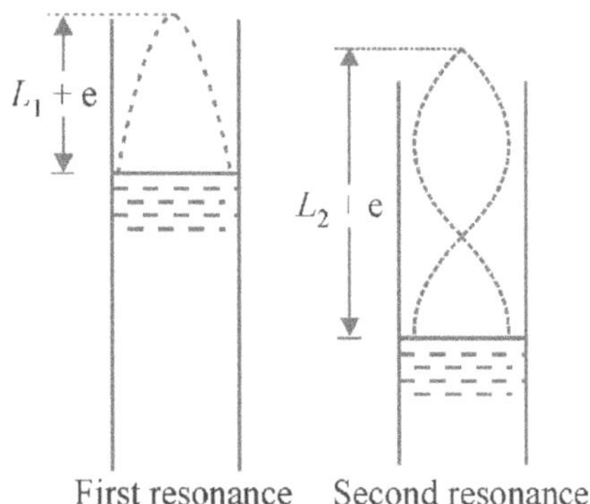

First resonance   Second resonance

Fig. 10.50

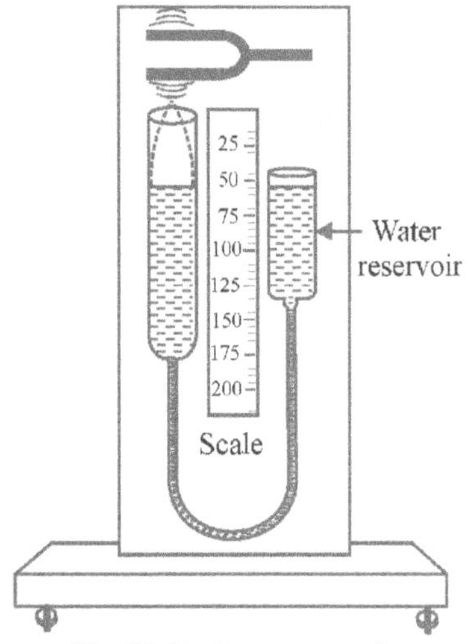

Fig. 10.51. Resonance tube.

or

$$\frac{2\pi}{\lambda} x = n\pi$$

$$x = n\frac{\lambda}{2}, \text{where } n = 0, 1, 2, 3, \ldots\ldots\ldots$$

$$\therefore \qquad x = 0, \frac{\lambda}{2}, \lambda, \frac{3\lambda}{2}, \ldots\ldots$$

These points of maximum pressure variation are called pressure antinodes (see *Fig. 10.49*). The pressure at these points varies from $(P - 2\Delta P_m)$ to $(P_0 + 2\Delta P_m)$.

Resonance tube : It is used to determine the speed of sound in air with the help of tuning fork of known frequency. It is a close pipe whose length can be changed by changing level of liquid in the tube. When a vibrating tuning fork is brought over its mouth, its air column vibrates longitudinally. If the length of the air column is varies until its natural frequency becomes equal to the frequency of fork, then resonance will occur and loud sound is heard.

For the first resonance $\qquad L_1 + e = \dfrac{\lambda}{4} \qquad \ldots (i)$

and for second resonance $\qquad L_2 + e = \dfrac{3\lambda}{4} \qquad \ldots(ii)$

Here L_1 and L_2 are the length of resonance columns and e is the end correction. After solving equations (i) and (ii), we get

$$\lambda = 2(L_2 - L_1)$$

and $\qquad e = \dfrac{L_2 - 3L_1}{2}$

If f is the frequency of the fork, then speed of sound in air

$$\boxed{v = f\lambda = 2f(L_2 - L_1)}$$

Ex. 24 The first overtone of an organ pipe beats with the first overtone of a close organ pipe with a beat frequency of 2.2 Hz. The fundamental frequency of the closed organ pipe is 110 Hz. Find the lengths of the pipes. Velocity of sound in air = 330 m/s.

Sol.

Suppose L_o and L_c are the lengths of open and close pipes respectively. Frequency of first overtone of open organ pipe,

$$f_o = \frac{2v}{2L_o} = \frac{v}{L_o}$$

Frequency of first overtone of close organ pipe

$$f_c = \frac{3v}{4L_c}$$

Given $\qquad f_o - f_c = 2.2$ Hz

$$\therefore \qquad \frac{v}{L_o} - \frac{3v}{4L_c} = 2.2$$

As $\dfrac{v}{4L_c} = 110$ Hz and $v = 330$ m/s

$$\therefore \qquad \frac{330}{L_o} - 3 \times 110 = 2.2$$

or $\qquad L_o = 0.99$m $\qquad$ *Ans.*

Ex. 25 Determine the possible harmonics in the longitudinal vibration of a rod clamped in the middle.

Sol. Consider a rod of length L clamped in the middle. It has one node in the middle and two antinodes at its free ends in the fundamental mode.

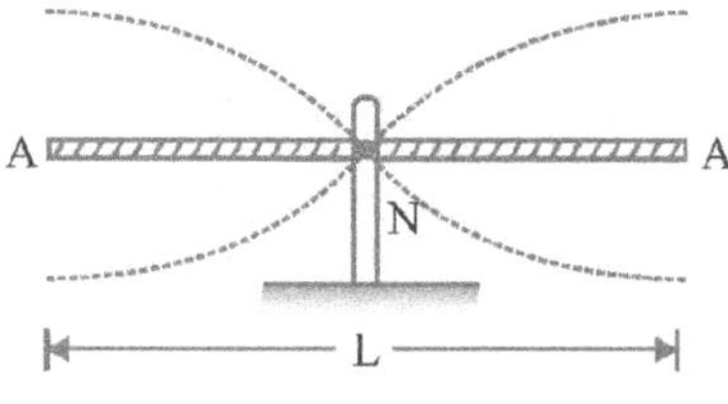

Fig. 10.52

Here $\qquad L = 2\dfrac{\lambda_1}{4}$ or $\lambda_1 = 2L$

Frequency of first harmonic

$$f_1 = \frac{v}{\lambda_1} = \frac{v}{2L}$$

Fig. 10.53

In the second mode of vibration

$$L = \frac{\lambda_2}{4} + \frac{\lambda_2}{2} + \frac{\lambda_2}{2} + \frac{\lambda_2}{4} = \frac{3\lambda_2}{2}$$

or

$$\lambda_2 = \frac{2L}{3}$$

Frequency,

$$f_2 = \frac{v}{\lambda_2} = \frac{3v}{2L} = 3f_1$$

This is called the third harmonic or first overtone .
Similarly for third mode

$$f_3 = 5f_1.$$

This is the fifth harmonic or second overtone.

Hence $\quad f_1 : f_2 : f_3 : \text{.......} \quad = \quad 1:3:5:\text{..........}$

Ex. 26 Three successive frequencies for a string are 75, 125, 175 Hz.

(a) State whether the string is fixed at one end or at both ends.
(b) What is the fundamental frequency?
(c) To which harmonics do these frequencies corresponds?
(d) Taking the speed of the transverse wave on the string as 400 m/s, determine the length of the string.

Sol.

(a) The given harmonics are in the ratio 1 : 3 : 5, so the string is fixed at one end.
(b) As the common maximum frequency in the harmonics is 25 Hz, so fundamental frequency = 25 Hz.
(c) The given harmonics are the third, fifth and seventh harmonics.

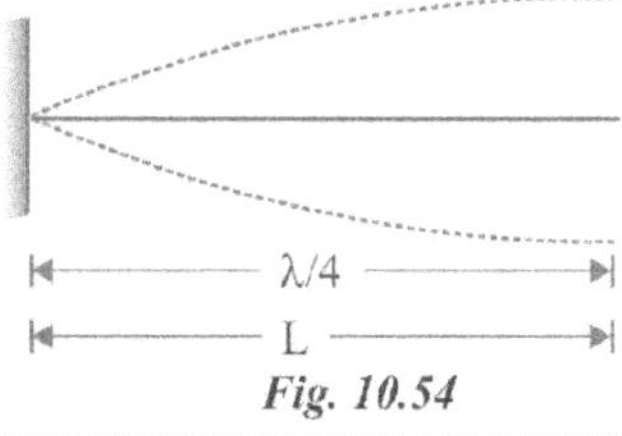

Fig. 10.54

(d)

$$f = \frac{v}{4L}$$

$$\therefore \quad L = \frac{v}{4f} = \frac{400}{4 \times 25} = 4\text{m} \qquad \textit{Ans.}$$

Ex. 27 Find the temperature T_0 at which the fundamental frequency of an organ pipe is independent of small variation in the temperature in terms of the coefficient of linear expansion (α) of the material of the tube.

Sol.

If L_0 is the length of the pipe at T_0, then its length at temperature T is

$$T = L_0[1 + \alpha(T - T_0)]$$

The speed of sound, $\quad v = \sqrt{\dfrac{\gamma RT}{M}}$

We have to find the temperature T_0 at which

$$f(T_0) = f(T) \text{ for small } (T - T_0)$$

$$\therefore \quad \frac{\sqrt{\dfrac{\gamma RT_0}{M}}}{2L_0} = \frac{\sqrt{\dfrac{\gamma RT}{M}}}{2L_0[1 + \alpha(T - T_0)]}$$

or

$$\sqrt{\frac{T}{T_0}} = 1 + \alpha(T - T_0)$$

or

$$\left[1 + \left(\frac{T - T_0}{T_0}\right)\right]^{1/2} = 1 + \alpha(T - T_0)$$

For small $(T - T_0)$, we can write

$$1 + \frac{1}{2}\left(\frac{T - T_0}{T_0}\right) = 1 + \alpha(T - T_0)$$

or

$$T_0 = \frac{1}{2\alpha} \qquad \textit{Ans.}$$

Kundt's tube : It is a long glass tube about 5 cm in diameter held horizontally. At one end it carries a disc of cork or board connected with a metal rod which is clamped at its middle. Other end of the tube is closed by a movable piston, so that its length can be adjusted. Lycopodium power is spread on the box of the tube. The free end of the rod rubbed along its length by resin cloth. The rod begins to vibrate longitudinally. These vibrations forced air inside tube through disc. And so stationary longitudinal vibrations are set-up in the tube. At resonance, frequency of vibration of rod becomes equal to frequency of vibration of air column inside tube.

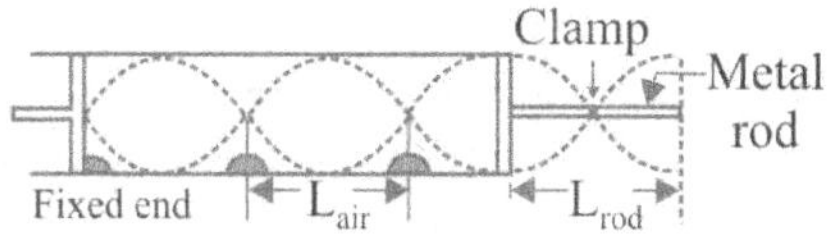

Fig. 10.55

For rod : $\qquad \dfrac{\lambda_{rod}}{2} = L_{rod} \Rightarrow \lambda_{rod} = 2L_{rod}$

For air : $\qquad \dfrac{\lambda_{air}}{2} = L_{air} \Rightarrow \lambda_{air} = 2L_{air}$

Since $\qquad f_{rod} = f_{air}$

$$\therefore \quad \frac{v_{rod}}{\lambda_{rod}} = \frac{v_{air}}{\lambda_{air}} \Rightarrow \frac{v_{rod}}{v_{air}} = \frac{\lambda_{rod}}{\lambda_{air}} = \frac{L_{rod}}{L_{air}}$$

By using Kundt's tube one can compare the speed of sound in different mediums.

Ex. 28 A long wire PQR is made by joining two wires PQ and QR of equal radii. PQ has length 4.8 m and mass 0.06 kg. QR has length 2.56 m and mass 0.2 kg. The wire PQR is under a tension of 80 N. A sinusodial wave-pulse of amplitude 3.5 cm is sent along the wire PQ from the end P. No power is dissipated during the propagation of the wave-pulse. Calculate

(a) the time taken by the wave-pulse to reach the other end R of the wire and

(b) the amplitude of the reflected and transmitted wave-pulse after the incident wave-pulse crosses the joint.

Sol. Mass per unit length of wire PQ

$$\mu_1 = \frac{0.06}{4.8}$$

```
P ————————————————————————————————— R
      4.8 m       Q        2.56 m
```

Fig. 10.56

$$= \frac{1}{80} \text{ kg/m}$$

and

$$\mu_2 = \frac{0.2}{2.56} = \frac{20}{256} \text{ kg/m}$$

Now

$$v_1 = \sqrt{\frac{F}{\mu_1}} = \sqrt{\frac{80}{1/80}} = 80 \text{ m/s}$$

and

$$v_2 = \sqrt{F/\mu_2} = \sqrt{\frac{80}{20/256}} = 32 \text{ m/s } \textbf{\textit{Ans.}}$$

(a) Time taken by wave-pulse to reach the other end of wire

$$t = \frac{4.8}{80} + \frac{2.56}{32} = 0.14 \text{ s}$$

(b)

$$A_r = A_i\left(\frac{v_2 - v_1}{v_1 + v_2}\right) = 3.5\left(\frac{32 - 80}{32 + 80}\right)$$

$$= -1.5 \text{ cm} \qquad \textbf{\textit{Ans.}}$$

and

$$A_t = A_i\left(\frac{2v_2}{v_1 + v_2}\right) = 3.5\left(\frac{2 \times 32}{80 + 32}\right)$$

$$= 2 \text{ cm} \qquad \textbf{\textit{Ans.}}$$

Ex. 29 An aluminium wire of cross-sectional area $1 \times 10^{-6}\text{m}^2$ is joined to a steel wire of the same cross-sectional area. This compound wire is stretched on a sonometer, pulled by a weight of 10 kg. The total length of the compound wire between the bridges is 1.5 m of which the aluminium wire is 0.6 m and the rest is steel wire. Transverse vibrations are set up in the wire by using an external source of variable frequency. Find the lowest frequency of excitation for which standing waves are formed, such that the joint in the wire is a node. What is the total number of nodes observed at this frequency, excluding the two at the ends of the wire? The density of the aluminium is 2.6×10^3 kg/m^3 and that of steel is 1.04×10^4 kg/m^3.

Sol.

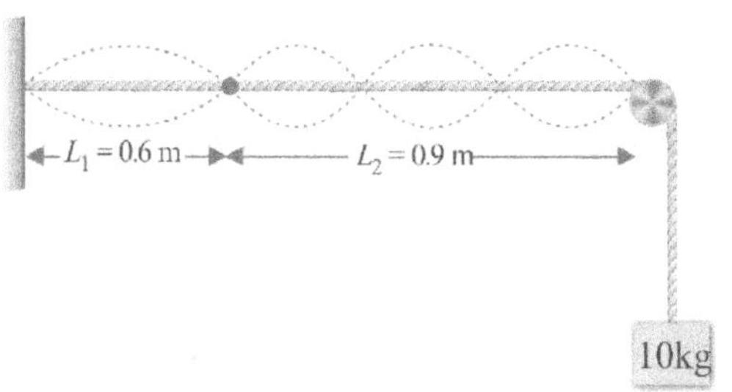

Fig. 10.57

Length of aluminium wire = 0.6 m.
Length of steel wire = 0.9 m
Mass per unit length of aluminium wire

$$\mu_1 = \frac{m}{\ell} = \rho a = 2.6 \times 10^3 \times 1 \times 10^{-6},$$

$$= 2.6 \times 10^{-3} \text{ kg/m}$$

Frequency of aluminium wire

$$f_1 = \frac{P_1}{2L_1}\sqrt{\frac{F}{\mu_1}}$$

For steel wire

$$\mu_2 = \rho a = 1.04 \times 10^4 \times 1 \times 10^{-6}$$

$$= 1.04 \times 10^{-2} \text{ kg/m}$$

$$f_2 = \frac{P_2}{2L_2}\sqrt{\frac{F}{\mu_2}}$$

For composite wire, $f_1 = f_2$

$$\therefore \quad \frac{P_1}{2L_1}\sqrt{\frac{F}{\mu_1}} = \frac{P_2}{2L_2}\sqrt{\frac{F}{\mu_2}}$$

or

$$\frac{P_1}{P_2} = \frac{L_1}{L_2}\sqrt{\frac{\mu_1}{\mu_2}}$$

$$= \frac{0.6}{0.9}\sqrt{\frac{2.6 \times 10^{-3}}{1.04 \times 10^{-2}}} = \frac{1}{3}$$

The minimum number of loops of aluminium wire = 1 and minimum number of loops of iron wire = 3 The total number of nodes in composite wire = 5 excluding two of the ends, there are = 5 – 2 = 3.

Lowest frequency

$$f_1 = \frac{P_1}{2L_1}\sqrt{\frac{F}{\mu_1}}$$

$$= \frac{1}{2 \times 0.6}\sqrt{\frac{10 \times 9.8}{2.6 \times 10^{-3}}} = 16.2 \text{ Hz } \textbf{\textit{Ans.}}$$

Ex. 30 A 3.6 m long vertical pipe resonates with a source of frequency 212.5 Hz. When water level is at certain height in the pipe. Find the heights of water level (from the bottom of the pipe) at which resonances occur. Neglect the correction. Now the pipe is filled to a height of H ($\simeq 3.6$m). A small hole is drilled very close to its bottom and water is allowed to leak. Obtain an expression for the rate of fall of water level in the pipe as a function of H. If the radii of the pipe and hole are 2×10^{-2} m and 1×10^{-3} m respectively, calculate the time interval between the occurrence of first two resonances. Speed of sound in air is 340 m/s and $g = 10$ m/s^2.

Sol. The wavelength of sound

$$\lambda = \frac{v}{f}$$

$$= \frac{340}{212.5} = 1.6 \text{ m}$$

The first resonance length

$$\ell = \frac{\lambda}{4}$$

$$= \frac{1.6}{4} = 0.4$$

Next resonance lengths are at $3\ell, 5\ell, 7\ell, 9\ell,$

$$= 1.2 \text{ m}, 2.0 \text{ m}, 2.8 \text{ m}, 3.6 \text{ m},$$

The water level in the pipe

$$h_1 = (3.6 - 0.4) = 3.2 \text{ m}$$
$$h_2 = (3.6 - 1.2) = 2.4 \text{ m}$$
$$h_3 = (3.6 - 2) = 1.6 \text{ m}$$
$$h_4 = (3.6 - 2.8) = 0.8 \text{ m}$$
$$h_5 = (3.6 - 3.6) = 0 \text{ m}$$

At any height H

$$A\left(-\frac{dH}{dt}\right) = av$$

$$= a\sqrt{2gH}$$

or

$$\left(-\frac{dH}{dt}\right) = \frac{a}{A}\sqrt{2g}H^{1/2}$$

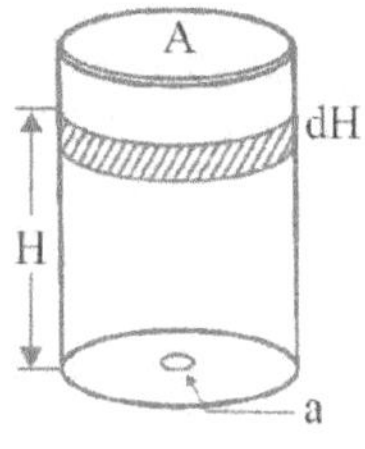

Fig. 10.58

$$= \frac{\pi r^2}{\pi R^2}\sqrt{2g}H^{1/2} = \frac{r^2}{R^2}\sqrt{2g}H^{1/2}$$

$$= \left(\frac{1\times10^{-3}}{2\times10^{-2}}\right)^2 \times \sqrt{2g} \times H^{1/2}$$

Rate of fall of level of water

$$\left(\frac{dH}{dt}\right) = 5\sqrt{5}\times10^{-3}H^{1/2} \qquad \textit{Ans.}$$

The time interval between two occurrence of resonance :

$$dt = \frac{A}{a\sqrt{2g}}\left(\frac{-dH}{H^{1/2}}\right)$$

or

$$t = \frac{-\pi R^2}{\pi r^2\sqrt{2\times10}}\int_{3.2}^{2.4} H^{-1/2} \, dH$$

$$= -\frac{R^2}{r^2\sqrt{20}}\frac{\left(\sqrt{2.4}-\sqrt{3.2}\right)}{(1/2)}$$

$$= 43 \text{ s} \qquad \textit{Ans.}$$

Ex. 31 The displacement of the medium in a sound wave is given by the equation $y_i = A\cos(ax + bt)$ where A, a, b are positive constants. The wave is reflected by an obstacle situated at $x = 0$. The intensity of the reflected wave is 0.64 times that of the incident wave.

(a) What are the wavelength and frequency of the incident wave?
(b) Write the equation for the reflected wave.
(c) In the resultant wave formed after reflection, find the maximum and minimum values of the particle speeds in the medium.
(d) Express the resultant wave as a superposition of a standing wave and a travelling wave. What are the positions of the antinodes of the standing wave? What is the direction of propagation of wave?

Sol.

(a) The given equation can be written in the form

$$y_i = A\sin(ax + bt + \pi/2)$$

Compare this equation with standard equation of travelling wave

$$y = A\sin(kx + \omega t), \text{ we have}$$

$$\therefore \quad k = a \text{ and } \omega = b$$

Frequency of wave

$$n = \frac{\omega}{2\pi} = \frac{b}{2\pi}$$

and wavelength $\quad \lambda = \dfrac{2\pi}{k} = \dfrac{2\pi}{a}$

(b) The amplitude of reflected wave $A_r = 0.80\, A_i$
$\therefore$ The equation of reflected wave

$$y_r = 0.80A_i\cos(-ax + bt + \pi)$$

$$y_r = -0.80A_i\cos(bt - ax) \qquad \textit{Ans.}$$

(c) Particle speed due to incident wave

$$v_1 = \frac{dy_i}{dt} = -Ab\sin(ax + bt)$$

$$\therefore \quad (v_1)_{max} = -Ab$$

Particle speed due to reflected wave

$$v_2 = \frac{dy_r}{dt} = 0.8\,Ab\sin(at - ax)$$

$$\therefore \quad (v_2)_{max} = -0.8Ab$$

The maximum value of particle speed in medium is

$$v_{max} = |v_1|_{max} + |v_2|_{max}$$

$$= Ab + 0.8Ab = 1.8\,Ab$$

The minimum value of particle speed in medium.

$$v_{min} = Ab - 0.8\,Ab = 0.2\,Ab$$

(d) The equation of resulting wave is

$$y = y_i + y_r$$

$$= A\cos(ax + bt) - 0.8A\cos(bt - ax)$$

$$= A\cos(ax + bt) - (A - 0.2A)\cos(bt - ax)$$

$$= A\cos(ax + bt) - A\cos(bt - ax)$$

$$\qquad\qquad + [0.2A\cos(bt - ax)]$$

$$= 2A\sin\left[\frac{ax + bt + bt - ax}{2}\right]$$

$$\sin\left[\frac{bt - ax - ax - bt}{2}\right] + [0.2A\cos(bt - ax)]$$

$$= -2A\sin bt.\sin ax + 0.2A\cos(bt - ax)$$

$$= \underbrace{-2A\sin ax\sin bt}_{\text{standing wave}} + \underbrace{0.2A\cos(bt - ax)}_{\text{travelling wave}}$$

The position of antinodes :

$$I \propto (-2A\sin ax)$$

Intensity is maximum, when $\sin ax = \pm 1$

or $\qquad ax = (2n+1)\dfrac{\pi}{2}, n = 0, 1, 2, \dots\dots$

or $\qquad x = (2n+1)\dfrac{\pi}{2a}$

$$= \dfrac{\pi}{2a}, \dfrac{3\pi}{2a}, \dfrac{5\pi}{2a}, \dots\dots$$

The travelling wave is moving along positive x-axis.

Ex. 32 Two radio stations broad-cast their programmes at the same amplitude A and at slightly different frequencies f_1 and f_2 respectively. A detector receives the signals from the two stations simultaneously. It can only detect signals of intensity $> 2A^2$. Find
(i)   time interval between successive maxima of the intensity of the signal received by the detector.
(ii)   Time for which the detector remains idle in each cycle of the intensity of signal.

Sol.

Assuming the detector is located at $x = 0$, then the equations of the waves broad-casting from the two stations

$$y_1 = A\sin\omega_1 t = A\sin 2\pi f_1 t$$

and $\qquad y_2 = A\sin\omega_2 t = A\sin 2\pi f_2 t$

The resultant wave

$$y = y_1 + y_2$$

$$= A\sin 2\pi f_1 t + A\sin 2\pi f_2 t$$

$$= 2A\sin\left(\dfrac{2\pi f_1 t + 2\pi f_2 t}{2}\right).$$

$$\cos\left(\dfrac{2\pi f_1 t - 2\pi f_2 t}{2}\right)$$

$$= 2A\sin 2\pi\left(\dfrac{f_1+f_2}{2}\right)t\cos\pi\left(f_1-f_2\right)t$$

or $\qquad y = R\sin 2\pi f_{av}t$,

where $\qquad R = 2A\cos\pi(f_1-f_2)t$

The intensity of resultant wave

$$I \propto R^2$$

$$\propto 4A^2\cos^2\pi(f_1-f_2)t$$

(i)   Intensity of the resultant wave is maximum $(4A^2 > 2A^2)$ for which

$$\cos\pi(f_1-f_2)t = \pm 1$$

or $\qquad \pi(f_1-f_2)t = n\pi$

$\therefore \qquad t = \dfrac{n}{(f_1-f_2)}$

or $\qquad t = 0, \dfrac{1}{(f_1-f_2)}, \dfrac{2}{(f_1-f_2)}, \dots\dots$

The time interval between successive maximas

$$\Delta t = \dfrac{1}{(f_1-f_2)} \qquad \textit{Ans.}$$

(ii)   As detector can detect the intensity $> 2A^2$, so

$$2A^2 = 4A^2\cos^2\pi(f_1-f_2)t$$

or $\quad \cos\pi(f_1-f_2)t = \pm\dfrac{1}{\sqrt{2}}$

or $\qquad \pi(f_1-f_2)t = \dfrac{\pi}{4}, \dfrac{3\pi}{4}, \dfrac{5\pi}{4}, \dots\dots$

$\therefore \qquad t = \dfrac{1}{4(f_1-f_2)}, \dfrac{3}{4(f_1-f_2)}, \dfrac{5}{4(f_1-f_2)}, \dots$

The time interval between two successive instants for which intensity remains $\leq 2A^2$ is

$$\Delta t = \dfrac{1}{2(f_1-f_2)} \qquad \textit{Ans.}$$

Ex. 33 A string under a tension of 129.6 N produces 10 beats/s when it is vibrated along with a tuning fork. When the tension in the string is increased to 160 N, it sounds in unison with the same tuning fork. Calculate the fundamental frequency of the tuning fork.

Sol.

Suppose f be the frequency of the tuning fork. The frequency of the string will be either $(f-10)$ or $(f+10)$. With the increase in tension its frequency becomes f, so initial frequency of the string is $(f-10)$. Thus

For $F = 129.6\,N$, $\quad (f-10) = \dfrac{1}{2L}\sqrt{\dfrac{129.6}{\mu}} \qquad \dots (i)$

and for $f = 160\,N$, $\quad f = \dfrac{1}{2L}\sqrt{\dfrac{160}{\mu}} \qquad \dots (ii)$

After solving equations (i) and (ii), we get
$$f = 100\text{ Hz} \qquad \textit{Ans.}$$

Ex. 34 A metal wire of diameter 1 mm is held on two knife edges separated by a distance of 50 cm. The tension in the wire is 100 N. The wire, vibrating with its fundamental frequency and a vibrating tuning fork together produces 5 beats/s. The tension in the wire is then reduced to 81N. When the two are excited, beats are heard at the same rate. Calculate
(i)   the frequency of the fork and
(ii)   the density of the material of wire.

Sol.

Suppose the frequency of the tuning fork is f, then the frequency of wire in first case be $(f+5)$. With the decreases in tension, the frequency of wire will decrease. So to give same number of beats/s, it should be $(f-5)$. Thus

$$f+5 = \dfrac{1}{2L}\sqrt{\dfrac{F}{\mu}}$$

or $\qquad f+5 = \dfrac{1}{2L}\sqrt{\dfrac{100}{\mu}} \qquad \dots (i)$

and $\qquad f-5 = \dfrac{1}{2L}\sqrt{\dfrac{81}{\mu}} \qquad \dots (ii)$

(i)   After solving equations (i) and (ii), we get
$$f = 95\text{ Hz}$$

(ii)   From equation (i)

$$95 + 5 = \frac{1}{2 \times 0.50}\sqrt{\frac{100}{\mu}}$$

After solving $\quad \mu = \dfrac{1}{100}$ kg/m

$\therefore$ Density $\quad \rho = \dfrac{\mu}{A} = \dfrac{\mu}{\pi r^2}$

$$= \frac{1}{100 \times \pi \times (0.5 \times 10^{-3})^2}$$

$$= 12.73 \times 10^3 \ \text{kg/m}^3 \qquad \textbf{\textit{Ans.}}$$

Ex. 35 A tube of certain diameter and of length 48 cm is open at both ends. Its fundamental frequency of resonance is found to be 320 Hz. The velocity of sound in air is 320 m/s. Estimate the diameter of the tube. One end of the tube is now closed. Calculate the lowest frequency of resonance for the tube.

Sol.

The tube with open ends is shown in figure.

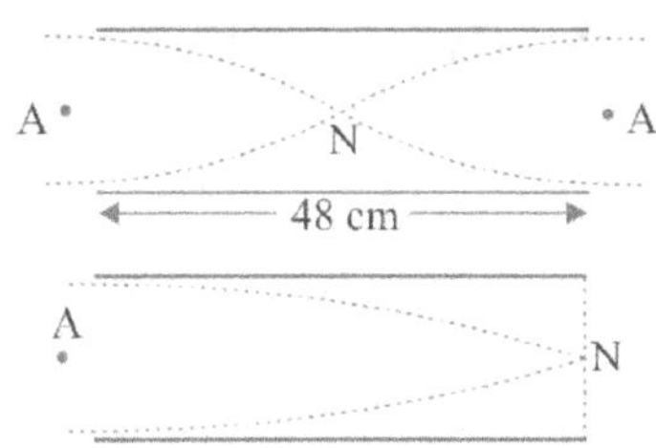

Fig. 10.59

Suppose the radius of the tube is r. The effective length of the tube open at both ends

$$\ell_e = \ell_0 + 2e = \ell_0 + 2 \times 0.6r = \ell_0 + 1.2r$$

or $\quad \dfrac{\lambda}{2} = 48 + 1.2r$

But $\quad \lambda = \dfrac{v}{f} = \dfrac{320}{320} = 1\text{m} = 100 \text{ cm}$

$\therefore \quad \dfrac{100}{2} = 48 + 1.2r$

or $\quad r = 1.67$ cm

Diameter $\quad d = 2r = 3.33$ cm $\qquad$ **Ans.**

When one end of the tube is closed, then

$$\frac{\lambda}{4} = \ell_0 + 0.6r$$

$$= 48 + 0.6 \times 1.67$$

$\therefore \quad \lambda = 196$ cm

Frequency, $\quad f = \dfrac{v}{\lambda} = \dfrac{320 \times 100}{196} = 163.3$ Hz $\quad$ **Ans.**

Ex. 36 A column of air at 51°C and a tuning fork produce 4 beats/s when sounded together. As the temperature of air column is decreased, the number of beats per second tends to decrease and when the temperature is 16°C then two produce one beat per second. Find the frequency of tuning fork.

Sol.

Suppose f be the frequency of the fork, then frequency of air column of 51°C be either $(f + 4)$ or $(f - 4)$. As the beat frequency decreases with decrease in temperature, so it must be $(f + 4)$. Thus

$$(f + 4) = \frac{v_{51}}{\lambda} \qquad \dots \text{(i)}$$

At 16°C, the frequency of the fork will be $(f + 1)$,

$$\therefore \qquad (f + 1) = \frac{v_{16}}{\lambda} \qquad \dots \text{(ii)}$$

Dividing equation (i) by (ii),

$$\frac{(f + 4)}{(f + 1)} = \frac{v_{51}}{v_{16}}$$

$$= \sqrt{\frac{273 + 51}{273 + 16}} = 1.06$$

After solving, $\qquad f = 49$ Hz $\qquad$ **Ans.**

Ex. 37 AB is a cylinder of length 1.0 m filled with a thin flexible diaphram C (see figure) at the middle and two other thin flexible diaphrams A and B at the ends. The portions AC and BC contain hydrogen and oxygen gases respectively. The diaphrams A and B are set into vibrations of same frequency. What is the minimum frequency of these vibrations for which the diaphram C is a node? Under the conditions of the experiment, the velocity of sound in hydrogen is 1100 m/s and in oxygen is 300 m/s.

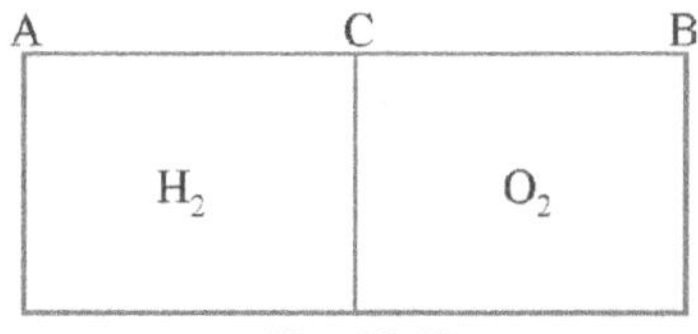

Fig. 10.60

Sol.

As ends A and B are set in vibrations, so displacement antinodes are formed at these ends. The fundamental

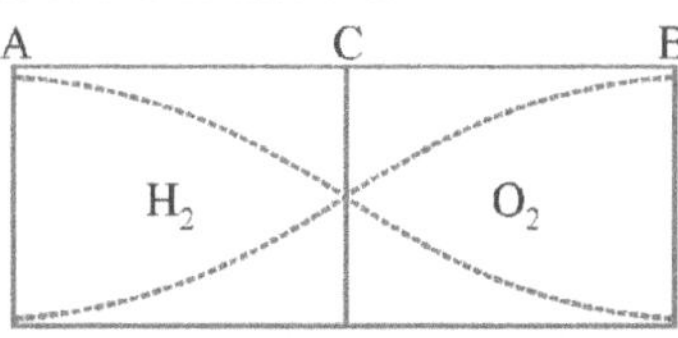

Fig. 10.61

frequency of each pipe is corresponding to one node and one antinode. If f_1 and f_2 be the fundamental frequencies of gases in AC and BC respectively, then

$$f_1 = \frac{v_1}{4L} = \frac{1100}{4 \times 0.5} = 550 \text{ Hz}$$

and $\qquad f_2 = \dfrac{v_2}{4L} = \dfrac{300}{4 \times 0.5} = 150 \text{ Hz}$

As the two frequencies are different, so the two columns are not vibrating in the fundamental mode. The close column of gas vibrates only in odd harmonics with frequencies $1 : 3 : 5 : 7 : \dots$. Thus we can write

$$\frac{f_1}{f_2} = \frac{550}{150} = \frac{11}{3}, \frac{22}{6}, \frac{33}{9}$$

or $\qquad 3f_1 = 11f_2$

The common minimum frequency

$$= 3f_1 = 3 \times 550 = 1650 \text{ Hz}$$

also $\qquad = 11f_2 = 11 \times 150 = 1650 \text{ Hz} \quad$ **Ans.**

Ex. 38 The first overtone of an open organ pipe beats with the first overtone of a closed organ pipe with a beat frequency of 2.2 Hz. The fundamental frequency of the closed organ pipe is 110 Hz. Find the lengths of the pipes.

Sol.

Let L_1 and L_2 be the lengths of open and close pipes respectively. The frequency of first overtone of an open organ pipe

$$= \frac{2v}{2L_1}$$

The frequency of first overtone of closed organ pipe

$$= \frac{3v}{4L_2}$$

Given fundamental frequency of closed organ pipe

$$\frac{v}{4L_2} = 110$$

or $\qquad \dfrac{330}{4L_2} = 110$

$\therefore \qquad\qquad L_2 = 0.75 \text{ m} \qquad\qquad$ *Ans.*

As the beats frequency is 2.2 Hz, so

$$\frac{2v}{2L_1} - \frac{3v}{4L_2} = 2.2$$

or $\qquad \dfrac{2 \times 330}{2L_1} - \dfrac{3 \times 330}{4 \times 0.75} = 2.2$

After solving

$$L_1 = 0.993 \text{ m} \qquad\qquad \textit{Ans.}$$

Also $\qquad \dfrac{3v}{4L_2} - \dfrac{2v}{2L_1} = 2.2$

or $\qquad \dfrac{3 \times 330}{4 \times 0.75} - \dfrac{2 \times 330}{2L_1} = 2.2$

After solving $\qquad L_1 = 1.006 \text{ m} \qquad\qquad$ *Ans.*

Review of formulae & Important Points

16. **Boundary effects :**

    (i) When wave is reflected from rigid boundary, the reflected wave will suffer a phase change of π radian. Thus if

    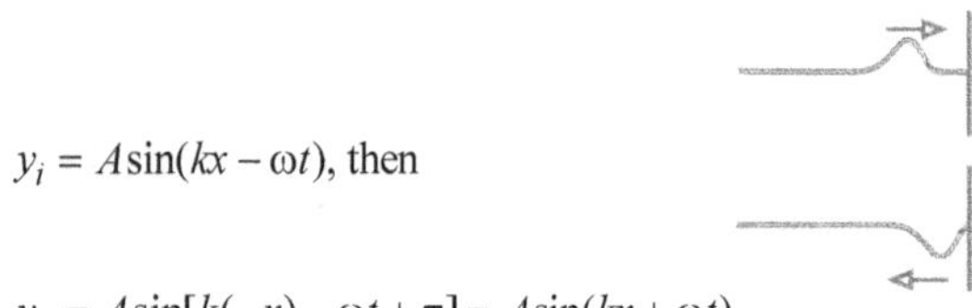

    $y_i = A\sin(kx - \omega t)$, then

    $y_r = A\sin[k(-x) - \omega t + \pi] = A\sin(kx + \omega t)$

    (ii) When wave is reflected from free boundary, the reflected wave suffers no phase change.

    Thus if

    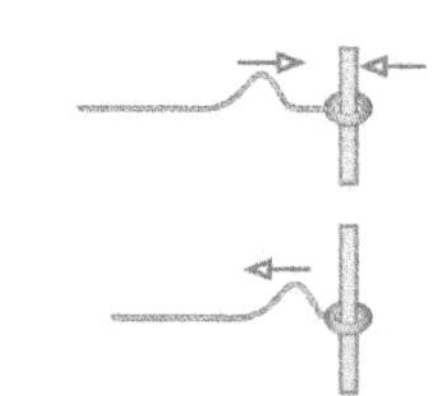

    $y_i = A\sin(kx - \omega t)$, *then*

    $y_r = A\sin(-kx - \omega t) = A\sin(kx + \omega t)$

17. **Principle of superpositoin :** If y_1, y_2, ... y_n are the displacements produced by waves acting separately, then the resultant desplacement

    $y = y_1 + y_2 + ... + y_n.$

    There are three types of superpositions.

18. **Interference :** When two or more waves of same frequency travel simultaneously in the same direction or nearly along the same direction in a medium, they superpose on each other and give rise new disturbance is called interference.

    If A_1 and A_2 are the amplitudes of the interfering waves, then resultant amplitude

    $$R = \sqrt{A_1^2 + A_2^2 + 2A_1 A_2 \cos\phi}$$

    (a) **Constructive interference :**

    $$\phi = 2\pi n, \ n = 0, 1, 2, ...$$

    or $\qquad\qquad \Delta x = n\lambda$

    $$R_{max} = (A_1 + A_2)$$

    (b) **Destructive interference :**

    $$\phi = (2n - 1)\pi, \ n = 1, 2, ...$$

    or $\qquad \Delta x = (2n - 1)\dfrac{\lambda}{2}$

    $$R_{min} = A_1 - A_2$$

    The ratio of maximum and minimum intensities

    $$\frac{I_{max}}{I_{min}} = \frac{(A_1 + A_2)^2}{(A_1 - A_2)^2}$$

19. In Quinke's tube, each x cm slide of tube will cause a path difference 2x. Thus for a mixima and next minima

    $$\frac{\lambda}{2} = x \quad \text{or} \quad \lambda = 4x.$$

20. **Beats :** In the superposition of two waves of slightly different frequencies

    $$y_1 = A_1 \sin 2\pi f_1 t$$

    and $\qquad\qquad y_2 = A_2 \sin 2\pi f_2 t$

    number of maximum per second are $f_1 \sim f_2$, and number of minimum per second are $f_1 \sim f_2$.

    Beats frequency, $\qquad \Delta f = f_1 \sim f_2.$

21. Stationary waves :

(a) Consider two waves travelling from opposite directions

$$y_1 = A \sin (kx - \omega t)$$

and $\quad\quad y_2 = A \sin (kx + \omega t)$

The resultant wave

$$y = y_1 + y_2 = [2A \sin kx] \cos \omega t$$

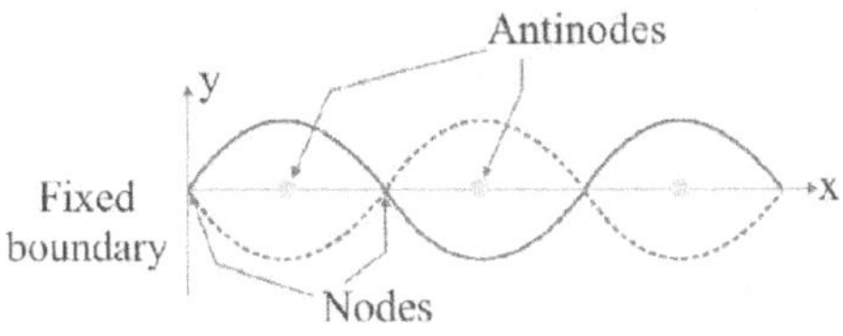

Positions of nodes : $\quad x = 0, \dfrac{\lambda}{2}, \lambda, \dots$

Positions of antinodes : $\quad x = \dfrac{\lambda}{4}, \dfrac{3\lambda}{4}, \dots$

(b) When wave is reflected from free boundary, then

$$y_1 = A\sin(kx - \omega t)$$

and $\quad\quad y_2 = A\sin(-kx - \omega t) = -A\sin(kx + \omega t)$

The resultant wave

$$y = [2A \cos kx] \sin \omega t$$

Positions of nodes : $\quad x = \dfrac{\lambda}{4}, \dfrac{3\lambda}{4}, \dots$

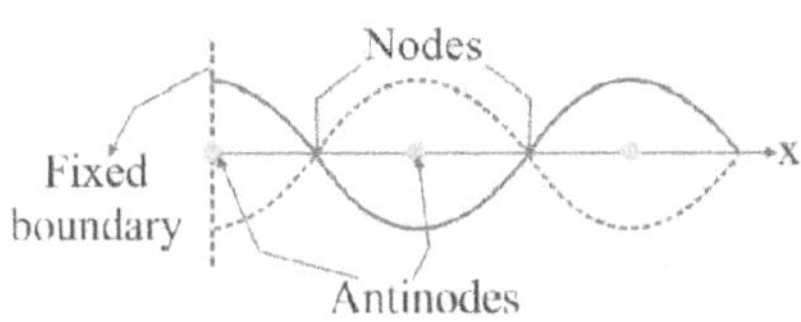

22. Resonance tube : It is used to determine the speed of sound in air.

For the two consecutive resonances

$$L_1 + e = \frac{\lambda}{4} \quad \text{and} \quad L_2 + e = \frac{3\lambda}{4}$$

$$\therefore \quad \lambda = 2(L_2 - L_1) \quad \text{and} \quad e = \frac{(L_2 - 3L_1)}{2}$$

Speed of sound $\quad v = f\lambda = 2f(L_2 - L_1)$

23. Vibrations of stretched string :

(a) Frequency of fundamental note

$$f_1 = \frac{1}{2L}\sqrt{\frac{F}{\mu}}$$

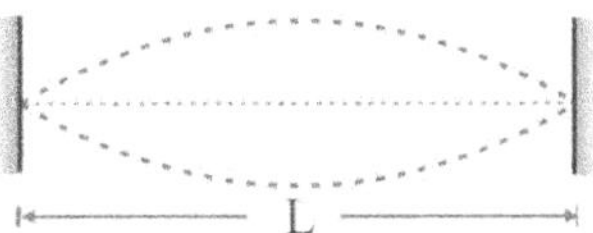

(b) If string vibrates in P loops, then

$$f_p = \frac{P}{2L}\sqrt{\frac{F}{\mu}}$$

24. Organ pipes

(a) Open organ pipe : The frequency of fundamental note

$$f = \frac{v}{2L}$$

Harmonics of frequencies ratio 1 : 2 : 3 : ..... are possible.

(b) Close organ pipe : The frequency of fundamental note

$$f = \frac{v}{4L}$$

Harmonics of frequencies ratio 1 : 3 : 5 : ..... are possible.

LEVEL - 1

Only one option correct

1. Two waves with the same amplitude and wavelength interfere in three different situations to produce resultant waves with the following equations :

(1) $y = 2 \sin (3x - 4t)$

(2) $y = 2 \sin (3x) \cos (4t)$

(3) $y = 2 \sin (5x + 4t)$

In which situation are the two combining waves travelling in opposite directions ?

(a) 1   (b) 2

(c) 3   (d) None

2. In the sixth harmonic on a string fixed at both ends, the number of nodes and antinodes are

(a) 5, 6   (b) 6, 6

(c) 6, 7   (d) 7, 6

3. Two standing waves are given by

$y_1 = (2 \text{ mm}) \sin (3x) \cos (4t)$

and $y_2 = (2 \text{ mm}) \sin (3x + \pi/6) \cos (4t)$.

If waves are confined in the same distance, then the distance between first node of wave y_1 and first node of wave y_2 is :

(a) 0   (b) $\dfrac{2\pi}{3}$

(c) $\dfrac{\pi}{3}$ (d) $\dfrac{\pi}{6}$

4. Figure shows sound waves of wavelength λ are emitted by a point source S and travel to a detector D directly along path 1 and via reflection from a panel along path 2. Initially, the panel is almost along path 1 and the waves arriving at D along the two paths are almost exactly in phase. Then the panel moved away from path 1 as shown until the waves arriving at D are exactly out of phase, the path difference Δx of the waves along the two paths

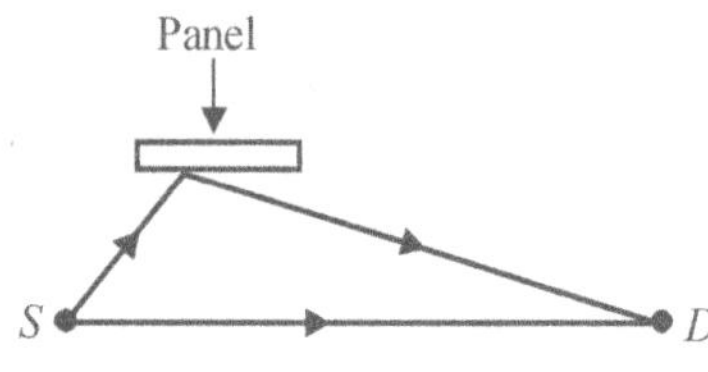

(a) 0   (b) $\dfrac{\lambda}{4}$

(c) $\dfrac{\lambda}{2}$ (d) $\dfrac{3\lambda}{2}$

5. A standing sound wave in a pipe has five displacement nodes and five antinodes. The harmonic number for the standing wave is

(a) 3   (b) 4

(c) 5   (d) 9

6. The tenth harmonic is set up in a pipe. The pipe is

(a) open pipe   (b) close pipe

(c) any of them   (d) none

7. For a particular tube, there are four of the six harmonic frequencies below 1000 Hz : 300, 600, 750 and 900 Hz. Two frequencies are missing from the list are

(a) 100, 200 Hz   (b) 150, 400 Hz

(c) 150, 450 Hz   (d) 450, 800 Hz

8. Pipe A has length twice the pipe B. Pipe A has both ends open and pipe B has one end open. Which harmonics of pipe A have a frequency that matches a resonance frequency of pipe B

(a) 1   (b) 2

(c) 3   (d) 4

9. A tuning fork arrangement (pair) produces 4 beat/s with one fork of frequency 288 cps. A little wax is placed on the unknown fork and it then produces 2 beat/s. The frequency of the unknown fork is

(a) 286 cps   (b) 292 cps

(c) 294 cps   (d) 288 cps

10. The equation $f(x, t) = j \sin \left(\dfrac{2\pi}{\lambda} vt\right)\cos \left(\dfrac{2\pi}{\lambda} x\right)$ represents

(a) transverse progressive wave

(b) longitudinal progressive wave

(c) longitudinal stationary wave

(d) transverse stationary wave

11. A wave represented by the given equation $y = a \cos (kx - \omega t)$ is superposed with another wave to form a stationary wave such that the point $x = 0$ is a node. The equation for the other wave is

(a) $y = a \sin (kx + \omega t)$ (b) $y = -a \cos (kx + \omega t)$

(c) $y = -a \cos (kx - \omega t)$ (d) $y = -a \sin (kx - \omega t)$

12. Standing waves can not be produced :

(a) on a string clamped at both the ends

(b) on a string clamped at one end and free at the other

(c) when incident wave gets reflected from a wall

(d) when two identical waves with a phase difference of π are moving in the same direction

Answer Key	1	(b)	3	(d)	5	(d)	7	(c)	9	(b)	11	(b)
Sol. from page 685	2	(d)	4	(c)	6	(a)	8	(a)	10	(d)	12	(d)

13. A standing wave having 3 nodes and 2 antinodes is formed between two atoms having a distance 1.21 Å between them. The wavelength of the standing wave is :

(a) 1.21 Å   (b) 2.42 Å
(c) 6.05 Å   (d) 3.63 Å

14. Two sinusoidal waves with same wavelengths and amplitudes travel in opposite directions along a string with a speed 10 m/s. If the minimum time interval between two instants when the string is flat is 0.5 s, the wavelength of the wave is

(a) 25 m   (b) 20 m
(c) 15 m   (d) 10 m

15. Standing waves are produced in a 10 m long stretched string. If the string vibrates in 5 segments and the wave velocity is 20 m/s, the frequency is

(a) 2 Hz   (b) 4 Hz
(c) 5 Hz   (d) 10 Hz

16. A string in musical instrument is 50 cm long and its fundamental frequency is 800 Hz. If a frequency of 1000 Hz is to be produced, then required length of string is

(a) 62.5 cm   (b) 50 cm
(c) 40 cm   (d) 37.5 cm

17. A man is watching two trains, one leaving and the other coming in which equal speed of 4 m/s. If they sound their whistles, each of frequency 240 Hz, the number of beats heard by the man (velocity of sound in air = 320 m/s) will be equal to

(a) 6   (b) 3
(c) 0   (d) 12

18. An open pipe is resonance in its 2nd harmonic with tuning fork of frequency f_1. Now it is closed at one end. If the frequency of the tuning fork is increased slowly from f_1 then again a resonance is obtained with a frequency f_2. If in this case the pipe vibrates n^{th} harmonics, then

(a) $n = 3, f_2 = \dfrac{3}{4} f_1$ (b) $n = 3, f_2 = \dfrac{5}{4} f_1$

(c) $n = 5, f_2 = \dfrac{5}{4} f_1$ (d) $n = 5, f_2 = \dfrac{3}{4} f_1$

19. An organ pipe is closed at one end has fundamental frequency of 1500 Hz. The maximum number of overtones generated by this pipe which a normal person can hear is

(a) 14   (b) 13
(c) 6   (d) 9

20. Two pulses in a stretched string whose centres are initially 8 cm apart are moving towards each other as shown in the figure. The speed of each pulse is 2 cm/s. After 2 s, the total energy of the pulses will be

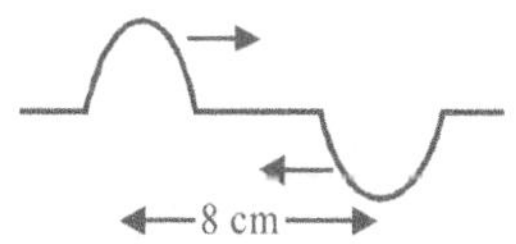

(a) Zero
(b) Purely kinetic
(c) Purely potential
(d) Partly kinetic and partly potential

21. A man is standing on a railway platform listening to the whistle of an engine that passes the man at constant speed without stopping. If the engine passes the man at time t_0. How does the frequency f of the whistle as heard by the man changes with time :

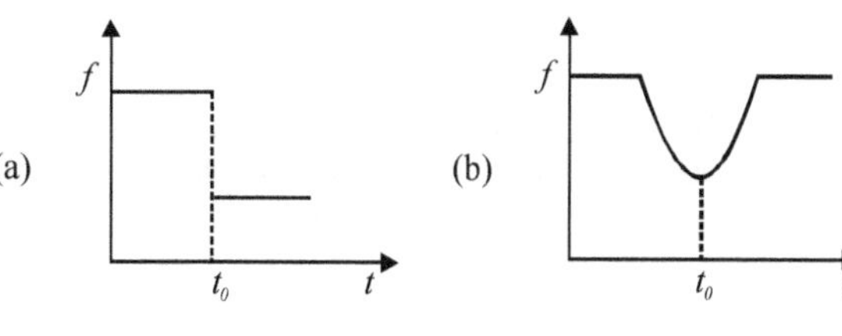
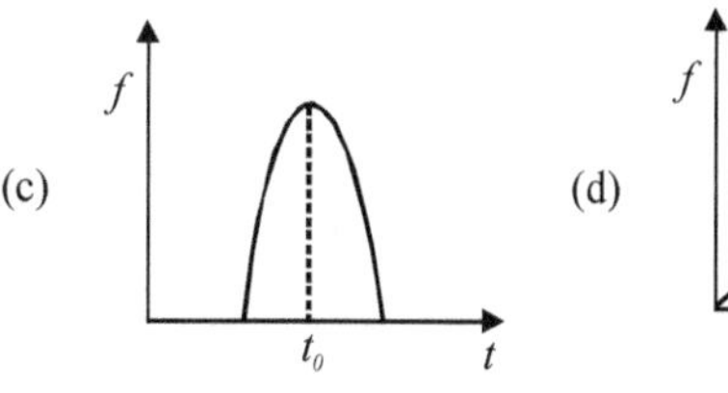
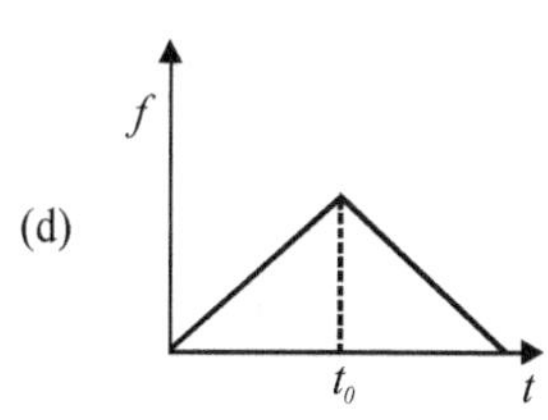

22. The figure shows four progressive waves A, B, C and D with their phases expressed with respect to the wave A. It can be concluded from the figure that

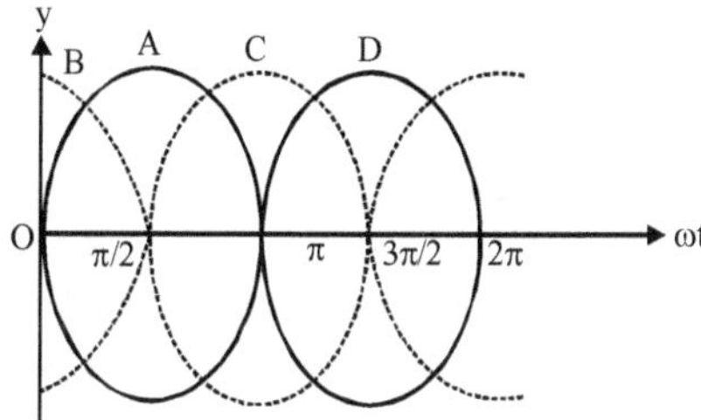

(a) The wave C is ahead by a phase angle of $\dfrac{\pi}{2}$ and the wave B lags behind by a phase angle of $\dfrac{\pi}{2}$

(b) The wave C is behind by a phase angle of $\dfrac{\pi}{2}$ and the wave B lags ahead by a phase angle of $\dfrac{\pi}{2}$

(c) The wave C is ahead by a phase angle of π and the wave B lags behind by a phase angle of π

(d) The wave C is behind by a phase angle of π and the wave B lags ahead by a phase angle of π

Answer Key	13	(a)	15	(c)	17	(a)	19	(c)	21	(a)
Sol. from page 685	14	(d)	16	(c)	18	(c)	20	(b)	22	(b)

23. The diagram below shows the propagation of a wave. Which points are in same phase

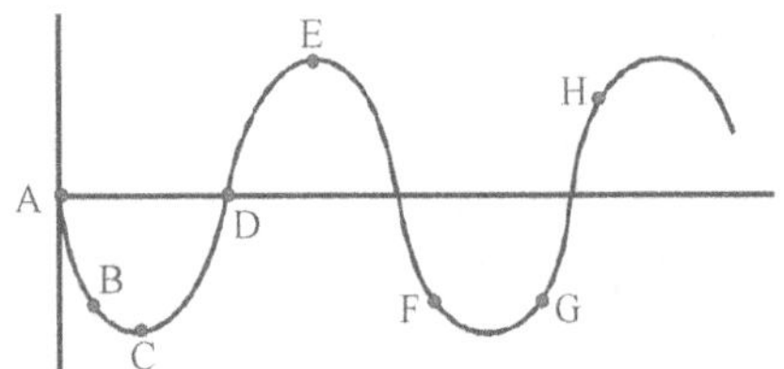

(a) F and G 　　　　　(b) C and E
(c) B and G 　　　　　(d) B and F

24. Two pulses travel in mutually opposite directions in a string with a speed of 2.5 cm/s as shown in the figure. Initially the pulses are 10 cm apart. What will be the state of the string after two seconds

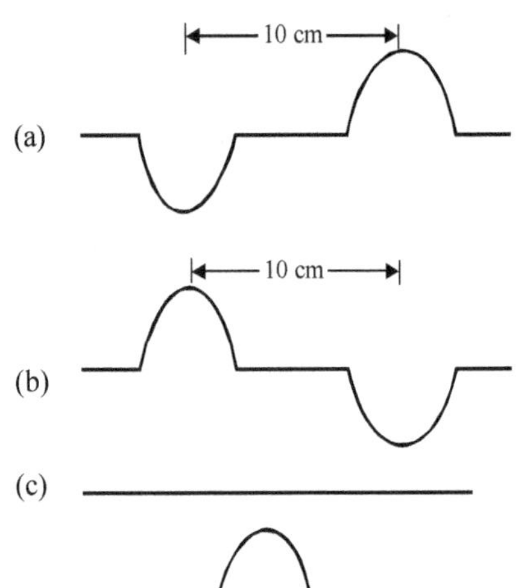

25. When two sound waves with a phase difference of $\pi/2$, and each having amplitude A and frequency ω, are superimposed on each other, then the maximum amplitude and frequency wave is

(a) $\dfrac{A}{\sqrt{2}} : \dfrac{\omega}{2}$ 　　　　　(b) $\dfrac{A}{\sqrt{2}} : \omega$

(c) $\sqrt{2}A : \dfrac{\omega}{2}$ 　　　　　(d) $\sqrt{2}A : \omega$

26. The displacement of the interfering sound waves are $y_1 = 4\sin\omega t$ and $y_2 = 3\sin\left(\omega t + \dfrac{\pi}{2}\right)$. What is the amplitude of the resultant wave

(a) 5 　　　　　(b) 7
(c) 1 　　　　　(d) 0

27. Which two of the given transverse waves will give stationary waves when get superimposed
$z_1 = a\cos(kx - \omega t)$ 　　　...(A)
$z_2 = a\cos(kx + \omega t)$ 　　　...(B)
$z_3 = a\cos(ky - \omega t)$ 　　　...(C)
(a) A and B 　　　　　(b) A and C
(c) B and C 　　　　　(d) any two

28. A standing wave is represented by $y = A\sin(100t)\cos(0.01x)$ where y and A are in millimetre, t is in seconds and x is in metre. The velocity of wave is
(a) 10^4 m/s
(b) 1 m/s
(c) 10^{-4} m/s
(d) Not derivable from above data

29. A stretched string of length l, fixed at both ends can sustain stationary waves of wavelength λ, given by

(a) $\lambda = \dfrac{f^2}{2l}$ 　　　　　(b) $\lambda = \dfrac{l^2}{2f}$

(c) $\lambda = \dfrac{2l}{f}$ 　　　　　(d) $\lambda = 2lf$

30. A string is rigidly tied at two ends and its equation of vibration is given by $y = \cos 2\pi t \sin 2\pi x$. Then minimum length of string is

(a) 1 m 　　　　　(b) $\dfrac{5}{2}$ m

(c) 5 m 　　　　　(d) 2π m

31. A source of sound placed at the open end of a resonance column sends an acoustic wave of pressure amplitude P_0 inside the tube. If the atmospheric pressure is P_A, then the ratio of maximum and minimum pressure at the closed end of the tube will be

(a) $\dfrac{(P_A + P_0)}{(P_A - P_0)}$ 　　　　　(b) $\dfrac{(P_A + 2P_0)}{(P_A - 2P_0)}$

(c) $\dfrac{P_A}{P_A}$ 　　　　　(d) $\dfrac{\left(P_A + \dfrac{1}{2}P_0\right)}{\left(P_A - \dfrac{1}{2}P_0\right)}$

32. A string fixed at both ends has consecutive standing wave modes for which the distances between adjacent nodes are 18 cm and 16 cm respectively. The minimum possible length of the string is
(a) 144 cm 　　　　　(b) 152 cm
(c) 176 cm 　　　　　(d) 200 cm

33. A note has a frequency of 128 Hz. The frequency of a note which is two octave higher than this is
(a) 256 Hz 　　　　　(b) 320 Hz
(c) 400 Hz 　　　　　(d) none of these

34. If the source is moving towards right, wave front of sound waves get modified to

(a) 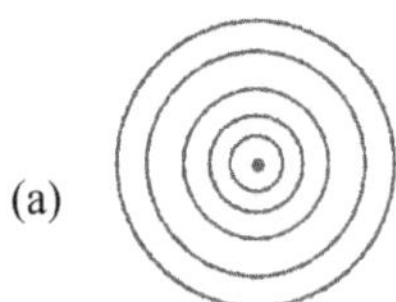 　　　　　(b) 

(c) 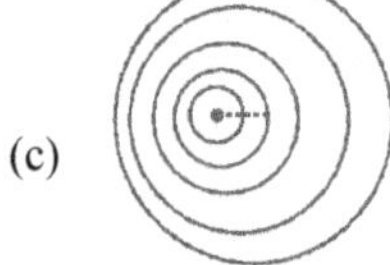 　　　　　(d) None of these

LEVEL - 2

Only one option correct

1. Figure shows a stretched string of length L and four pipes of length L, $2L$, $L/2$ and $L/2$ respectively. The string's tension is adjusted until the speed of waves on the string equals the speed of sound waves in the air. The fundamental mode of oscillation is then set up on the string. In which pipe will the sound produced by the string cause resonance

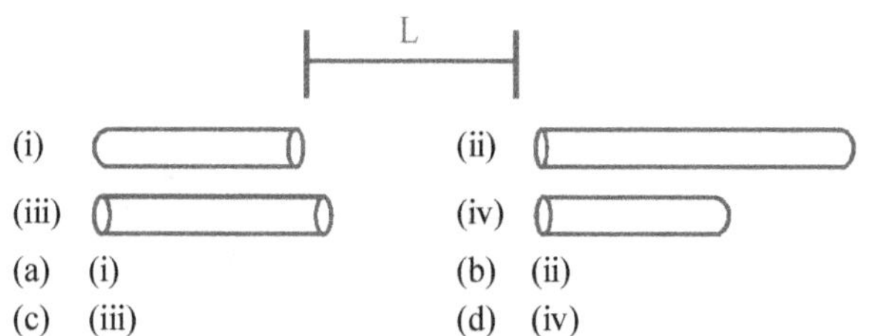

(a)   (i)
(b)   (ii)
(c)   (iii)
(d)   (iv)

2. The superposing waves are represented by the following equations $y_1 = 5 \sin 2\pi (10\,t - 0.1\,x)$, $y_2 = 10 \sin 2\pi (20\,t - 0.2\,x)$. Ratio of intensities $\dfrac{I_{max}}{I_{min}}$ will be

(a)   1
(b)   9
(c)   4
(d)   16

3. Equation of motion in the same direction is given by $y_1 = A \sin(\omega t - kx)$, $y_2 = A \sin(\omega t - kx - \theta)$. The amplitude of the medium particle will be

(a) $2\,A\cos\dfrac{\theta}{2}$
(b) $2\,A\cos\theta$
(c) $\sqrt{2}\,A\cos\dfrac{\theta}{2}$
(d) $1.2\,f, 1.2\,\lambda$

4. A tuning fork of known frequency 256 Hz makes 5 beat/s with the vibrating string of a piano. The beat frequency decreases to 2 beat/s when the tension in the piano string is slightly increased. The frequency of the piano string before increasing the tension was

(a) $256 + 5$ Hz
(b) $256 + 2$ Hz
(c) $256 - 2$ Hz
(d) $256 - 5$ Hz

5. The equation of stationary wave along a stretched string given by $y = 5 \sin \dfrac{\pi x}{3} \cos 40\,\pi t$, where x and y are in cm and t in second. The separation between two adjacent nodes is

(a)   1.5 cm
(b)   3 cm
(c)   6 cm
(d)   4 cm

6. A sonometer wire resonates with a given tuning fork forming standing waves with five antinodes between the two bridges when a mass of 9 kg is suspended from the wire. When this mass is replaced by a mass M, the wire resonates with the same tuning fork forming three antinodes for the same positions of the bridges. The value of M is

(a)   25 kg
(b)   5 kg
(c)   12.5 kg
(d)   1/25 kg

7. A tuning fork of frequency 392 Hz, resonates with 50 cm length of a string under tension (T). If length of the string is decreased by 2 %, keeping the tension constant, the number of beats heard when the string and the tuning fork made to vibrate simultaneously is :

(a)   4
(b)   6
(c)   8
(d)   12

8. Two vibrating strings of the same material but lengths L and $2L$ have radii $2r$ and r respectively. They are stretched under the same tension. Both the strings vibrate in their fundamental modes, the one of length L with frequency f_1 and the other with frequency f_2. The ratio f_1/f_2 is given by

(a)   2
(b)   4
(c)   8
(d)   1

9. If in an experiment for determination of velocity of sound by resonance tube method using a tuning fork of 512 Hz, first resonance was observed at 30.7 cm and second was obtained at 63.2 cm, then maximum possible error in velocity of sound is (consider actual speed of sound in air is 332 m/s)

(a)   204 cm/s
(b)   110 cm/s
(c)   58 cm/s
(d)   80 cm/s

10. The ends of a stretched wire of length L are fixed at $x = 0$ and $x = L$. In one experiment, the displacement of the wire is $y_1 = A \sin \dfrac{\pi x}{L} \sin \omega t$ and energy is E_1, and in another experiment its displacement is $y_2 = A \sin \dfrac{2\pi x}{L} \sin 2\,\omega t$ and energy is E_2. Then :

(a) $E_2 = E_1$
(b) $E_2 = 2\,E_1$
(c) $E_2 = 4\,E_1$
(d) $E_2 = 16\,E_1$

11. In a large room, a person receives direct sound waves from a source 120 m away from him. He also receives waves from the same source which reach him, being reflected from the 25 m high celling at a point halfway between them. The two waves interfere constructively for wavelength of

(a) $20, \dfrac{20}{3}, \dfrac{20}{5}$ etc
(b)   10, 5, 2.5 etc
(c)   10, 20, 30 etc
(d)   15, 25, 35 etc

12. In the experiment for the determination of the speed of sound in air using the resonance column method. The length of the air column that resonates in the fundamental mode, with a tuning fork is 0.1 m. When this length is changed to 0.35 m, the same tuning fork resonates with the first overtone. The end correction is

(a)   0.012 m
(b)   0.025 m
(c)   0.05 m
(d)   0.024 m

Answer Key	1	(d)	3	(a)	5	(b)	7	(c)	9	(d)	11	(a)
Sol. from page 686	2	(b)	4	(d)	6	(a)	8	(d)	10	(c)	12	(b)

13. A string of length 0.4 m and mass 10^{-2} kg is tightly clamped at its ends. The tension in the string is 1.6 N. Identical wave pulses are produced at one end at equal intervals of time Δt. The minimum value of Δt which allows constructive interference between successive pulses is

(a) 0.05 s   (b) 0.10 s

(c) 0.20 s   (d) 0.40 s

14. A police car moving at 22 m/s, chases a motorcyclist. The policeman sounds his horn at 176 Hz, while both of them move towards a stationary siren of frequency 165 Hz. The speed of the motorcycle, if it is given that he does not observe any beats is

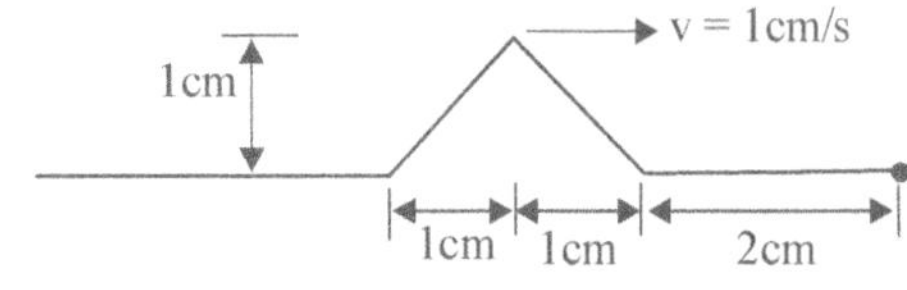

(a) 33 m/s   (b) 22 m/s

(c) zero   (d) 11 m/s

15. The equation of displacement of two waves are given as

$$y_1 = 10 \sin\left(3\pi t + \frac{\pi}{3}\right); \quad y_2 = 5 (\sin 3\pi t + \sqrt{3} \cos 3\pi t).$$ Then what is the ratio of their amplitudes

(a) 1 : 2   (b) 2 : 1

(c) 1 : 1   (d) None of these

16. Two identical straight wires are stretched so as to produce 6 beats per second when vibrating simultaneously. On changing the tension in one of them, the beat frequency remains unchanged. Denoting by T_1, T_2, the higher and the lower initial tension in the strings, then it could be said that while making the above change in tension

(a) T_2 was decreased   (b) T_2 was increased

(c) T_1 was increased   (d) T_1 was kept constant

17. A metal wire of linear mass density of 9.8 g/m is stretched with a tension of 10 kg weight between two rigid supports 1 m apart. The wire passes at its middle point between the poles of a permanent magnet, and it vibrates in resonance when carrying an alternating current of frequency f. The frequency f of the alternating source is

(a) 25 Hz   (b) 50 Hz

(c) 100 Hz   (d) 200 Hz

18. An earthquake generates both transverse (S) and longitudinal (P) sound waves in the earth. The speed of S waves in about 4.5 km/s and that of P waves is about 8.0 km/s. A seismograph records P and S waves from an earthquake. The first P wave arrives 4.0 min. before the first S wave. The epicenter of the earthquake is located at a distance about

(a) 25 km   (b) 250 km

(c) 2500 km   (d) 5000 km

19. A glass tube 1.0 m length is filled with water. The water can be drained out slowly at the bottom of the tube. If a vibrating tunning fork of frequency 500 c/s is brought at the upper end of the tube and the velocity of sound is 330 m/s, then the total number of resonances obtained will be

(a) 4   (b) 3

(c) 2   (d) 1

20. A wave pulse on a string has the dimension shown in figure. The wave speed is $v = 1$ cm/s. If point O is a free end, the shape of wave at time $t = 3$ s is

(a)

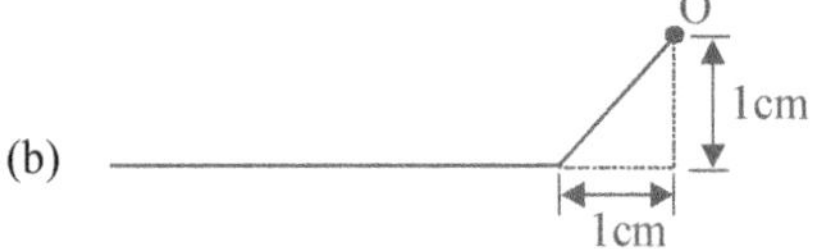

(b)

(c)

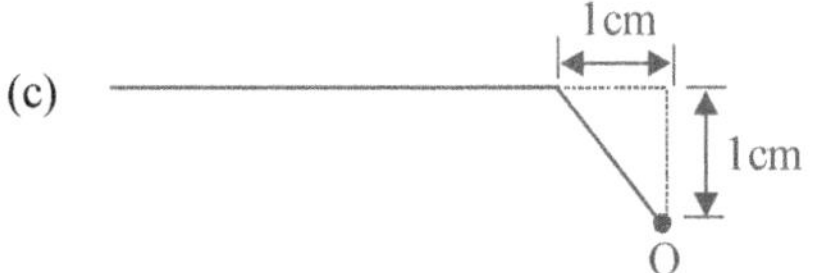

(d)

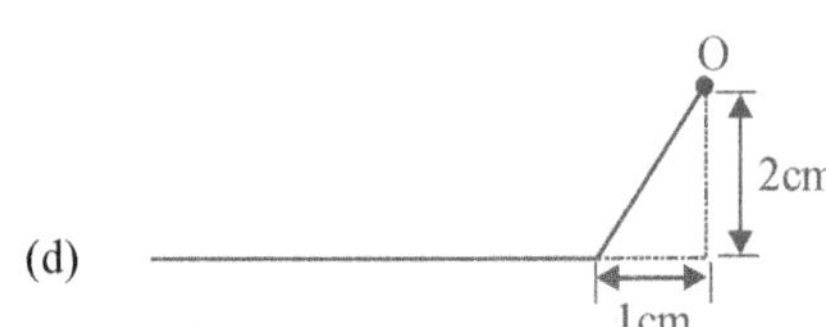

21. Two waves are propagating to the point P along a straight line produce by two sources A and B of simple harmonic and of equal frequency. The amplitude of every wave at P is 'a' and the phase of A is ahead by $\pi/3$ than that of B and the distance AP is greater than BP by 50 cm. Then the resultant amplitude at the point P will be, if the wavelength is 1 meter

(a) $2a$ (b) $a\sqrt{3}$

(c) $a\sqrt{2}$ (d) a

22. The amplitude of a wave represented by displacement equation

$$y = \frac{1}{\sqrt{a}} \sin \omega t \pm \frac{1}{\sqrt{b}} \cos \omega t \quad \text{will be}$$

(a) $\dfrac{a+b}{ab}$ (b) $\dfrac{\sqrt{a}+\sqrt{b}}{ab}$

(c) $\dfrac{\sqrt{a}\pm\sqrt{b}}{ab}$ (d) $\sqrt{\dfrac{a+b}{ab}}$

Answer Key	13	(b)	15	(c)	17	(b)	19	(b)	21	(d)
Sol. from page 686	14	(b)	16	(b)	18	(c)	20	(d)	22	(d)

23. Two travelling waves $y_1 = A \sin [k(x-ct)]$ and $y_2 = A \sin [k(x+ct)]$ are superimposed on string. The distance between adjacent nodes is
    (a) ct/π (b) $ct/2\pi$
    (c) $\pi/2k$ (d) π/k

24. A transverse sinusoidal wave moves along a string in the positive x-direction at a speed at 10 cm/s. The wavelength of the wave is 0.5 m and its amplitude is 10 cm. At a particular time t, the snapshot of the wave is shown in figure. The velocity of point P when its displacement is 0.05 m, is

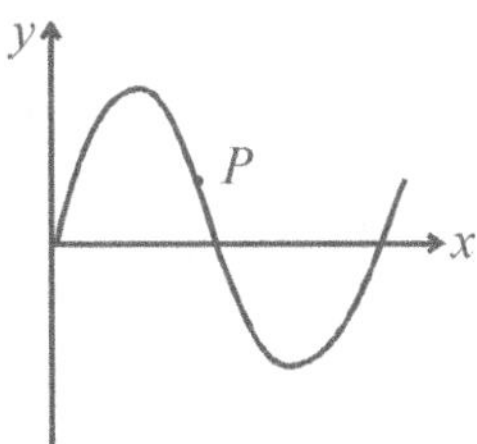

    (a) $\dfrac{\sqrt{3}\pi}{50}\hat{j}\, m/s$ (b) $-\dfrac{\sqrt{3}\pi}{50}\hat{j}\, m/s$

    (c) $\dfrac{\sqrt{3}\pi}{50}\hat{i}\, m/s$ (d) $-\dfrac{\sqrt{3}\pi}{50}\hat{i}\, m/s$

25. The stationary wave $y = 2a \sin kx \cos \omega t$ in a closed organ pipe is the result of the superposition of $y = a \sin (\omega t - kx)$ and
    (a) $y = -a \cos (\omega t + kx)$ (b) $y = -a \sin (\omega t + kx)$
    (c) $y = a \sin (\omega t + kx)$ (d) $y = a \cos (\omega t + kx)$

26. While measuring the speed of sound by performing a resonance column experiment, a student gets the first resonance condition at a column length of 18 cm during winter. Repeating the same experiment during summer, she measures the column length to be x cm for the second resonance. Then
    (a) $x > 54$ (b) $54 > x > 36$
    (c) $36 > x > 18$ (d) $18 > x$

27. The equation of a plane progressive wave is $y = 0.9\sin 4\pi\left[t - \dfrac{x}{2}\right]$.

    When it is reflected at a rigid support, its amplitude becomes $\dfrac{2}{3}$ of its previous value. The equation of the reflected wave is

    (a) $y = 0.6\sin 4\pi\left[t + \dfrac{x}{2}\right]$ (b) $y = -0.6\sin 4\pi\left[t + \dfrac{x}{2}\right]$

    (c) $y = -0.9\sin 8\pi\left[t - \dfrac{x}{2}\right]$ (d) $y = -0.6\sin 4\pi\left[t - \dfrac{x}{2}\right]$

28. A tube U–shaped has a uniform cross–section with arm lengths ℓ_1 and ℓ_2 $(\ell_2 < \ell_1)$. Tube has a liquid of density ρ_1 filled to a height h. Another liquid of density $\rho_2 = \dfrac{\rho_1}{2}$ is poured in arm A. Both liquids are immiscible. The length of the second liquid that should be poured in A so that first overtone of A is in unison with fundamental tone of B is

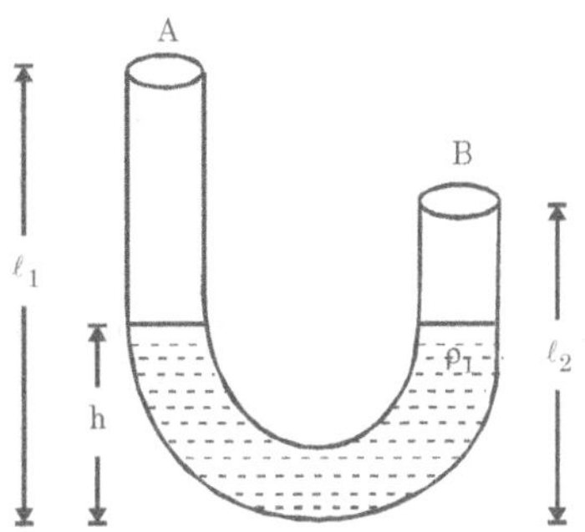

    (a) $\dfrac{3}{2}(\ell_1 - 3\ell_2 - 2h)$ (b) $\dfrac{3}{2}(\ell_1 - 3\ell_2 + 2h)$

    (c) $\dfrac{2}{3}(\ell_1 + 3\ell_2 + 2h)$ (d) $\dfrac{2}{3}(\ell_1 - 3\ell_2 + 2h)$

29. A massless rod is suspended by two identical strings AB and CD of equal length. A block of mass m is suspended from point O such that BO is equal to x.
    Further, it is observed that the frequency of 1st harmonic (fundamental frequency) in AB is equal to 2nd harmonic frequency in CD. Then length of BO is

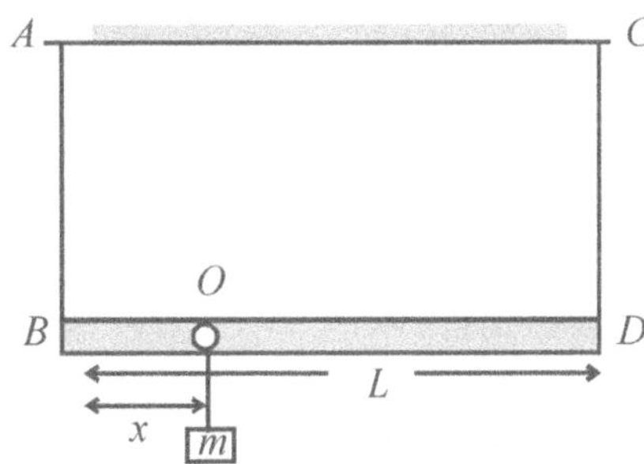

    (a) $\dfrac{L}{5}$ (b) $\dfrac{4L}{5}$

    (c) $\dfrac{3L}{4}$ (d) $\dfrac{L}{4}$

30. A vibrating string of certain length l under a tension T resonates with a mode corresponding to the first overtone (third harmonic) of an air column of length 75 cm inside a tube closed at one end. The string also generates 4 beats per second when excited along with a tuning fork of frequency f. Now when the tension of the string is slightly increased the number of beats reduces to 2 per second. Assuming the velocity of sound in air to be 340 m/s, the frequency f of the tuning fork in Hz is
    (a) 344   (b) 336
    (c) 117.3   (d) 109.3

31. Three waves of equal frequency having amplitudes 10 mm, 4 mm and 7 mm arrive at a given point with successive phase difference of $\dfrac{\pi}{2}$. The amplitude of the resulting wave in mm is given by :
    (a) 7   (b) 6
    (c) 5   (d) 4

Answer Key	23	(d)	25	(b)	27	(b)	29	(a)	31	(c)
Sol. from page 686	24	(a)	26	(a)	28	(d)	30	(a)		

Wave -II   MCQ Type 2   *Exercise 10.2*

Multiple options correct

1. The displacement of a particle in string stretched in x direction is represented by y. Among the following expressions for y, those describing wave motions are
   (a) $\cos kx \sin \omega t$
   (b) $k^2 x^2 - \omega^2 t^2$
   (c) $\cos(kx + \omega t)$
   (d) $\cos(k^2 x^2 - \omega^2 t^2)$

2. Two point sources S_1 and S_2, which are out of phase, emit sound waves of wavelength 2.0 m. The phase difference between the waves arriving at point P if $x_1 = 18$ m and $x_2 = 19$ m

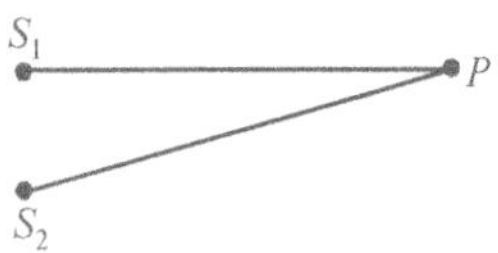

   (a) 0
   (b) $\dfrac{\pi}{2}$
   (c) π
   (d) 2π

3. Coherent sources are characterized by the same
   (a) Phase and phase velocity
   (b) Wavelength, amplitude and phase velocity
   (c) Wavelength, amplitude and frequency
   (d) Wavelength and phase

4. Standing waves can be produced
   (a) On a string clamped at both the ends
   (b) On a string clamped at one end and free at the other
   (c) When incident wave gets reflected from a wall
   (d) When two identical waves with a phase difference of π are moving in the same direction

5. It is desired to increase the fundamental resonance frequency in a tube which is closed at one end. This can be achieved by
   (a) Replacing the air in the tube by hydrogen gas
   (b) Increasing the length of the tube
   (c) Decreasing the length of the tube
   (d) Opening the closed end of the tube

6. A wave disturbance in a medium is described by $y(x, t) = 0.02 \cos\left(50\pi t + \dfrac{\pi}{2}\right) \cos(10\pi x)$, where x and y are in metres and t in seconds
   (a) A displacement node occurs at $x = 0.15\ m$
   (b) An antinode occurs at $x = 0.3\ m$
   (c) The wavelength of the wave is 0.2 m
   (d) The speed of the wave is 5.0 m/s

7. A student performed the experiment to measure the speed of sound in air using resonance air-column method. Two resonances in the air-column were obtained by lowering the water level. The resonance with the shorter air-column is the first resonance and that with the longer air-column is the second resonance. Then,
   (a) The intensity of the sound heard at the first resonance was more than that at the second resonance
   (b) The prongs of the tuning fork were kept in a horizontal plane above the resonance tube
   (c) The amplitude of vibration of the ends of the prongs is typically around 1 cm
   (d) The length of the air-column at the first resonance was somewhat shorter than 1/4th of the wavelength of the sound in air

8. Standing waves are produced on a stretched string of length L with fixed ends. When there is a node at a distance $L/3$ from one end, then
   (a) minimum and next higher number of nodes excluding the ends are 2, 5 respectively
   (b) minimum and next higher number of nodes excluding the ends are 2, 4 respectively
   (c) frequency produced may be $v/3L$
   (d) frequency produced may be 3v/2L

9. The equation of a stationary wave in a string is $y = (4\text{mm}) \sin[(3.14\ \text{m}^{-1})\,x] \cos \omega t$
   Select the correct alternative(s):
   (a) The amplitude of component waves is 2 mm
   (b) The amplitude of component waves is 4 mm
   (c) The smallest possible length of string is 0.5 m
   (d) The smallest possible length of string is 1.0 m

10. In a resonance tube experiment, a close organ pipe of length 120 cm resonates when tune with a turning fork of frequency 340 Hz. If water is poured in the pipe then (given $v_{\text{air}} = 340$ m/sec)
    (a) minimum length of water column to have the resonance is 45 cm
    (b) the distance between two successive nodes is 50 cm
    (c) the maximum length of water column to create the resonance is 95 cm
    (d) none of these

11. A transverse sinusoidal wave of amplitude a, wavelength λ and frequency f is traveling on a stretched string. The maximum speed of any point on the string is $v/10$ where v is the speed of propagation of the wave. If $a = 10^{-3}$ m and $v = 10$ ms^{-1}, then λ and f are given by
    (a) $\lambda = 2\pi \times 10^{-2}\,\text{m}$
    (b) $\lambda = 10^{-3}\,\text{m}$
    (c) $f = 10^3/(2\pi)\ \text{Hz}$
    (d) $f = 10^4\ \text{Hz}$

Answer Key	1	(a, c)	3	(a, d)	5	(a, c, d)	7	(a, d)	9	(a, d)	11	(a, c)
Sol. from page 688	2	(a, d)	4	(a, b, c)	6	(a, b, c, d)	8	(a, d)	10	(a, b, c)		

12. A closed organ pipe of length 1.2 m vibrates in its first overtone mode. The pressure variation is maximum at

(a) 0.8 m from the open end   (b) 0.4 m from the open end

(c) closed end   (d) 1.0 m from the open end

13. For a certain stretched string, three consecutive resonance frequencies are observed as 105, 175, 245 Hz respectively. Then select the correct alternatives(s)

(a) The string is fixed at both ends

(b) The string is fixed at one end only

(c) The fundamental frequency is 35 Hz

(d) The fundamental frequency is 52.5 Hz

14. An air column in a pipe, which is closed at one end will be in resonance with a vibrating tuning fork of frequency 264 Hz, then the length of the column in cm is

(a) 31.25   (b) 62.50

(c) 93.75   (d) 125

15. A wave is travelling along a string. At an instant, shape of the string is as shown in figure. At this instant, point A is moving upwards. Which of the following statements is / are correct :

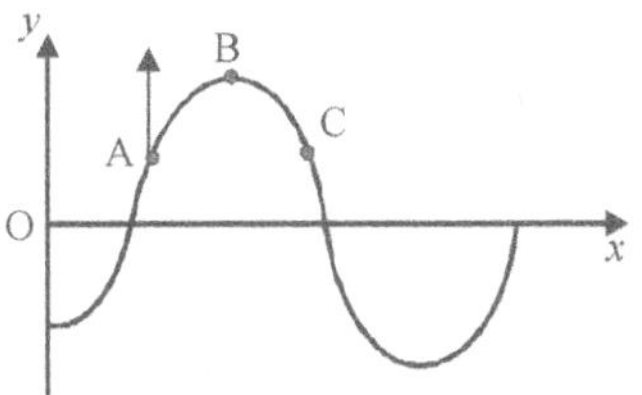

(a) The wave is travelling to the right.

(b) Displacement amplitude of the wave is equal to displacement of B at this instant.

(c) At this instant velocity of C is also directed upwards.

(d) Phase difference between A and C may be equal to $\dfrac{\pi}{2}$.

16. The (x, y) coordinates of the corners of a square plate are $(0, 0)$, $(L, 0)$, (L, L) and $(0, L)$. The edges of the plate are clamped and transverse standing waves are setup in it. If $u(x, y)$ denotes the displacement of the plate at the point (x, y) at some instant of time, the possible expression (s) for u is (are) (a = positive constant)

(a) $a \cos \dfrac{\pi x}{2L} \cos \dfrac{\pi y}{2L}$ (b) $a \sin \dfrac{\pi x}{L} \sin \dfrac{\pi y}{L}$

(c) $a \sin \dfrac{\pi x}{L} \sin \dfrac{2\pi y}{L}$ (d) $a \cos \dfrac{2\pi x}{L} \cos \dfrac{\pi y}{L}$

Answer Key	**12**	(b, c)	**14**	(a, c)	**16**	(b, c)
Sol. from page 688	**13**	(b, c)	**15**	(b, d)		

Wave - II Statement Questions *Exercise 10.3*

Read the two statements carefully to mark the correct option out of the options given below:
(a) If both the statements are true and the *statement - 2* is the correct explanation of *statement - 1*.
(b) If both the statements are true but *statement - 2* is not the correct explanation of the *statement - 1*.
(c) If *statement - 1* true but *statement - 2* is false.
(d) If *statement - 1* is false but *statement - 2* is true.

1. **Statement -1**
Principle of superposition can be used for any physical quantity.
Statement -2 Principle of superposition can be used only when amplitude of quantity is small.

2. **Statement -1**
It is not possible to have interference between the waves produced by two independent sources of same frequency.
Statement -2
For interference of two waves the phase difference between the waves remain constant.

3. **Statement -1**
To hear distinct beats, difference in frequencies of two sources should not be greater than 10.
Statement -2
Persistance of human ear is 10 per second.

4. **Statement -1**
Sound produced by an open organ pipe is richer than the sound produced by a closed organ pipe.
Statement -2
Outside air can enter the pipe from both ends, in case of open organ pipe.

5. **Statement -1**
In the case of a stationary wave, a person hear a loud sound at the nodes as compared to the antinodes.
Statement -2
In a stationary wave all the particles of the medium vibrate in phase.

6. **Statement -1**
The fundemental frequency of an open organ pipe increases as the temperature is increased.
Statement -2
As the temperature increses, the velocity of sound increases more rapidly than length of the pipe.

7. **Statement -1**
Velocity of particles, while crossing mean position in case of stationary waves varies from maximum at antinodes to zero at nodes.
Statement -2
Amplitude of vibration at antinodes is maximum and at nodes, the amplitude is zero, and all particles between two successive nodes cross the mean position together.

8. **Statement -1**
Like sound, light can not propagate in vacuum.
Statement -2
Light waves are transverse in nature.

9. **Statement -1** Speed of wave $= \dfrac{\text{Wave Length}}{\text{time period}}$.
Statement -2
Wavelength is the distance between two nearest particles in phase.

10. **Statement -1**
The flash of lightening is seen before the sound of thunder is heard.
Statement -2
Speed of sound is greater than speed of light.

11. **Statement -1**
When a beetle moves along the sand within a few tens of centimeters of a sand the scorpion immediately turn towards the beetle and dashes to it.
Statement -2
When a beetle disturbs the sand, it sends pulses along the sands surface one set of pulses is longitudinal while other set is transverse.

12. **Statement -1**
The reverberation time dependent on the shape of enclosure, position of source and observer.
Statement -2
The unit of absorption coefficient in MKS system metric sabine.

Answer Key	1	(d)	3	(a)	5	(c)	7	(a)	9	(b)	11	(a)
Sol. from page 690	2	(a)	4	(b)	6	(a)	8	(d)	10	(c)	12	(d)

Passage & Matrix

Exercise 10.4

PASSAGES

Passage for (Q. 1 - 3) :

Waves $y_1 = A\cos(0.5\pi x - 100\pi t)$ and $y_2 = A\cos(0.46\pi x - 92\pi t)$ are travelling along x-axis. (Here x is in m and t is in second)

1. The number of times intensity is maximum in time interval of 1 sec
   - (a) 4
   - (b) 6
   - (c) 8
   - (d) 10
2. The wave velocity of louder sound is
   - (a) 100 m/s
   - (b) 192 m/s
   - (c) 200 m/s
   - (d) 96 m/s
3. The number of times $y_1 + y_2 = 0$ at $x = 0$ in 1 sec is
   - (a) 100
   - (b) 46
   - (c) 192
   - (d) 96

Passage for (Q. 4 - 6) :

A pulse is started at a time $t = 0$ along the $+x$ direction on a long, taut string. The shape of the pulse at $t = 0$ is given by function $f(x)$ with

$$f(x) = \begin{cases} \dfrac{x}{4}+1 & for & -4 < x \le 0 \\ -x+1 & for & 0 < x < 1 \\ 0 & & otherwise \end{cases}$$

Here f and x are in centimeters. The linear mass density of the string is 50 g/m and it is under a tension of 5N.

4. The shape of the string is drawn at $t = 0$ and the area of the pulse enclosed by the string and the x-axis is measured. It will be equal to
   - (a) 2 cm^2
   - (b) 2.5 cm^2
   - (c) 4 cm^2
   - (d) 5 cm^2
5. The vertical displacement of the particle of the string at $x = 7$ cm and $t = 0.01$ s will be
   - (a) 0.75 cm
   - (b) 0.5 cm
   - (c) 0.25 cm
   - (d) zero
6. The transverse of the particle at $x = 13$ cm and $t = 0.015$ s will be
   - (a) – 250 cm/s
   - (b) – 500 cm/s
   - (c) 500 cm/s
   - (d) – 1000 cm/s

Passage for (Q. 7 - 9) :

A string of linear mass density 0.5 g/cm and a total length 30 cm is tied to a fixed wall at one end and to a frictionless ring at the other end. The ring can move on a vertical rod. A wave pulse is produced on the string which moves towards the ring at a speed of 20 cm/s. The pulse is symmetric about its maximum which is located at a distance of 20 cm from the end joined to the ring.

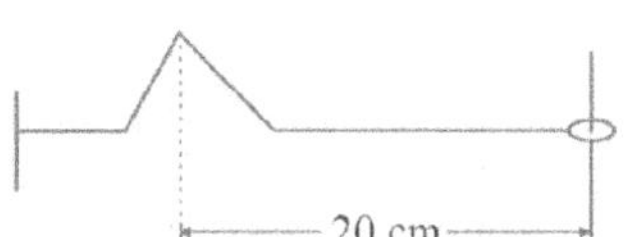

7. Assuming that the wave is reflected from the ends without loss of energy, the time taken by the string to regain its shape is
   - (a) 3 s
   - (b) 6 s
   - (c) 2 s
   - (d) 4 s
8. The shape of the string changes periodically with time. The time period is
   - (a) 3 s
   - (b) 5 s
   - (c) 4 s
   - (d) 2 s
9. The tension in the string is
   - (a) 1×10^{-3}N
   - (b) 1.5×10^{-3}N
   - (c) 1.8×10^{-3}N
   - (d) 2×10^{-3}N

Passage for (Q. 10 - 11) :

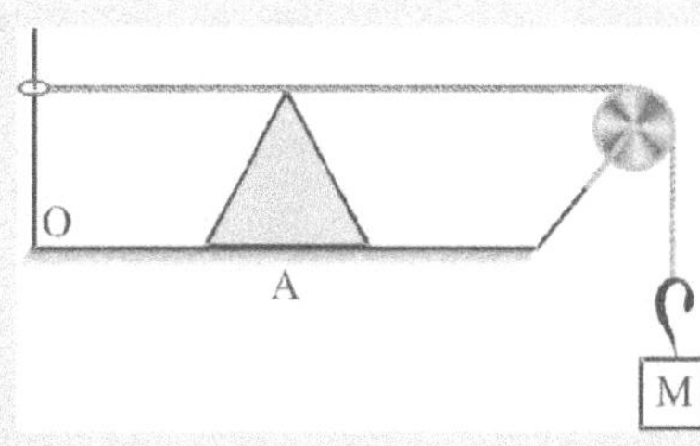

10. A sonometer wire 1 m long and weighing 1.25 g is in unison with a tuning fork of frequency 212 Hz when a wooden bridge is placed at position A such that $OA = 40$ cm. If the weight is fully immersed in water. The bridge A has to be moved towards O, 5 cm to regain unison. The density of material of weight M is
   - (a) 4267 kg/m^3
   - (b) 3000 kg/m^3
   - (c) 2800 kg/m^3
   - (d) None of these
11. If two wires are stretched on a sonometer each wire with length $OA = 40$ cm, one having mass in air and other in water and both vibrate simultaneously what will be the number of beats produced
   - (a) 26.2 Hz
   - (b) 20.2 Hz
   - (c) 24.4 Hz
   - (d) 30.6 Hz

Answer Key	1	(a)	3	(d)	5	(c)	7	(a)	9	(d)	11	(a)
Sol. from page 690	2	(c)	4	(b)	6	(a)	8	(b)	10	(a)		

12. Two identical speakers emit sound waves of frequency 660 Hz uniformly in all directions. The audio output of each speaker is 1 mW and the speed of sound in air 330 m/s. A point P is a distance 2m from one speaker and 3m from the other. Match the columns :

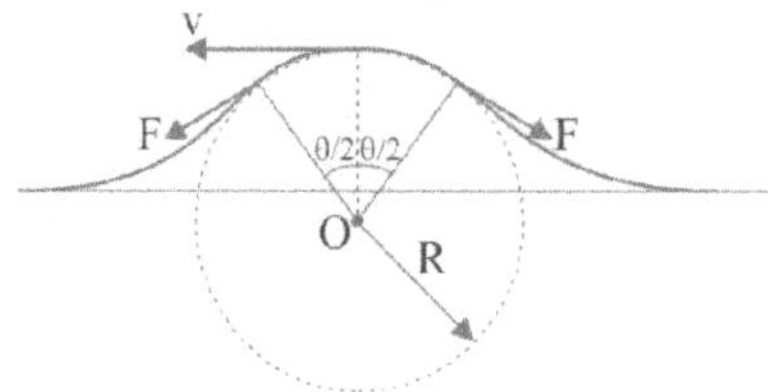

	Column I		Column II
A.	Intensity of speaker S_1 at P	(p)	55.3×10^{-6} W/m^2
B.	Intensity of sound at P, if the speakers are driven coherently and in phase	(q)	19.90×10^{-6} W/m^2
C.	Intensity of sound at P, if speakers are incoherent and out of phase by 180°	(r)	28.7×10^{-6} W/m^2
D.	Intensity of sound at P, if speakers are incoherent.	(s)	2.2×10^{-6} W/m^2

13. The air column in a pipe closed at one end is made to vibrate in its second overtone by a tuning fork of frequency 440 Hz. The speed of sound in air is 330 m/s. End correction may be neglected. Let P_0 denotes the mean pressure at any point in the pipe and ΔP_0 the maximum amplitude pressure variation. Then the columns :

	Column I		Column II
A.	The length of the air column	(p)	0.75 m
B.	The amplitude of pressure variation at the middle	(q)	0.94 m
C.	Maximum pressure at open end	(r)	$\Delta P_0/\sqrt{2}$
D.	Minimum pressure at closed end	(s)	P_0
		(t)	$(P_0 - \Delta P_0)$

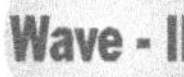 **Wave - II**

Subjective Integer Type

Exercise 10.5

Solution from page 692

1. In an experiment it was found that the string vibrated in three loops when 8 g were placed on the scale pan. What mass must be placed on the pan to make the string vibrate in six loops ? Neglect the mass of the string and the scale pan.

Ans. 2 g.

2. A fork of unknown frequency when sounded with one of frequency 288 Hz gives 4 beats/s and when loaded with a piece of wax again gives 4 beats/s. How do you account for this and what was the unknown frequency ?

Ans. 292 Hz.

3. Two sitar strings A and B playing the note 'Ga' are slightly out of tune and produce beats of frequency 6 Hz. The tension in the string A is slightly reduced and the beat frequency is found to reduce to 3 Hz. If the original frequency of A is 324 Hz, what is the frequency of B ?

Ans. 318 Hz.

4. At 16°C, two open end organ pipes, when sounded together produce 34 beats in 2 second. How many beats per second will be produced, if the temperature rises to 51°C ? Neglect the increase in length of the pipes.

Ans. 18 s^{-1}.

5. A column of air and a tuning fork produced 4 beats/s when sounded together. The tuning fork gives the lower note. The temperature of air is 15°C. When the temperature falls to 10°C, the two produce 3 beats/s. Find the frequency of the fork.

Ans. 110 Hz.

6. A guitar string is 90 cm long and has a fundamental frequency of 124 Hz. Where should it be pressed to produce a fundamental frequency of 186 Hz ?

Ans. 60 cm.

7. A string,fixed at both ends, vibrates in a resonant mode with a separation of 2.0 cm between the consecutive nodes. For the next higher resonant frequency, this separation is reduced to 1.6 cm. Find the length of the string.

Ans. 8.0 cm.

8. Figure shows an aluminium wire of length 60 cm joined to a steel wire of length 80 cm and stretched between two fixed supports. The tension produced is 40 N. The cross–sectional area of the steel wire is 1.0 mm^2 and that of the aluminium wire is 3.0 mm^2. What could be the minimum frequency of a tuning fork which can produce standing waves in the system with the joint as a node ? The density of aluminium is 2.6 g/cm^3 and that of steel is 7.8 g/cm^3.

80 cm	60 cm
Steel	Aluminium

Ans. 180 Hz.

9. A source emitting sound of frequency 180 Hz is placed in front of a wall at a distance of 2 m from it. A detector is also placed in front of the wall at the same distance from it. Find the minimum distance between the source and the detector for which the detector detects a maximum of sound. Speed of sound in air = 360 m/s.

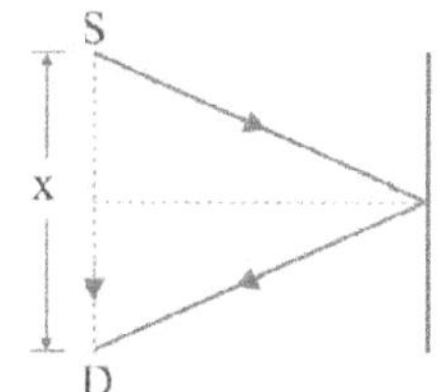

Ans. $x = 3$.

10. A heavy string is tied at one end to a movable support and to a light thread at the other end as shown in figure. The thread goes over a fixed pulley and supports a weight to produce a tension. The lowest frequency with which the heavy string resonates is 120 Hz. If the movable support is pushed to the right by 10 cm so that the joint is placed on the pulley, what will be the minimum frequency at which the heavy string can resonate ?

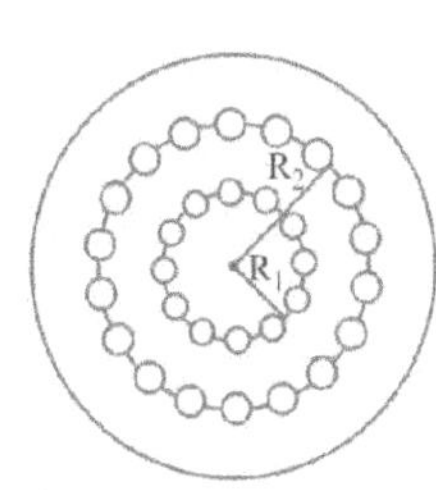

Ans. 240 Hz .

11. A rotating disc contains two sets of holes in the form of equally spaced concentric circles.

The area of innermost circle is equal to area between two circles.

A jet of air directed on the inner set of holes produces a note, of frequency 100Hz. What will be the frequency of note produced when a jet of of air is directed on the outer set of holes ? The spacingbetween inner and outer set of holesis same.

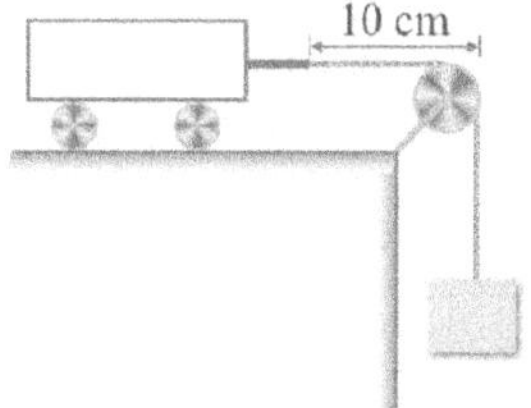

Ans. 1414Hz.

12. A column of air at 51°C and a tuning fork produce 4 beats/s when sounded together. As the temperature of air column is decreased the number of beats per second tends to decrease and when temperature is 16°C the two produce 1 beat/s. Find the frequency of tuning fork.

Ans. 50 Hz.

Wave -II | Subjective | *Exercise 10.6*

Solution from page 693

1. Stationary waves are set up by the superposition of two waves given by $y_1 = 0.05 \sin (5\pi t - x)$ and $y_2 = 0.05\sin (5\pi t + x)$

where x and y are in metre and t in second. Find the displacement of a particle situated at a distance $x = 1$m.

Ans. 0.054 m.

2. The transverse displacement of a string (clamped at its two ends) is given by

$$y (x, t) = 0.06 \sin (2\pi x/3) \cos (120 \pi t),$$

where x, y are in m and t is in s.

(i) Do all the points on the string oscillate with the same (a) frequency, (b) phase and (c) amplitude ?

Explain your answers. (ii) What is the amplitude of a point 0.375 m away from one end ?

Ans. (i) (a) same (b) same (c) not same (ii) 0.042 m.

3. (i) Write the equation of a wave identical to the wave represented by the equation : $y = 5 \sin \pi (4.0\, t - 0.02\, x)$ but moving in opposite direction. (ii) Write the equation of stationary wave produced by the composition of the above two waves and determine the distance between two nearest nodes. All the distances in the equation are in mm.

Ans. (i) $y = 5 \sin \pi (4.0\, t + 0.02\, x)$

(ii) $y = 10 \cos 0.02\, \pi x \sin 4.0\, t$, 50 mm.

4. A wire stretched between two rigid supports vibrates in its fundamental mode with a frequency of 45 Hz. The mass of the wire is 3.5×10^{-2} kg and its linear density is 4.0×10^{-2} kg/m. What is

(i) the speed of a transverse wave on the string, and

(ii) the tension in the string ?

Ans. (i) 248 N (ii) 78.75 m/s.

5. A stone hangs in air from one end of a wire which is stretched over a sonometer. The wire is in unison with a certain tuning fork when the bridges of the sonometer are 45 cm apart. Now the stone hangs immersed in water at $4°C$ and the distance between the bridges has to be altered by 9 cm to re–establish unision of the wire with the same fork. Calculate the density of the stone.

Ans. 2.778 g/cm^3.

6. A wire having a linear mass density of 5.0×10^{-3} kg/m is stretched between two rigid supports with a tension of 450 N. The wire resonates at a frequency of 420 Hz. The next higher frequency at which the same wire resonates is 490 Hz. Find the length of the wire.

Ans. 2.14 m.

7. A pipe 30.0 cm long is open at both ends. Which harmonic mode of the pipe is resonantly excited by a 1.1 kHz source ? Will resonance with the same source be observed if one end of the pipe is closed ? Take the speed of sound in air as 330 m/s.

Ans. Second harmonic of the open pipe, No resonance will be observed with the source.

8. A metre–long tube open at one end, with a movable piston at the other end, shows resonance with a fixed frequency source (a tuning fork of frequency 340 Hz), when the tube length is 25.5 cm or 79.3 cm. Estimate the speed of sound in air at the temperature of the experiment. Ignore edge effect.

Ans. 346.8 m/s.

9. A steel rod 100 cm long is clamped at its middle. The fundamental frequency of longitudinal vibrations of the rod is given to be 2.53 kHz. What is the speed of sound in steel ?

Ans. 5.06 km/s.

10. *A* set of 24 tuning forks is arranged in a series of increasing frequencies. If each fork gives 4 beats/s with the preceding one and the last sounds the octave of the first, find the frequencies of the first and the last forks.

Ans. 92 Hz, 184 Hz.

11. The two parts of sonometer wire divided by a movable knife differ by 2 mm and produce one beat per second when sounded together. Find their frequencies if the whole length of the wire is one metre.

Ans. 249.5 Hz, 250.5 Hz.

12. Figure shows two wave pulses at $t = 0$ travelling on a string in opposite directions with the same wave speed 50 cm/s. Sketch the shape of the string at $t = 4$ ms, 6 ms, 8 ms and 12 ms.

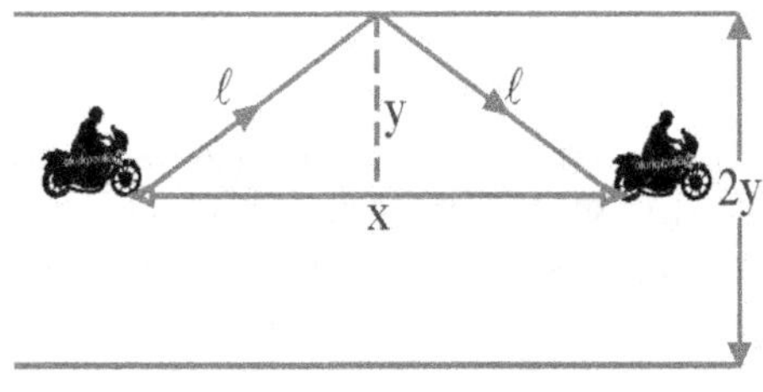

13. A string of length L fixed at both ends vibrates in its fundamental mode at a frequency f and a maximum amplitude A. (a) Find the wavelength and the wave number k. (b) Take the origin at one end of the string and the x–axis along the string. Take the y–axis along the direction of the displacement. Take t = 0 at the instant when the middle point of the string passes through its mean position and is going towards the positive y–direction. Write the equation describing the standing wave.

Ans. (a) $2L$, π/L (b) $y = A \sin (x\pi/L) \sin (2\pi ft)$.

14. In a Quinke's experiment, the sound intensity has a minimum value I at a particular position. As the sliding tube is pulled out by a distance of 16.5 mm, the intensity increases to a maximum of $9I$. Take the speed of sound in air to be 330 m/s (a) find the frequency of the sound source (b) find the ratio of the amplitudes of the two waves arrivingat the detector assuming that it does not change much between the positions of minimum intensity and maximum intensity.

Ans. (a) 5.0 kHz (b) 2.

15. Two stereo speakers are separated by a distance of 2.40 m. A person stands at a distance of 3.20 m directly in front of one of the speakers as shown in figure. Find the frequencies in the audible range (20–20000 Hz) for which the listener will hear a minimum sound intensity. Speed of sound in air = 320 m/s.

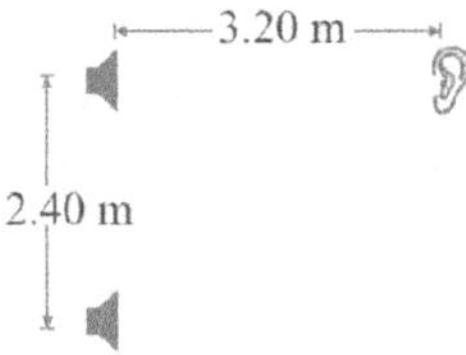

Ans. 200 $(2n + 1)$ Hz, where $n = 0, 1, 2,.......49$.

16. Consider the situation shown in figure. The wire which has a mass of 4.00 g oscillates in its second harmonic and sets the air column in the tube into vibrations in its fundamental mode. Assuming that the speed of sound in air is 340 m/s, find the tension in the wire.

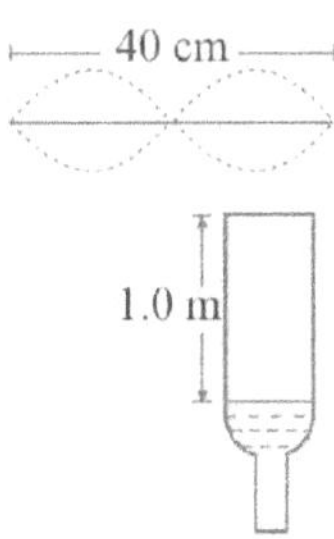

Ans. 11.6 N.

17. Show that if the room temperature changes by a small amount from T to $T + \Delta T$, the fundamental frequency of an organ pipe changes from f to $f + \Delta f$, where $\Delta f / f = \dfrac{1}{2} \dfrac{\Delta T}{T}$.

18. A tuning fork of frequency 256 Hz produces 4 beats per second with a wire of length 25 cm vibrating in its fundamental mode. The beat frequency decreases when the length is slightly shortened. What could be the minimum length by which the wire be shortened so that it produces no beats with the tuning fork?

Ans. 0.39 cm.

19. A violin player riding on a slow track plays a 440 Hz note. Another violin player standing near the track plays the same note. When the two are close by and the train approaches the person on the ground, he hears 4.0 beats per second. The speed of sound in air = 340 m/s. (a) Calculate the speed of the train. (b) What beat frequency is heard by the player in the train?

Ans. (a) 11 km/h (b) a little less than 4 beats/s.

20. A particular guitar wire is 30.0 cm long and vibrates at a frequency of 196 Hz when no finger is placed on it. The next higher notes on the scale are 220 Hz, 247 Hz, 262 Hz and 294 Hz. How far from the end of the string must the finger be placed to play these notes ?

Ans. 26.7 cm, 23.8 cm, 22.4 cm, and 20.0 cm.

21. A wave is propagating along the length of a string taken as positive x–axis. The wave equation is given by $y = Ae^{-\left(\frac{t}{T} - \frac{x}{\lambda}\right)^2}$ where $A = 5$mm, $T = 1.0$ s and $\lambda = 8.0$ cm.

(a) Find the velocity of the wave.

(b) Find the function $f(t)$ representing the displacement of particle at $x = 0$.

(c) Find the function $g(x)$ representing the shape of the string of $t = 0$.

(d) Plot the function $g(x)$ at the string at $t = 0$ and $t = 5$ s.

Ans. (a) 8 cm/s (b) $Ae^{-(t/T)^2}$ (c) $Ae^{-\left(\frac{x}{\lambda}\right)^2}$

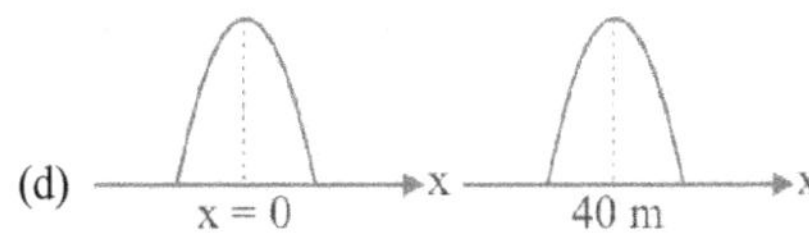

22. Two speakers connected to the same source of fixed frequency are placed 2.0 m apart in a box. A sensitive microphone placed at a distance of 4.0 m from their mid–point along the perpendicular bisector shows maximum response. The box is slowly rotated till the speakers are in a line with the microphone. The distance between the midpoint of the speakers and the microphone remains unchanged. Exactly 5 maximum responses are observed in the microphone in doing this. Calculate the wavelength of sound wave.

Ans. 0.4 m.

23. In a large room a person receives direct sound wave from a source 120 m away from him. He also receives wave from the same source which reach him being reflected from the 25 m high ceilling at a point half way between them. For which wavelength will these two sound waves interfere constructively ?

Ans. 10, 5, $\dfrac{10}{3}$, 2.5m, ...

24. Two waves are represented by pressure changes

$$P_1(x,t) = p_0 \cos\left(kx - \omega t + \frac{\pi}{4}\right),$$

$$P_2(x,t) = \frac{p_0}{2}\sin\left(kx - \omega t + \frac{\pi}{4}\right),$$

with $k = \dfrac{2\pi}{\lambda}$. What is the total pressure at (i) $x = \lambda$ and $t = 0$ (ii) $x = \lambda$ and $t = 2\pi / 3 \,\omega$. Also calculate the amplitude of total pressure.

Ans. $\dfrac{3}{2\sqrt{2}} p_0$, Pressure amplitude = maximum pressure = $\dfrac{\sqrt{5}}{2} P_0$.

25. The fundamental frequency of a sonometer wire increases by 6 Hz if its tension is increased by 44%, keeping the length constant. Find the change in the fundamental frequency of the sonometer wire when the length of the wire is increased by 20%, keeping the original tension in the wire.

Ans. 30Hz, 5Hz (decrease).

26. A sonometer wire is stretched by a hanging a mass of 50.7 kg from the open end of the wire. The volume of the hanging mass is 0.0075 m³ and the fundamental frequency of the wire is 260 Hz. If the hanging mass is completely immersed in water, what will be the fundamental frequency of the wire ?

Ans. 240 Hz.

27. A string of mass per unit length μ is clamped at both ends such that one end of the string is at $x = 0$ and the other end at $x = L$. When string vibrates in fundamental mode, amplitude of the

midpoint of string is a 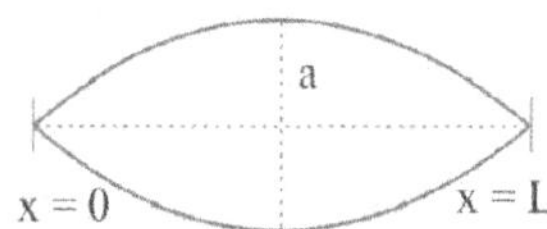

and tension in string is F. Find the total oscillation energy stored in the string.

Ans. $\dfrac{\pi^2 a^2 F}{4L}$.

28. A metal wire of diameter 1 mm is held on two knife edges by a distance 50 cm. The tension in the wire is 100 N. The wire vibrating with its fundamental frequency and a vibrating tuning fork together produce 5 beats/s. The tension in the wire is then reduced to 81 N. When the two are excited, beats are heard at the same rate. Calculate (i) frequency of a fork and (ii) the density of material of wire.

Ans. (i) 95 cycles/s (ii) 12.7×10^3 kg/m³.

29. A metallic rod of length 1 m is rigidly clamped at its mid point. Logitudinal stationary waves are set up in the rod in such a way that there are two nodes on either sides of mid–point. The amplitude of antinode is 2×10^{-6} m. Write the equation of motion at a point 2 cm from the mid–point and those of the constituents waves in the rod. (Young's modulus = 2×10^{11} N/m², density = 8000 kg/m³).

Ans. $y = 2 \times 10^{-6} \cos 0.6 \pi \sin 25000 \pi t$, $y_1 = 1 \times 10^{-6} \sin (25000 \pi t - 5 \pi x)$, $y_2 = 1 \times 10^{-6} \sin (25000 \pi t + 5 \pi x)$.

30. The following equations represent transverse waves :
$z_1 = A \cos (kx - \omega t)$, $z_2 = A \cos (kx + \omega t)$, $z_3 = A \cos (ky - \omega t)$
Identify the combination(s) of waves which will produce (i) standing wave(s) (ii) a wave travelling in the direction making an angle of 45° with the positive x and positive y axes. In each case, find the position at which the resultant intensity is always zero.

Ans. (i) z_1 = A cos $(kx - \omega t)$ and z_2 = A cos $(kx + \omega t)$
(ii) $(x - y) = (2n + 1) (\pi/k)$ $n = 0,1,2,3,..........$

31. A movable bridge divides a sonometer wire into two parts , which differ in length by 1 cm and produce 4 beats /s when sounded together. If the whole length is 100 cm, find the frequencies of the parts.

Ans. 202, 198 Hz.

32. Two narrow cylindrical pipes A and B have the same length. Pipe A is open at both ends and is filled with a monoatomic gas of molar mass M_A. Pipe B is open at one end and closed at the other end and is filled with a diatomic gas of molar mass M_B. Both gases are at the same temperature.

(a) If the frequency to the second harmonic of the fundamental mode in pipe A is equal to the frequency of the third harmonic of the fundamental mode in pipe B; determine the value of M_A / M_B .

(b) Now the open end of pipe B is also closed (so that pipe B is closed at both ends). Find the ratio of the fundamental frequency in pipe A to that in pipe B.

Ans. (a) (400 / 189), (b) (3 / 4).

33. A tube is of shape shown in figure. The straight line portion $l_1 = 100$ cm and the side tube measures $l_2 = 185$ cm. Find the audible frequencies for which this device acts as a silencer (speed of sound = 340 m/s).

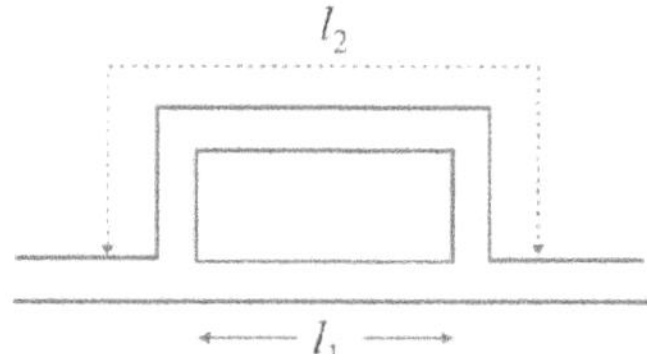

Ans. 200, 600, 900, ... 19800 Hz.

34. In figure S is a sound source and O an observer at a horizontal distance D, the direct wave from S and the wave reflected from point A, at a horizontal level at altitude H are in same phase. When the layer rises a distance h and the wave is reflected from point B, no signal is detected at O. Given that the incident and the reflected rays make the same angle with the reflecting layer. Find an expression for the wavelength λ of the waves in terms of D, H and h.

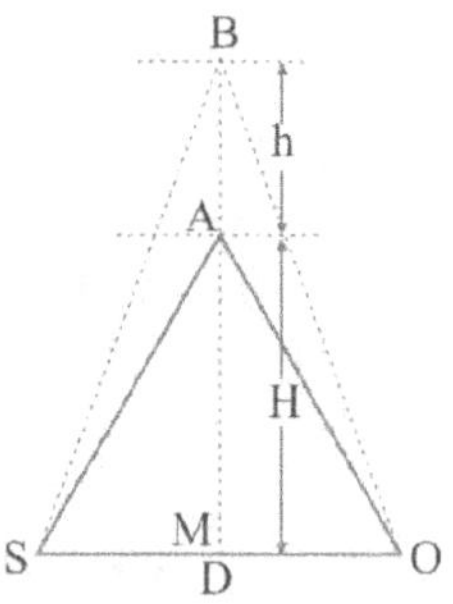

Ans. $\lambda = 2\sqrt{4(H + h)^2 + D^2} - 2\sqrt{(4H^2 + D^2)}$.

35. A particle oscillates in a wave according to the law $y = 4 \cos^2 0.5t \sin 1000t$. How many harmonic components are there in the complex wave and what are their frequencies ?

Ans. Three, 999, 1000, 1001Hz.

Hints & Solutions

1. (b) Equation $y = 2 \sin (3x) \cos (4t)$ is the combination of two wave equations.

2. (d) In sixth harmonic, there are six loop and so, there are 7 nodes and 6 antinodes.

3. (d)

4. (c) For $\Delta\phi = \pi$, $\Delta x = \dfrac{\Delta\phi\lambda}{2\pi} = \dfrac{\pi \times \lambda}{2\pi} = \dfrac{\lambda}{2}$

5. (d) Equal number of nodes and antinodes occur in close pipe. It is corresponding to ninth harmonic.

6. (a) The even number of harmonics possible in open pipe.

7. (c) Six harmonics are; 150, 300, 450, 600, 750 and 900 Hz.

8. (a) $f_A = \dfrac{v}{2(2\ell)}$ and $f_B = \dfrac{v}{4\ell}$

   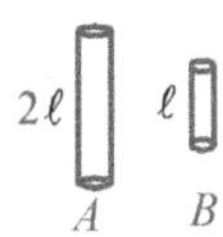

   Clearly first harmonic of both the pipes have equal frequency.

9. (b) $f = 288 + 4 = 292$ Hz or 284 Hz.

   Suppose, $f = 292$ Hz; On waxing, let its frequency becomes 290, which on known tuning fork gives 2 beats/s. So f must be 292 Hz.

10. (d) The wave is going along x direction, while particles are oscillating along y direction, so it represents transverse stationary wave.

11. (b) $\quad y_1 = a\cos(kx - \omega t)$, if we take

    $\quad y_2 = -a\cos(kx + \omega t)$, then

    $\quad y = y_1 + y_2 = 2a\sin kx \cos\omega t$

    $\quad\quad = A\cos\omega t$

    For $x = 0$, $A = 0$, which represents node.

12. (d) For stationary wave, two waves must be from opposite directions.

13. (a) The wavelength

    $\lambda = \ell = 1.21$ Å

14. (d) $T/2 = 0.5$ s, $\therefore$ $T = 1$ s

    $\lambda = \dfrac{v}{f} = vT = 10 \times 1 = 10$ m.

15. (c) $5\dfrac{\lambda}{2} = 10$, $\therefore$ $\lambda = 4$ m.

    Now $f = \dfrac{v}{\lambda} = \dfrac{20}{4} = 5$ Hz.

16. (c) As $f = \dfrac{1}{2\ell}\sqrt{F/\mu}$,

    $\therefore$ $\dfrac{f_1}{f_2} = \dfrac{\ell_2}{\ell_1}$

    or $\ell_2 = \dfrac{f_1}{f_2}\ell_1 = \dfrac{800}{1000} \times 50 = 40$ cm.

17. (a) $f_1 = f\dfrac{v}{v - v_s} = 240\left(\dfrac{320}{320 - 4}\right) = 243$ Hz.

    and $f_2 = f\dfrac{v}{v + v_s} = 240\left(\dfrac{320}{320 + 4}\right) = 237$ Hz.

    $\therefore$ Beats frequency $f_b = f_1 \sim f_2 = 6$ Hz.

18. (c) $\quad f_1 = 2\left(\dfrac{v}{2\ell}\right)$

    $\quad f_2 = n\left(\dfrac{v}{4\ell}\right)$

    $\therefore \quad f_2 = \dfrac{n}{4}f_1$; (where n is odd number.)

    As $f_2 > f_1$, $\therefore$ $n = 5$.

19. (c) A person can hear sound of frequency $f \geq 20000$ Hz.

    $\therefore \quad n \times 1500 = 20000$

    or $\quad n = \left[\dfrac{20000}{1500}\right]$; where n is an odd number

    $\quad\quad = 13.33$

    $\therefore \quad n = 13$.

    It is 13th harmonic or 6 overtones.

20. (b) After 2 s, the each wave travels a distance $= 2 \times 2 = 4$ m. The wave shape is shown in figure. Thus energy is purely kinetic.

21. (a) $f_1 = f\left(\dfrac{v}{v - v_s}\right)$ and $f_2 = f\left(\dfrac{v}{v + v_s}\right)$; so the frequency of whistle suddenly changes from f_1 to f_2.

22. (b) For wave B, $y = A$ and so $\varphi = \pi/2$.

    For wave C, $y = -A$ and so $\varphi = -\pi/2$.

23. (d) The displacement of the points B and F are equal in magnitude and sign. So these points are in same phase.

24. (c) After 2 second, each wave travels a distance $= 2.5 \times 2 = 5$ m and so the shape in figure (c) is correct one.

25. (d) The resultant amplitude

    $R = \sqrt{A_1^2 + A_2^2} = \sqrt{A^2 + A^2} = \sqrt{2}A$,

    but frequency remains the same.

26. (a) $R = \sqrt{A_1^2 + A_2^2} = \sqrt{4^2 + 3^2} = 5$

27. (a) Two identical waves from opposite directions will form stationary wave.

28. (a) On comparing with standard equation of stationary wave,

    $y = A \sin\omega t \cos kx$, we get

    $\omega = 100$, $k = 0.01$

    $\therefore \quad v = \dfrac{\omega}{k} = \dfrac{100}{0.01} = 10^4$ m/s

29. (c) For stationary waves in stretched string,

$$\eta\frac{\lambda}{2} = \ell \; ; \therefore \lambda = \frac{2\ell}{\eta}.$$

30. (b) On comparing with standard equation, we get

$$\omega = 2\pi \text{ and } k = 2\pi$$

or $$\frac{2\pi}{\lambda} = 2\pi \; , \therefore \lambda = 1 \text{ m}.$$

Thus $$\ell = \frac{\lambda}{2} = 0.5 \text{ m}.$$

So the length of the string will be in integral multiple of 0.5, which is 2.5 m.

31. (a) The maximum pressure is $= P_0 + P_A$, at the closed end and minimum pressure is $P_A - P_0$, at the open end.

32. (a) $$\frac{\lambda}{2} = (18 - 16) = 2$$

$$\therefore \qquad \lambda = 2 \times 2 = 4 \text{ cm}.$$

The length of the string must be in integral multiple of $\frac{\lambda}{2}$.

The minimum of the given values is 144 cm.

33. (d) $f = 128$ Hz.
The required frequency $= 3f = 3 \times 128 = 384$ Hz.

34. (b) For a moving source, $\lambda' < \lambda$ (normal wavelength).

Solutions EXERCISE 10.1 LEVEL -2

1. (d) The fundamental frequency of the wire is

$$f = \frac{v}{2L}.$$

The frequency of pipes are :

$$f_1 = \frac{v}{4L} \; ; \; f_2 = \frac{v}{4(2L)} \; ; \; f_3 = \frac{v}{2(L/2)} \; ; \; f_4 = \frac{v}{4(L/2)}$$

Thus the frequency of fourth pipe resonates with the frequency of wire.

2. (b) $A_1 = 5$ and $A_2 = 10$.

$$\therefore \qquad \frac{I_{max}}{I_{min}} = \frac{(A_1 + A_2)^2}{(A_1 - A_2)^2} = \frac{(5+10)^2}{(5-10)^2} = 9$$

3. (a) $$R = \sqrt{A^2 + A^2 + 2AA\cos\theta}$$
$$= 2A\cos\theta/2$$

4. (d) The frequency of piano wire may be
$$f = 256 \pm 5 = 261 \text{ Hz or } 251 \text{ Hz}.$$
Suppose $f = 261$ Hz; After increasing tension the frequency of wire may be 262 Hz, which will produce more number of beats with the fork. So the frequency of wire must be 251 Hz.

5. (b) $y = 5 \sin\frac{\pi x}{3} \cos 40 \pi t$. On comparing with standard equation of standing wave, $y = R \sin kx \cos \omega t$, we get

$$k = \pi/3 \text{ and } \omega = 40 \pi$$

or $$\frac{2\pi}{\lambda} = \pi/3, \therefore \lambda = 6 \text{ cm}.$$

The separation between two adjacent nodes $= \lambda/2 = 3$ cm.

6. (a) $$f = \frac{5}{2\ell}\sqrt{\frac{F}{\mu}} = \frac{5}{2\ell}\sqrt{\frac{9g}{\mu}} \qquad \text{........(i)}$$

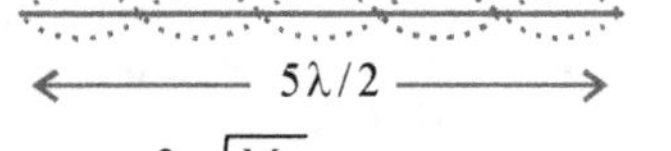

$$\longleftarrow 5\lambda/2 \longrightarrow$$

and $$f = \frac{3}{2\ell}\sqrt{\frac{Mg}{\mu}} \qquad \text{............(ii)}$$

From above equations, we get $M = 25$ kg.

7. (c) The frequency of tuning fork, $f = 392$ Hz.

Also $$392 = \frac{1}{2 \times 50}\sqrt{F/\mu} \qquad \text{..........(i)}$$

After decreasing the length by 2%, we have

$$f' = \frac{1}{2(49)}\sqrt{F/\mu} \qquad \text{..........(ii)}$$

From above equations,

$$f' = 400 \text{ Hz}.$$
$$\therefore \text{ Beats frequency} = 8 \text{ Hz}.$$

8. (d) $$\frac{f_1}{f_2} = \frac{l_2 r_2}{l_1 r_1} = \frac{2L}{L} \times \frac{r}{2r} = 1$$

9. (d) $$\frac{\lambda}{4} = 30.7 \text{ and } \frac{3\lambda}{4} = 63.2 \text{ cm}$$

$$\therefore \qquad \lambda = 65 \text{ cm}.$$

The velocity of sound in air

$$v = f\lambda = 512 \times 0.65 = 332.8 \text{ m/s}.$$

As actual velocity of sound is 332 m/s, so the maximum error in this can be 0.8 m/s.

10. (c) As $I \propto f^2$; or $I \propto \omega^2$.

$$\therefore \qquad \frac{E_1}{E_2} = \frac{\omega^2}{(2\omega)^2} = \frac{1}{4}.$$

11. (b) The path difference,

$$\Delta x = 2 \times 65 - 2 \times 60 = 60 \text{ m}.$$
For constructive interference
$$\Delta x = 10 = n\lambda$$

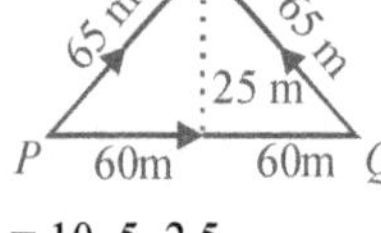

$$\therefore \lambda = \frac{10}{n} \; ; \text{For } n = 1, 2, 3, \dots ; \; \lambda = 10, 5, 2.5\dots$$

Ceiling here acts as free boundary, so do not add phase difference due to reflection.

12. (b) $$\ell_1 + e = \frac{\lambda}{4}$$

or $$0.1 + e = \frac{\lambda}{4} \qquad \text{.........(i)}$$

and $\quad 0.35 + e \quad = \quad \dfrac{3\lambda}{4}$ ....(ii)

From above equations, we get
$$e \quad = \quad 0.025 \text{ m}$$

13. (b) $\quad \mu \quad = \quad \dfrac{m}{\ell} = \dfrac{10^{-2}}{0.4} = 2.5 \times 10^{-2} \text{ kg/m.}$

and $\quad f \quad = \quad \dfrac{1}{2\ell}\sqrt{\dfrac{F}{\mu}} = \dfrac{1}{2\times0.4}\sqrt{\dfrac{1.6}{2.5\times10^{-2}}}$

$$= \quad \dfrac{1}{0.8}\times\dfrac{4}{5}\times10 = 10 \text{ Hz.}$$

$$\Delta T \quad = \quad \dfrac{1}{f} = \dfrac{1}{10} = 0.10 \text{ s.}$$

14. (b) $\quad 176\left(\dfrac{v - v_0}{v - 22}\right) \quad = \quad 165\dfrac{v + v_0}{v}$

Here $\quad v \quad = \quad 330$ m/s, after simplifying , we get
$\qquad\quad v_0 \quad = \quad 22$ m/s

15. (c) $\quad y_1 \quad = \quad 10 \sin\left(3\pi t + \pi/3\right),$

and $\quad y_2 \quad = \quad 5\sin 3\pi t + 5\sqrt{3}\cos 3\pi t$.

Amplitude, $\quad A_1 \quad = \quad 10$ unit

and $\quad A_2 \quad = \quad \sqrt{5^2 + \left(5\sqrt{3}\right)^2} = 10$ unit.

$$\therefore \quad \dfrac{I_1}{I_2} \quad = \quad \dfrac{A_1^2}{A_2^2} = 1.$$

16. (b) $\quad f \quad = \quad \dfrac{1}{2\ell}\sqrt{\dfrac{T_1}{\mu}}$ ......(i)

and $\quad f \pm 6 \quad = \quad \dfrac{1}{2\ell}\sqrt{\dfrac{T_2}{\mu}}$ ......(ii)

As $T_1 > T_2$, $\therefore$ second equation must be

$$f - 6 \quad = \quad \dfrac{1}{2\ell}\sqrt{\dfrac{T_2}{\mu}}.$$

On increasing T_2, the frequency of it may be $(f + 6)$, which again gives 6 beats/s.

17. (b) $\quad f \quad = \quad \dfrac{1}{2\ell}\sqrt{\dfrac{F}{\mu}} = \dfrac{1}{2\times1}\sqrt{\dfrac{10g}{9.8\times10^{-3}}}$

$$= \quad 50 \text{ Hz.}$$

18. (c) If x be the distance of epicentre from the seismograph, then

$$\dfrac{x}{v_s} - \dfrac{x}{v_p} \quad = \quad 4 \times 60$$

or $\quad \dfrac{x}{4.5} - \dfrac{x}{8} \quad = \quad 4 \times 60$

on simplifying, we get
$$x \quad \simeq \quad 2500 \text{ km}$$

19. (b) $\quad \lambda \quad = \quad \dfrac{v}{f} = \dfrac{330}{500} = 0.66 \text{ m}$

The resonance lengths are :

$\ell_1 \quad = \quad \dfrac{\lambda}{4} = 0.165$ m,

$\ell_2 \quad = \quad \dfrac{3\lambda}{4} = 0.495$ m,

$\ell_3 \quad = \quad \dfrac{5\lambda}{4} = 0.825$ m,

and $\quad \ell_4 \quad = \quad \dfrac{7\lambda}{4} = 1.155$ m

As ℓ_4 is greater than 1 m, so allowed resonances are only three.

20. (d) At $t = 3$ s, the wave pulse will reach at the free end. At the free end the displacement after superposition becomes
$$R \quad = \quad 2\,A = 2 \times 1 = 2 \text{ cm.}$$

21. (d) As $\lambda = 1$ m

so, 0.5 m $\to \lambda/2$.

The total phase difference

$$\Delta\phi = \pi - \pi/3 = 2\pi/3 = 120°$$

The resultant amplitude,

$$A = \sqrt{a^2 + a^2 + 2aa\cos 120°} = a.$$

22. (d) $\quad A = \sqrt{\left(\dfrac{1}{\sqrt{a}}\right)^2 + \left(\dfrac{1}{\sqrt{b}}\right)^2} = \sqrt{\dfrac{1}{a} + \dfrac{1}{b}} = \sqrt{\dfrac{a+b}{ab}}$.

23. (d) $\quad y = A \sin(kx - kct) + A \sin(kx + kct)$

$$= 2\,A\sin\left(\dfrac{kx - kct + kx + kct}{2}\right)\cdot\cos\left(\dfrac{kx - kct - kx - kct}{2}\right)$$

$$= 2\,A\sin(kct).\cos kx.$$

Thus $\dfrac{2\pi}{\lambda} = k$, $\therefore \lambda = \dfrac{2\pi}{k}$

The distance between adjacent nodes $= \dfrac{\lambda}{2} = \dfrac{\pi}{k}$

24. (a) $\quad f \quad = \quad \dfrac{v}{\lambda} = \dfrac{10}{50} = \dfrac{1}{5}$ Hz.

$$\therefore \quad \omega \quad = \quad 2\pi f = \dfrac{2\pi}{5}.$$

The particle velocity,

$$v_p \quad = \quad \omega\sqrt{A^2 - y^2} = \dfrac{2\pi}{5}\sqrt{10^2 - 5^2}$$

$$= \quad \dfrac{5\sqrt{3}\times 2\pi}{5} = 2\sqrt{3}\pi \text{ cm/s}$$

$$= \quad \dfrac{\sqrt{3}\pi}{50} \text{ m/s.}$$

25. (b) The superposition of $y = a\sin(\omega t + kx)$ together with

$$y \quad = \quad -a\sin(\omega t - kx) \text{ will give}$$

$$y_R \quad = \quad a\sin(\omega t + kx) - a\sin(\omega t - kx)$$

$$= \quad 2a\sin kx\cos\omega t.$$

26. (a) The second resonance length will be slightly greater than three times the first in summer.

Thus $x > (3 \times 18) = 54$ cm

27. (b) The equation of reflected wave is

$$y = \frac{2}{3} \times 0.9 \times \sin 4\pi \left[t + \frac{x}{2} + \pi \right]$$

$$= -0.6 \sin 4\pi (t + x/2)$$

28. (d) Let y be the length of second liquid poured in A. Let the first liquid come down by a level x in arm A and rises by x in arm B.

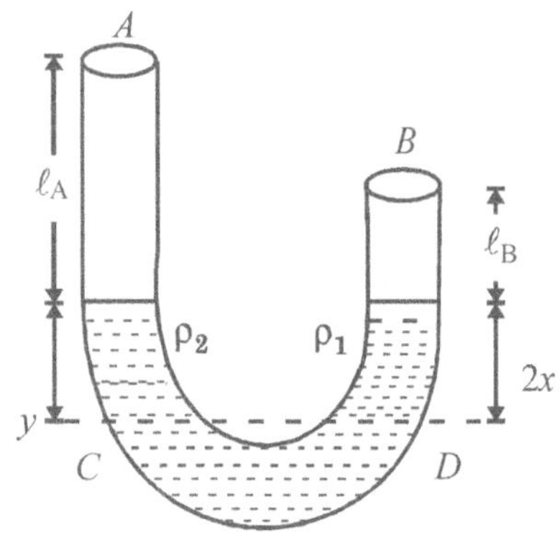

$\therefore$ Pressure at C = Pressure at D

$\therefore$ $\rho_2\, g\, y = \rho_1\, g\,(2x) \;\Rightarrow\; x = \dfrac{\rho_2}{2\rho_1}\, y = \dfrac{y}{4}$

$$\left(\because \rho_2 = \frac{\rho_1}{2} \right)$$

Length of air column in arm A is

$\Rightarrow$ $\ell_A = (\ell_1 - h) - \left(y - \dfrac{y}{4}\right) = \ell_1 - h - \dfrac{3y}{4}$

Length of air column in arm B is $\ell_B = \ell_2 - h + \dfrac{y}{4}$

Since first overtone of arm A is in unison with fundamental tone of B.

$\therefore$ $3\dfrac{v}{4\,\ell_A} = \dfrac{v}{4\,\ell_B}$

$\Rightarrow \ell_A = 3\,\ell_B \;\Rightarrow\; \ell_1 - h - \dfrac{3y}{4} = 3\left(\ell_2 - h + \dfrac{y}{4}\right)$

$\Rightarrow y = \dfrac{2}{3}(\ell_1 - 3\,\ell_2 + 2h)$

29. (a) If F_1 and F_2 are the tension forces in strings AB and CD respectively, then

$$\frac{1}{2\ell}\sqrt{\frac{F_1}{\mu}} = \frac{2}{2\ell}\sqrt{\frac{F_2}{\mu}} \qquad \text{........(i)}$$

and $F_1 x = F_2\,(L - x)$ ....(ii)

After solving above equations, we get

$x = L/5$.

30. (a)

$$f = 3\frac{v}{4\ell} = 3 \times \left(\frac{340}{4 \times 0.75} \right)$$

$$= 340 \text{ Hz.}$$

The frequency of fork may be $= 340 \pm 4$ Hz.

With the increase in tension in the string, beats frequency decreases, so the frequency of fork must be $= 340 + 4 = 344$ Hz.

31. (c) $R = \sqrt{3^2 + 4^2} = 5$ mm

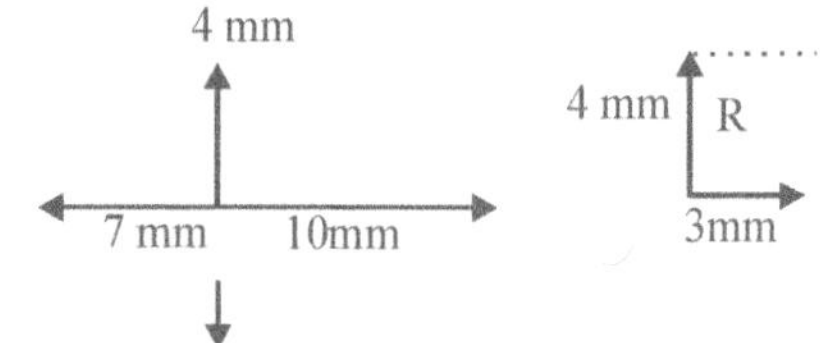

1. (a,c) Explained in the theory of the chapter.

2. (a,d) $\Delta x = 19 - 18 = 1$m

As $\lambda = 2,$

$\therefore$ 1m $= \sfrac{\lambda}{2}$, or $\phi = \pi$ rad

So $\Delta\phi = \pi - \pi = 0$ or $\Delta\phi = \pi + \pi = 2\pi$.

3. (a,d) For coherent sources, waves must have same frequency and constant phase difference.

4. (a,b,c) Standing waves can be produced by the two identical waves from opposite directions. It is possible in case (a), (b) and (c).

5. (a,c,d) $f = \dfrac{v}{2L}$; so the fundamental frequency can be increased either by increasing wave velocity or by decreasing length of pipe. As $v = \sqrt{\dfrac{\gamma RT}{M}}$, so lighter gas will have large value of v.

6. (a,b,c,d) On comparing the given wave with the standard equation of wave, we have

$\omega = 50\pi$ and $k = 10\pi$

$\therefore$ $v = \dfrac{\omega}{k} = \dfrac{50\pi}{10\pi} = 5$ m/s.

Also $\dfrac{2\pi}{\lambda} = 10\pi \Rightarrow \lambda = 0.2$ m.

At node, $R = 0$

or $\cos(10\pi x) = 0 \Rightarrow 10\pi x = \sfrac{\pi}{2}, \; \sfrac{3\pi}{2}, ...$

$\therefore$ $x = 0.05$m, 0.15m, ...

At antinode, $R =$ maximum

or $\cos(10\pi x) = \pm 1$

or $10\pi x = 0, \pi, 2\pi,$

$\therefore$ $x = 0, 0.1$ m, 0.2 m, ...

7. (a,d) The intensity of second resonance will be smaller than intensity of sound of first resonance. Consider end correction, the length of air column is slightly less than $\sfrac{\lambda}{4}$.

8. (a,d)

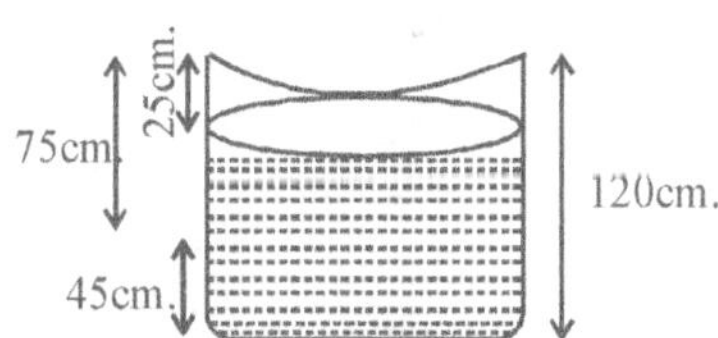

$$\frac{3\lambda}{2} = L$$

$$\therefore \quad \lambda = \frac{2L}{3}$$

so $\quad f = \frac{v}{\lambda} = \frac{3v}{2L}$

9. (a,d) On comparing the given wave with the standard equation of standing wave, we get

$$R = 2A = 4 \text{ mm},$$

$$\therefore \quad A = 2\text{mm}$$

Also $\quad k = 3.14$ or $\frac{2\pi}{\lambda} = 3.4$

$$\therefore \quad \lambda = 2\text{m}$$

As $\quad l = 2\lambda \Rightarrow \lambda = \frac{\ell}{2} = 1 \text{ m.}$

10. (a,b,c)

As $\quad v = \nu\lambda$

$$\lambda = \frac{v}{\nu} = \frac{340}{340} = 1\text{m}$$

First resonance light

$$R_1 = \frac{\lambda}{4} = \frac{1}{4} \text{ m} = 25 \text{ cm.}$$

$$\therefore \quad R_2 = \frac{3\lambda}{4} = \frac{3}{4} \text{ m} = 25 \text{ cm.}$$

$$\therefore \quad R_3 = \frac{5\lambda}{4} = \frac{5}{4} \text{ m} = 125 \text{ cm.}$$

i.e.,third resonance does not establish.

Now H_2O is poured,

$\therefore$ Minimum length of H_2O column to have the resonance $= 45$ cm.

$\therefore$ Distance between two successive nodes

$$= \frac{\lambda}{2} = \frac{1}{2} \text{ m} = 50 \text{ cm.}$$

and maximum length of H_2O column to create resonance i.e., $120 - 25 = 95$ cm.

11. (a,c) $\quad y = a\sin\frac{2\pi}{\lambda}(vt - x)$

Particle velocity $\dfrac{dy}{dt} = a \cdot \dfrac{2\pi}{\lambda} v \cos\dfrac{2\pi}{\lambda}(vt - x)$

$$\left|\frac{dy}{dt}\right|_{max} = a \cdot \frac{2\pi}{\lambda} = \frac{v}{10}$$

$\therefore$ Amplitude $\quad a = \dfrac{\lambda}{2\pi \times 10}$

or, $\quad \lambda = 20\pi \cdot a = 2\pi \times 10^{-2}$ m

Frequency $\quad f = \dfrac{v}{\lambda} = \dfrac{10}{2\pi \times 10^{-2}} = \dfrac{10^3}{2\pi}$ Hz.

12. (b, c) $\quad l = \dfrac{3\lambda}{4}$

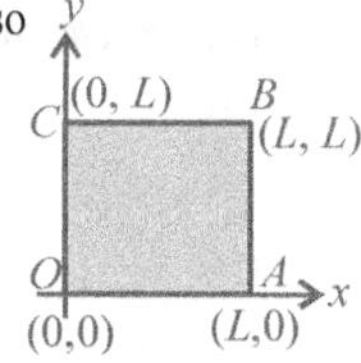

$$\therefore \quad \frac{\lambda}{4} = \frac{l}{3} = 0.4 \text{ m}$$

Pressure variation will be maximum at displacement nodes i.e., at 0.4 m from the open end and at closed end.

13. (b, c) As $f_1 : f_2 : f_3 = 3 : 5 : 7$ is fixed at one end. Its fundamental frequency is

$$\therefore \quad f_0 = \frac{f_1}{3} = \frac{105}{3} = 35 \text{ Hz}$$

14. (a,c) For closed organ pipe,

$$f = n\left(\frac{v}{4l}\right) \text{ where } n = 1, 3, 5...$$

$$l = \frac{nv}{4f}$$

For $n = 1$, $l_1 = \dfrac{nv}{4f} = \dfrac{(1)(330)}{4 \times 264} = 100$ cm $= 31.25$ cm

For $\quad n = 3, l_3 = 3l_1 = 93.75$ cm

For $\quad n = 5, l_5 = 5l_1 = 156.25$ cm.

15. (b,d) The separation between them is nearly

$$\Delta x \simeq \frac{\lambda}{4}, \quad \therefore \Delta\phi \simeq \frac{\pi}{2}$$

The amplitude of A or any other point will be equal to that of B.

16. (b,c) Since edges of the plate are clamped, so

$$U(x,y) = 0 \text{ for}$$

$OA; \quad y = 0, 0 \le x \le L$

$AB; \quad x = L; 0 \le y \le l$

$BC; \quad x = L, 0 \le y \le L$

$OC; x = 0, 0 \le y \le L$

Above conditions are satisfied in (b) and (c).

Solutions EXERCISE-10.3

1. (d) Principle of superposition can be used for vector quantity or tensor quantity.

2. (a) In case of independent sources, the phase difference between them does not remain constant.

3. (a) Statement-2 is the answer of statement-1.

4. (b) Open pipe can produce more number of harmonics in comparison to close pipe.

5. (c) At displacement nodes, pressure is maximum and so loud sound is heard.

In stationary waves, particles in the same loop vibrate in phase.

6. (a) As $f = \dfrac{v}{2l}$; and so with increase in temperature v increases more than l.

7. (a) Statement-2 is the answer of statement-1.

8. (d) Sound can not propagate in vacuum.

9. (b) Both the statements are self explanatory.

10. (c) Speed of light is very much greater than speed of sound.

Solutions EXERCISE-10.4

Passage (Q.1 – 3) :

1. (a)   2. (c)   3. (d)

The equations are y_1 = A cos $(0.5\ \pi x - 100\ \pi t)$ and $y_2 = A$ cos $(0.46\ \pi x - 92\ \pi t)$ represents two progressive wave travelling in the same direction with slight difference in the frequency. This will give the phenomenon of beats.

Comparing it with the equation

$y = A$ cos $(kx - \omega t)$, we get

$\omega_1 = 100\ \pi \Rightarrow 2\pi f_1 = 100\ \pi \Rightarrow f_1 = 50$ Hz and

$k_1 = 0.5\ \pi \Rightarrow \dfrac{2\pi}{\lambda_1} = 0.5\pi \ \lambda_1 = 4$ m

Wave velocity = $\lambda_1 f_1 = 200$ m/s [Alternatively use $v = \dfrac{\omega}{k}$]

$\omega_2 = 92\ \pi \Rightarrow 2\pi f_2 = 92\ \pi \Rightarrow f_2 = 46$ Hz

Therefore beat frequency $= f_1 - f_2 = 4$ Hz and

$k_2 = 0.46\ \pi \Rightarrow \dfrac{2\pi}{\lambda_2} = 0.46\pi \Rightarrow \lambda_2 = \dfrac{200}{46}$

Wave velocity = $\dfrac{200}{46} \times 46 = 200$ m/s

Note : Wave velocity is same because it depends on the medium in which the wave is travelling.

Now, at $x = 0$,

$y_1 + y_2 = (A$ cos $10\ \pi t) + (A$ cos $92\ \pi t) = 0$

$\Rightarrow$ cos $100\ \pi t = -$ cos $92\ \pi t =$ cos $(-92\ \pi t)$

$=$ cos $[(2n + 1)\pi - 92\ \pi t \Rightarrow t = \dfrac{2n+1}{192}$

when $t = 0$, $n = -\dfrac{1}{2}$ and when $t = 1$,

$n = \dfrac{191}{2} = 95.2$

$\Rightarrow$ net amplitude is zero for $n = 96$ times (the nearest answer).

Passage (Q.4 – 6) :

4. (b) Shape of the pulse at $t = 0$

That is a triangular pulse

Area of the pulse $= \dfrac{1}{2}[(4 \times 1) + (1 \times 1)] = \dfrac{5}{2}$ cm^2

5. (c) $v = \sqrt{\dfrac{T}{\mu}} = 10$m/s

Solution of the wave equation that gives displacement of any piece of the string at any time

$$y = f(x, t) = \begin{cases} \dfrac{(x - vt)}{4} + 1 & \text{for } vt - 4 < x \leq vt \\ -(x - vt) + 1 & \text{for } vt < x < vt + 1 \\ 0 & \text{otherwise} \end{cases}$$

Using $v = 1000$ cm/s, $t = 0.01$ s $\Rightarrow vt = 10$ cm.

as $(vt - 4) < (x = 7$ cm$) < vt$

$\Rightarrow \quad y = \dfrac{1}{4}(7 - 10) + 1 = \dfrac{1}{4}$cm. $= 0.25$ cm.

6. (a) Transverse velocity $= \dfrac{\partial y}{\partial t}$

at $t = 0.015$ s, $vt = 15$ cm.

as for $x = 13$ cm., $(vt - 4) < x < vt$

therefore, $\dfrac{\partial y}{\partial t} = -\dfrac{v}{4} = -250$ cm/s

Passage for (Q.7 – 9) :

7. (c) The situation is shown in figure. The distance travelled

$x \quad = \quad 20 + 20$

$= \quad 40$ cm

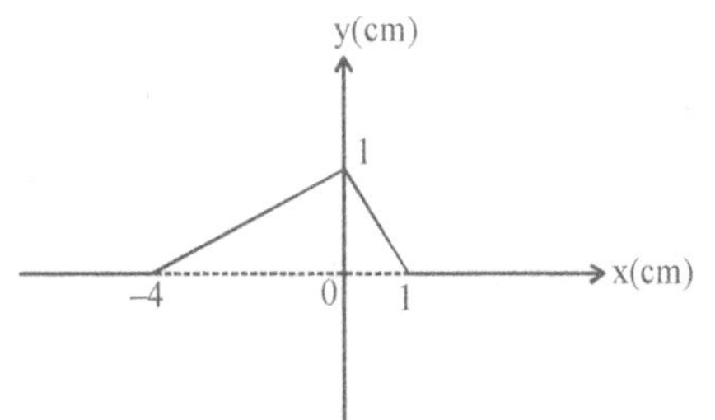

The time required $\quad t \quad = \quad \dfrac{x}{v}$

$= \quad \dfrac{40}{20}$

$= \quad 2$s.

8. (a) The distance travelled by the pulse to start from the same position

$x \quad = \quad 20 + 20 + 10 + 10$

$= \quad 60$ cm

Thus time period $T \quad = \quad \dfrac{x}{v}$

$= \quad \dfrac{60}{20} = 3$s.

9. (d) We have $v = \sqrt{\dfrac{F}{\mu}}$

$\therefore\quad F = v^2\mu$
$= 0.20^2 \times 0.5 \times 10^{-1}$
$= 2 \times 10^{-3}$ N.

Passage for (Q.10 – 11) :

10. (a) The frequency of sonometer wire

$$f = 212 = \dfrac{1}{2 \times 0.40}\sqrt{\dfrac{F}{\mu}}$$

$$= \dfrac{1}{2 \times 0.40}\sqrt{\dfrac{Mg}{\mu}}.$$

Here $\quad \mu = \dfrac{m}{\ell} = \dfrac{1.25 \times 10^{-3}}{1}$

$$= 1.25 \times 10^{-3}\,\text{kg/m}.$$

Again $\quad 212 = \dfrac{1}{2 \times 0.35}\sqrt{\left[\dfrac{Mg - V\rho_\omega g}{\mu}\right]}$ ...(ii)

After solving above equations, we get

$$\rho = \dfrac{M}{V} = 4267 \text{ kg/m}^3.$$

11 (a) If f' is the frequency when mass is in water, then

$$f' = \dfrac{1}{2 \times 0.4}\sqrt{\left[\dfrac{Mg - V\rho_\omega g}{\mu}\right]}$$ ...(iii)

From equations (ii) and (iii), we get beats frequency
$= 26.2$ Hz.

12. **A→(q); B→(p); C→(s); D→(r)**
(A) Intensity due to a source emitting sound uniformly in all directions is given by

$$I = \dfrac{P}{4\pi r^2}$$

So $\quad I_1 = \dfrac{1 \times 10^{-3}}{4\pi(2)^2} = 19.90 \times 10^{-6}$ W/m^2

$\quad I_2 = \dfrac{1 \times 10^{-3}}{4\pi(3)^2} = 8.85 \times 10^{-6}$ W/m^2

(B) The resultant intensity is given by

$$I = I_1 + I_2 + 2\sqrt{I_1 I_2}\cos\phi$$

where $\quad \phi = \dfrac{2\pi}{\lambda}\Delta x$.

Here $\lambda = \dfrac{v}{f} = \dfrac{330}{660} = \dfrac{1}{2}$ and $\Delta x = 3 - 2 = 1$ m

$\therefore\quad \phi = \dfrac{2\pi}{(1/2)} \times 1 = 4\pi$

$$I = I_1 + I_2 + 2\sqrt{I_1 I_2}\cos 4\pi$$

$$= I_1 + I_2 + 2\sqrt{I_1 I_2}$$

or $\quad I = (\sqrt{I_1} + \sqrt{I_2})^2$

$$= (\sqrt{19.9} + \sqrt{8.85})^2 \times 10^{-6}$$

$$= 55.3 \times 10^{-6} \text{ W/m}^2$$

(C) In the case $\quad \phi_0 = \pm\pi$ rad

$\therefore\quad I = [\sqrt{I_1} + \sqrt{I_2} + 2\sqrt{I_1 I_2}\cos(4\pi \pm \pi)]$

$$= (\sqrt{I_1} - \sqrt{I_2})^2$$

$$= (\sqrt{19.9} - \sqrt{8.85})^2 \times 10^{-6}$$

$$= 2.2 \times 10^{-6} \text{ W/m}^2$$

(D) For incoherent sources

$$I = I_1 + I_2$$

$$= (19.9 + 8.85) \times 10^{-6}$$

$$= 28.7 \times 10^{-6} \text{ W/m}^2$$

13. **A→(q); B→(r); C→(s); D→(t)**
(A) The frequency of vibration
$$f = 440 \text{ Hz}$$

$\therefore$ Wavelength $\quad \lambda = \dfrac{v}{f} = \dfrac{330}{440} = 0.75$ m

For the second overtone in closed pipe

$$L = \dfrac{5\lambda}{4} = \dfrac{5}{4} \times 0.75$$

$$= 0.9375 \text{ m} = 0.94 \text{ m}$$

(B) Equation of stationary wave with x from close end
$$\Delta P = -2\Delta P_m \cos(kx)\sin(\omega t)$$

Pressure amplitude
$$R = [2\Delta P_m \cos(kx)|$$

Given $\quad 2\Delta P_m = \Delta P_0$

$\therefore\quad R = |\Delta P_0 \cos(kx)|$

$$= \left|\Delta P_0 \cos\left(\dfrac{2\pi x}{\lambda}\right)\right|$$

At the middle of the pipe,

$$x = L/2 = \dfrac{15}{32} \text{ m}$$

$\therefore\quad R = \Delta P_0 \cos\left[\dfrac{2\pi}{(3/4)} \times \dfrac{15}{32}\right]$

$$= \Delta P_0 \cos\left(\dfrac{5\pi}{4}\right)$$

$$= \dfrac{\Delta P_0}{\sqrt{2}}$$

(C) At the open end of the pipe, there is pressure node
$\therefore$ Pressure there $\quad R = P_0$

(D) At the closed end of the pipe, pressure antinode is formed, so

$$R_{max} = P_0 + \Delta P_0$$
$$R_{min} = P_0 - \Delta P_0$$

Solutions **EXERCISE-10.5**

1. For the given string, we have

$$F_1 P_1^2 = F_2 P_2^2,$$

$$\therefore \quad F_2 = \left(\frac{P_1}{P_2}\right)^2 F_1$$

$$= \left(\frac{3}{6}\right)^2 \times 8$$

$$= 2\,g$$

2. The unknown frequency
$$f' = 288 \pm 4$$
$$= 292 \text{ or } 284 \text{ Hz}.$$
Suppose $f' = 292$ Hz.
After waxing this frequency will decrease and so this may give 4 beat/s again when its frequency becomes 284 Hz. Thus unknown frequency will be 292 Hz.

3. Given, $f_A = 324$ Hz.
The frequency $f_B = 324 \pm 6$
$$= 330 \text{ Hz}.$$
or $$= 318 \text{ Hz}.$$
When string A is waxed, its frequency will decrease and may give 3 beats for the frequency 318 Hz. Thus
$$f_B = 318 \text{ Hz}.$$

4. $$f_{\text{beat}} \propto v$$

$$\therefore \quad \frac{f_{beat_1}}{f_{beat_2}} = \frac{v_1}{v_2}$$

$$= \sqrt{\frac{273+16}{273+51}} \quad [f_{beat_1} = 17]$$

$$\therefore \quad f_{beat_2} = 18 \text{ beat/s}$$

5. If f be the frequency of the fork, then frequency of air column
$$= f \pm 4$$

$$= \frac{v}{4L}$$

As with decrease in temperature, beats frequency decreases, so

$$f + 4 = \frac{v_{15}}{4L}$$

Also $$f + 3 = \frac{v_{10}}{4L}$$

$$\therefore \quad \frac{f+4}{f+3} = \frac{v_{15}}{v_{10}}$$

$$= \sqrt{\frac{273+15}{273+10}}$$

$$\therefore \quad f \approx 110 \text{ Hz}.$$

6. We have, $$f_1 = \frac{1}{2L}\sqrt{\frac{F}{\mu}}$$

or $$124 = \frac{1}{2 \times 0.90}\sqrt{\frac{F}{\mu}} \qquad ...(i)$$

Also $$186 = \frac{1}{2L'}\sqrt{\frac{F}{\mu}} \qquad ...(ii)$$

From above equations, we get
$$L' = 0.6 \text{ m}$$

7. If P and $(P+1)$ be the number of loops corresponding to two consecutive resonances, then length of string
$$L = P \times 2$$
$$= (P+1) \times 1.6$$
$$\therefore \quad P = 4$$
and $$L = 8.0 \text{ cm}$$

8. If P_1 and P_2 are the number of loops in aluminium wire and steel wire respectively then

$$f = \frac{P_1}{2L_1}\sqrt{\frac{F}{\mu_1}}$$

$$= \frac{P_2}{2L_2}\sqrt{\frac{F}{\mu_2}}$$

or $$\frac{P_1}{P_2} = \frac{L_1}{L_2}\sqrt{\frac{\mu_1}{\mu_2}} \qquad ...(i)$$

Here $$\frac{\mu_1}{\mu_2} = \frac{2.6 \times 3}{7.8 \times 1}$$
$$= 1$$

$$\therefore \quad \frac{P_1}{P_2} = \frac{60}{80}\sqrt{1}$$

$$= \frac{3}{4}.$$

Thus $$f = \frac{3}{2 \times 0.6}\sqrt{\frac{40}{2.6 \times 3 \times 10^{-3}}}$$
$$= 180 \text{ Hz}.$$

9. The wavelength of the sound wave

$$\lambda = \frac{v}{f}$$

$$= \frac{360}{180}$$

$$= 2 \text{ m}$$

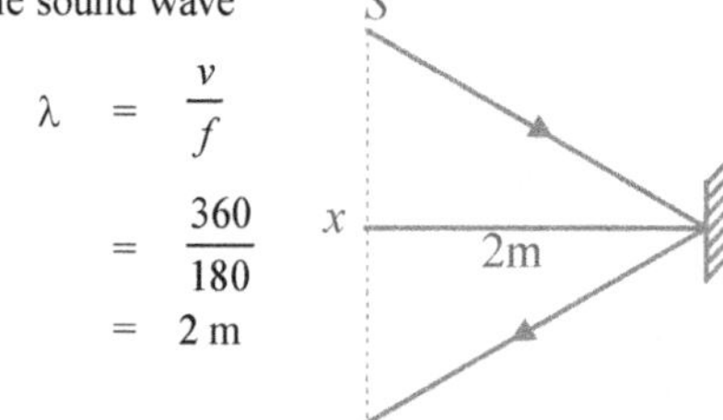

The path difference between reflected sound and direct sound

$$\Delta x = 2\sqrt{\left(\frac{x}{2}\right)^2 + 2^2} - x$$

For maximum of sound,
$$\Delta x = \lambda$$

or $$2\sqrt{\left(\frac{x}{2}\right)^2 + 2^2} - x = \lambda$$

$$= 2$$

$$\therefore \quad x = 3 \text{ m}.$$

10. In the first case, the joint is the antinode, and so

$$120 = \frac{v}{4L} \qquad .... \text{ (i)}$$

In the second case, the joint becomes the node, and so

$$f = \frac{v}{2L} \qquad .... \text{ (ii)}$$

From equations (i) and (ii), we get
$$f = 240 \text{ Hz}.$$

11. The number of holes in inner circle

$$n_1 = \frac{2\pi R_1}{d},$$

and in outer circle $\quad n_2 = \dfrac{2\pi R_2}{d}.$

Given $\qquad \pi R_1^2 = \pi(R_2^2 - R_1^2)$

$\therefore \qquad R_2 = \sqrt{2}R_1.$

Thus $\qquad \dfrac{f_1}{f_2} = \dfrac{n_1}{n_2} = \dfrac{R_1}{R_2} = \dfrac{1}{\sqrt{2}}$

or $\qquad f_2 = \sqrt{2}f = \sqrt{2}f.$

12. If f be the frequency of tuning fork, then

$$\frac{v_{51}}{4L} - f = \pm 4$$

When temperature decreases, beats frequency also decreases, so

$$\frac{v_{51}}{4L} - f = +4 \qquad \qquad ...(i)$$

At 16°C, we have $\quad \dfrac{v_{16}}{4L} - f = +1 \qquad ...(ii)$

Here $\qquad v_{16} = \sqrt{\dfrac{\gamma R(273+16)}{M}}$

and $\qquad v_{51} = \sqrt{\dfrac{\gamma R(273+51)}{M}}$

On solving above equations, we get

$$f = 50 \text{ Hz}.$$

Solutions EXERCISE-10.6

1. The equation of stationary wave is

$$\begin{aligned} y &= y_1 + y_2 \\ &= 0.05 \sin(5\pi t - x) + 0.05 \\ &\quad \sin(5\pi t + x) \\ &= 0.1 \sin 5\pi t \cdot \cos x. \\ &= (0.1 \cos x) \sin 5\pi t \end{aligned}$$

The amplitude of the wave is

$$R = 0.1 \cos x.$$

The displacement of the particle situated at

$$x = 1$$
$$R = 0.054 \text{ m}.$$

2. (i) Frequency and phase of all the points on the string are same but amplitude depends on the distance of the particle.

(ii) Given,

$$y = 0.06 \sin\left(\frac{2\pi x}{3}\right)\cos(120\pi t).$$

The amplitude, $\quad R = 0.06 \sin\dfrac{2\pi x}{3}$

$$= 0.06 \sin\left(\frac{2\pi \times 0.375}{3}\right)$$

$$= 0.042 \text{ m}.$$

3. (i) Given, $\quad y_1 = 5\sin\pi(4.0t - 0.02x).$

The equation of the wave moving in opposite direction will be

$$y_2 = 5\sin\pi(4.0t - 0.02x).$$

(ii) The equation of stationary wave is,

$$\begin{aligned} y &= y_1 + y_2 \\ &= 5\sin\pi(4.0t - 0.02x) \\ &\quad + 5\sin\pi(4.0t + 0.02x) \\ &= 10\cos 0.02\pi x \sin 4.0t. \end{aligned}$$

On comparing with,

$$y = R\cos\frac{2\pi x}{\lambda}\cdot\sin\frac{2\pi t}{T},$$

we have $\quad \lambda = 100 \text{ mm}.$

The distance between two nearest nodes

$$= \frac{\lambda}{2} = 50 \text{ mm}.$$

4. The length of the wire, $\ell = \dfrac{3.5\times10^{-2}}{4.0\times10^{-2}} = 0.875 \text{ m}$

Thus for fundamental mode of vibration

$$\frac{\lambda}{2} = \ell$$

$\therefore \qquad \lambda = 2\ell = 1.75 \text{ m}.$

The speed of transverse wave

$$v = f\lambda = 45 \times 1.75 = 78.75 \text{ m/s}.$$

We have $\qquad v = \sqrt{\dfrac{F}{\mu}}$

$\therefore \qquad \begin{aligned} F &= \mu v^2 \\ &= 4 \times 10^{-2} \times (78.75)^2 \\ &= 248 \text{ N}. \end{aligned}$

5. Let V be the volume and ρ be the density of the stone. In air tension in wire

$$F = V\rho g.$$

When hanged in water, then tension in the wire

$$F' = V\rho g - V\rho_\omega g$$

For two lengths L and L', we have

$$\frac{1}{2L}\sqrt{\frac{V\rho g}{\mu}} = \frac{1}{2L'}\sqrt{\frac{V(\rho - \rho_\omega)g}{\mu}}$$

or $\qquad \dfrac{L'}{L} = \sqrt{\dfrac{\rho - \sigma}{\rho}}$

or $\qquad \dfrac{36}{45} = \sqrt{\dfrac{\rho - 1}{\rho}}$

$\therefore \qquad \rho = 2.778 \text{ g/cm}^3.$

6. Suppose P^{th} and $(P+1)^{th}$ be the number of loops corresponding to the resonance frequencies 420 Hz and 490 Hz respectively. Then

$$420 = \frac{P}{2L}\sqrt{\frac{F}{\mu}} \qquad ...(i)$$

and $\qquad 490 = \dfrac{P+1}{2L}\sqrt{\dfrac{F}{\mu}} \qquad ...(ii)$

$$\therefore \qquad \frac{490}{420} = \frac{P+1}{P}$$

or $\qquad P = 6.$

Substituting this value in equation (i), we get

$$420 = \frac{6}{2 \times L} \sqrt{\frac{450}{5 \times 10^{-3}}}$$

$$\therefore \qquad L = 2.14 \text{ m}$$

7. The fundamental frequency

$$f_1 = \frac{v}{4L}$$

$$= \frac{330}{4 \times 0.30} = 550 \text{ Hz.}$$

Second harmonic, $\quad f_2 = 2 \times 550 = 1100$ Hz.

and $\qquad f_3 = 3 \times 550 = 1650$ Hz .

Clearly, a source of frequency 1.1 k Hz will resonantly excite the second harmonic of the open pipe.

If one end of the pipe is closed, then fundemental frequency

$$f_1' = \frac{v}{4L}$$

$$= \frac{330}{4 \times 0.30} = 275 \text{ Hz.}$$

Third harmonic $\quad f_3' = 3f_1' = 825$ Hz.

and $\qquad f_5' = 5f_1' = 1375$ Hz.

No resonance will be observed.

8. We know that the frequency of nth mode of vibration of closed end pipe is

$$f = \frac{(2n-1)v}{4L}$$

where $\qquad n = 1, 2, \ldots\ldots$

For two resonance lengths, L_1 and L_2, we have

$$f = \frac{(2n_1 - 1)v}{4L_1}$$

$$= \frac{(2n_2 - 1)v}{4L_2}$$

or $\qquad \dfrac{2n_1 - 1}{2n_2 - 1} = \dfrac{25.5}{79.3} \approx \dfrac{1}{3}$

If $\qquad n_1 = 1,$

then $\qquad n_2 = 2$

Thus $\qquad f = 340$

$$= \frac{(2 \times 1 - 1)v}{4 \times 25.5}$$

$\Rightarrow \qquad v = 346.8$ m/s.

9. The wavelength $\quad \lambda = 2L$

$$= 2 \times 1$$

$$= 2 \text{ m.}$$

The speed of sound $\quad v = f\lambda$

$$= 2.53 \times 10^3 \times 2$$

$$= 5.06 \times 10^3 \text{ m/s.}$$

10. If f be the frequency of first fork, then frequency of last fork will be

$$f' = f + (24 - 1) \times 4$$

$$= f + 92$$

Given $\qquad f' = 2f$

or $\qquad f + 92 = 2f$

$\therefore \qquad f = 92$ Hz

and $\qquad f' = 184$ Hz.

11. If L_1 and L_2 be the lengths of two points of the wire, then

$$L_1 + L_2 = 1000 \text{ mm}$$

and $\qquad L_1 - L_2 = 2 \text{ mm}$

$\therefore \qquad L_1 = 499$ mm

and $\qquad L_2 = 501$ mm

They produce the frequency

$$f_1 = \frac{v}{2L_1}$$

and $\qquad f_2 = \dfrac{v}{2L_2}$

or $\qquad 1 = v\left[\dfrac{1}{2 \times 0.499} - \dfrac{1}{2 \times 0.501}\right]$

$\therefore \qquad v = 250$ m/s.

Thus $\qquad f_1 = 250.5$ Hz

and $\qquad f_2 = 249.5$ Hz

12. The distance travelled by the pulses in 4 ms

$$= 500 \times 4 \times 10^{-3} = 2 \text{ mm.}$$

The shape of the string is shown in figure

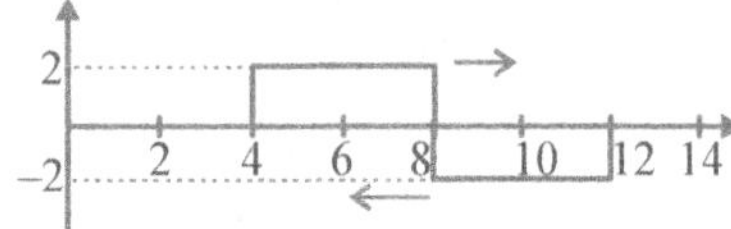

Do the other part of the problem accordingly.

13. (a) In this case $\qquad \dfrac{\lambda}{2} = L$

or $\qquad \lambda = 2L$

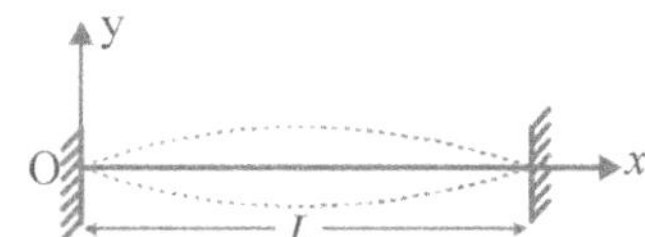

Wave number, $\quad k = \dfrac{2\pi}{\lambda}$

$$= \frac{2\pi}{2L}$$

$$= \frac{\pi}{L}.$$

(b) We have $\qquad y = A\sin\dfrac{2\pi x}{\lambda}.\cos(\omega t + \phi)$

Given, At $\qquad t = 0$

$$x = \frac{L}{2}$$

$$y = 0$$

$\therefore \qquad 0 = A\sin\dfrac{2\pi\frac{L}{2}}{2L}\cos(0 + \phi)$

or $\qquad \cos\phi = 0$

or $\qquad \phi = \dfrac{\pi}{2}.$

Now $\qquad y = A\sin\dfrac{2\pi x}{2L}\cos(2\pi f t + \pi/2)$

$\qquad\qquad = A\sin\dfrac{\pi x}{L}\sin(2\pi f t)$

14. (a) The distance between minimum to next maximum
$\qquad\qquad = 2 \times 16.5 = 33$ mm.

This distance must be equal to $\dfrac{\lambda}{2}.$

Thus $\qquad \dfrac{\lambda}{2} = 33$

or $\qquad \lambda = 2 \times 33$
$\qquad\qquad = 66$ mm.

Frequency of sound

$\qquad f = \dfrac{v}{\lambda} = \dfrac{330}{66\times 10^{-3}} = 5$ kHz.

(b) Given, $\dfrac{(a_1 - a_2)^2}{(a_1 + a_2)^2} = \dfrac{1}{9}$

$\qquad \dfrac{a_1 - a_2}{a_1 + a_2} = \dfrac{1}{3}$

$\therefore \qquad \dfrac{a_1}{a_2} = 2$

15. The path difference between two sounds
$\qquad \Delta x = 4 - 3.20$
$\qquad\qquad = 0.80$ m.

For minimum sound intensity

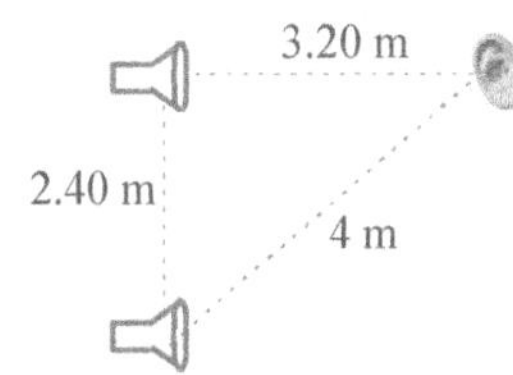

$\qquad \Delta x = (2n+1)\dfrac{\lambda}{2}$

or $\qquad 0.80 = (2n+1)\dfrac{\lambda}{2};$

$\qquad n = 0, 1, 2,....$

$\therefore \qquad \lambda = \dfrac{1.60}{(2n+1)}$

The frequency, $\qquad f = \dfrac{v}{\lambda} = \dfrac{320}{1.60(2n+1)}$

$\qquad\qquad = 200\,(2n+1)$

16. The frequency of second harmonic of the wire

$\qquad f = \dfrac{2}{2L}\sqrt{\dfrac{F}{\mu}}$

Here, $\qquad \mu = \dfrac{m}{L} = \dfrac{4\times 10^{-3}}{0.40} = 10^{-2}$ kg/m

The frequency of fundamental mode of vibration of the air column

$\qquad\qquad = \dfrac{v}{4L'} = \dfrac{340}{4\times 1} = 85$ Hz

Given, $\qquad 85 = \dfrac{2}{2L}\sqrt{\dfrac{F}{\mu}} = \dfrac{1}{0.40}\sqrt{\dfrac{F}{10^{-2}}}$

$\therefore \qquad F = 11.6$ N

17. The fundamental frequency of organ pipe is given by

$\qquad f = \dfrac{v}{\lambda} = \dfrac{1}{\lambda}\sqrt{\dfrac{\gamma RT}{M}}$

$\qquad\qquad = \dfrac{1}{\lambda}\left(\dfrac{\gamma R}{M}\right)^{1/2} T^{1/2}$

Thus we can write, $\dfrac{\Delta f}{f} = \dfrac{1}{2}\dfrac{\Delta T}{T}.$

18. The frequency of fundamental mode of wire $= \dfrac{1}{2L}\sqrt{\dfrac{F}{\mu}}.$

According to the given condition,

$\qquad \dfrac{1}{2L}\sqrt{\dfrac{F}{\mu}} = 256 \pm 4$

With the decrease in length of the wire its frequency increases and beats frequency decreases, so

$\qquad \dfrac{1}{2L}\sqrt{\dfrac{F}{\mu}} = 256 - 4 = 252 \qquad .... (i)$

For L' length of the wire, we have

$\qquad \dfrac{1}{2L'} = \sqrt{\dfrac{F}{\mu}}$

$\qquad\qquad = 256 \qquad .... (ii)$

Dividing equation (i) by (ii), we have

$\qquad \dfrac{L'}{L} = \dfrac{252}{256} = 0.984$

$\therefore \qquad L' = 0.984 \times 25 = 24.61$ cm

Thus $\qquad (L - L') = 25 - 24.61 = 0.39$ cm.

19. The frequency heard by the person on the ground will be
$\qquad f' = 440 + 4$
$\qquad\qquad = 444$ Hz.

If v_s be the speed of the train, then

$\qquad\qquad 444 = 440\left(\dfrac{v}{v - v_s}\right)$

After putting, $\qquad v = 340$ m/s,
and solving, we get $\quad v_s \simeq 3$ m/s $\simeq 11$ km/h

20. Given, $\qquad 196 = \dfrac{1}{2\times 30}\sqrt{\dfrac{F}{\mu}} \qquad .... (i)$

If x is the required distance for 220 Hz, then

$\qquad\qquad 220 = \dfrac{1}{2x}\sqrt{\dfrac{F}{\mu}} \qquad .... (ii)$

Dividing equation (i) by (ii), we get
$\qquad\qquad x = 26.7$ cm

Do the other parts similarly.

21. Given,

$$T = 1 \text{ s}$$

and so

$$f = \frac{1}{T} = \frac{1}{1} = 1 \text{ Hz}.$$

$$\lambda = 8.0 \text{ cm}.$$

(a) The velocity of wave,

$$v = f\lambda = 1 \times 8.0 = 8 \text{ cm/s}$$

(b) For $x = 0$,

$$y = Ae^{-\left(\frac{t}{T}\right)^2}$$

(c) For $t = 0$,

$$y = Ae^{-\left(\frac{x}{\lambda}\right)^2}$$

22. The path difference, $\Delta x = 2$ m

According to the given condition

$$\Delta x = 5\lambda$$

or

$$2 = 5\lambda$$

$$\therefore \quad \lambda = 0.4 \text{ m}$$

23. The path length SAP $= 2\sqrt{60^2 + 25^2} = 130$ m

The path difference $\Delta x = 130 - 120$

$$= 10 \text{ m}$$

For constructive interference

$$\Delta x = n\lambda$$

or

$$10 = n\lambda$$

$$\therefore \quad \lambda = \frac{10}{n};$$

$$n = 1, 2, \ldots\ldots\ldots\ldots$$

24. The resultant pressure

$$P = P_0 \cos\left(kx - \omega t + \frac{\pi}{4}\right) + \frac{P_0}{2}\sin\left(kx - \omega t + \frac{\pi}{4}\right)$$

Substituting, $P_0 = A\sin\phi$

and

$$\frac{P_0}{2} = A\cos\phi$$

Thus $P = A\sin\phi\cos\left(kx - \omega t + \frac{\pi}{4}\right) + A\cos\phi\sin\left(kx - \omega t + \frac{\pi}{4}\right)$

or

$$P = A\sin\left(kx - \omega t + \frac{\pi}{4} + \phi\right).$$

where

$$A = \sqrt{P_0^2 + \left(\frac{P_0}{2}\right)^2} = \frac{\sqrt{5}P_0}{2},$$

and $\tan\phi = 2$

or $\phi = \tan^{-1}(2)$

$$\therefore P = \frac{\sqrt{5}P_0}{2}\sin\left(kx - \omega t + \frac{\pi}{4} + \tan^{-1} 2\right) \quad \ldots\ldots\ldots \text{ (i)}$$

(i) At $x = \lambda$, $t = 0$

$$P = \frac{\sqrt{5}P_0}{2}\sin\left(2\pi + \frac{\pi}{4} + \phi\right)$$

$$= \frac{\sqrt{5}P_0}{2}P_0\sin\left(\frac{\pi}{4} + \phi\right)$$

$$= \frac{\sqrt{5}P_0}{2}\left(\sin\frac{\pi}{4}\cos\phi + \cos\frac{\pi}{4}\sin\phi\right)$$

$$= \frac{\sqrt{5}P_0}{2\sqrt{2}}\left(\cos\phi + \sin\phi\right)$$

As $\tan\phi = 2$,

$$\therefore \quad \sin\phi = \frac{2}{\sqrt{5}}$$

and $\cos\phi = \frac{1}{\sqrt{5}}$

$$\therefore \quad P = \frac{\sqrt{5}P_0}{2\sqrt{2}}\left(\frac{1}{\sqrt{5}} + \frac{2}{\sqrt{5}}\right) = \frac{3}{2\sqrt{2}}P_0 \; \textbf{\textit{Ans.}}$$

(ii) At $x = \lambda$, $t = \frac{2\pi}{3\omega}$

$$\therefore \quad P = \frac{\sqrt{5}P_0}{2}\sin\left(2\pi - \frac{2\pi}{3} + \frac{\pi}{4} + \phi\right)$$

$$= -\frac{\sqrt{5}P_0}{2}P_0\sin\left(\frac{5\pi}{12} - \phi\right)$$

$$= -0.224 \, P_0$$

25. For L length of the sonometer wire, its fundamental frequency

$$f = \frac{1}{2L}\sqrt{\frac{F}{\mu}} \quad \ldots\ldots\ldots\ldots \text{ (i)}$$

When tension is incresed by 44%, it becomes

$$F + 0.44\,F = 1.44\,F$$

Thus, $f + 6 = \frac{1}{2L}\sqrt{\frac{1.44F}{\mu}} \quad \ldots\ldots\ldots\ldots \text{ (ii)}$

From equations (i) and (ii), we get

$$f = 30 \text{ Hz}.$$

When length of the sonometer wire is increased to $L + 0.2\,L = 1.2\,L$, its frequency

$$f' = \frac{1}{2(1.2L)}\sqrt{\frac{F}{\mu}} \quad \ldots\ldots\ldots\ldots \text{ (ii)}$$

From equations (i) and (iii), we get

$$f' = 25 \text{ Hz}.$$

$\therefore$ Decrease in frequency

$$= 5 \text{ Hz}.$$

26. The fundamental frequency is given by

$$f = \frac{1}{2L}\sqrt{\frac{F}{\mu}} = \frac{1}{2L}\sqrt{\frac{Mg}{\mu}}.$$

When mass is immersed in water, the tension in the wire becomes $= (Mg - V\rho_\omega g)$,

and freguency, $f' = \frac{1}{2L}\sqrt{\frac{Mg - V\rho_\omega g}{\mu}}$

After substituting the given values, we get

$$f' = 240 \text{ Hz}$$

27. For fundamental mode of vibration
$$\lambda = 2\ell$$
The equation of stationary wave is
$$y = a \sin kx \cos \omega t,$$
where
$$k = \frac{2\pi}{\lambda} = \frac{2\pi}{2\ell} = \frac{\pi}{\ell}.$$
The amplitude of wave is given by
$$A = a \sin kx.$$
The mass of dx length of string,
$$dm = \mu \, dx$$
The total energy stored in the string can be calculated as :
$$dE = \frac{1}{2}(dm)v^2 = \frac{1}{2}(\mu dx)\omega^2 A^2$$
$$= \frac{\mu\omega^2}{2}(a\sin kx)^2 \, dx$$
$$\therefore \quad E = \int_0^\ell \frac{\mu\omega^2}{2}a^2 \sin^2 kx \, dx$$
$$= \frac{1}{4}\mu a^2 \omega^2 \ell$$
Also,
$$\omega = 2\pi f = 2\pi\frac{v}{\lambda} = 2\pi\frac{\sqrt{F/\mu}}{2\ell}$$
$$\therefore \quad \omega^2 = \frac{\pi^2 F}{\ell^2\mu}.$$
Now
$$E = \frac{1}{4}\mu a^2\left(\frac{\pi^2 F}{\ell^2\mu}\right) = \frac{\pi^2 a^2 F}{4\ell}$$

28. If f is the fundamental frequency of the wire, then
$$f+5 = \frac{1}{2L}\sqrt{\frac{F}{\mu}} = \frac{1}{2L}\sqrt{\frac{F}{\pi r^2\rho}}$$
$$= \frac{1}{2\times 0.5}\sqrt{\frac{100}{\pi r^2\rho}}$$
and
$$f-5 = \frac{1}{2L}\sqrt{\frac{F'}{\pi r^2\rho}} = \frac{1}{2\times 0.5}\sqrt{\frac{81}{\pi r^2\rho}}.$$
Here
$$f = 95 \text{ cycles/s,}$$
and
$$\rho = 12.7 \times 10^3 \text{ kg/m}^3.$$

29. The situations is shown in figure.

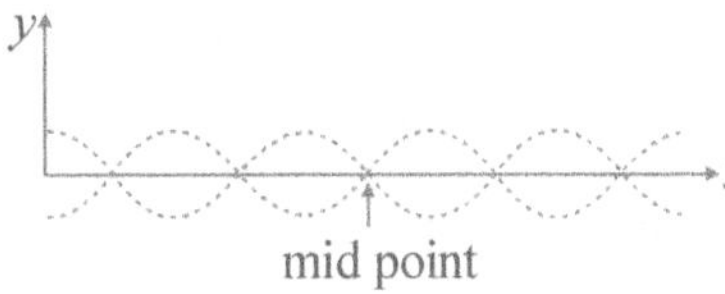

Clearly
$$\frac{5\lambda}{2} = \ell = 1 \text{ m}$$
$$\therefore \quad \lambda = 0.4 \text{ m}$$
Speed of wave,
$$v = \sqrt{\frac{\lambda}{\rho}} = \frac{5000}{0.4} = 12500 \text{ Hz..}$$

The equation of stationary wave can be written as:
$$y = 2a\cos\frac{2\pi x}{\lambda}.\sin 2\pi ft$$
$$= 2\times 10^{-6}\cos\frac{2\pi x}{0.4}\sin(2\pi\times 12500t)$$
$$= 2\times 10^{-6}\cos 5\pi x\sin(25000t)$$
At a point 2 cm from the mid point to the right,
$$x = 50+2 = 52 \text{ cm}$$
$$\therefore \quad y = 2\times 10^{-6}\cos(5\pi\times 0.52)\sin(25000\pi t)$$
$$= 2\times 10^{-6}\cos(0.6\pi)\sin(25000\pi t).$$
The equations of constitutent waves are
$$y_1 = 1\times 10^{-6}\sin(25000\pi t - 5\pi x)$$
and
$$y_2 = 1\times 10^{-6}\sin(25000\pi t + 5\pi x).$$

30. **(i)** For standing wave the two waves must travel from opposite directions. Thus these waves are;
$$z_1 = A\cos(kx - \omega t),$$
and
$$z_2 = A\cos(kx - \omega t).$$
The resulting wave is given by
$$z = z_1 + z_2$$
$$= A\cos(kx - \omega t) + A\cos(kx + \omega t)$$
$$= 2A\cos kx\cos\omega t. = R\cos\omega t.$$
where
$$R = 2A\cos kx.$$
The intensity of resulting wave
$$I = R^2$$
$$= 4A^2\cos^2 kx$$
The intensity is zero, when
$$\cos^2 kx = 0$$
or
$$\cos kx = 0$$
or
$$kx = (2n+1)\frac{\pi}{2},$$
$$n = 0, 1, 2,.....$$
or
$$x = (2n+1)\frac{\pi}{2k}$$
$$n = 0, 1, 2,.....$$
(ii) For a wave propagating in a direction making an angle 45° with positive x and positive y-axis, the component waves must be of equal amplitude. These are;
$$z_1 = A\cos(kx - \omega t),$$
and
$$z_3 = A\cos(ky - \omega t).$$
The resultant wave is $z = z_1 + z_3$
$$= A\cos(kx - \omega t) + A\cos(ky - \omega t)$$
$$= 2A\cos\left[\frac{k(x+y)}{2} - \omega t\right].\cos\frac{k}{2}(x - y)$$
$$= 2A\cos\frac{k(x-y)}{2}\cos\left[\frac{k(x+y)}{2} - \omega t\right]$$
$$= R\cos\left[\frac{k(x+y)}{2} - \omega t\right]$$
where
$$R = 2A\cos\frac{k(x-y)}{2}$$
Intensity
$$I = R^2 = 4A^2\cos^2\frac{k(x-y)}{2}$$

For zero intensity

$$\cos\frac{k(x-y)}{2} = 0$$

or

$$\frac{k(x-y)}{2} = (2n+1)\frac{\pi}{2},$$

$$n = 0, 1, 2,......$$

31. If ℓ_1, ℓ_2 be the lengths of two parts of the wire, then

$$\ell_1 + \ell_2 = 100$$

and

$$\ell_1 - \ell_2 = 1,$$

$\therefore$

$$\ell_1 = 50.5 \text{ cm}$$

and

$$\ell_2 = 42.5 \text{ cm.}$$

The frequency

$$f_1 = \frac{1}{2\ell_1}\sqrt{\frac{F}{\mu}}$$

$$= \frac{1}{2\times 50.5}\sqrt{\frac{F}{\mu}} \qquad ...(i)$$

and

$$f_2 = \frac{1}{2\times 49.5}\sqrt{\frac{F}{\mu}} \qquad ...(ii)$$

Given $\qquad f_2 - f_1 = 4$

After solving above equations, we get

$$f_1 = 198 \text{ Hz and } 202 \text{ Hz.}$$

32. (a) The frequency of second harmonic of pipe A

$$f_A = \frac{2v_A}{2L},$$

and frequency of third harmonic of pipe B

$$f_B = \frac{3v_B}{4L}.$$

According to given condition

$$f_A = f_B$$

or

$$\frac{2v_A}{2L} = \frac{3v_B}{4L}$$

$\therefore$

$$\frac{v_A}{v_B} = \frac{3}{4}$$

$$\frac{\sqrt{\dfrac{\gamma_A RT}{M_A}}}{\sqrt{\dfrac{\gamma_B RT}{M_B}}} = \frac{3}{4}$$

where

$$\gamma_A = \frac{5}{3}$$

and

$$\gamma_B = \frac{7}{5}$$

$\therefore$

$$\frac{\sqrt{5/3 M_B}}{\sqrt{7/5 M_B}} = \frac{3}{4}$$

or

$$\frac{M_A}{M_B} = \frac{400}{189}$$

(b) When pipe B is closed at both ends, its frequency

$$f'_B = \frac{v_B}{2L}$$

Thus

$$\frac{f_A}{f'_B} = \frac{v_A}{v_B} = \frac{3}{4}.$$

33. The path difference,

$$\Delta x = \ell_2 - \ell_1 = 185 - 100 = 85 \text{ cm}$$

For silence (zero intensity of sound)

$$\Delta x = (2n-1)\frac{\lambda}{2},$$

$$n = 1, 2, ...$$

or $\qquad 0.85 = (2n-1)\frac{\lambda}{2}$

$\therefore$

$$\lambda = \left(\frac{1.70}{2n-1}\right)$$

The frequency, $\quad f = \dfrac{v}{\lambda} = \dfrac{340}{1.70/(2n-1)}$

$$= 200\,(2n-1)$$

Thus for $\qquad n = 1, 2,.....$

$$f = 200, 600, 900, \text{ Hz. .....}$$

34. The length of the path SBO,

$$x_1 = 2\sqrt{(H+h)^2 + \left(\frac{D}{2}\right)^2},$$

and the length of the path SAO,

$$x_2 = 2\sqrt{H^2 + \left(\frac{D}{2}\right)^2}.$$

Thus path difference,

$$\Delta x = x_2 - x_1$$

$$= 2\sqrt{(H+h)^2 + \left(\frac{D}{2}\right)^2} - 2\sqrt{H^2 + \left(\frac{D}{2}\right)^2}$$

For no signal detected (destructive interference)

$$\Delta x = \frac{\lambda}{2}$$

or $\quad \dfrac{\lambda}{2} = 2\sqrt{(H+h)^2 + \left(\dfrac{D}{2}\right)^2} - 2\sqrt{H^2 + \left(\dfrac{D}{2}\right)^2}$

or $\quad \lambda = 2\sqrt{4(H+h)^2 + D^2} - 2\sqrt{4H^2 + D^2}$

35. Given, $\qquad y = 4\cos^2 0.5t / \sin 1000t$

$$= 2[2\cos^2 0.5t]\sin 1000t$$

$$= 2(\cos t + 1)\sin 1000t$$

$$= 2\cos t \sin 1000t + 2\sin 100t$$

$$= \sin(100\,t) + \sin(999\,t)$$
$$+ 2\sin 1000\,t$$

Clearly, there are three waves of frequencies 999, 1000 and 1001 Hz.